Prai...
New York Times bestselling author
Brenda Jackson

"[A] heartwarming romance."
—*Library Journal* on *Love in Catalina Cove*

"The only flaw of this first-rate, satisfyingly sexy tale is that it ends."
—*Publishers Weekly*, starred review, on *Forged in Desire*

"[Jackson's] signature is to create full-sensory romances that deliver on the heat, and she duly delivers.... Sure to make any reader swoon."
—*RT Book Reviews* on *Forged in Desire*

"Leave it to Jackson to take sizzle and honor, wrap it in romance and come up with a first-rate tale."
—*RT Book Reviews* on *Temptation*

"Brenda Jackson is the queen of newly discovered love... If there's one thing Jackson knows how to do, it's how to pluck those heartstrings and stir up some seriously saucy drama."
—*BookPage* on *Inseparable*

"This deliciously sensual romance ramps up the emotional stakes and the action.... Sexy and sizzling."
—*Library Journal* on *Intimate Seduction*

"Jackson does not disappoint... First-class page-turner."
—*RT Book Reviews* on *A Silken Thread*, 4½ stars, Top Pick!

"Jackson is a master at writing."
—*Publishers Weekly* on *Sensual Confessions*

BRENDA JACKSON

Forget Me Not

HQN™

ISBN-13: 978-1-335-90612-0

Recycling programs for this product may not exist in your area.

Forget Me Not

Copyright © 2019 by Brenda Streater Jackson

To the love of my life.
The man who will always be my everything.
Gerald Jackson Sr.

To all my readers who are enjoying the
Catalina Cove series. This book is for you.

To my family and friends
who continue to support me in all that I do.

For he beholdeth himself, and goeth his way, and
straightway forgetteth what manner of man he was.
—*James* 1:24 KJV

Forget Me Not

Live with no excuses and love with no regrets.

—Montel

PROLOGUE

"DELIVERY FOR ASHLEY RYAN."

Ashley glanced over her shoulder and did a double take. A man was standing in the doorway of StayNTouch, her social media network firm, carrying the largest arrangements of flowers she'd ever seen. There had to be at least five dozen red roses in that vase. And sitting pretty in the middle of the roses was a single sunflower.

She shook her head. "He wouldn't."

Her business partner and best friend since college, Emmie Givens, chuckled. "He would. It's your fifth wedding anniversary and you know as well as I do that your husband likes doing everything in a big way, so don't act surprised."

Emmie was right—she shouldn't be surprised, although she hadn't expected anything so outlandishly extravagant. She would be the first to admit the first two years had been challenging, and all because of a pact they'd made on their wedding night.

While in their hotel room in Jamaica, naked in bed and a little tipsy on wine, love and sex, they'd made goals for their marriage. Goals they intended to achieve by their fifth wedding anniversary. They pledged to be successful in their chosen occupations and finances, which would require hard work, dedication and sacrifices. For her, the biggest sacrifice had been agreeing not to start a family until after the fifth year. But Devon had promised that when they reached the five-year mark and had accomplished all their goals, they would return to Jamaica to not only celebrate fulfilling all their accomplishments but to make their baby.

Those first two years would not have put such a strain on their marriage if she and Devon hadn't been two success-driven individuals. But they had been, and for a time, instead of competing against outside forces, they started opposing each other. That was when things seemed to start falling apart in their marriage.

There was never any doubt in her mind, even through all their difficult times, that Devon loved her. Just like he'd known she loved him. When they saw their marriage headed for serious trouble, they had sought marriage counseling. Doing so had helped and for the past three years they'd worked hard to put their marriage first and their ambitions second. In the end, what had saved their marriage was their love and commitment to each other.

"Where do you want these, lady?" the deliveryman asked.

"In my office. Please follow me."

Moments later, alone in her office, Ashley sat behind the desk and stared at the huge floral arrangement. She'd counted and just as she'd thought there were sixty roses. A dozen for every year of their lives together. One rose for every month. And the single sunflower had a special meaning all its own.

The night they'd met on a blind date at Harvard, he'd given her a single sunflower. She'd been working on her MBA, and Devon had been working through dual graduate degrees in computer technology and finance. He was four years older and for her it had been love at first sight. Devon always said it had been likewise for him. He'd graduated two years before she had and landed a job with a technology firm in New York. They'd gotten married a year after she'd graduated from college.

Devon had grown up in Hardeeville, South Carolina, located less than an hour's drive from the shores of Hilton Head. More than anything, he loved being out on the ocean. One of their first indulgences had been to buy a boat. Well, it had been his and she'd given in to his expensive whim. However, she would admit she'd enjoyed their weekends spent out on the water. She'd discovered those were their most relaxing times, when they could put the outside world on hold and connect with each other.

She reached for the card that accompanied the flowers and read it.

Ashley, you are the love of my life and on our fifth anniversary I cherish you. You are my sunflower and marrying you has been my greatest accomplishment. Happy fifth anniversary, baby.
Love always,
Devon

She placed the card next to her heart, feeling the love. He had left three days ago on a business trip and she always missed him like crazy when he was away. Their anniversary wasn't until tomorrow but this sort of thing was just like Devon. He was always surprising her. She wondered what he had in store for their anniversary, and couldn't help remembering the promise they'd made to each other on their wedding night. She'd patiently waited for a baby. This was their year to start a family.

He knew how hard it was for her whenever her married girlfriends became mothers. And her parents were anxious to be grandparents and hadn't made things any easier either. She dealt with the pressure by telling herself that her time was coming. What they hadn't counted on was Devon starting his own technology company a year and a half ago; a company he'd been putting a lot of time into. A company he was convinced would make them millions—they could retire as early as their forties and wouldn't have to work again. They could spend every free moment out on the ocean. And children were a big part of that equation. But still, a part of her wanted to believe he hadn't forgotten.

"You, Devon Ryan, are a tough negotiator."

Devon leaned back in his chair. This meeting with Robert Banner was going just as he'd hoped. For the past two days he and Banner had been hashing out the terms of an agreement, and Devon was certain he'd finally made the man an offer he couldn't refuse.

There was no way Banner would let him walk out that door and run the risk of him making the same offer to someone else. Namely, Banner's competitor.

"It's not that I'm a tough negotiator, Mr. Banner. It's just that I know the value of what I'm offering. In one year, I was able to build this company from the ground up. Now I need you to take it to the next level. And as long as I get to retain a sufficient number of shares in the company, I'll be satisfied."

The older man raised a brow. "And then you'll do what? You're only thirty-two. Way too young to retire."

Devon chuckled. "And I don't plan to. But I want to do something that doesn't require all my time and energy." No need to tell the man there were promises he'd made to his wife that he intended to keep.

"If I agree with your terms, it will make you a very wealthy man, Ryan. Both now and later."

Devon chuckled. "No, it would make me *and* my wife a very wealthy couple. She's my partner in all things."

Banner nodded. "That's another thing I like about you."

"That's the way it should be." There was no need to tell the man it had been a lesson he'd learned by almost losing Ashley. That had been his wake-up call.

Banner glanced at the woman sitting beside him. Candace Jenkins was Banner's personal attorney. Devon also had a feeling she was a lot more than that. "So, as my attorney, what do you think, Candace? Should we take the deal he's offering?"

"You would be a fool not to, Robert. He's asking for a considerable number of shares on top of what you'll be giving him up front upon signing, but on that he's not budging and the two of you have been at it for two days," the woman was saying, as if Devon wasn't in the room. "However, in the end, I believe his company will make you millions."

"It will become *my* company," Banner reminded her. "He'll just retain a number of hefty shares. Way too many to suit me."

It was obvious the man still found that a sore spot. "But you realize the investment." Devon didn't present it as a question.

Banner smiled. "Yes, I realize the investment." And then without saying another word, the man signed the documents.

DEVON ENTERED HIS hotel room with a very happy grin on his face. He'd done it. He had secured his and Ashley's future for life. His wife knew this deal was important, but not the true magnitude of it. He hadn't wanted her to worry over what might happen if he failed. But when he left for Chicago three days ago he'd felt confident he could pull things off, and he had. He couldn't wait to surprise Ashley with the news.

Tomorrow was their wedding anniversary and this business deal was just one of many surprises he had for her. She should have gotten the flowers by now, which was probably the reason she'd called. Twice. He hated that he'd missed her calls but at the time he'd been in the middle of contract negotiations and had had Banner just where he'd wanted him.

But he would remedy that now, he thought, pulling his phone out the pocket of his jacket and dialing Ashley's number. She should be home from work now and, probably like him, was about to strip for a shower. Damn, he wished he could be there with her.

"Devon?"

Why after all these years did her saying his name still turn him on? "Yes, Sunflower, it's me," he said, putting her on speaker before placing the phone aside to start undressing.

"Now, why would you call me that when I'm not there to do anything about it?"

He smiled. Normally, he would call her by the pet name he'd given her during their most intimate moments. "We can always have phone sex."

"Won't do any good, Devon. I'm too hot. When are you coming home? And please tell me you will be here tomorrow."

"I intend to," he said, stripping down to his last piece of clothing. "I'm about to take a shower. And speaking of being hot, if you were here I'd cool you off."

"I wanted to come with you and you wouldn't let me," she said with a pout in her voice.

"Too close to our anniversary. I have other plans for you."

"Do tell. And the flowers were beautiful, by the way. So many of them."

"Not enough for you. And I got good news."

"You made the deal with Robert Banner?"

"Yes." He grinned, knowing that she had no idea just how good a deal he'd made. "I'll tell you about it when I get home. It will be just another reason to celebrate."

"And when will you be home?"

"By tomorrow, like I promised. I fly out in the morning and I should be home by three."

"And I will be here waiting on you since I'm taking the day off."

His grin widened. "In that case, I want you naked in bed when I get there. We can start the celebrating a little early." Which suited Devon just fine as there was so, so much they had to celebrate.

"WHAT DID YOU SAY?" Devon asked, staring at the woman, certain he'd heard her wrong. She stared back at him with an annoyed look on her face at having to repeat herself.

"I said that due to the snowstorm headed our way, all flights out of both O'Hare and Midway have been canceled."

"What snowstorm?"

The woman looked at him as if he was crazy. "Surely you've heard about the massive storm in Minnesota."

"What does that have to do with my flight that's going south to South Carolina?"

"A lot, sir. When one flight is delayed all flights get delayed, regardless of their destinations. In the next couple of hours there's expected to be at least twelve inches of snow here in some areas. Once that happens this airport will close and it will be another day before it reopens."

That was not what he wanted to hear. "Look, I have to leave for Hilton Head today. It's important that I get home today." He refused not to be with Ashley today, of all days. "It's my fifth wedding anniversary," he said, with all the disappointment he felt. "I made special plans for my wife." He glanced at his watch.

"Oh, that's so nice."

He glanced back at the woman. The look of annoyance in the woman's eyes had been replaced with a romantic look. "I'd hate for you to miss your wedding anniversary. Some men wouldn't care if they made it back home or not. Let me see what I can do. I can't get you a flight out of here, but I might be able to suggest something that could get you home."

He didn't say anything as she clicked several keys into her computer with an intense look on her face. Moments later she smiled. "Okay, this might work. Cincinnati is approximately a five-hour drive from here. There's a straight flight leaving Cincinnati to Hilton Head at three. That will give you time to get there with two hours to spare. You'll land in Hilton Head around six thirty."

He nodded enthusiastically. "That will work."

"Good. Now, if you hold on a minute, I'll book that flight out of Cincinnati for you."

"Thanks."

A short while later Devon was walking quickly to the car rentals area.

ASHLEY RAISED A concerned brow as Devon spoke on the other end of the line. "Devon, are you sure you want to make the five-hour drive to Cincinnati? You hate driving long distances."

"Right now I'm frustrated more than anything. I had to wait a half hour for this rental. I'm not the only one trying to beat the storm out of here. This is the last place where I want to be stranded."

Chicago was the last place where she would want him stranded, too, but his safety came first. She, of all people, knew her husband hated long-distance driving. Five hours wasn't bad, but for Devon, it might as well be ten. "I don't know, Devon. I don't feel good about you being on the road for five hours."

"Sweetheart, I'll be fine. I will drink as much coffee as I need to. Besides, it's daytime and not night. I'll be okay. Will it make you feel better if I call you when I'm at the halfway point?"

She smiled. "Yes, then I could sing to you."

He chuckled. "On second thought, maybe I won't call you. Your talents are not with your voice."

"Thanks a lot."

"Just keeping it honest, Mrs. Ryan. God, I can't wait until I'm home."

"And I can't wait for you to get here. I can't believe it's number five for us. When you look back over the years, what means the most to you?"

"Hmm, that's easy. Although there were lots of things, I believe my most cherished moment was our wedding day."

She recalled that day vividly. It had been an outdoor wedding at her parents' home and everything had cooperated, especially the weather, to make it a perfect day. "What do you remember the most?"

"The moment you walked down the aisle on your father's arm to me. Looking into your face, seeing you smile, your happiness in getting married to me… That moment touched me deeply, profoundly. My mind blotted out everything and everyone and just focused on you. Only you were the center of my attention. My universe. You still are."

"You're mine, too." Devon's words touched her deeply. She needed to get off the phone before she got all emotional on him. "Drive carefully, and whenever you do make a stop, call me. Or else I'll worry."

"And the last thing I want you to do is worry. My plane from Cincinnati lands a little after six, so I should be home around seven. I still want you in bed when I get there. Now, that's where your true talent lies."

Ashley threw her head back and laughed. "Horny man."

"Can't help it, baby. Love you. Bye."

"Love you back. Bye."

Ashley clicked off the phone and smiled. Devon had yet to tell her of his plans for their fifth anniversary—she knew he was planning something. Emmie was right when she said Devon liked doing things in a big way. He also liked surprising her. She had no problem with it because she always liked his surprises.

She was about to go into the kitchen to pour

another cup of coffee when her doorbell sounded.
Ashley quickly moved toward the door and glanced
out the peephole to see a woman standing there with
a huge beautifully wrapped gift box.

"May I help you?" she asked, before opening the
door.

"Yes, I have a delivery for Ashley Ryan."

Smiling, Ashley opened the door. After she signed
the log, the woman handed her a gift-wrapped box.
Moments later Ashley was quickly tearing off the
bow to see what was inside. There was an envelope
and inside were plane tickets to Jamaica, with the
flight leaving in two days. Joy swept through her, although two days barely gave her much time to pack,
but she would manage.

Also inside was a smaller wrapped box. She tore
off the tissue paper and her breath caught when she
saw a pair of yellow baby booties with a matching
bib. Tears came to her eyes when she read the card.

I'm ready to start making babies in Jamaica.
There's not another woman I'd want as the
mother of my sons and daughters.
Love,
Devon

DEVON PULLED INTO a roadside stop. He hadn't eaten
breakfast and wanted something else in his stomach
other than coffee. He was making good time and
so far wasn't feeling tired. Luckily, he was keeping

his mind revved up by thinking of all the plans he had for Ashley when he got home.

He grabbed a bagel and coffee and was back on the interstate. A half hour later he was thanking God for GPS when he had to take a detour due to heavy rain in the area that had left several streets flooded. Eventually he made it back onto the interstate.

It stopped raining and he was glad. He slowed down for the slippery roads and couldn't believe how fast semis were flying by regardless of the wet conditions as they headed back toward the interstate.

Devon adjusted the volume on the radio when he saw the hitchhiker standing ahead with a backpack. It looked as if there would be another downpour any minute and he hated the thought that the man would get caught out in it. Typically, he never picked up strangers, but considering his good luck of yesterday, he was still in a great mood. He'd never had to hitchhike and figured everybody had a story. He tried not to be judgmental and the guy seemed harmless.

Before he could talk himself out of doing so, Devon pulled to the shoulder of the road, rolled the window down and asked, "Where are you headed?"

The stranger smiled as he leaned in the window. "To Cincinnati, but I'm grateful to go as far as you can take me."

Devon smiled back. "You're in luck. I'm headed to Cincinnati as well. I'll give you a lift." Devon figured at least he'd have company the last leg of the drive.

A broad grin covered the man's face. "Hey, thanks."

"I'M DEVON, by the way," he said to the man, who refused to look at him. Instead he preferred looking straight ahead. When the man didn't say anything, didn't even nod, Devon asked, "And you are?"

It was then that the man glanced over at him. "Tom."

Devon nodded. "So, Tom, where are you from?"

The man was staring out the windshield again. "Nowhere in particular."

Devon nodded again. "You have family in Cincinnati?"

The man glanced over at him again. "No. You?"

"No. I'm just trying to get to the airport. To catch a plane home."

The man nodded. "And where is home for you?"

"South Carolina."

The man stared out the window again and Devon decided to keep his eyes on the road and conversation at a minimum. So much for thinking he'd picked up a passenger who would be company for him. This man only talked when spoken to and then you had to almost pull the words out of him.

He drove for another fifteen to twenty miles when suddenly the man said, "Take the next exit."

Devon lifted a brow. Why would the man want him to get off the interstate? And then the obvious quickly came to mind. He needed a bathroom break. "There's nothing at the next exit if you need a bathroom break. I'll probably need to drive till the next one."

"No. You need to get off that exit now," the man said with an edge to his voice.

Devon didn't appreciate the man's tone of voice. Who the hell did he think he was talking to? If Devon got off at the next exit, it would be to tell the ingrate to get the hell out of the car and find another way to Cincinnati.

He looked at the man to tell him just that and froze when he saw the gun pointed at him.

CHAPTER ONE

Three years later

"Happy birthday, Ashley."

Ashley smiled across the breakfast table at Emmie, Kim and Suzanne. Three women whom she considered her closest and dearest friends. She honestly didn't know what she would have done without them for the past three years. They had been her rock and, in some cases, her sanity. Yesterday Kim and Suzanne, whom she'd known since her high school days in Topeka, Kansas, had arrived in town to celebrate her thirtieth birthday with her.

What she appreciated more than anything was that none of them ever said the words "We know just what you're going through." Because they didn't. No one did. But at least they had given her their shoulders to cry on and there had been a lot of crying times.

Emmie was the only one who lived in Hardeeville. Suzanne lived in Atlanta and Kim in Dallas. "Go ahead and open your gift," Kim was saying, smiling brightly.

Ashley smiled back. The box was wrapped so

prettily, she hated untying the bow. There was no telling what these three had bought her and she decided to try to guess. "Is it something I can eat?"

Emmie laughed. "No."

"Umm, something I can wear?"

"Nope," Suzanne said, grinning. "Just open the darn box, and I'm telling the waiter to bring us another bottle of wine."

"Open it, Ash, before Suzanne drinks the whole bottle by herself," Kim said, chuckling.

"Oh, all right." Ashley began untying the bow and used the edge of her polished fingernail to carefully ease off the wrapping paper. Inside the box and buried beneath tissue paper was an envelope with her name sprawled across it in beautiful cursive. *Ashley Ryan.* Sometimes her mother would suggest that she go back to using her maiden name of Hardwick, and it upset her every time—as if she could just erase those five years with Devon from her life.

She slid her fingernail along the flap to open the envelope. "Ohh, wow…"

It was a gift certificate for a two-week stay at Shelby by the Sea. She'd heard reservations at the exclusive bed-and-breakfast in Catalina Cove, a quaint shipping town an hour's drive from New Orleans, were booked for a full year in advance.

"We're doing a girls' trip," Ashley said, smiling over at them.

Suzanne shook her head. "No, it's not a girls' trip."

Ashley's forehead bunched in confusion. "It's not?"

"No," Kim said.

"We know how hard these past three years have been for you, Ash," Emmie was saying in a soft voice. "And we know you have decisions you need to make about a number of things."

Since they were her best friends, they were well aware that her mother was determined to get her back into the dating scene. Ashley was satisfied just being left alone. It seemed no one but her best friends understood that. Her mother, Imogene Hardwick, certainly didn't. All she was concerned about was becoming a grandmother while she was young enough to enjoy her grandkids. Ashley had even overheard her mother whisper to her father that if Devon had to die at least he could have left her pregnant.

Her parents' moving to Hardeeville from Topeka was supposed to be temporary to give their daughter support, but Ashley saw it as just the opposite and wished they would return home. At least she'd gotten them out of her house after she'd come home from work one day to find her mother had removed all the framed photographs that Ashley and Devon had taken together. That had been the last straw and she'd asked them to leave that night.

Her father had given her an appreciative nod. Although he hadn't supported his wife's foolishness, he was a weakling when it came to standing up to her. Instead of returning to Topeka like Ashley had hoped they would do, they had moved to an apartment across town, and three years later Imogene was still in Hardeeville, causing havoc in Ashley's life.

Ashley studied the gift certificate. "What will I do there for two weeks by myself?"

"Definitely not what I'd do for two weeks by myself," Suzanne said, wiggling her brows. Since Suzanne was a divorcée who swore never to marry again but to just have fun with men, they could imagine what she'd do.

Emmie rolled her eyes before giving Ashley a pointed look. "For starters, you'll get a break from your mother."

"True," Ashley said, taking a sip of her coffee. Everyone chuckled since they all knew what a handful Imogene Hardwick could be.

"You can relax and enjoy yourself." Kim smiled and then added, "Jon Paul and I went to Catalina Cove for our honeymoon and loved it. I understand the original owner died and the owner's niece inherited it. I heard she's kept those things that made the bed-and-breakfast unique, yet she modernized some things that you can appreciate."

Ashley nodded. Since Kim and Jon Paul had gone there for their honeymoon, she wouldn't be surprised if there were a number of honeymooners there. How would she feel sharing space with them when they were starting their lives together, and hers had ended the day she lost Devon on their fifth anniversary? However, Ashley knew why they were sending her there. She couldn't grieve for Devon forever. At some point she needed to get on with her life. A life without the man she loved. But she wasn't sure she'd ever be ready to move on and allow another man into her life.

"We know what you're thinking, Ash, and it's okay if you come back with the same mind-set that you have now about things. But you can't continue to work as hard as you do," Emmie said, reaching out and touching her arm. "You haven't taken any time off. You can't continue to do so without giving your body and mind a break."

Ashley drew in a deep breath. Emmie was right. Since losing Devon, she'd thrown herself into her work. StayNTouch had become her lifeline. She had started the company with Emmie six years ago. They connected friends as most social media companies did. But they went a little further by planning periodic trips for their members; sending reminders of important events such as birthdays, weddings and reunions; and becoming a huge support group when needed. And for the past three years it had been a support for her as well.

The membership was growing by leaps and bounds with Emmie handling the day-to-day operations and Ashley handling the daily blog pieces. They were a great team that worked well together. Throwing herself into her work meant less time to dwell on her pain. But the hurt was still there when she went home to an empty house. She'd thought of selling but she couldn't when the place contained so many memories of her and Devon's time together.

"We want you to be happy, Ash."

She tried smiling through the heartache she still felt. "I know, but two weeks is a long time."

Suzanne chuckled. "If we could have gotten away with giving you a month, we would have. You need time to yourself, Ash. Away from your job, your house, your mother and those men she's trying to shove down your throat every chance she gets."

The latter in and of itself was enough to make her want to pack tonight and leave for two weeks. She glanced at the gift certificate and then back at her friends, smiled and asked, "So, how soon can I leave?"

RAY SULLIVAN EASED up to sit on the side of the bed and rubbed his hand down his face. The morning sun was shining bright through a slit in the blinds as he glanced at the calendar pinned to the wall. The date was June 10. Why did he feel this date should have some meaning to him?

It was days like this that he hated with a vengeance the situation he'd been in for the last three years. He was a man without a memory, and the sad thing was that he had no clue as to why or how he'd gotten in this predicament.

The only thing he remembered was waking up in a hospital room after being told he'd been in a coma for three weeks. According to the doctor, he had been found by a jogger in a wooded area severely beaten. From the depth of his injuries, specifically the condition of his hands, wrists and knuckles, he'd put up a good fight, but in the end, he'd been pistol-whipped into unconsciousness. Massive brain trauma had resulted in retrograde amnesia. In other words, he had awakened from his coma a man with no memory of his past life.

Due to the severity of his head injuries, there was a chance that he would never regain his memory. And since he hadn't had any identifying articles on him, they couldn't even contact the family who might be looking for him. The indentation on the third finger of his left hand led them to believe he was a married man. In fact, the doctors had told him that whoever assaulted him had almost broken Ray's finger in forcing the ring off his hand.

He had no recollection of a wife. There was a strong possibility she believed he was dead and there was a chance after all this time she had moved on with her life. If that was the case, what was stopping him with moving on with his?

He'd asked himself that question countless times and always came back to the same answer. The last thing he wanted was to meet someone and fall in love, only to get his memory back and be in love with another woman. It wouldn't be fair to either woman. So he'd made the decision to remain a single man with no involvements.

He had remained in the hospital three months before he'd been well enough to leave. He'd been well physically, but he doubted he would ever be well mentally again. How could he when he couldn't remember anything…but one thing? He loved being out on the water.

That was how he'd ended up in Catalina Cove, Louisiana. One of his doctors had reached out to a college friend who owned a shipping company in the small town. He'd been given the new identity of Ray Sullivan and was hired by Chambray Seafood Unlimited Shipping Company without so much as an interview.

He had arrived a few days later in what Ray thought had to be the most breathtaking town he'd ever remembered seeing, but since he had no memory, that really hadn't meant much. But still, he knew the job here was a godsend.

From the townsfolk, he'd learned the parcel of land the cove sat on that backed out to the gulf had been a gift to the notorious pirate Jean Lafitte, from the United States of America for his role in helping the states fight for independence from the British during the War of 1812. Some believed he wasn't buried at sea in the Gulf of Honduras like history claimed but was buried somewhere in the waters surrounding Catalina Cove.

For years because of Lafitte's influence, the cove had been a shipping town. It still was, which was evident by the number of fishing vessels that lined the piers in what was known as the shipping district. The Moulden River was full of trout, whiting, shrimp and oysters. Tourists would come from miles around to sample the town's seafood, especially the oysters. Ray had been hired by Chambray to harvest all that seafood from the ocean.

The man who'd picked him up from the airport

that day had been Kaegan Chambray, the owner of the company. Ray hadn't a clue to his real birthday, only the one he'd been given before leaving the hospital, but he figured that he and Kaegan were pretty close in age.

Over the past three years Kaegan hadn't just been his boss but had become a close friend. In fact, Kaegan and the town's sheriff, Sawyer Grisham, were the only two people in Catalina Cove who knew about his memory loss. Everyone else assumed he was a thirty-four-year-old divorcé whom Kaegan had known prior to returning to the cove to take over his family's shipping company.

That assumption worked in Ray's favor, although most people—namely, the single women in town—couldn't understand why he wasn't interested in dating even if remarrying wasn't on his mind. For him there was no way he could ever commit to a new life with a woman when he knew nothing about his old life. To avoid being caught in such a situation he'd decided the best thing for him was to avoid all personal involvements with women. So far that situation suited him just fine, even if it was a little lonely.

He stood and stretched, knowing that except for the loss of his memory he had a lot to be thankful for. For the past two and a half years he'd work hard for Kaegan and saved most of his earnings. With Kaegan as cosigner, two months ago Ray became the owner of Ray's Tours, a company that offered private ocean tours around the cove.

Now he woke up every morning with a purpose

and before going to bed at night he would record that day's activities in his journal. As he headed for the bathroom he was again bothered by a niggling thought that although he didn't have a clue why, for some reason he believed that today used to be an important one for him.

"I CAN'T BELIEVE you aren't telling me and Dad where you'll be for two weeks. What if an emergency comes up? What if I want to tell Elliott where you are in case he wanted to join you? What if—?"

"How dare you think you can invite a man I barely know to join me anywhere," Ashley said, not able to control her anger as she moved around her bedroom, packing. She knew she'd made the right decision in not telling her parents where she would be for two weeks.

"Honestly, Ashley, I don't understand why you're getting upset. According to Elliott, the two of you have talked on the phone a couple of times."

Ashley's anger escalated. Elliott Booker was the latest single guy her mother was trying to shove at her. She'd met him a mere month ago when he'd conveniently shown up at her parents' place for dinner one Sunday. Since then the man had called her a couple of times after getting her phone number from her mother.

"You turned thirty last week," her mother was saying. "I read those magazines for today's women and know casual affairs are the thing now for single women your age. Do you really think your friends expect you to spend two weeks alone?"

"Yes. In fact, I know they do, and do you know why?" Without waiting for her mother to respond, she said, "Because they know what I'm ready for and what I am not ready for, which is something you evidently don't know about me, your own daughter."

"It's been three years, Ashley. I think it's time for you to move on."

"I decide when it's time, Mom, not you or anyone else. I'll call you after I get back. If an emergency comes up and you need to reach me, Emmie will know how to contact me. Goodbye, Mom." She hung up the phone.

Ashley continued packing, refusing to dwell on yet another argument she'd had with her mother. Instead she wanted to think about the two weeks she would be spending in Catalina Cove doing whatever she wanted to do. And unlike what her mother thought, it wouldn't involve a man.

Ashley twisted her wedding ring on her finger. A ring she refused to take off even after three years. She would never forget that night when instead of Devon returning home, she'd gotten a visit from her local police department after having been contacted by authorities in Cincinnati. Because of heavy rains and icy roads, the rental car Devon was driving had skidded and he'd lost control on the Langley Memorial Bridge and gone through a guardrail to plunge into the Ohio River.

Ashley had screamed so loud that her neighbors

had come to see what had happened. When her parents had arrived in town the next day, Ashley was still in a state of shock. To this day she didn't know how she'd managed to get through the following week. Traffic cameras had shown the exact moment Devon had lost control. Because of the depth of the river, they never recovered the car or Devon's body. However, his briefcase with all his papers inside, including the anniversary card he had gotten for her, had floated to the top a couple of weeks later. It was only then that she accepted her husband was not coming back.

Deep down she, of all people, knew it was time to move on and Devon would have wanted her to do so, but she couldn't. His clothes were still in his closet and his belongings were where he'd left them. The only person it bothered was her mother, who was ready for her to move on, but Ashley didn't care what her mother was ready for because she wasn't.

Ashley went into the living room and glanced around. The plants she'd managed to keep alive since Devon's funeral would be taken care of by Emmie, who had a key to her place. Emmie would also collect her mail while she was gone. Now more than ever, Ashley was glad her mother had no idea where she was going.

She paused before going into the kitchen to gaze at the sunflower, the last one Devon had given her for their anniversary, the one that had been with all those roses. Emmie had gotten the huge sunflower freeze-dried and placed in a beautiful crystal case for her to have forever. A constant reminder of the love she and Devon had shared.

After eating dinner, Ashley put on the videos she'd been watching a lot lately. The one of her and Devon's wedding. She also watched a video Suzanne had had made, which contained a collection of every photograph Ashley and Devon had ever taken together, set to some of their favorite songs.

An hour later after watching the videos, Ashley's shirt was wet from her tears. She knew she couldn't continue on this way. Maybe she should have done as the grief counselor suggested and retained a therapist to help her through the healing process. But a part of her hadn't wanted to heal because doing so meant moving on without Devon and she wasn't ready for that.

But maybe the two weeks she would spend at Shelby by the Sea would be a start.

CHAPTER TWO

RAY COULD ONLY shake his head at Kaegan Chambray and Sheriff Sawyer Grisham. As most mornings, the two had joined him for coffee and blueberry muffins at the Witherspoon Café, a popular eating place in town.

Sawyer's wife, Vashti, had given birth to their son, Cutter, six months ago and already Sawyer was anticipating having another. Their oldest daughter, Jade, would be leaving for college in the fall. Since Sawyer had been away in the military during the first six months of Jade's life, he had missed out on all the newborn baby stuff he was experiencing with Cutter.

"I hope Vashti is in agreement," Kaegan was saying. "I'm sure that's nothing you can spring on a woman."

Sawyer gave them a devilish grin. Too devilish for a man who was the town's sheriff. "I got everything under control, trust me." He glanced over at Ray. "How have you been doing? Did you ever contact your therapist?"

Ray knew why he was asking. He'd mentioned to Kaegan and Sawyer about waking up last week on a day he felt should have meant something to him. They suggested that he call the therapist whom he'd routinely visited every six months up until the beginning of this year. Now he would contact him on an as-needed basis.

"Yes, I called Dr. Martin. He said June tenth probably meant something in my prior life, just like I thought."

"Does he think that means your memory might be returning?" Kaegan asked, before biting into his blueberry muffin.

Ray shook his head. "No, he doesn't think that," he said, trying to keep the disappointment from his voice. "However, he did suggest that I make a note of it in my journal."

"I hear business is going well," Sawyer said.

Ray nodded, knowing Sawyer was intentionally changing the subject to talk about a positive in Ray's life. He also knew where Sawyer had heard that from. Vashti owned and operated Shelby by the Sea, a bed-and-breakfast in town, and she had encouraged Ray to print brochures to place in the inn's welcome packet. That had been a great idea and a number of his new customers were people staying at Shelby.

"Yes, it is. I'm averaging a good ten to twelve trips a day. That's why I'm thinking of getting an additional boat."

"You should," Kaegan said, looking over at him, but only for a short while.

Kaegan's attention was drawn to Bryce Witherspoon, the daughter of the owners of the café, as she appeared from the back. Bryce, who owned a real-estate office in town, often helped her parents at the café by assisting with the breakfast and dinner crowds. Bryce had also worked for a while as assistant manager at Shelby by the Sea that first year to help Vashti, who was her best friend, get things off the ground, and had remained through Vashti's maternity leave. It hadn't been hard to figure out that there had been something between Kaegan and Bryce a while back that obviously hadn't ended well.

"Time for me to start the day," Sawyer said, standing and then leaving with a nod of farewell.

Ray knew it was time for him to start the day as well, but decided to get a refill on his coffee first. He figured sooner or later Bryce would mosey over to their table.

He didn't have long to wait when she approached their table with a smile. "Want a refill, Ray?"

He returned her smile. "I sure do, Bryce. Thanks."

She then turned to Kaegan and Ray didn't miss the glare that appeared in her eyes. "What about you, K-Gee?"

Ray tensed. K-Gee had been Kaegan's nickname while growing up, and apparently when he returned to town a few years ago to take over his family's shipping company, Kaegan had made it known that he would no longer answer to that name. He was certain Bryce had deliberately used it anyway and saw Kaegan's jaw tighten.

"No, I don't want a refill."

"Fine," Bryce all but snapped.

Ray figured this was a good time to leave before sparks started to fly more than they already were. Clearing his throat, he stood and said, "I just remembered there's somewhere I need to be. Can I get mine to go?"

Bryce smiled at him. "Sure thing, Ray."

When she walked off, Kaegan turned to him. "One day, do you know what I'm going to do to her?"

Ray chuckled. "No, and since you're best friends with the sheriff, I would suggest you forget that thought. See you later."

He decided to walk over to the counter to save Bryce the trouble of coming back to their table. That was the least he could do to keep Kaegan out of trouble.

ASHLEY GLANCED AROUND her studio bedroom at Shelby by the Sea. Her friends had really outdone themselves in sending her here and making sure her room that faced the cove was spacious and accommodating. Even with the closed windows, the sound of the ocean filled her ears.

Placing her luggage aside, she moved toward the huge picture window to appreciate the panoramic view of the gulf. Below she could also see a boardwalk that led down the marshy path to the cove. She could see herself spending a lot of her time beneath the huge gazebo reading and had brought several books with her to get her started.

She liked this place already and a deep feeling of peace and tranquility flowed through her for the first time in years. Three, to be exact. The drive from the airport had initiated those feelings. The route connecting New Orleans to Catalina Cove had been scenic to the point where she'd pulled to the shoulder of the road and sat there to stare at the giant oak trees lining both sides of the highway. Through the low-hanging branches you could see the sea marshes and the gulf. The closer you got to Catalina Cove, the highway merged from four lanes to two, and even more tall oaks were perfectly strung along the roadway, providing a countryside effect.

The first thing she noticed when she drove into town was how Catalina Cove's downtown area was a close replica of New Orleans's French Quarter. She couldn't help but like the stately older homes, most of them of the French Creole style, that lined the residential streets with pristine manicured lawns.

She moved away from the window to begin unpacking. Another thing she liked was the friendliness of the owner and staff. Vashti Grisham had greeted her at the door with so much enthusiasm in her voice that Ashley had felt totally welcomed before taking one step over the threshold. The woman had explained that everyone here was on a first-name basis unless she chose otherwise. She didn't.

Vashti had invited her down for blueberry muffins and tea once she got settled. Looking forward to that, Ashley finished unpacking.

"THANKS FOR BRINGING these here, Ray," Vashti said as he walked through the back door of the inn. "It was nice of you to help Kaegan out."

"No problem," Ray said, placing the huge box into the freezer. "I don't have another tour until three. I knew one of Kaegan's guys was out today, so I told him I would deliver this to you." He appreciated Vashti for teaming up with local businesses to provide goods and services to the inn. Kaegan's company provided all the seafood she needed.

"I didn't expect to find you in the kitchen. Where's Ms. Livingston?" he asked about the fifty-year-old woman who was the chef at the inn.

"She went grocery shopping. We have another full house. Five more people checked in today and one of them will be here for two weeks."

"Is there anything you need done while I'm here?"

She shook her head. "No, but thanks anyway. You're okay?"

He knew why she was asking. Since marrying Sawyer, she'd learned the details of Ray's memory loss. He didn't mind and knew she would keep those details private just like Kaegan and Sawyer were doing. "I'm fine, Vashti. How's the baby?" he asked, quickly changing the subject.

For the next ten minutes he listened while she told him how great motherhood was and shared that she wanted another baby. He was tempted to tell her Sawyer was on the same page, but figured she would find that out soon enough.

He glanced at his watch. "Time to go so I'll be there when my three o'clock tour arrives."

"Okay, and thanks again."

"No problem," Ray said, heading for the back door. "See you later."

"Okay," Vashti said, already moving through the swinging door of the kitchen.

His eye caught the barest glimpse of a woman coming down the stairs, and he overheard Vashti say, "You've settled in?"

CHAPTER THREE

ASHLEY WOKE UP bright and early the next morning, determined to make the most of her time in Catalina Cove. Breakfast would be served between eight and ten, and she figured most people wouldn't go down to eat right at eight like she intended to do. Hopefully that would give her a few private moments to reflect.

She had enjoyed her muffins and tea with Vashti Grisham yesterday. She'd learned Vashti was married to the town's sheriff and had given birth six months ago to a little boy. The couple also had an eighteen-year-old daughter. When Ashley had inquired why the couple had waited so long to have another child, Vashti had smiled and said it was a rather long story. Ashley had a feeling it would be a rather interesting story as well.

When Ashley had joined everyone in the dining room for dinner yesterday evening, just as she'd suspected, the majority of the people staying at Shelby by the Sea were couples. Four were there on their honeymoon, three were celebrating anniversaries, and a few others were renewing their vows. Then there was a group of five women, occupying the other studio room on the fourth floor, who were there for a girls' trip.

Being around the couples reminded her so much of what she had lost. It also reminded her of what she'd had and how lucky she had been to have been married to Devon. She'd known before coming here that she would encounter emotions of both longings and regrets. However, what she was determined to do was dwell on the happiness she knew Devon would want her to feel. Happiness at the memories that were hers and his. Memories that would always make her smile no matter what.

Before retiring for bed last night she had checked in with Emmie, and just like she'd suspected, her mother had called, trying to get Emmie to tell her where Ashley was, but Emmie respectfully refused to do so. Thank goodness.

Ashley was looking forward to her day. This morning she would be taking a two-hour boat tour around the cove at eleven. Tomorrow she had signed up to do a tour of the city's historical district on one of those double-decker buses. She couldn't wait to take a tour of the mansion that had once belonged to the famous pirate Jean Lafitte. Leaving her suite, she headed down for breakfast.

"DO YOU STILL need me to take care of your eleven o'clock appointment, Ray?"

Ray glanced over at Tyler Clinton, the man he had hired to work with him at his boat tour company. Tyler had been born in Catalina Cove and had left when he joined the navy after graduating from high school. He had returned to the cove last year and had worked the night shift at the LaCroix Blueberry Plant, the largest employer in town. When Tyler got married a few months ago, he preferred working during the daytime. He had been the first one to apply for the job of Ray's assistant and he'd been hired immediately. Ray never regretted doing so. Tyler was a hard worker, dependable and a fast learner.

Ray didn't understand how he personally had come to know so much about boats. He often wondered if in his previous life, the one he couldn't remember, he'd been in the navy, worked as a merchant marine or spent a lot of time in a shipyard. Then there was his love of numbers and his ability to handle finances. While employed with Kaegan, Ray had worked on the boat, working the nets to pull shrimp, fish and oysters from the ocean, until Kaegan discovered how good he'd been with numbers. It wasn't long before he'd been offered a job inside the office. Because he much preferred being out on the ocean, he had countered Kaegan's offer. Instead of being stuck inside the office five days a week, he would split his time out on the ocean and in the office. Kaegan had agreed to his terms and things had worked out fine until Ray had decided to go into business for himself.

"No. That conference call ended earlier than I thought it would." Ray pulled a clipboard from the rack and scanned it. A woman by the name of Ashley

Ryan had signed up for the boat tour at eleven. He checked his watch and noted he had a full hour before she arrived. "I'm going over to Smithy's Tackle Shop to get a rod tip replacement and will be back in a minute."

"Sure thing, Ray."

A few minutes later Ray was standing in the checkout line behind a family of four. It was obvious the couple had no control over their two young sons under the age of five, who were horseplaying around. Already the boys had knocked over a display of tackle boxes, and from the expression on Smithy's face, Ray could tell the man was ready to finalize their purchase and get them out the store before the kids could do any more damage.

Ray switched his gaze away from Smithy to glance out the window, and suddenly his breath was snatched from his lungs. A woman had paused on the boardwalk to read one of the markers. The first thought that came to his mind was that she was beautiful. Even with a baseball cap on her head, she looked good with shoulder-length hair and striking features on tawny brown skin.

This wasn't the first time a woman had caught his attention. After all, he was a man, memory or no memory. However, this was the first time a woman had stirred this strong a reaction within him. A deep attraction. Sadly it was an attraction that couldn't go anywhere.

"That's all for you, Ray?"

Ray turned his attention back to Smithy. "Yes,

that's all," he said, placing the rod tip kit on the counter. "Looks like you've been busy this morning."

"I was. However, I'm glad that couple took their kids out the store before they caused more damage. Those kids tossed all my bits out that basket onto the floor and those people didn't say anything."

Ray shook his head. "I noticed."

"I don't know why some people don't make their kids behave. If one of mine had acted that way when they were young, I would have taken a strap to them."

Ray knew Smithy's kids, a boy and a girl, who were in high school. They worked with him at the tackle shop on the weekends and both seemed to be good kids. Very respectful to adults.

A short while later he left the tackle shop and was headed back across the walkway to the docks. He glanced ahead and saw the woman. The one he'd noticed earlier. At that moment he saw something else. Those two kids had gotten away from their parents and were running ahead, tearing through the crowd, not caring who or what was in their way. Up ahead was a group of teens headed toward them on skateboards. In order to avoid hitting the kids they would have to swerve to the right. If they went to the left they would crash into one of the buildings. To go right meant colliding with a woman who had paused at the edge of the boardwalk—the section not protected by a railing—to look down into the water.

He knew what was about to happen and shouted, "Hey, lady, look out!"

Instead of getting out the way, she snapped her head around and looked at him just seconds before the group of boys on skateboards tore past her like a mighty whirling tornado, causing her to lose her balance and tumble into the ocean waters.

Not knowing whether she could swim, Ray raced to where the woman had fallen in. He glanced down to search the waters and didn't see her anywhere. Tossing aside the bag from Smithy's, he kicked off his shoes, snatched his T-shirt over his head and tossed his cell phone on top of the pile, before diving into the water after her.

Is this what dying feels like?

The cold water surrounded Ashley, pulling her deep. Still too stunned by the apparition of her husband, she made no move to reach for the surface. And he'd called out to her. She wasn't sure what he'd said but hearing the sound of Devon's voice was what had made her turn. She'd looked right into his face just seconds before losing her balance to tumble into the rough waters. Was she meant to take her last breath under water like he'd done?

Suddenly she felt someone catch her around the waist to tug her back to the surface. Why was she being saved when she was supposed to die this way? If she wasn't supposed to die this way, then why had she seen Devon?

Ashley felt her body being turned and she realized she was no longer under the water but was on her back with the sun shining down bright on her face. She felt herself gliding through the water and then being tugged out of it.

Unable to open her eyes, she felt a hard surface at her back. She heard someone shout that help had been called just moments before warm lips were placed over her mouth while someone was pinching her nose and breathing air into her lungs.

And then she heard that voice again. Devon's voice. He sounded angry and he was demanding her to breathe. If she began breathing, did that mean she would be joining him, wherever he was? She tried opening her eyes but couldn't. It was as if something heavy was weighing her eyelids down. Nor could she breathe like Devon wanted her to do. Her body felt full, tight, almost lifeless. Then suddenly warm lips were placed over hers again, and she immediately recognized them as Devon's lips. And he was pinching her nose again while forcing deep gulps of his breath into her lungs.

"BREATHE, DAMMIT," RAY demanded as he repeated the process, attempting to force air past any blockage in the woman's passageway and lungs. He then put his ear near her mouth while watching her chest for any sign of breathing.

He didn't see any movement and quickly began the process again, ignoring the crowd that had gathered around them. After a few more tries, Ray was relieved when the woman began coughing up water and then breathing.

The crowd of people around them cheered. *Thank God*, he thought. Obviously she couldn't swim because she hadn't put up a fight against the water. He prayed that help arrived soon. Catalina Cove had one fire department and a hospital.

The woman stopped coughing and slowly opened her eyes and stared at him. She then tried moving her mouth. "Don't try talking, ma'am. Help is on the way."

Ray noticed the woman was looking at him strangely. "You fell into the water," he said, not sure if she was confused about what had happened.

She kept looking at him and he figured the woman was in shock. It was understandable if she was. Although she hadn't been in the water that long, she'd managed to get a lot of water in her lungs. He glanced around. The skateboarders were there with petrified looks on their faces, but the couple with those misbehaving kids was nowhere to be found. Go figure.

He glanced back down at the woman who was still staring at him. He had checked her head earlier and hadn't seen where she might have hit it, but still, she needed medical help. What was taking the paramedics so long to get here?

Ray studied the features looking back at him. Even after her ordeal in the water she was totally wet but still beautiful. He saw the wedding ring on her finger. She wasn't anyone from the cove, he was certain of it, and figured she was probably a visitor in town. Was her husband in the cove with her?

"Coming through!"

He heard the paramedics. Great! They were finally there. "What happened?" one of the paramedics asked, although Ray thought it was pretty damn obvious.

"A couple of kids racing around on the boardwalk caused the skateboarders to swerve to avoid hitting them. Made this woman lose her balance and tumble into the water. I dived in and pulled her out—she wasn't in the water long," he said, making a move to get out the way to let the paramedics take over.

The woman grabbed hold of his arm. "Don't go," she whispered in a hoarse, barely audible voice.

He looked down on the hand holding his arm and then gazed back at her. "Is there someone I can call, ma'am? Your husband?"

He saw something flash in her eyes, and instead of answering, she said with choppy breath, "Please. Don't go."

He figured she was still in some semblance of shock. Instead of disengaging her hand from his arm, he shifted positions where the paramedics could check on her without being in their way. Even when they pulled her up in a sitting position, she held tight to his arm and continued to stare at him.

"Ma'am," one of the paramedics said. "Do you know who you are?"

Without taking her gaze off Ray, the woman nodded a slow affirmative before saying in a hoarse voice, "Ashley Ryan."

Ray heard her and immediately remembered the name. Ashley Ryan was on his log to take the boat tour at eleven. He also knew she'd been one of Vashti's referrals, which meant she was staying at Shelby by the Sea.

"Ma'am, is there someone here in the cove with you? Someone we should call? Your husband?" the paramedic asked.

She shook her head no.

Ray wondered why she was still staring at him that way.

"As a precaution, we need to take you to the hospital so they can check you over."

She finally broke eye contact with Ray to look at the paramedic and then shook her head furiously. "No hospital," she said, forcing the words out in a breathless rush.

"You do need to let them take you to the hospital, ma'am," Ray decided to speak up and say.

She switched her gaze from the paramedic and back to him. Tightening her grip on his arm, in a low voice she asked, "You'll go with me? Please."

Ray was surprised by her question and hesitated a minute before saying, "Yes, I'll go to the hospital with you."

Satisfied, she released his arm.

"Here's your shirt, Ray."

"Thanks." Someone handed him his T-shirt and he turned to put it on. Then someone else handed him his shoes and cell phone. He stood and got out the paramedics' way, keeping his eyes on the woman whose eyes were now closed.

He pulled out his cell phone, called Shelby by the Sea and told Vashti what had happened. He then called Tyler to tell him what had happened as well and to handle things with the tours because Ray was on his way to the hospital with the woman who'd been their eleven o'clock customer.

CHAPTER FOUR

ASHLEY HEARD THE movements just seconds before she heard the voices, a masculine voice and then a feminine one.

"How is she, Nurse Corker?"

"Resting comfortably, Dr. Frazier."

She then heard papers shifting right before the masculine voice asked, "I understand she was pulled from the water unresponsive."

"Yes, and after several attempts she was revived."

Then the room got quiet again as if the doctor and the nurse had left. Ashley wasn't sure the amount of time that had passed before she knew the two people had returned. She wanted to open her eyes but couldn't find the strength to do so just yet. Then suddenly what had been said earlier came back to her, nearly shocking her brain in the process.

She recalled Devon's voice telling her to look out. Then she'd seen him just seconds before she'd lost her balance to tumble into the murky waters of the cove. Devon's ghost had been a sign that her life was about to end, and that her husband had come for her to join him. Ashley had discovered she was fine with that because all she'd done for the past three years was grieve his death.

Then suddenly she'd gotten pulled out the water and the man who'd saved her had been Devon. She remembered and knew for a fact she hadn't been hallucinating. Devon had come back from the dead and was walking among the living. Suddenly she felt a pain in her head at the thought of something so preposterous.

"Ms. Ryan, I'm Dr. Frazier. Can you hear me?"

Ashley slowly opened her eyes and was nearly blinded by the brightness of the hospital lights. She quickly closed her eyes, and when she reopened them it was to stare into the face of the man towering over her.

"Ms. Ryan, can you hear me?"

She forced her mouth to move. "Yes."

"Do you know where you are?" Dr. Frazier asked her.

"Yes."

But her mind was still on Devon. He was alive.

After being revived on the boardwalk, she'd opened her eyes and looked into his face, and she knew it wasn't the trauma of hitting the water. When he'd put on his T-shirt, she'd seen his tattoo—the word *sunflower* written in script by his shoulder blade. Instead of the word, she had a design of a sunflower on her hip. Seeing that tattoo had been the confirmation she hadn't been hallucinating.

So why hadn't he recognized her when she clearly recognized him? Granted, he had a beard, looked a bit more rugged, his nose looked like it had gotten broken, and because his skin had darkened some, it was apparent he spent more time out in the sun. But she would recognize her husband anywhere. In fact, all those changes in his features made him even more handsome. Nothing could erase those gorgeous bedroom brown eyes, the sensual shape of his mouth and the deep, husky tenor of his voice.

"Ms. Ryan?"

The concerned look in the doctor's eyes gave her pause and she knew she needed to pay attention to whatever the doctor was asking her. "Could you repeat that?" she asked him.

He nodded. "Do you remember falling into the water off the boardwalk?"

"Yes, I remember."

"Do you remember being revived?"

"Yes." She definitely remembered that part and had known the exact moment Devon had placed his mouth over hers to force air into her lungs.

"You were pulled from the water unresponsive. The man who rescued you is Ray Sullivan. He owns the boat touring company here, Ray's Tours."

Ray's Tours? That was where she'd been headed for a two-hour tour around the cove. She didn't care what the man called himself, she was convinced he was Devon. "Where did he come from?"

Dr. Frazier lifted a brow. "Who? Ray?"

When she nodded, he said, "Lucky for you, he was on the boardwalk and went into action the moment he saw you fall in the water."

Ashley let out a frustrated breath. That wasn't an answer to the question she'd asked. Before she could rephrase the question, the doctor said, "I'm admitting you overnight and if you do okay you can leave tomorrow."

Her brows shot up. "Tomorrow?"

"Yes. Because of the amount of water that got into your lungs, we need to observe you for the next twenty-four hours."

She swallowed. "I need to see him. Ray Sullivan."

The doctor smiled. "You can thank him for saving your life later. Right now I need to get you over to the radiology department for a chest X-ray. Afterward, you will be assigned to a room."

Before she could say anything else, the doctor was gone, leaving her with the nurse, who smiled over at her. "Hi. I'm Paula Corker. I need to take your vitals."

Ashley nodded and then said, "I want to see the man called Ray Sullivan."

The nurse, who looked to be in her midtwenties, gave her a dreamy look, grinned and said, "Hey, don't we all? There's a slew of women who would have loved to have gotten rescued by him. But on a serious note, he's really concerned about you. Last time I looked he was still in the waiting room, awaiting word on your condition."

Devon was still at the hospital? Would he try to explain why he'd faked his death? Why he was pretending not to know her? The shock of seeing him hadn't completely worn off but she was trying to deal with it as best she could without getting hysterical.

"Your pressure is up a little," the nurse said after taking her blood pressure.

That was no surprise there, Ashley thought, not knowing how to stay calm while dealing with the magnitude of emotions she felt. Happiness, confusion, anger and shock. She then asked the nurse the same question she'd asked the doctor earlier, hoping for a different response. "Where did he come from?"

Paula glanced over at her. "Ray?"

Ashley nodded.

"Like Dr. Frazier told you," Paula said, checking her pulse. "He was on the boardwalk and saw you fall in, and it's a good thing he did. For years we've tried to get the mayor to put a rail up. You might want to sue. That would get their attention. You being a tourist and all."

Ashley didn't want to sue. What she wanted was answers, and she decided to rephrase her question. "Has he always lived in the cove?"

The perky nurse scrunched up her forehead as if she was in deep thought trying to remember. "Umm, Ray moved here a little over three years ago. Not sure where he came from but he's good friends with Kaegan Chambray, who owns the shipping company here. I think they were military buddies. Ray's also good friends with Sheriff Grisham."

Ashley didn't say anything for a minute, and then

she asked, "Is he married?" She hadn't even looked at his ring finger.

"No, he's divorced, but just a little warning. I wouldn't get my hopes up about him if I were you, no matter how much concern he's showing toward you."

"Why would you say that?"

"Because Ray's a loner and doesn't date. Trust me, a number of women have tried seducing him, and they have all failed," Paula said, grinning.

Ashley wondered if Paula was one of those women, and as if Paula read her mind, she said, "It's a good thing I married Alan right out of high school. My hubby is the love of my life, so I was never caught up in all the single ladies vying for Ray's attention. Right now, he and Kaegan are the two most eligible bachelors in town, now that the sheriff has gotten married."

Paula lowered her voice to a whispered tone and said, "Personally, I think Ray Sullivan is still pining over his wife. Otherwise, why wouldn't he get involved with another woman? He must have loved her a lot."

Not if he was trying to pretend she didn't exist. It didn't make any sense. Ashley was about to say something when a tall, gangly guy arrived.

"I came to wheel her up for her chest X-ray," he said.

"Good timing, Charles," Paula said.

"How is she, Ray?"

Ray glanced up as Vashti rushed in with Sheriff Grisham by her side. "She's being seen by the ER doctor now. I told Ms. Ryan that I would come here with her and I didn't want to leave until she knows that I kept my word. She indicated to the paramedics that her husband isn't here in the cove with her. Did she fill out any papers referencing how to contact him in case of an emergency?"

"She told me her husband died a few years ago in a car accident," Vashti said sadly.

"Oh," Ray said, nodding his head. "I guess they assumed she was still married since she's still wearing a wedding band."

"It's a good thing you were there," Sawyer said. "From the stories I'm hearing, she nearly drowned. Word is spreading fast around town how you jumped in to save her."

Vashti shook her head. "Ashley Ryan can swim, so I don't understand why she didn't."

Sawyer glanced over at his wife. "What makes you think she can swim?"

"She told me yesterday, when we talked while having tea and muffins. She couldn't wait to take a swim in the gulf and said she was once the captain of her swim team in college." She then turned to Ray. "Are you sure she didn't hit her head and pass out or something?"

"I didn't see any sort of injury, but then, I didn't check her all over."

"I did and there's no head injury." They turned and saw Dr. Frazier approach.

"How is she, Gil?" Vashti rushed to ask. Vashti and Dr. Gil Frazier had been born in Catalina Cove and attended school together. He had moved back to town last year to be closer to his aging parents.

"Ms. Ryan appears okay, but I'm keeping her overnight for observation. She did consume a lot of water into her lungs. I heard what you guys said about her ability to swim. The reason she didn't could be attributed to a number of reasons. The first one could be the shock of falling into the water. That section has the coldest temperatures. I'm glad you're an excellent swimmer, Ray. Otherwise, we could have lost you both."

Ray didn't say anything as he remembered jumping into the water. Gil was right—the water had been freezing cold. But he'd ignored the temperature, determined to pull Ashley Ryan out.

"So she's alert?" Sawyer asked Gil, intruding into Ray's thoughts.

"Yes, and she asked about you, Ray," Gil said, smiling. "I figured you would be the one person she remembers because you saved her life. I believe she wants to thank you. And don't be surprised if she's feeling a high degree of hero worship about now."

"That's not necessary," Ray said, filled with embarrassed discomfort. "I'm just glad the woman is okay."

"It will be necessary to her," Gil said. "It happens, trust me. It's a normal psychological occurrence after a lifesaving incident such as this. I've seen it before."

Well, Ray hoped that wasn't the case with her because he didn't want anyone to think of him as a hero. He'd done what anyone else would have under the circumstances. "Is there any way I can see her before I leave?" he asked. He'd made a promise to her that he would come to the hospital with her and he wanted to let her know he'd kept that promise. He didn't want to question why such a thing was important.

"She's being taken up for X-rays, but I should have her in a room in thirty minutes if you can wait awhile."

Ray felt his chest tighten. Gil had just given him the perfect excuse to leave. All he had to say was that he couldn't wait because he had a business to run. Gil could let Ms. Ryan know he'd been there. But for some reason that wouldn't suffice for him. He wanted to see for himself that she was all right. But more than that, he'd seen the haunted look in her eyes. The look of someone regaining consciousness to discover they'd come close to death. He'd experienced such a thing. "I can wait."

CHAPTER FIVE

ASHLEY GLANCED AROUND her hospital room and thought it was pretty. Sterile looking but pretty just the same. Instead of blinds there were fluffy white curtains, and instead of the plain white blanket on the bed, hers was a bright yellow that matched the throw rug and hospital robe draped across her bed.

She'd only been in Catalina Cove a couple of days but it was easy to tell everyone ran a pretty clean and neat operation, and the hospital was no exception. Even when she'd been wheeled to radiology, she had expected an hour wait time. But they had seen her the moment she'd arrived.

More than anything, she wanted to call Emmie and tell her what had happened. Every single detail, especially about Devon. She doubted Emmie was going to believe her since Ashley had a hard time believing it herself.

Ashley hadn't seen Paula anymore. It had taken every ounce of control Ashley had not to tell the woman that his name was Devon Ryan and not Ray Sullivan and that the man was her husband and not some stranger.

Ashley drew in a deep breath, thinking how weird

all that sounded. But she was convinced it was true. But what if it wasn't? What if the man she thought was Devon really wasn't and she'd only been hallucinating after all? She had experienced quite a bit of trauma, which could account for her thinking that...

No! Ashley refused to let her mind play crazy tricks on her. But what if it had been playing tricks on her all along? What she thought she saw didn't make sense. Her dead husband saving her life. She closed her eyes for a second, trying to calm her racing heart. No matter what, until she saw this man named Ray Sullivan again, she was sticking to what she believed.

There was a knock on her hospital door. Her heart began pounding even faster since to her way of thinking, the sound had been too hard to be made by a female's hand. Drawing in a deep breath, she said, "Come in."

The door opened and in walked a tall man wearing the badge of the law with Vashti by his side. Ashley knew, although they hadn't met yet, the man was Vashti Grisham's husband. The sheriff.

Vashti rushed over to the bed. "You're okay?"

Ashley nodded, glad to see a familiar face. "Yes, I'm fine."

Vashti then introduced the man at her side. "This is my husband, Sawyer. Sawyer, this is Ashley Ryan."

Sawyer offered his hand and she took it. "Nice meeting you," she said.

"Same here. I just hate it's under these circumstances," Sawyer said, smiling grimly. "I'm glad you're okay."

"Thanks." Ashley thought Sawyer was a handsome man and that he and Vashti made a striking couple.

She then recalled what Paula had said earlier. The man standing by her bed was one of Ray Sullivan's close friends. How much did he know about Devon? He was the sheriff. Could she ask him? No, she wouldn't ask anyone anything else until she got a chance to talk to Devon herself. If he didn't show up at the hospital, then she would seek him out the minute she was discharged.

"I got your purse, Ashley," Vashti was saying. "Unfortunately, your cell phone got wet and can't be used. Is there anyone you want me to call for you?"

Ashley knew that more than anything she wanted to call Emmie, Kim and Suzanne, but she couldn't do it now. "No, thanks. That's not necessary, but if you don't mind, could you go to my room and bring me some clothes that I can wear when I get released from here tomorrow?"

"Of course I can."

Ashley thought of something else. "And I left my rental car parked near the marina. I'm sure I've gotten a parking fine by now."

"You don't have to worry about it," the sheriff said. "I will void it under the circumstances."

"Thanks."

"And I'll make sure the car is taken care of," he added.

"I appreciate that."

Vashti glanced at her watch. "We need to go, but I will be back in the morning with your clothes."

"Thanks."

Ashley wanted to ask if Devon was still at the hospital but discovered she didn't have to when Vashti said, "The man who pulled you from the water, Ray Sullivan, had to place a call. But he'll be in to see you after."

A few moments later the couple left, closing the door behind them. Ashley glanced out the hospital window, anticipation building inside her at the thought that she'd be seeing Devon again soon.

She recapped in her mind all that had happened since leaving Shelby by the Sea to make her eleven o'clock appointment with Ray's Tours. Even if their paths hadn't crossed when she fell into the water, Devon and she would have eventually encountered each other when she showed up for the cruise around the cove. What were the chances of her coming here and seeing her husband, who'd supposedly died almost three years ago? The odds were too far-fetched to be real.

But it was real. And what was even crazier was that the reason she'd come here in the first place was to finally get the strength and peace of mind to move on.

Now her mind filled with memories of her three years of courtship and five years of marriage with Devon. At some point she began feeling tired. She closed her eyes, deciding to rest for just a minute.

She was sleeping.

Ray knew he should leave, but for some reason he couldn't. Rubbing a hand down his face, he wondered what the hell was wrong with him. The only excuse he could come up with was that he'd come close to watching this woman die today, and he felt a desperate need to know she was truly okay.

Fear, greater than anything he'd ever felt before, had gripped him when she hadn't responded and then the sense of rippling relief he felt when she finally had… It was a feeling he doubted he would ever forget. And then when she'd opened her eyes and looked at him—stared at him, really—there was something about the look in her eyes that he recognized. The stare of a person realizing how close they'd come to dying. It was probably the same look he'd given the nurse when Ray had awakened after coming out of a three-week coma. Only difference was that she was able to identify herself.

But still, he knew the feeling. He knew how it felt to be at someone's mercy. To believe that you owed your life to another person. He hadn't wanted the feeling for himself and he didn't want it for her. Definitely not her.

Those eyes that had stared at him had almost looked into his soul and he'd felt a bond between two people whose lives had been saved but in different ways. She didn't know him and he didn't know her, but what he did know was that at that moment in time, he had felt an affinity to her. Based on fear, vulnerability, unsettling consciousness or otherwise, it didn't matter. The connection was there whether he wanted it or not. That was why he was here. Nothing more. Nothing less. Nothing personal.

Although he would admit to a keen sense of awareness of the woman sleeping in that hospital bed. A degree he didn't want to feel.

He needed to remedy that and the only way he could was to ease her vulnerability. In easing hers, he would be doing the same with his own.

Ray shoved his hands into the pockets of his jeans as he glanced around. He appreciated Kaegan for dropping off a dry pair of jeans at the hospital for him. Walking around in wet clothes had been uncomfortable as hell, but he had refused to leave even for a moment.

Drawing in a deep breath, he sat down in the chair. If Ms. Ryan didn't wake up within the next hour, he would leave. Visiting hours would be over anyway. He would leave her a note that he had been there and that would be it.

At least, he hoped so.

ASHLEY SLOWLY OPENED her eyes and immediately felt another presence in the room. She moved her head and saw him. He was there, sitting in a chair on the opposite side of the room, and his gaze was fixed on her. Wordlessly, she stared back.

He was staring at her with intense dark eyes, and she maybe had been imagining it, but she was certain that she could feel the impact of his gaze in every part of her body. It suddenly occurred to her that although he was staring at her, it wasn't with any kind of recognition but rather with a fascination he was trying hard not to show but was a little too pronounced not to do so.

She knew her husband and the one thing he'd never been able to hide, even from the first, was his interest in her. But now that interest was not as the woman who'd been his wife, but as a woman he was concerned about and, yes, also attracted to.

At that moment it occurred to her that Devon was not acting. He honestly didn't know who she was and that could mean only one thing. Devon didn't know her because he had somehow lost his memory. The thought of something like that happening seemed so ludicrous, but what other possible reason could there be? Still, she felt the need to test her theory.

"Ray Sullivan?"

He smiled as he stood from the chair to approach her. "I'm surprised you remembered."

"How could I forget the man who saved my life?" she said, forcing a smile. "Thank you."

"You don't have to thank me. I'm just glad that I was there at the time."

"I'm glad you were, too."

"I was hoping you would wake up before I left, Ms. Ryan," he said in that deep, husky voice that always had the ability to make her pulse soar. Devon's voice, looks and build had always been turn-ons for her. It seemed they still were. There was nothing average about his looks. Her husband was a very handsome man. And no matter what, as far as she was concerned, he was still her husband. Whether he knew it or not.

She felt totally at a loss and she didn't want to feel that way. She should be overjoyed and inwardly she was. However, there were a number of questions that only he could provide the answers to. Or could he, when it was obvious he couldn't remember anything? He couldn't remember her?

"Well, I'll be seeing you."

"Wait!" she said, not wanting him to leave yet. There were so many questions she wanted to ask. So many answers she wanted to demand of him. Then she wanted to scream her joy. Cry her relief. Throw herself in his arms and make him remember her. Force him to do so, but she held back because all it took was for her to remember that incident with Carolyn Jacobs.

Carolyn Jacobs had been a member of their swimming team at Harvard. While home on spring break, she had jumped into a friend's pool and somehow hit her head, resulting in memory loss. The doctors had warned Carolyn's parents that the worst thing they could do to a person with amnesia was to try to force their memory back on them.

As much as Ashley wanted to tell Devon who she was and who and what he was to her, she couldn't. At least not until she found out how Devon hadn't died when the car he'd driven had gone off that bridge. Someone had to know something about what had happened and how he'd ended up in Catalina Cove.

What had Paula Corker told her about Devon being good friends with Sheriff Grisham and someone name Kaegan Chambray? She had met the sheriff earlier when he and Vashti had dropped by her hospital room. He was a man of the law. Of course, when she told him her true relationship to Devon, that the man who'd saved her life wasn't just a Good Samaritan, but her husband, it would be hard for anyone to believe, but it was the truth.

"Yes, Ms. Ryan?"

"Please call me Ashley."

He nodded. "Okay, Ashley." His face softened a little and her heart began pounding when he said her name, just the way he'd always pronounced it. In a way that could get her blood stirring.

"I need to know everything that happened. From the beginning."

He nodded again, and then he pulled the chair closer to the bed, and she became filled with so much joy, she could weep. She wanted to touch him, hug him, kiss him and make love to him. More than anything, she wanted him to remember she was his woman like he was her man.

She watched him ease down in the chair and bit down on her lower lip to keep from moaning out loud. Why did he have to look so good? Why was the way his jeans tightened across masculine thighs such a turn-on to her?

He began talking and the sound of his voice comforted her, made her believe in miracles and in the power of prayers. She had been given another chance with her husband, and it didn't matter what he was calling himself now—she would take that second chance.

Every so often she would interrupt his narrative to ask him a question or to get him to clarify something he'd said. It didn't matter one iota if he thought the near-drowning incident had fogged up her brain's ability to comprehend. The bottom line was she wasn't ready for him to go. She wanted to ask him questions about himself but knew she couldn't risk him getting suspicious.

He glanced at his watch. "Visiting hours ended a while ago," he said, standing.

Ashley had to tilt her head back to look at him. More than anything, she wanted to ask him when she could see him again, but there was no way she could do so without it sounding like a come-on.

An idea then popped into her head. "I was on my way to take a tour around the cove on your boat."

He nodded, holding her gaze. "Yes, I know. I recognized your name."

Hope sprang to life inside of her. Had seeing her name triggered something in his mind? "You recognized my name?"

"Yes. Earlier I'd gone over the day's tour log and saw your name. When you gave it to the paramedics, I remembered it."

Ashley tried not to let disappointment settle around her heart. "I hope I can reschedule," she said, pasting a smile to her face.

"No reason you shouldn't. Just let Vashti know

and she can arrange it. Either me or my assistant, Tyler Clinton, will be able to take you."

Only someone as close to him as she was could realize what he was doing. According to what the nurse had told her, he hadn't shown interest in any of the women in Catalina Cove, yet he was showing interest in her whether he wanted to or not.

If it was his intent to pass her over to his assistant, that wasn't acceptable. He would find that out soon enough. "I will."

"Goodbye, Ashley."

He hadn't said "I'll be seeing you later" but he'd said "Goodbye," which sounded so final. She fought back the wave of disappointment she felt. "Goodbye." She couldn't call him Devon and she refused to call him Ray. At least, not right now.

He turned and left without looking back. She didn't want to cry but she did so anyway. She was overwhelmed and distraught at the same time. Her husband was back and that should be the only thing that mattered. But he didn't know her and for her that realization hurt more than anything, more than almost dying.

CHAPTER SIX

"Morning."

Kaegan and Sawyer glanced up when Ray slid into the booth with them. "Morning," they greeted him simultaneously.

"Did you get to see Ms. Ryan before visiting hours ended yesterday?" Sawyer asked, taking a sip of his coffee.

"Yes, I saw her," Ray said, and appreciated when Bryce Witherspoon appeared with a cup of coffee just the way he liked it. "Thanks, Bryce."

"You're welcome, Ray."

Out of habit he glanced at Kaegan and watched how his gaze was on Bryce when she refilled Kaegan's and Sawyer's cups. The two men thanked her but it was only Sawyer whom she acknowledged by name. Her usual slight didn't appear to bother Kaegan. Ray figured chances were he was pretty used to it by now.

"You're quiet, Ray."

"Is that a crime, Sheriff?"

Sawyer chuckled. "No. In fact, I wish Jade would practice it sometime."

Ray couldn't help but grin. Jade was Sawyer and Vashti's teenage daughter. She was in her last year of high school with plans to attend college some-where in Nevada in the fall. At least, according to Sawyer that was the plan now, but it could change.

"You've taken my position as town hero," Kae-gan said, causing them to remember how Kaegan had raced into a burning house last winter to save an old man who'd fallen asleep while smoking. "Ev-eryone is talking about how you jumped into the ocean to save that woman. According to old lady Kitty Barnwell, you stripped naked before you dived in."

Ray rolled his eyes. The one thing that amazed him about Catalina Cove was how fast news trav-eled and usually how inaccurate. People liked to embellish details, and it was always the older resi-dents doing it more so than the young. "I didn't strip naked. Didn't come close. I took off my T-shirt and shoes. Since you brought me a dry pair of jeans to the hospital yesterday to put on, then you know I kept my pants on, Kaegan."

Kaegan shrugged. "Just telling you the story that's out there, and since it's Ms. Kitty who's put-ting it out, it's going to get around quickly."

With little credibility, Ray hoped. "Whatever." He glanced over at Sawyer. "Tell me what you know about Ashley Ryan."

The lifting of Sawyer's brow denoted his sur-prise and Ray knew why. In the three years he'd known Sawyer, Ray had never asked the man any specifics about a woman before. "What makes you think I know anything?"

Ray rolled his eyes. "You're the sheriff, for starters, and then you're married to Vashti, who has befriended the woman."

Sawyer smiled. "Vashti befriends anyone who stays at Shelby by the Sea." He paused a moment and asked, "What do you want to know, Ray?"

Ray took another sip of his coffee and waited until after Bryce delivered a plate of hot blueberry muffins and left before saying, "She's wearing a wedding ring. However, according to Vashti, she's a widow and her husband died a few years back in a car accident."

Sawyer nodded before biting into a hot muffin. After chewing a minute, he said, "Obviously, she hasn't fully gotten over her grief and still wears her rings. No crime in that."

RAY DIDN'T SAY ANYTHING. If that was true, why had he felt her interest in him? He could say the reaction was mutual because he'd felt it in the way she had looked at him, which was the basically the same way he'd looked at her. But the attraction wouldn't last.

As far as he knew, he'd never saved anyone's life before, and maybe the way he was feeling, a sense of attachment, was merely a normal reaction and vice versa.

"Where is she from?" Ray asked.

Both Kaegan and Sawyer stared at him and then Kaegan asked, "Are you interested in her?"

Ray shook his head. "No. I can't be interested in any woman—you know that."

"Only because you won't allow yourself to be," Kaegan countered.

"Only because I can't" was his response.

"She's from South Carolina. Not sure of the city," Sawyer said, then paused and asked, "Any reason you didn't ask her any of these questions when you saw her?"

Ray shrugged. "I didn't want to tire her out. She'd been through enough."

"So what did the two of you talk about?" Kaegan asked curiously.

Ray took a sip of his coffee. "She wanted details of exactly what happened. I guess she didn't remember much of it."

Sawyer nodded. "That makes sense. Most victims can't remember details of trauma."

Ray, of all people, knew that. "She's pretty."

Why he'd said that, he wasn't sure. But it was the truth. Ashley Ryan was pretty. He had first noticed her while in Smithy's Tackle Shop. When he saw Kaegan and Sawyer staring at him, he said, "I didn't mean anything by that. It's just an observation."

"Don't offer any explanations, Ray. Memory or no memory, you're still a man. And there are times when men want things they know just aren't good for them."

Ray noticed Kaegan was staring across the café at Bryce Witherspoon, who was serving another customer.

"Ms. Ryan is going to be in town for two weeks," Sawyer said.

Ray took a sip of his coffee. "Is she?"

"Yes. Just in case you want to know."

Ray shrugged. "I shouldn't want to."

"But you do," Kaegan said, grinning. "Like Sawyer said, you're a man. Glad to know you're not really made of stone where women are concerned."

Ray lifted a brow. "You thought I was?"

Kaegan chuckled. "Sometimes I wondered. I've seen some real nice-looking women flirt with you and I've watched your lack of interest."

Ray lifted a brow. "Hmm, I've seen you act the same way, Kaegan." There, he'd called his friend out. It was obvious whether Kaegan wanted to admit it or not, and regardless of what might have happened between Kaegan and Bryce years ago, Kaegan still had the hots for her.

"Anyone want a refill?"

Ray glanced up and Bryce was at their table. "No, I'm fine," he said.

Sawyer wanted a refill. Kaegan didn't say anything. He wouldn't even look at her, but then watched her walk off.

"Time for me to go," Ray said, placing enough money on the table for his coffee, muffins and a tip.

"I understand Ms. Ryan was on her way to take a tour on your boat when the accident happened," Sawyer said.

Ray nodded.

"Think she'll reschedule?" Kaegan asked.

"Not sure," Ray said.

"Don't be surprised if she doesn't. She might not want to go anywhere near a lot of water for a while," Sawyer said.

That might be true but for some reason Ray wanted to believe Ashley Ryan was a fighter and would not let what happened yesterday defeat her. "If she does, fine, and if she doesn't, that's fine, too." He stood. "I'll see you guys later. And, Kaegan, my last tour is around two. I'll stop by your place to see if you need an extra man on one of your boats."

Kaegan smiled. "Thanks. I'd appreciate it if you do. I have a big order that's going to New Orleans. One of the hotels in the French Quarter is hosting a huge convention of seafood lovers. They've asked for four times their usual order."

"Then I'll make it my business to drop by and help. See you guys later."

"THANKS FOR EVERYTHING you've done, Vashti," Ashley said when they drove up the long driveway to Shelby by the Sea. The doctor had discharged her that morning and Vashti had arrived with her clothes and everything she needed to leave the hospital.

"You're welcome. I'm glad you're okay and hope you'll get some rest today."

Ashley knew there was no way she could do that. She had too much to do and she had to hit the ground running. First, she needed to replace her mobile phone and then call Emmie, Suzanne and

Kim and tell them about Devon. They would think she was crazy, but no matter what it took, she had to convince them she wasn't insane. Then she needed to make sure they didn't converge on Catalina Cove. The situation with Devon was one she had to handle on her own. She would need their support but not their interference.

"I need to get a new phone," she said as she followed Vashti through the door.

"Done," Vashti said, smiling over at her and reaching into the pocket of her jeans to bring out a phone. "Here's your new phone."

Ashley's brows shot up. "Thanks," she said, accepting the phone. "But how could you get it without me?"

Vashti chuckled. "I couldn't but Sawyer could. Being sheriff comes with certain privileges."

"And I'm forever grateful," Ashley said, slipping the phone into the back pocket of her jeans.

Vashti grinned. "However, Sawyer drew the line about replacing your purse. Decided to let you handle that yourself."

Ashley let out a laugh. "I do understand."

Moments later Ashley was up in her suite and pulling out her new phone. She gave a sigh of relief when she saw all her apps, contacts and photos had gotten transferred over. She placed a call to Emmie. "If you're calling me you can't be having much fun, Ash," Emmie said.

"We need to have a four-way," she quickly said.

"You connect with Suzanne and I'll grab Kim and merge calls."

"Oh, okay. Is something wrong?"

"It depends on how you look at it. Now get Suzanne on the call."

It wasn't long before all four of them were on the phone. "Okay, I need to tell you guys something you might find hard to believe. As hard as it might be, I want you guys to listen and know I haven't lost my mind. And please hold your questions or comments until after I'm finished. Okay?"

"Okay," agreed all three.

Taking a deep breath, Ashley said, "I saw Devon." Then she started at the beginning. Unlike what they had agreed to, they didn't wait until she was finished to make comments or ask questions. Of course they thought she'd slipped into insanity. They told her they'd sent her to Catalina Cove to relax, enjoy herself and make decisions about her future—not sink deeper into the past.

It took Ashley a full thirty minutes of answering their questions and repeating certain aspects of what she'd told them, especially the part about her almost drowning and Devon saving her, before they began crying. In fact, the four of them cried together. They were happy for her and afraid for her as well. If Devon did have amnesia, what if he didn't regain his memory?

For Ashley, that was a no-brainer. She intended to be a part of his life regardless.

But of course Kim had to play devil's advocate

and ask her the one question she couldn't answer: What if he didn't want her as part of his life? The life he had now?

After swearing her best friends to secrecy and promising to keep them updated with every single detail—big or small—she was finally able to end the call. A part of her felt better sharing every element of the past twenty-four hours with them. After clicking off the phone she went into the bathroom to wash her tearstained face.

She stared at herself in the mirror. Talking to her friends, she'd relived the moments of the day herself. Especially waking up to find Devon sitting in her hospital room waiting for her. She doubted that she would ever forget how he'd been looking at her. There had been concern in his eyes but she was convinced there had been something else as well. Had his mind been trying to recall other times he'd watched her sleep? If that had been the case, he hadn't let on. She distinctly hadn't seen any kind of recognition in his gaze. Only male interest. Considering what the nurse had said about his reluctance to show interest in any woman in town, should that give her hope?

Ashley moved away from the mirror to leave her suite, deciding not to get her hopes up about anything. What she decided to do and what her best friends had agreed she should do was to find out every bit of detail she could about how Devon was alive when she and everyone else had thought him dead.

The combined aroma of coffee and blueberry muffins greeted Ashley the moment she stepped off the stairs and headed toward Vashti's office. The serving of breakfast had ended a half hour ago, but she hoped there were leftovers somewhere since she hadn't eaten anything.

She knocked on Vashti's office door. "Come in."

"I hope I'm not disturbing you, Vashti."

Vashti smiled as she stood. "You aren't. And you look like you could use a cup of coffee," she said, heading for the coffeepot. "And what about a blueberry muffin?"

"I was hoping you would ask. I've fallen in love with them," Ashley said, grinning.

"Well, we are the blueberry capital of the nation," Vashti said proudly, pouring coffee into cups and then filling small plates with muffins.

Ashley took the plate and cup Vashti handed her. "Thanks."

"You're welcome. I think I'll join you with coffee and a muffin myself. And let's sit over here." Vashti led Ashley over to a sitting area with a love seat and chair.

Ashley recalled Vashti telling her that for years she'd worked for a five-star hotel in New York before moving back here to reopen the inn she'd inherited upon the death of her aunt. Even after a few days Ashley could tell Vashti was good at what she did and was a person she could talk to. It stood to reason since Vashti's husband was close friends with Devon that Ashley should start here with her.

Hopefully, Vashti could shed some light on a few things, and if she couldn't, certainly Vashti's husband could.

Ashley took a sip of her coffee and then said, "I hate taking you away from your work, but I have a few questions I'd like to ask you."

Vashti's brows rose. "Oh? About what?"

"Not what, but who. Ray Sullivan," Ashley said, then watched Vashti over the rim of her cup.

"What about Ray?"

"I'd like for you to tell me everything you know about him."

Vashti didn't say anything for a minute and then she placed her coffee cup aside. "Why? Do you like him?"

Ashley shook her head. "No, I *love* him."

"Love him?"

"Yes."

Vashti didn't say anything for a moment and then she said, "I can understand you might believe that since he saved your life yesterday, but—"

"It's more than that," Ashley interrupted to say.

Vashti's brows arched. "How so?"

Ashley sighed deeply while ignoring the way her stomach tightened. In her heart she believed Vashti was someone she could trust. Someone who could help her put the pieces of the puzzle together so she could understand how Devon was still alive when she'd thought him dead for three years.

She met Vashti's inquisitive gaze and said, "For me it should be pretty simple but in truth it's rather complicated."

When Vashti didn't say anything but sat there waiting for Ashley to continue, she said, "The man you know as Ray Sullivan… Well, I am his wife."

CHAPTER SEVEN

"HIS WIFE?" VASHTI EXCLAIMED, jumping to her feet.

"Yes," Ashley said, clearly trying to remain calm. "Yesterday he saved my life and didn't even recognize me. I recognized him, right before I tumbled over in the water. Since he didn't know who I was, I can only assume he's somehow lost his memory after the car accident."

Car accident? Vashti began pacing when she recalled what Sawyer had told her about how Ray had lost his memory and had come to live in Catalina Cove. It hadn't been a car accident.

When she heard sobbing, she turned to Ashley and saw tears in the woman's eyes. Vashti immediately went to her, dropping down on the sofa beside her and wrapping her arms around her shoulders. She knew how important and comforting hugs were and she gave her a fierce one. When Ashley's sobs eased up somewhat, Vashti asked, "What happened?"

In a teary voice Ashley told Vashti everything, ending with how hard it had been for her over the past three years.

"Oh, my God!" Vashti said, imagining that memories of that day were coming back full blast. "You got word that your husband was dead on your fifth wedding anniversary?"

Ashley just nodded as tears continued to flow down her cheeks. "And he doesn't know me, Vashti. I talked to him last night when he came to the hospital to see me, to make sure I was doing okay. He looked at me but didn't recognize me. Do you know how that hurts?"

Vashti couldn't rightly say that she did. She'd gone through plenty of drama in her own life but nothing like this. "No, I don't know," she said honestly.

Ashley wiped at her eyes. "Please tell me what you know about Devon."

Vashti's brow went up. "Devon?"

"Yes. The man you know as Ray Sullivan is Devon Ryan. I need to know how a man everybody in Hardeeville, South Carolina, believes is dead is very much alive in Catalina Cove, Louisiana."

Vashti didn't know everything about how Ray came to live in Catalina Cove, but she knew two men who did. "I can tell you what I know, but you really need to talk to Sawyer and Kaegan."

She moved away from the sofa to grab the phone off her desk, punched in a number and then waited for an answer. "Hello, sweetheart. What's up?" the male voice on the other end asked.

"Hi, Sawyer. I need you to come to Shelby immediately. And please bring Kaegan with you."

"Why? What's wrong?"

"I'll explain things when you get here."

VASHTI WASN'T SURPRISED when Sawyer arrived with Kaegan in less than five minutes. They rushed inside Shelby by the Sea like they expected to find the inn on fire. Since she'd been expecting them, she was there to open the door before they got a chance to knock. "Come in, guys. Sorry to interrupt your breakfast."

Sawyer leaned down to give her a peck on the lips. "Sweetheart, you can interrupt me at any time."

"Well, you can't interrupt me anytime. I have a lot of work to do today," Kaegan said, moving past Vashti and Sawyer to enter her office. He headed in that direction, but stopped when he saw Ashley standing there.

Ashley had stood when the men entered the room.

"Hello, excuse my manners. Good morning," Kaegan said, smiling and moving toward her. Vashti didn't miss the way he checked out Ashley's hand and noticed her wedding ring. She knew he would assume she was off-limits and would respect that.

"Hello and good morning," Ashley replied, accepting the hand he offered in a friendly handshake.

"It's good seeing you again, Ashley," Sawyer said, walking over to her to shake her hand as well. "Glad you're out of the hospital and doing well."

"Ashley?" Kaegan asked, as if surprised. "Ray's Ashley?" Then as if he might have said something he should not have, he said, "What I mean is that you're the woman Ray saved from drowning yesterday, right?"

"Yes, I am," Ashley said. "I'm Ashley Ryan."

Kaegan gave her a friendly smile. "Glad to see you up and about after yesterday."

"Thanks."

He then turned to Vashti. "So what's up, Vash? Why did you have us rush over here?"

Vashti moved to stand beside Ashley. "What you let slip moments ago, Kaegan, is pretty close to the truth."

Sawyer stared at his wife. "What do you mean?"

Vashti glanced at her husband and Kaegan. They were Ray's closest friends and fiercely loyal to him. She looked at Ashley, giving her a supportive smile, before glancing back over at them. "I want you guys to meet Ray's wife."

ALMOST AN HOUR later Ashley drew in a deep breath. She hadn't been bothered by Kaegan and Sawyer's relentless questions. They needed to verify she was who she claimed to be before they would tell her anything. She hadn't taken it personally. In fact, it made her feel good that Devon had such loyal friends.

It had been Sawyer who asked the most questions. She hadn't been surprised to learn he was a former FBI agent. She'd shown them her photo album that had been transferred to her new phone that included tons of pictures of her and Devon, even their wedding picture.

Then on Vashti's computer, she was able to pull up Devon's obituary and news articles about his death. There was also a news article about the foundation she'd established in his name and the number of college scholarships the foundation gave out each year.

"Although Ray couldn't remember a single thing about his past," Kaegan was saying, taking a sip of his coffee while sitting across from Vashti's desk, "I knew in my gut he was well educated, with an IQ that would astound a lot of people. But all he wanted to do was be on a boat in the ocean. And I often wondered why his family wasn't looking for him. Now I know."

Ashley nodded. "The reason we didn't look for him was because we had no reason to suspect that wasn't him in that car. Had I known differently, no amount of money would have kept me from searching for him. I gave the Ohio sheriff hell for not sending divers into that river to find him and bring up his car."

"To give law enforcement credit, they didn't have reason to think it wasn't Ray driving that car," Sawyer said. "And I'm not just saying that because I'm a cop."

"Please tell me what you guys know," she said softly. "How did he end up here in Catalina Cove?"

"I know the answer to that," Kaegan said. "After he came out of his coma and went through various evaluations, the one thing his doctor discovered about Ray was that he loved being near water. His doctor, Dennis Riggins, was a college friend of mine. We've stayed in touch and he knew I had returned to Catalina Cove to take over my family's shipping company. I got a call from him one day and he told me about Ray and what happened to him. Dennis thought Ray would not only be a good fit for my company but also for the town. He thought the cove was just the place Ray needed to start over. I hired him over the phone just on Dennis's recommendation without even talking to Ray. After he was given a new identity and enough funds just to make do, I picked him up from the airport."

Kaegan took another sip of his coffee. "We hit it off immediately. I told him that instead of living in an apartment, he could move in with me and use one of my spare bedrooms until he was up on his feet. To keep people from asking too many questions about his past, we decided to let people assume he was an old military friend of mine. The only person we leveled with was Sawyer. Only because being a cop made him curious and suspicious by nature."

"Whose idea was it to claim he was a divorced man?" Ashley asked.

"It was Ray's idea. Although he had no recollection of his past, he was convinced it included a wife. When he came out of the coma, the indentation of where his wedding ring used to be was obvious. Dennis figured at some point he'd gotten robbed by gunpoint of everything. He was found unconscious by a jogger in the woods. He was badly beaten with a broken jaw and nose as well as several hard blows to the head from the butt of a gun."

Ashley fought back tears upon hearing all Devon

had gone through without her. "Is there any way for me to talk to Dr. Riggins? To get a clear understanding of how to move forward. It's obvious Devon has no idea who I am."

"That might be true but he does feel a connection to you," Sawyer said.

Ashley's heart leaped. "How do you know that?"

"He told us. He thinks it's an attraction."

Her stomach contracted when she remembered how she had awakened last night to find him sitting in her hospital room and staring at her. She'd been certain the look in his eyes had been of male interest. The look he'd seen in hers certainly had been feminine interest. If he'd been capable of reading her thoughts like Devon could, then he would know for her it was more than interest and all about love.

"But you don't think that's what it is?" she asked Sawyer.

He shrugged. "I can't say. All I know is that from the time he's been in the cove there hasn't been a woman who's caught his interest."

"Sawyer is right about that," Kaegan said, standing to stretch his legs. "Ray even brought you up at breakfast this morning. Personally, I just assumed he felt an affinity toward you for saving your life. But like Sawyer, now I'm not sure. What if he's slowly regaining his memory and feeling a connection to you is the first sign?"

Kaegan pulled his cell phone from his jean pocket. "I'll put you in touch with Dennis. I know for a fact he'd want to talk to you. He calls me from time to time just to see how Ray's doing."

When Dr. Dennis Riggins came on the line, Ashley placed the call on speaker for all of them to hear. He was able to provide her with the details about Devon from the time he'd been brought into the ER, a man barely alive, and how he'd remained in a coma for three weeks. He told her everything had been done to determine Ray's identity. News about him had been placed in newspapers around the country and he was funneled through the national missing persons database with no luck. The authorities had even done a fingerprint check. Since Ray didn't have a criminal record, nothing came back.

Profound regret washed over Ashley. Had she thought for one second that Devon had been missing instead of dead as the police had claimed, there was no way she would not have searched for her husband. That made her wonder who had been driving Devon's car when it had gone off the bridge.

Dr. Riggins further explained retrograde amnesia and how there was a chance Devon would never regain his memory, but then, there was an equal chance that he might. Also, he couldn't guarantee any connection that Devon felt to her had anything to do with his memory returning.

He warned her against shocking Devon into remembering her, no matter how tempting it might be to do so, explaining that with some amnesia cases, doing such a thing might work, but with Devon it could backfire and cause him to have a setback.

"If you tell him that you're his wife," the doctor was saying, "he's going to feel guilty that he has no idea who you are and that emotions he should be feeling for you aren't there."

"Then what am I supposed to do? I can't just leave my husband here and go back home and pretend I didn't see him and he's still dead. I love Devon and the thought that he might never get his memory back is unacceptable to me."

"Yes, but it's a reality you might have to face. Fifty percent of those with retrograde amnesia don't ever get their memory back. The other half does. Not enough studies have been conducted to determine the reason why some regain their memory while others don't. But statistics have shown those who don't ever get their memory back are usually those whose families try to force their memory on them. The brain can't accept what is being told to them and reacts negatively."

Ashley drew in a deep breath. That was not what she wanted to hear and she fought back her tears. She had cried enough over the last three years and now she had to be strong, for both her and Devon. "Then what should I do?" she asked in a shaky voice, although she was determined not to feel defeated.

"You love your husband regardless of whether he's Devon Ryan or Ray Sullivan, right?"

"Yes," she said softly. There was no question in her mind or heart that she did.

"Then get to know Ray Sullivan as Ray Sullivan and not as Devon Ryan. Get to know him and let him get to know you. According to what Kaegan said earlier, Ray is attracted to you, although he might not know why. That's a start. It could be that those same qualities you possessed that captured his heart before might recapture it again. In other words, give him a chance to know you, not as the woman he *should* be in love with, but as the woman he would want to be in love with. If he gets his memory back, then you'll be both his first and second love."

Ashley brightened at that, but Kaegan said, "There's something you should know, though. There's a chance that although Ray might be interested in you, he will never act on it. He believes he was married in his former life, and because there's a fifty-fifty chance he might regain his memory, he's decided not to get involved with another woman. He has a strong sense of doing what's right. He'll probably resist anything between the two of you. Put all kinds of roadblocks in the way. Whatever you do, you're going to have to make it seem like pursuing you is his idea and you're not a stalker."

Ashley didn't say anything. From the looks on Sawyer's face, he agreed. They, of all people, should know since Devon was their friend. Now what the nurse at the hospital had said made sense. That was why he wasn't dating any of the single women in town.

Sawyer gave a half smile. "I would hate for Ray

to file a complaint against you for stalking. Then I'd have to arrest you."

Ashley knew even with the sheriff's smile that he was dead serious. Ray had rights, and if he thought those rights were being violated or threatened, he would have the law on his side. That could get ugly, especially if, as a result, she was forced to reveal Ray's true identity. She had to figure out a way to ensure Ray became interested in her again without him feeling she was a threat or manipulating the process.

"What happens if he wants to get to know me and information I share about myself starts him remembering things?" she asked the doctor.

"Then that's good. Being told who you are and figuring out who you are on your own are two different things. There's a possibility the information you share might trigger some type of memory, and if so, that's good."

The doctor paused a minute and then added, "If you decide to give him the chance to get to know you, it's imperative that you be truthful with him as much as you can. If he asks, tell him the truth that you're a widow. If he asks your husband's name and how he died, tell him."

Ashley nodded and then asked, "What if I'm able to break through this wall Devon has erected? If he falls in love with me all over again, then can I tell him the truth about who I am?"

"Telling him at that point could be less traumatic for him. Although he still won't remember a life with you, I believe having you in his life in that situation would be more acceptable because he has fallen in love with you all over again. However, I would caution you to know for sure he's at that point. You shouldn't assume emotions Ray might not be feeling."

In other words, Ashley knew the doctor was warning her not to assume Devon had fallen in love with her just because that was what would be best for her. She decided he'd have to tell her he loved her outright. "Thanks, Dr. Riggins, for all the information you've provided."

"I'm sure I've given you a lot to think about."

"Yes. I love Devon, and if I have to get to know him as Ray Sullivan, then I will. Even if he never gets his memory back or doesn't fall in love with me a second time, it doesn't matter. I will always love him." She drew in a deep breath. "Why does life have to be so complicated?"

Nobody answered her and then Dr. Riggins said, "Please solve this mystery for me regarding Ray."

Ashley's brow bunched. "What mystery is that?"

"That tattoo on his back. He had no idea why it's there and what it means."

A smile touched Ashley's lips as she remembered the day they'd gone to the tattoo parlor together. "Sunflower is Devon's pet name for me. It's written in script across his back, and I have an actual design of one someplace else." No need to share with them that she had a design of a sunflower on her upper hip.

"Mystery solved," Dr. Riggins said, chuckling.

"And just so you're not taken by surprise in case you reschedule that tour around the cove on Ray's boat, the name of his boat is the *Sunflower*," Kaegan told her.

Ashley's breath caught. "It is?"

"Yes. He figured the word evidently meant something since he had it tattooed on his back and decided to give that name to his boat."

"We also have a mystery that needs solving," Sawyer said when the room got quiet again.

Ashley lifted a brow. "What mystery is that?"

"A couple of weeks ago Ray mentioned to me and Kaegan that he woke up feeling that particular day should mean something to him."

"What date was it?"

"June 10," Kaegan said.

Ashley stared at the two men. "That's my birthday."

Nobody said anything for a moment. Then Vashti asked in a hopeful voice, "Could that mean something vital, Dr. Riggins?"

"I still can't say. It could, but again, there's no guarantee even with that."

"But what if he asks when my birthday is?"

"Tell him. He's either going to think it's a coincidence or it might help in his memory's reclamation process. If you need more information from me, just get my number from Kaegan and call me at any time."

"Thanks, Dr. Riggins," she said and hung up.

Vashti crossed the room to Ashley, gave her a hug and said, "As Ray's friends who love him and want what's best for him, we're hoping you're able to break through those barriers he has erected, Ashley."

Ashley smiled through tears she'd tried to hold back and said, "I hope so, too. I intend to do whatever it takes and I truly do thank you guys for being there for Devon."

"I'm going to warn you that it won't be easy since he has pretty much made it up in his mind to be a loner," Vashti said. "But then, I know firsthand how strong an attraction between two people can be," she said, glancing over at her husband and giving him a smile. She then looked back at Ashley. "A strong attraction is hard to resist."

"So, what's the first thing you plan to do?" Kaegan asked.

For several seconds, Ashley stood there in front of them, the three people she'd discovered were her husband's closest friends. "I guess the first thing I need to do is wrap my mind around the fact that he's not Devon Ryan now but Ray Sullivan. I have to get used to calling him that."

AT THE END of his workday, Ray opened the door to his truck and slid behind the wheel. After buckling his seat belt and before turning the key in the ignition, he paused a moment and just sat there, fighting the urge to call Vashti to see how Ashley Ryan was doing.

He was certain Vashti would know since she'd

volunteered to take Ms. Ryan back to Shelby by the Sea after she was released from the hospital this morning. Sawyer had driven the rental car to the inn after someone had turned Ms. Ryan's purse in after it had gotten fished out the water.

If something went wrong and the woman had a relapse or something, Vashti would have called him. But then, why would she? He was not a relative of the woman. Nor could he be considered a friend. He was only the man who'd pulled her from the ocean, doing what anyone else would have done under the circumstances.

He rubbed a frustrating hand down his face. Today shouldn't be any different from any other day. He would go home, get a beer out the fridge and enjoy the drink before diving into his microwave dinner. Then he would jog a few miles around the neighborhood, return home, take a shower, make entries into his journal and then get ready for bed.

Every now and then instead of eating alone at home, he would join Kaegan at the café, but tonight he didn't want to do that either. He wanted to find out how Ashley Ryan was doing. Baffled by this obsession yet giving into it anyway, he pulled his phone out the pocket of his shirt and punched in Vashti's number. She answered immediately.

"Hey, Ray."

"Hey, Vashti. You okay?"

"I'm doing fine. What about you?"

"Doing okay. I was wondering if Ashley Ryan is back at Shelby by the Sea."

"Yes. I picked her up from the hospital this morning."

Ray raked a hand over his head. "How is she doing?"

"She's been resting up most of the day like the doctor suggested. She joined me for breakfast, but I haven't seen her anymore today."

"Oh."

"Is something wrong, Ray?"

"No, nothing is wrong. I was just checking on her."

"That's kind of you. In fact, why don't you stop by on your way home from work and see how she's doing for yourself?"

"There's no way I can do that."

"Why not?"

He truly couldn't answer that. "Look, Vashti, I've got to go. I'll talk to you later." He quickly clicked off the phone.

Leaning back in his seat, he tilted his head against the headrest and closed his eyes. His thoughts had been filled with Ashley Ryan today. Why? He knew the decision he'd made three years ago and until now sticking to it hadn't been an issue. So, what was there about Ms. Ryan that was different? Why had he felt like a goner the moment she had opened her eyes and looked at him?

Ray knew he had to get a grip. There was no way he could become involved with a woman when he might have a wife and family out there somewhere. He didn't want to think of the drama such a thing would cause if his memory ever returned. He went to bed every night praying that it would return. But lately he'd noted that particular prayer wasn't as strong as it used to be. He was getting used to being Ray Sullivan and living a comfortable life in the cove.

Catalina Cove had a way of growing on a person and it had definitely grown on him. Granted, he didn't go out of his way to make friends, but the ones he'd made were solid and trustworthy. Even the single women in town had finally gotten the message and backed off.

He liked it here and couldn't see himself leaving to live anyplace else. But he might have to if his memory ever returned. Then he would be thrust back into another life. Had he liked that life? What if he no longer wanted to be part of that world?

It had been three years, going on four. What if his wife had moved on and was involved with someone else? What if she had remarried? His therapist had suggested such a possibility to him. Just because he had refused to become involved with another woman didn't mean she hadn't become involved with another man. Especially if she assumed he was dead.

For a whole year he'd checked the various missing persons sites on the internet, hoping to see his picture. But no such report ever appeared. Why? If his wife loved him, wouldn't she be looking for him? Then maybe he hadn't been a good husband and she was glad he was gone. The thought that he had no idea what sort of person he'd been in his previous life twisted his insides.

He opened his eyes when a devastating scenario torpedoed through his mind. It was one where he had to choose between the life he once had and the one he had now. His chest tightened, not wanting to think about having to make such a choice. But he had to accept that one day he might. He could not have lived on this earth for as long as he had without people knowing him.

So why was he yet to be identified by anyone? Granted, he'd rarely left Catalina Cove since moving here, except for those times when he made trips to Baton Rouge for his therapist appointments. One thing was for certain: he'd had a lot to write in his journal last night.

He drew in a deep breath as he put his key into the ignition and turned it. It was time to go home to an empty house and later tonight to an empty bed. But then, that was the way he'd chosen to live and there wasn't anything he could do about it.

CHAPTER EIGHT

ASHLEY CHECKED HER appearance in the mirror one final time before hurrying down the stairs. She knew the rest of the residents of Shelby by the Sea were still asleep but she'd awakened early, intent on going through with her plan.

She had talked with Vashti, Sawyer and Kaegan, and the last thing she wanted was for Ray to feel as if he was suddenly being stalked. But she needed to make sure their paths crossed on more than one occasion. She would sign up again to take the tour around the cove on his boat and she would attend the cove's annual Blueberry Festival this weekend.

According to Sawyer and Kaegan, Ray joined them for breakfast every morning at a place called Witherspoon Café. Today they intended to be there. They would intentionally cut their time with him short so if he saw her and wanted to talk to her, he could do so without having the feel of them looking over his shoulder. But they had warned her that although he might speak to her, there was a chance he would not sit down with her and chat. She was prepared for that but she wouldn't give up. If not today, then perhaps another day.

She had talked to Emmie, Suzanne and Kim last night. The three had gone on the internet to look up Ray's Tours, and when they saw Devon's face on his website, the three had cried again. She had ended up crying right along with them. She'd agreed with the three that he looked more handsome than ever with that beard, a rough maturity shining in his features.

Ashley told them of her plans and they asked the question she couldn't yet answer. What would happen when her two weeks in Catalina Cove ended and he still didn't know her? She didn't want to think that far ahead, although deep down she didn't expect anything to change with him in two weeks. But their inquiries made her realize she had decisions to make.

"You're on your way to see Ray?"

At the sound of Vashti's voice, Ashley had to take a deep breath to slow down the racing of her heart before looking in Vashti's direction. She nodded and smiled. "Yes, I'm on my way to see Ray." There. She'd said it. She had called him by his new name. His current name. The only name he knew.

"I hope things turn out all right today."

"And if they don't, I'll try again," Ashley said, her chin firm with determination. "I love him, Vashti. So much. I know I have to accept he's not the same man and I will."

Vashti's lips curved into a supporting smile. "Sure you will. I can feel the love."

Ashley wondered if Devon…Ray…would be able to feel the love as well. If not, she had enough love piled up for the both of them. She wouldn't lie and say she wasn't nervous because she was. What if she called him Devon? What if he suspected something was up with her and put up his guard? What if...?

"Hey, don't start doubting yourself," Vashti said, reaching out to take her hand. "Ray's friends are behind you and will help in any way we can."

"Thanks." Ashley looked at her watch, which had been a gift from Devon. "Time for me to go. I'll see you later." Her stomach tightened as she moved toward the door.

Making decisions about how she would deal with Devon had been the easy part. Executing those plans would be difficult.

"SOMETHING ON YOUR MIND, Ray?"

Ray glanced over at Sawyer. He'd discovered since the time they'd become friends that not only was Sawyer a good judge of character, the man was also good at reading people. Ray figured it was a skill from his days with the FBI.

"Don't have much to say right now. I'm just thinking."

"What about? That new boat you plan on buying?" Kaegan asked.

Ray wished buying that boat was the only thing on his mind. Hell, he hadn't thought about buying the boat since...

"Hey, isn't that the woman whose life you saved the other day?"

It was a wonder Ray didn't get whiplash with the speed he jerked his head around to see Ashley

Ryan walk into the café. Seeing her unexpectedly this morning made him wish he was drinking something a lot stronger than coffee. She looked beautiful. Too beautiful. Gone was the ponytail. Now her hair flowed in silky waves down her back. And instead of the shorts set, she was wearing a pair of capri pants and a peasant blouse.

He forced his gaze away from her when Ms. Witherspoon escorted her to a table, and wouldn't you know it, it was in line of sight of his. "How did you know it was Ashley Ryan? I didn't know the two of you had met," he said to Kaegan.

Kaegan smiled. "We met yesterday morning when I stopped by Shelby by the Sea for something. She was enjoying coffee and muffins with Vashti. I talked to her for a brief minute. She seems to be a nice lady. Glad she recovered okay."

Ray was glad, too. In a way he was hoping that she would swing her gaze in his direction, but instead she was studying the menu. "I wonder what brought her away from the inn. They serve a pretty good breakfast there," Ray said absently.

"There's nothing wrong with variety," Sawyer said, taking a sip of his coffee. "Besides, Vashti encourages those staying at the inn to eat at other places. That way they can see all that the cove has to offer." He looked at his watch. "I've got to go."

"So soon?" Ray asked.

"Yes. I told Vashti I would swing by the inn and pick up a box she wants to give to Trudy," Sawyer said. Trudy Caldwell was the sheriff's office manager.

"And I need to go, too," Kaegan said, finishing off the rest of his coffee. "Getting ready for that audit next week."

Ray nodded. "How's that going?"

"Great, thanks to you. Glad you found that surplus."

Ray nodded again. "Glad I was able to help." He'd suggested that Kaegan let him go over the company's books a couple of weeks ago. It hadn't been a big deal to Ray since that had been one of his duties while working for Kaegan. Within an hour he'd found a mistake that would have resulted in a huge tax bill at the end of the year.

Now Ray sat alone. A part of him felt the urge to leave as well, but then another part wanted to just sit right there with his eyes on Ashley Ryan. She hadn't looked his way, so chances were she hadn't seen him yet. That was fine and dandy since he was seeing her and liked what he saw. Too much.

"More coffee, Ray?"

He smiled up at Bryce. "Yes, thanks."

"I see your comrades left you," she said.

He chuckled, knowing the only comrade she was interested in was Kaegan. One day he would just come out and ask his friend what had happened between him and Bryce. Then again, maybe not. He had a feeling the less he knew the better. He liked Kaegan and he liked Bryce and refused to take sides.

Bryce refilled his cup and Ray sat there, taking slow, long sips while keeping his gaze on Ms. Ryan.

Now she was giving one of the waitresses her order. He knew he should stop staring. She could catch him doing it any moment.

No sooner had he thought that than she looked over at him and smiled—and he nearly stopped breathing.

ASHLEY SLOWLY INHALED a deep breath. When her gaze lit on Ray she'd somehow managed to look surprised. At least she'd pulled that off and now for the rest.

She broke eye contact with him and tried looking bored and alone. Would he take the bait and invite her to join him at his table or join her at hers? Or he very well might do neither and just finish off his coffee and leave.

Then again, she could go over to his table and invite herself to join him. She didn't like the idea of being that forward with a guy. But this wasn't just any guy; this was her husband. She glanced over in his direction again. He had stood. Was he about to leave? He was sitting close to the door and wouldn't have to pass by her table. If he came over to her, he would have to do so purposely.

The waitress returned with her coffee, and when Ashley glanced back over in Ray's direction, she saw he was walking toward her.

"Good morning, Ms. Ryan. Good seeing you out and about."

"Good morning, Ray." Ignoring the magnitude of nerves flowing through her, she greeted him with a smile. "And I feel awkward calling you Ray when you call me Ms. Ryan, so please call me Ashley."

He smiled. "Okay, Ashley."

She felt like she'd melt into a puddle on the floor at his feet with the way he'd said her name. Devon had been born in the South and always had a Southern twang to his words. Even when he said her name. She'd always loved hearing him say it.

"Vashti told me you called yesterday evening to see how I was doing. I appreciate you doing so. That was kind of you. Thank you."

"No need to thank me. Anyway, I was just on my way out and wanted to come over and say hello."

"And I'm glad you did. I plan to reschedule my boat tour for next week."

"I'm glad to hear it. Well, I'll let you get back to your breakfast. Have a good day, Ashley."

"And you do the same, Ray."

He nodded, smiled and then walked away.

She watched him leave while thinking her husband still had that fine ass. She giggled to herself, thinking she had one up on all the women she noticed watching him leave. She knew all about those tight buns and masculine thighs in those jeans, up close and personal.

She should feel disappointed he hadn't wanted to join her but she didn't. At least he'd made the effort to come say hello to her and that was a start. Thanks to Kaegan, she knew what time he got off work at the marina. Not today and maybe not tomorrow, but she intended for their paths to cross again, real soon.

IT TOOK EVERY amount of Ray's control to walk out the café door and not look back over his shoulder at Ashley. He wasn't sure what perfume she was wearing but it most certainly smelled good on her.

When he made it to his truck, he opened the door and slid over the seat. Before starting the ignition, he took a long breath. Fortunately, he'd maintained his cool while talking to her, but he'd felt anything but relaxed. Never had his nerves gotten the best of him.

He wondered if he'd always been this way with a woman. Cautious. Guarded. He wanted to believe he hadn't and what he was going through was self-induced.

He visited his therapist on an as-needed basis. He wondered if perhaps it was time for another session. Maybe Dr. Martin would be able to explain why he was so attracted to Ashley. There had to be a reason and he knew it went beyond having saved her life.

He was so taken with her that he'd actually dreamed about her last night. He hadn't dreamed about a woman, especially not making love to one, ever. And for some reason he wasn't feeling guilty when he knew he should. Shouldn't he? Hell, he was certain he would dream of making love to his wife, if he could recall how she looked. But every time he tried to remember, his memory went blank. It was like a void in his mind he couldn't fill.

At least he'd gotten to talk to Ashley. Had heard from her own lips how she felt. And they were a pair of nice lips. Full and sexy. He could say the same thing about her breasts that had been pressed against the material of her blouse. And they were firm, too. Shapely. He could just imagine the feel of them in his hands, the taste of the nipples on his tongue...

What the hell! He shouldn't be thinking about stuff like that. He was a married man, for heaven's sake! At least, he thought he was.

Beginning to feel frustrated, he rubbed his hand down his face. At no time during the last three years had he felt such a magnitude of lust for a woman, and that wasn't good.

Pulling his cell phone out the pocket of his shirt, he speed-dialed his therapist. Someone picked up on the second ring. "Dr. Martin's office. May I help you?"

"Yes. This is Ray Sullivan. I was wondering if I could see the doctor."

"And how soon would you like to set your appointment, Mr. Sullivan?"

"As soon as I can" was Ray's quick response.

"You're in luck. Dr. Martin's last appointment for today, scheduled for four o'clock, canceled. Would you like to take it?"

The driving distance from the cove to Baton Rouge would take two and a half hours. Since he was getting ahead of evening traffic between New Orleans and Baton Rouge, he should be fine. And the tour schedule was light today. Tyler could handle things while he was gone.

"Yes, I'll take it."

CHAPTER NINE

"DON'T YOU THINK you need to come up with a plan in case nothing happens before you leave Catalina Cove?"

Ashley raked a hand through her hair, refusing to feel frustrated although she knew that very thing might occur. She doubted very seriously that seeing her was triggering anything in Devon's mind and he would miraculously get his memory back. Again what she saw in his eyes hadn't been recognition but male interest. Not that she was complaining, mind you. She would take what she could get.

"Yes, I know I should, Emmie, but I don't want him to think I'm some crazy woman who is beginning to stalk him or anything like that. That's why I'm keeping my distance most of the time."

"How will that help when you only have two weeks there?"

Good question, Ashley thought as she stirred her lemonade. She stared in the direction of a couple walking along the shore, holding hands and stealing kisses. She could recall days when she and Devon had done that same thing. She turned her attention back to Emmie's question when the couple stole another kiss. "I don't know. I honestly don't know."

"Hey, don't start getting overwhelmed, Ash. Just think about it. The man you love and who you thought was dead is really alive. The fact that he's lost his memory is nothing more than a little inconvenience."

A little inconvenience? "Oh, I think it's more than that, Emmie."

"What I mean is that it's nothing that will defeat you, right? You've decided that regardless of whether Devon remembers you or not, you intend to be around."

Yes, that had been her decision, but how could she accomplish that if Devon didn't give her any indication that he wanted her around? Granted, he was nice to her this morning, but that was all. Was she expecting too much too soon?

"You know what I think you should do, Ash?"

"No. What do you think I should do?"

"Go ahead and make plans to stay beyond the two weeks."

Ashley lifted a brow. "And how am I supposed to do that? Have you forgotten I have work to return to?"

"No, but you and I know that you can work from anywhere. I suggest you check out places in town to remain the entire summer. And just so he won't think he has anything to do with your decision, let word get out now of what you plan to do. So if things start heating up between the two of you, he won't suspect your hanging in town has anything to do with him since you would have made the decision beforehand."

Ashley gave Emmie's idea some thought and then she thought of a big issue she might face. Her mother. "Mom almost flipped when I told her I was leaving town for two weeks without telling her where I was going. How do you think she'll handle it if I decide to stay here the entire summer? If I told her where I was she might show up unexpectedly. Can you imagine how she would handle it if she came and saw Devon? I can't let that happen, Emmie."

"Okay, I agree. But weren't your parents returning to Kansas most of the summer anyway to check on their property there?"

"Yes."

"Then tell her you're traveling this summer, living various places. It won't be one hundred percent true but close enough."

"Hmm, let me give it some thought. I'll let you know what I decide."

A short while later Ashley left the beach to return to the inn. When she got halfway across the boardwalk she realized she truly liked this place. And she definitely liked how the boardwalk connected Shelby by the Sea to the beach. She'd noticed how the evening lanterns were timed to come on at dusk to light a path to the beach. Last night she had sat on the boardwalk steps for hours to stare out at the ocean and think.

Returning to the inn, she smiled when she met Vashti coming out of her office. "Hi, Vashti."

"Enjoy the beach?" Vashti asked her, returning her smile.

"Yes. It cheered me up some." When she had returned to the inn from the café, she'd told Vashti she was a little disappointed Devon hadn't at least joined her for a cup of coffee.

"I'm glad."

Emmie's suggestion then came back to Ashley's mind. "There's an idea my friend came up with that I'd like to run by you. Do you have time to talk after I take a shower and freshen up a bit?"

"Sure. I'll see you then."

"DID YOU WANT to see me because you woke up again feeling a date meant something to you, Ray?" Dr. Martin asked, leaning back in his office chair.

"No," Ray said, shaking his head. "It's something else entirely."

"Oh? Tell me about it."

One of the things Ray liked about Dr. Martin, in addition to his calming air, was his willingness to listen before giving his thoughts on any given situation. And he was a patient man. The first time Ray had come to him, Ray had been filled with a lot of negative emotions and frustrations. Over the months of therapy it had taken to release them all, Dr. Martin had not once made Ray feel less of a man or human for what he was going through.

"I saved a woman's life."

That blunt statement had Dr. Martin straightening up in his chair. "When?"

"Two days ago."

"What happened?"

Ray provided details and Dr. Martin said, "My goodness, the woman was lucky you were where you were and acted quickly."

"I had seen her before the accident, when she was walking around the marina. I thought she was pretty."

"Nothing wrong with that, Ray. You are a man, after all."

"Yes, but things have gotten worse," Ray said.

Dr. Martin raised a brow. "Worse? In what way?"

"No woman has filled my mind the way she has. In a way she's taken over it. I think of her all the time. Last night I even dreamed about her. I saw her this morning when she was having breakfast at the same café I was and I couldn't stop looking at her."

"Like I said, Ray, you're a man. Sooner or later it was bound to happen. I told you that. It's like the law of gravity. You can't avoid letting nature take its course."

"I don't want it to take any course. I've always been able to control my attraction to a woman, so why can't I do so this time?"

"Only you can answer that. I guess I'm wondering why such a thing is bothering you so. Just because you're attracted to her doesn't mean you have to act on it."

He met Dr. Martin's stare. "But that's just it—I

want to act on it. You don't know how hard it was not to slide in the booth beside her and converse with her. Find out everything about her. Ask her out."

"There's no reason you can't."

"There is a reason. You know my history."

"I know the history you've formulated in your mind about yourself. You think you're a married man."

"Yes, and I've told you why I think it. But lately I've been thinking other things. Things I've never given much thought to before."

"Such as?"

"What if the reason my wife hasn't found me is because she doesn't want to find me? What if I was a prick of a husband? Someone she would have wanted out of her life anyway. What if she's married again and has gotten on with her life? What if I never get my memory back?"

Dr. Martin didn't say anything for a minute and then said, "Those are questions I can't answer, but then, neither can you. Sounds to me you're reaching deep into your inner self, the self you're not even sure about, to come up with reasons why it might be acceptable to pursue this woman without any guilt, when in actuality the only guilt you'd face is what you put on yourself. If you are married and get your memory back, and you discover your wife, who thought you dead or missing, has someone else in her life, would you fault her for not waiting? Do you think she should have held on to a possible belief—no matter how small—that you would return?"

He thought about Dr. Martin's question. Then he answered, "No."

"Then why are you? Why are you holding yourself to a marriage you have no memory of?"

"Because one day my memory might return. Then I could have deep feelings for two women."

"I think you'll only truly love one. Keep in mind, when and if you get your memory back, you won't forget the present and just remember the past. Even if there's a time when you discover your true identity, you would have been a man who'd lived two lives. Your old and new. Your before and after. What you're trying hard to do, Ray, is deny there is a new and an after."

"I don't think I'm doing that."

"Think about it for a second. You've done everything to try to move on. You've moved to a new town and have taken on a new job, which probably isn't the occupation you did in your previous life. You've moved on. However, when it comes to the opposite sex, you've stood still to the point where you've refused to even date."

"I don't want to ever hurt anyone. I don't want any woman to get involved with me knowing they won't have a future."

Dr. Martin nodded. "Then be up-front with them if you detect things are getting serious. Trust them enough to let them know your situation. I know you have your circle of friends you feel comfortable with and only they know your past. Would it be so bad to slowly let others in? Others you feel you can trust?"

Ray didn't say anything for a minute. Then Dr. Martin added, "About this woman, the one whose life you saved, the one you can't seem to forget. Maybe you need to get to know her and find out why she, of all women, can push your buttons? What is there about her that is drawing you in?"

Ray gave the doctor a wary glance. "She's pretty."

Dr. Martin chuckled. "I'm sure there is more about her than a pretty face, Ray. Just remember," he said, "at some point you will have to move on in all aspects of your life and not just in some."

"I THINK YOU staying in Catalina Cove for the summer would be a wonderful idea," Vashti said, smiling.

"You do?"

"Yes. You don't come across as the type of woman to give up easily. But just remember what Dr. Riggins said about retrograde amnesia. There's a fifty-fifty chance of the memory returning."

"I remember but I believe I have a chance again with my husband, even as Ray Sullivan. This morning when he stood beside my table, I felt something. I'm convinced *we* felt something. I'm even more convinced he's trying to fight it and I refuse to let him."

"I don't blame you."

Ashley smiled, glad Vashti agreed. "You once mentioned you had a friend in town who is a Realtor. Is there any way I can talk to her about finding me a nice rental? It doesn't have to be too big but I want it close to the marina and in a somewhat secluded area."

"Why secluded?"

"Because Ray comes across as a private person who wouldn't want the entire town in his business."

Vashti nodded. "You do have a point. My best friend's name is Bryce Witherspoon, and I'll make sure the two of you connect today."

Ashley drew in a deep breath, happy with her decision. "Thanks, and there's something else I need to do."

"What?"

"Reschedule my time with Ray's Tours."

CHAPTER TEN

"I THINK IT's wonderful that you've decided to spend the entire summer in Catalina Cove, Ash. While you're there, if you happen to meet someone who might interest me, please send them my way. I could always use some more FWM time."

A couple of days later, Ashley rolled her eyes as she strolled along the boardwalk while talking to Suzanne. Would her friend ever think about anything other than "fun with men" time when it came to the opposite sex? "Whatever, Suzanne." They talked a little while longer before Ashley said, "I will chat with you later. Bye." She clicked off the phone then dropped it into her cross-body purse.

Regardless of what had nearly happened to her in this area of the pier, she'd decided this was one of her favorite parts of town. It had nothing to do with the numerous shops on one side of the boardwalk with the ocean on the other; it was just the atmosphere. It was so relaxing. No one seemed in a hurry to get anyplace. That was why she'd taken her time to shop and had several bags to show for it. When she deliberately ran into Ray later, he wouldn't know anything had been preplanned.

She couldn't help but wonder what would happen if in the interim his memories returned. He would know immediately that she had misled him and hadn't been totally up-front about who she was. Would he see that as deception on her part or would he understand she'd been desperate enough to want to do things this way? She wanted to think if that happened Devon would know her enough to believe she'd done what she thought was best for them.

She appreciated Kaegan telling her what time Ray's workday usually ended and what path he took to get to his truck. Unless he changed his MO, he would have to walk by the area where she was. She knew that although more than anything Sawyer and Kaegan wanted Ray's memory to return, they didn't want to participate in anything that might be perceived as being disloyal to Ray. That meant there was only so much information they would give her. She understood the two men's position.

Vashti, on the other hand, was all in. She wanted Ray to do more than regain his memory. She wanted him to fall madly in love with his wife all over again and thought nothing could be more romantic than for him to do so. She appreciated Vashti's positive attitude.

Ashley had met with Vashti's best friend, Bryce Witherspoon, who'd told her about a rental place that had come on the market just that week. It sounded like the place Ashley was looking for and Bryce would be picking her up from Shelby tomorrow to take her to see it.

Ashley finally reached her spot in front of the huge bronze statue of Jean Lafitte erected in front of an eatery called Lafitte Seafood House. Then she pretended to be studying the huge menu posted beside the statue while shifting the shopping bags containing gifts for her three best friends to her other arm.

She refused to think that being here was a manipulative move on her part. As far as she was concerned, she was in a fight for her life. If Ray didn't remember her one way, then she was determined he would remember her in another. She refused to sit back and wait for a miracle to happen. She was determined to execute her own miracles.

"Need help carrying those bags, ma'am?"

She glanced over her shoulder to see the man who came to stand by her. He was nice looking, but she was certain he, like the other two men who'd asked the same thing before him, noticed she was wearing her wedding ring. And it wasn't something dainty that could easily be missed. Devon had made sure she had a ring on her finger that could be seen. She was certain Ray had seen it as well but hadn't questioned her about the missing Mr. Ryan. When he did, she would follow Dr. Riggins's advice and be honest with Ray. If he eventually put two and two together, then there was nothing she could do about it.

"No, thanks. I got this," she said.

"You're sure? I'll be glad to assist you."

"Thanks. I'm positive."

Ashley was grateful he nodded and moved on.
She checked her watch again and figured Devon—
Ray—should be walking by within the next few
minutes. He might ignore her and keep walking, he
might speak and keep walking, or he might be like
those other gents and offer to carry her bags. Honestly, she didn't think he would do the latter, but she
was hoping he would at least stop and hold a conversation, no matter how short. Any amount of time
spent in her husband's presence was worth it to her.

Suddenly, the hand holding her shopping bags
began to tremble and she knew without moving an
inch that Ray was in the vicinity, possibly walking
her way. Her profile was to him but there was no
reason he wouldn't recognize her. Would he stop?
She hoped, wished, prayed that he would.

Her heart began pounding and a rush of heat
seemed to overtake her on what was already a hot
day. But she was determined to keep her cool even
if things didn't work out the way she wanted.

The powerful sound of a pair of fisherman's
boots seemed to echo across the wooden planks
and she fought back a smile at the familiar heavy
noise Devon's boots would make. The man couldn't
tiptoe even if he tried.

"Ashley?"

She said a silent prayer of thanks before turning
around, and there he stood, Devon Ryan, aka Ray
Sullivan, looking as handsome as ever and automatically arousing her like only he could do. She forced
her face from breaking into too bright a smile. In-

stead she gave him what she hoped was a surprised smile. "Hey, Ray."

She couldn't ignore the shiver that passed through her when he came near. Nor could she ignore the feeling of total and complete love when she looked into his face. She fought back the urge to race to him and throw herself in his arms and tell him of that love and to cry out her relief at seeing him again and knowing she truly hadn't lost him. Ashley knew she couldn't do any of those things. The stakes were too high for her to make any mistakes now.

"I see you've been shopping," he said, looking at her with a smile. She felt that smile all the way to her toes. His smile had always had an effect on her and nothing had changed.

"Yes, my three girlfriends who sent me here for my birthday. I thought the least I could do was make sure I pick them up souvenirs."

"Yes, that's the least you can do. And now it appears you're about to enjoy dinner."

"Yes," she said, breaking eye contact with him to look back at the menu. "They have so many entrées to choose from." She looked back at him. It was hard keeping her eyes off him. "Have you eaten here before?" she asked him.

"Yes, several times," he said, in a deep, husky voice that was sexier than she remembered. Now it had a sort of rough tenor to it that had the ability to make certain parts of her quiver. "They serve good food."

"Then what do you suggest?" she asked, breaking eye contact with him to glance at the posted menu again.

"Their lobster definitely, but then, people come from miles around just for their crab cakes."

"And I love crab cakes," she said excitedly, turning back to him. Devon used to be able to read her like a book. She was glad Ray didn't seem capable of it.

"So do I," he said, giving that Devon Ryan grin she missed so much. Now it was a Ray Sullivan grin but she didn't care. She would take it no matter.

Then as if she'd just thought of the idea, she said, "Would you join me? I'd love some company."

She could tell from the look on his face that her invitation surprised him, and at first he didn't know what to say. He quickly recovered and said, "That won't be a problem. If you're sure you want my company."

Her smile brightened. "I'm sure."

He glanced down at the canvas duffel bag. "I need to put this in my truck first. I'll be right back."

"All right."

He was about to walk off and then he said, "If the waitress comes around before I get back, just tell her I want the number twenty-two. That's what I usually get whenever I eat here."

Ashley nodded. "Number twenty-two. Got it."

He then turned and sprinted toward the parking lot. She watched him, thinking he was agile as ever and still filled out a pair of jeans better than any man she knew.

When he was no longer in sight, she headed toward an empty table, trying not to let giddiness overtake her at the thought of sharing a meal with her husband.

BY THE TIME Ray reached his truck he was having second thoughts about dining with Ashley. He didn't want her to get any ideas about anything. Hell, who was he kidding? He was the one who shouldn't get any ideas about anything. There was something about her that unsettled him, although it wasn't her fault. Mainly it was because he found her so darn desirable.

He blew out a frustrated breath as he opened the door to his truck and tossed his duffel bag onto the back seat. Even if he did decide he shouldn't eat with her, he owed her the courtesy of letting her know and not just leaving. Especially after he'd told her what to order him off the menu.

He might as well eat with her. There would be no harm in that. It would be up to him to make sure things stayed impersonal. But then, what was impersonal? He really wanted to know about her, especially why she was still wearing her wedding ring if her husband had died a few years ago.

He recalled when Faith Forsythe's husband died when he'd been working with her at Kaegan's company. Her old man hadn't been dead a good six months when she'd stopped wearing her wedding ring and a year later she had married again. But then, according to the talk he'd heard from some of their coworkers, Faith hadn't had a good marriage and her husband had cheated on her a couple of times. Now she was Faith Harris and was happily married to someone else.

Ray wondered if the reason Ashley was still wearing her ring was because, unlike Faith, she'd had a good marriage. One she still couldn't move on from.

As he headed back toward Lafitte Seafood House, he figured the thought of that should please him because that meant she wouldn't be interested or expect anything serious with a guy. People ate together all the time without expecting anything. Besides, if she only intended to spend two weeks in the cove, then the first week was almost over. When she left here, chances were he would never see or hear from her again. Then his life could get back to normal and he could forget all about her.

He shook his head, wondering who he was kidding. Ashley Ryan wasn't a woman a man could easily forget.

When Ray walked into the restaurant he quickly spotted her at a table. The moment their gazes connected, his chest tightened. Not for the first time he wondered what there was about Ashley that could hammer at his common sense. The intensity of his attraction to her did more than mystify him. It had his mind going in circles. The last place he should be was here with her, but all he had to do was stare at the shape and fullness of her lips and the beauty of her brown eyes, and he knew he wasn't going anywhere.

He moved in her direction, tuning out everyone around him.

"That didn't take you long," she said when he slid into the booth seat across from her. "I placed your order, but I wasn't sure if you wanted your draft beer or not."

One of his brows went up. "How do you know I prefer draft beer?"

She seemed surprised by his question and he could tell she was thinking of what to say. Why? For several seconds she didn't say anything, and then in a soft voice, she said, "I apologize for assuming you did. It's just that was my husband's favorite and he once told me all real men drink draft beer."

He nodded, understanding completely. "Your husband was right, but you better not let Kaegan hear you say that. He prefers drinking his beer from a can. I guess you can say I do, too, when I'm home, but whenever I eat out, it's draft beer for me."

She smiled. "I promise I won't say a word."

"And speaking of Kaegan, I understand you met him the other day."

"How do you know that?"

Was he imagining it or did he just detect a slight nervousness in her voice? "He mentioned it at breakfast the other day when you walked into the café. He said the two of you had met."

She nodded. "Yes, we met. He seems to be a nice guy."

"He is." He then turned and got the waitress's attention and ordered his draft beer. When he turned back to Ashley, he found her staring at him in the same way she'd looked at him that day he'd revived her. "You okay?"

As if embarrassed she'd been caught staring, she said, "Sorry. I didn't mean to stare. I was just trying to figure out your age without asking."

"I have no problem with you asking. I'm thirty-four."

Now he decided to stare at her, even tilting his head to one side to study her features, which he'd been doing on the sly anyway. Up close she was even more beautiful. The gold flecks in her dark eyes even more profound, the fullness of her lips that much more striking. "Hmm, you're still in your twenties, right?"

She chuckled and the sound was a sensuous scrape across his spine. "I wish. I turned thirty a couple of weeks ago.

"Happy belated birthday."

"Thanks."

"And your girlfriends didn't want to join you?" he asked, remembering what she'd told him earlier.

"No. They thought I needed two weeks here in Catalina Cove."

"And did you need two weeks here?" He watched as the intensity in her eyes shifted, and although she tried to quickly recover, he'd felt the impact of the question he'd asked her just the same.

"Yes. In fact, I like it so much I'm thinking about staying."

His chest tightened. "Staying? As in moving here?"

She shook her head. "No. I'm thinking of extending my stay through the summer."

"What about your job? Your family?" Ray wasn't sure he should be elated or bothered at the thought she would be hanging around the cove longer than he'd expected.

"I live in Hardeeville, South Carolina, and I'm co-owner of a social media site. I handle the daily blogs and that's something I can do from anywhere. I'm working on a book. I discovered the cove is the perfect place to do both. It's so peaceful and relaxing here. And as far as my family goes, I'm the only child and my parents' home is in Kansas."

The waitress interrupted them to place his beer in front of him. He quickly took a swig and noticed she was watching him again. He wondered what there was about him that seemed to fascinate her. Not that he was complaining since she had the ability to fascinate him as well.

"I understand you lost your husband a few years back. Sorry to hear that."

"Thank you. Devon was killed in a drowning accident."

"He drowned? I thought he was killed in a car accident."

He watched as she used the tip of her tongue to wet her lips and felt his boner get bigger. "He was. The car he was driving hit a patch of ice in the road.

He lost control and crashed through the guardrail and plunged into the river off a bridge."

"Wow. I'm sure that was difficult for you."

"Yes, it was. Although it happened three years ago, it still is."

"Is that why you still wear your wedding ring?" A part of Ray knew he had no right to ask her that, but curiosity had gotten the best of him.

Nervously, she began toying with her ring before looking back at him. "Yes. I guess the biggest reason is because I haven't met a man since Devon who has charmed me enough into taking it off."

CHAPTER ELEVEN

ASHLEY APPRECIATED THAT the waitress chose that moment to bring out their food, eliminating the need for conversation for a while. She wasn't sure what comment could be made directly after saying what she had. He had asked and she'd been honest. She hadn't realized how truthful she'd been until she'd spoken the words. Truthful but not totally.

Her mother had shoved a lot of men at her and she'd never been able to feel a connection to any of them. She hadn't given them the chance to be charming or otherwise because she couldn't imagine any man in her life other than Devon, so all other men had been found lacking.

"Food looks good," she said, in a way to regain conversation.

He glanced over at her, smiled and said, "It is good. I can't wait for you to try those crab cakes. I see you ordered the same thing I did."

She chuckled. "Yes, I figured if number twenty-two worked for you, then it should work for me." She then bit into a french fry. "These are great."

"Best in town and we have some pretty good eating places here. I think what I like is that this place doesn't use frozen potatoes. They grow their own."

"Potatoes?"

"Yes. They even grow their own cabbage and carrots for the coleslaw. They have a garden out back."

Ashley thought that was simply fascinating. "I tried my hand at a garden once," she said, squirting ketchup on her fries.

"You did? How did it turn out?"

Devon would not have asked how things had turned out. He would have remembered since he had given her encouragement even when it was obvious her effort had been a flop.

"Not so good. In fact, nothing was edible. My husband blamed the soil and not anything I did as the result."

Ray grinned. "And I'm sure he was right."

For several seconds they said nothing else while they ate. She noticed a table of four women staring at them. She'd noticed the same four women's attention had been drawn to Ray when he'd walked in. Honestly, nothing new there. Even before the accident, he would draw feminine interest. It never bothered her before and it shouldn't bother her now but it did. In the past she'd known her husband loved her and only her. She couldn't make such a claim now.

"Tell me about Hardeeville, South Carolina. Were you born there?"

Ashley glanced over at Ray. "No, I'm a Kansas

girl all the way. Was born in Topeka. Went to Harvard, met Devon, and we were married a year after I graduated. His home was Hardeeville and he needed to go home to look after his elderly grandmother. I liked the place and we decided to stay after Nana passed away." She took a sip of her drink, studying him for some sign that anything she'd just said was triggering a memory. There was no indication whatsoever that it did.

"How long were you married?"

She placed her glass down and absently began fiddling with her ring again. "Five years, to be exact. The police showed up on my doorstep the night of our anniversary. I was waiting for Devon to return home from a business trip so we could celebrate but he never came home."

"I'm sorry. I should not have asked that. I didn't mean to make you relive what have to be painful memories."

Ashley picked up her fork and looked over at him. "What about you, Ray? Where are you from?"

HE WAS HOPING that she wouldn't ask him that. But then, what did he expect when he'd asked her the same thing? He remembered the information the government had fabricated for him and he would stick to it now, although doing so made him feel like a liar. There was no way he would admit to having amnesia and not knowing a single thing about himself.

"Tulip, Indiana." Since that was the place he'd

been found barely alive, that was where he claimed as a starting point in the life he knew now.

"I've never heard of the place."

Neither had he. "It's a small town outside of Chicago as you head toward Ohio's state line. Not much to see or do there."

She nodded. "Your parents still alive?"

He had no idea, but his answer was "No." And then to switch the conversation off him back to her, he said, "Tell me about your job."

She began talking and he listened attentively... at least, most of the time. The other time was spent watching her mouth and how on occasion she would swipe across those lips with her tongue.

He wasn't sure she realized they had an audience. Several locals who were probably surprised to see him out dining with a woman. Usually, whenever he came here or any other restaurants in town, he either dined alone or with Sawyer and Kaegan.

In the years he'd lived here he'd never dated a woman and he knew what he and Ashley were sharing could be construed as a date. They were all wrong about that. It wasn't a date. The only reason he had accepted her invitation was because he had a feeling she'd truly wanted company.

Wanting to keep her talking, he asked, "What prompted your decision to remain in the cove over the summer months?"

She took a sip of her drink before answering. "I like it here and I refuse to let what happened to me make me want to pack up and leave. Accidents happen, and thanks to you, I'm alive. Since being here I've discovered that Catalina Cove is a friendly town. I'm hoping Bryce Witherspoon finds me a place to rent near the water. I would love waking up to a sunrise over the ocean each morning."

"It is a beautiful sight. One I could never get tired of seeing," he said. "Both sunrise and sunset."

The waitress came to remove their plates and to give them dessert menus.

"I don't think I can eat another thing," Ashley said, placing the menu aside.

"Well, I happen to like their blueberry cheesecake."

She smiled over at him. "Is everything in this town made of blueberries?"

"Just about. Share a slice with me and you'll see why."

ASHLEY SHARED A slice of cheesecake with Ray and could see why he liked it so much. It was delicious. She wished she could tell him how much he used to detest blueberries. That was obviously something he didn't remember.

A couple of times she'd nearly bit her tongue watching him eat. He'd never been a slow eater before, and what a total turn-on it was. She wondered if it had to do with the broken jaw Kaegan had told her about.

When the waitress brought them separate checks, he offered to pay for hers but she refused him, saying, "I prefer you didn't. If you did, it would seem like a date."

For a moment he sat there and stared at her, his gaze locked with hers while the meaning of her words sank in. It was important to her for him to think she had ground rules about men like he did with women. If for one minute he thought they were on what she considered an official date he would make sure it didn't happen again. But if she left him with the impression that she wasn't interested in a man any more than he was in a woman, he could possibly let his guard down.

After the waitress took their credit cards, he said, "I wouldn't have minded paying for your meal, Ashley."

"Thanks, but I'd rather you didn't. I can't help it since my husband taught me to be independent." That was definitely true.

"Do you think you'll ever remarry?"

"I'm not sure. What about you? Think you'll ever marry?"

"I was married."

"Oh. Then I guess I should ask if you'll ever remarry."

He shrugged massive shoulders. "Like you, I'm not sure." The waitress returned with their credit cards. He quickly signed his slip and asked, "Ready to leave?"

"Yes."

They left walking side by side to the parking lot. A number of shops were still open and a band had set up in the middle of the boardwalk between the hamburger stand and the game store. Dusk had settled in and the lights from the marina were reflecting off the ocean's water. Under any other circumstances, walking by his side in such a beautiful setting would have been romantic.

"I enjoyed your company, Ray," she decided to say.

"Thanks, and I enjoyed yours."

Did that mean he had no problem with them doing it again sometime? "I still plan to reschedule my tour with your company."

"Whenever you get ready, we'll be there."

"Thanks."

"That's my truck," he said, pointing to a black truck with huge tires. She couldn't help but smile. This truck was a big change from the Mercedes-Benz convertible that he used to own. "Where are you parked? I'll make sure you get to your vehicle before leaving."

Always the gentleman and I'm glad that hasn't changed, she thought. "That's my rental vehicle over there," she said, raising her hand to point out the dark blue two-door.

"I don't know why I imagined another color for you," he said, leading her out of harm's way when a kid on a bicycle breezed by them.

He'd only lightly touched her arm but the contact to her was electrifying nonetheless. She looked up at him. "What color did you imagine my car would be?"

He shrugged his shoulders again. "Hmm, I don't know. Green maybe."

Ashley almost missed her step. Green was her favorite color. She couldn't get her hopes up about anything. Hadn't she told herself that over and over when she'd decided on this course of action for herself? She had talked to Dr. Riggins again yesterday, wanting to make sure she wouldn't say or do anything to cause Devon a relapse. The doctor had stressed to her again not to get her hopes up about anything.

She smiled up at Ray. "Green? Now, wouldn't you know that's my favorite color. However, since this is a rental, I just took what color they had."

They continued walking and then she asked, "What's your favorite color?"

His lips curved into a smile. "Not sure I have one."

Ashley wished she could remind him that it used to be blue. "Everyone has a favorite color."

He laughed, and the sound was such a Devon Ryan laugh. "In that case I'd say green."

"Green? Why green?"

They had reached her car and he shoved his hands into the pockets of his jeans. "Because it's your favorite color."

She moistened her suddenly dry lips. It was either lick her own or reach up and grab hold of his shoulders and lick his. She doubted he had any idea how nice what he said was or how much it meant to her. He was claiming the color green as his favorite only because it was hers. She was feeling all gushy inside.

Slow down, Ashley, she told herself. *To him it probably means nothing.* Too bad, because for her it meant everything.

"I enjoyed dining with you tonight, Ashley."

"Same here, Ray. You saved me from dining alone and I appreciate your company."

He tilted his head to look at her. "A meal at Shelby by the Sea isn't so bad."

She smiled. "No, it's quite good, actually. However, I wanted to get out and try something different. I had hoped to do the lighthouse before I left town but I understand you have to make reservations months in advance."

"Yes, that's what I heard. I've never been there. I guess you can say it's way too classy for my taste."

She didn't say anything as she absorbed what he said. For Devon Ryan, the classier the better. She tipped her head back and looked at him. "Hmm, I don't know, Ray Sullivan. I take you as a pretty classy guy."

"Thanks. Now I better let you go. I'd hate for Vashti to do a bed check and find you missing."

She couldn't help but laugh at that. "Staying there is like being part of a family and I like that. And for these two weeks I need that. Good night, Ray. I hope to see you around again."

"You probably will, especially if you decide to reschedule that tour on my boat."

"And I do intend to."

When she unlocked the car door, he opened it for her and she slid inside.

"Good night to you, Ashley."

She closed the car door and he stood back when she drove off.

Ashley glanced back in her rearview mirror and saw him still standing there with his hands shoved into his pockets while watching her leave. She would sleep well tonight because all her dreams would be filled with the time she had spent with him tonight.

CHAPTER TWELVE

WHILE BRUSHING HIS teeth the next morning, Ray stared at himself in the mirror wondering just who the man was staring back at him. A part of him wished he knew. Then there was that other part, the one who liked his life now and had totally enjoyed Ashley Ryan's company last night. The part that preferred he didn't know.

And he *had* enjoyed her company. There was a lot of things he'd wanted to know and had refused to ask for fear of getting too personal. On the flip side, he would not have been prepared had she inquired about him. What could he say? *I really don't know who I am but I'll be glad to provide you with the made-up version?*

The main takeaway from last night was that Ashley was a woman who was still in love with her deceased husband. It was obvious she hadn't moved on.

However, neither had Ray. For him it wasn't that he didn't want to move on. He just couldn't. Not when there was a chance his past and future could one day collide.

So what was last night all about? Why, against

his better judgment, had he taken a chance? Was joining her for dinner the first step in moving forward, when one day it could blow up in his face?

Ray rinsed out his mouth and looked back into the mirror, again wishing the person staring back at him could shed some light onto his former life or at least help him find closure. He closed his eyes and an image of Ashley came to mind.

She was filling his thoughts and he wanted to see her again. She had been easy to talk to and she wasn't someone looking for an involvement with a man. Far from it. He could see her becoming another friend. Someone to pass the time with while she was in the cove.

A friend? Honestly? How could something like that work when he was so attracted to her? He didn't have to be a rocket scientist to figure that out. But was being attracted to her a big deal when it was an attraction that he didn't have to worry about going anywhere?

He drew in a deep breath when he remembered what she'd told him about her decision to stay in the cove all summer. Just because she remained in town didn't mean their paths had to cross. And if they did, so what?

Satisfied he had his head screwed on straight, he finished dressing and went to work. He had talked to Kaegan last night and promised to help him with some paperwork before the audit was due. That meant Tyler would be handling things by himself most of the day.

As he headed for the door to leave, he knew that although he had enjoyed being with Ashley last night, he refused to think about her any longer.

"So, what do you think of this place?"

Ashley glanced around at the four-bedroom house Bryce Witherspoon had taken her to see. It was not too big and not too small. It was just the size she needed. It also had a beautiful view of the ocean from the bedrooms. She liked the set of the kitchen and eating areas. And there was an enclosed patio off the kitchen if she decided to dine out there to enjoy the gulf.

Ashley turned to Bryce, smiled and said, "I like it."

When Bryce had picked her up for their appointment, she had been surprised to see the woman she remembered from the café the other day. Bryce explained her parents owned the café but it was a family affair. Her brothers worked there full-time, but she only helped out in the mornings and evenings whenever she could. Like Vashti, she was born and raised in Catalina Cove.

"Great, but I might as well warn you that Mrs. Landers's family is asking a lot for this rental because it's on the water. There's a chance they might sell it, and if they do, I think it will be a good buy for someone who wants to tear this place down and rebuild something larger since it sits on two acres."

Ashley nodded. Bryce had told her the previous owner, Gertie Landers, had been the town's midwife and had died a couple of years ago. Her son had recently renovated the place and decided to rent it out for a while before deciding what he would do with it. She liked that it was on a secluded dead-end road with only three other houses. All three were sitting back off the road with long driveways.

"I'll take it," she said quickly.

Bryce chuckled. "You didn't ask how much he wanted each month."

Ashley smiled. "It doesn't matter. It's perfect."

"I'm glad you think so," Bryce said, smiling. "I got the paperwork in my car. How about if we final- ize things over lunch? There's this place that I know for a fact has a good lunch menu," she added, grin- ning. "And today happens to be fried chicken day."

Ashley threw her head back and laughed. "That's just what this Mid-Western turned Southern girl wants to hear."

A short while later they walked into the Wither- spoon Café and grabbed a booth. After placing their order, Bryce pulled the paperwork out her briefcase and in minutes Ashley had finalized the rental agree- ment. She didn't want to think what would happen if by the end of August she hadn't made any progress in a relationship with Ray.

"This calls for a celebration," Bryce said. "What's on your schedule tonight?"

Ashley wished she could say Ray was on her sched- ule but she could not. In fact, she doubted if she would even see him today. "Nothing."

"Then how would you like to join me at Taters?"

Ashley recalled the name. Taters was a popular bar and grill in town. "I'd love to." After one of Bryce's brothers brought them glasses of water and left, she asked, "So when can I move in?"

After taking a sip of water through her straw, Bryce asked, "When do you want to move in? You have another week at Shelby's, right?"

"Yes, and then I'd like to move in after that." Ashley knew that was moving fast but she didn't have time to waste. She would have to return home and check on things and repack, but that shouldn't take her more than a few days.

"No problem."

She liked Bryce. She was friendly with a bubbly personality, and because she'd lived in the cove all her life, except for the time she had left for college, it was easy to see from the way everyone greeted her that she was well liked.

"I heard about your accident at the beginning of the week and how Ray jumped in after you. I'm glad you're okay."

Since it seemed Bryce was on a first-name basis with Ray, Ashley couldn't help wondering if she was one of those women in town the nurse, Paula Corker, had told her about. One of the ones who'd been interested in dating him. There was only one way to find out. "You know Ray?" she tried asking in what she hoped was a nonchalant tone.

"Yes, Ray and I are friends. He's a real nice guy."

He's also a married guy, Ashley wanted to say but didn't. She couldn't tell from Bryce's response if there was any interest there. For all she knew, Bryce could have a boyfriend somewhere.

"Speak of the devil. Look who just walked in."

Ashley glanced toward the entrance of the café to see Ray and Kaegan walk in.

RAY COULDN'T IGNORE the quiver that ran down his spine the moment his gaze connected with Ashley's. She'd smiled when she saw him and automatically his lips curved into a smile as well.

"Hey, Ray, where are you going?" Kaegan asked. "There's an empty table over there."

He stopped and met Kaegan's gaze. "I see Ashley and want to say hello."

"She's sitting with Bryce."

Ray tipped his head and lifted a brow. "And?"

"Nothing."

Ray frowned. "For you, there is something, and I think whatever it is, Kaegan, you and Bryce need to deal with it."

"There's nothing to deal with. What used to be is over and done with."

"If that's true, then don't you think you should act like it? You don't have to go over there with me." He smiled and said, "You can grab that empty table over there to hide out if you like." Ray knew Kaegan well enough to know what he'd just said had hit a nerve. Hopefully, his friend would take a look at his and Bryce's attitude toward each other and admit enough was enough.

He moved toward the table where Ashley and

Bryce sat and wasn't surprised to see Kaegan right on his heels. "Ashley. Bryce. How are you ladies doing?" he asked when he reached them.

"Fine," they both said simultaneously.

Kaegan came to stand beside him. "Ashley. Bryce."

Ray watched Ashley smile up at Kaegan, but Bryce barely moved her mouth. "Kaegan."

"You look happy," Ray said to Ashley. "Did you find a place?"

"Yes, I did, thanks to Bryce."

Kaegan lifted a brow. "You're moving to town?" he asked, surprised.

Ashley looked at him. "I like this town so much, I've decided to extend my time here through the summer."

Kaegan nodded. "Oh, I see."

"Would you guys like to join us?" she asked.

"No!" That quick response came from Kaegan and Bryce.

Ashley glanced over at Ray, who merely shrugged his shoulders before saying, "We have a table over there, so we'll see you guys later. Congratulations, Ashley."

"Thanks, and good seeing you again, Kaegan."

"Same here, Ashley. See you." Then without even looking at Bryce, Kaegan walked off.

Ignoring Kaegan's awkward departure, Ray said, "Well, great news, Ashley, and it's always good seeing you, Bryce."

Bryce smiled. "Same here, Ray."

When Ray reached their table, he asked Kaegan, "You want to talk about it?"

"No, not now. In fact, I'm not hungry after all," he said, standing. "Thanks for your help today."

"You don't have to thank me, Kaegan."

"Hey, you're leaving?" Sawyer said, suddenly appearing and sliding down into one of the chairs at the table.

"Yes, I'm leaving. I'll see you guys later." Kaegan walked off.

"What's going on with him?" Sawyer asked.

Ray knew he could sum it up in one word. "Bryce."

CHAPTER THIRTEEN

"Good morning, Ray."

"Morning, Tyler," Ray greeted him, holding his coffee cup with one hand and grabbing the clipboard off the rack with the other. "How was your weekend?"

"Great. How was yours?"

"Good. Got some fishing in with Kaegan around Buccaneer Sound," he said, scanning the clipboard. He immediately saw Ashley's name listed as his first cruiser for that day.

He sipped his coffee while recalling that he hadn't seen her since he ran into her when she'd been having lunch with Bryce. That had been two days ago. He wished he could claim out of sight was out of mind, but that hadn't been the case. He had thought about Ashley over the weekend, whether he'd wanted to or not.

"I think our first cruiser is headed this way."

He glanced toward the boardwalk and saw her. In fact, he did more than see her; his gaze was drinking in every inch of her. His groin seemed to tighten with every step she took. She was wearing a pair of cutoffs and a T-shirt. A huge floppy straw hat was on her head, sandals on her feet and sunglasses on her eyes. Damn, she looked good.

"You want me to take her out, right?" Tyler asked.

Usually that was how it worked. Tyler would take out the first cruiser of the day while Ray stayed behind in the office to get as much paperwork done as he could. Today, of all days, he needed to stick with that routine since he had volunteered his time at Kaegan's office Friday morning.

"Ray?"

He shifted his gaze off Ashley. "No, I'll take her out. Make sure everything is ready."

"Okay."

He glanced back to Ashley, finished off the last of his coffee and set the cup aside before sliding on his sunglasses.

ASHLEY FELT GOOSE bumps cover her arms when she glanced at the boat and nearly missed her step at the name written on the side of it. The *Sunflower*. Kaegan had given her a heads-up about it, yet seeing it did something to her nonetheless.

She was glad she was wearing sunglasses. Not only did they protect her eyes from the glare of the sun but she could look her fill at the man standing at the ramp of the boat. Why did he have to look so handsome standing there in a pair of jeans and a snug blue T-shirt that promoted Ray's Tours? Devon never wore snug T-shirts but she would admit it fit him well. Showed all his muscles.

He was wearing sunglasses as well. She wondered if Ray was checking her out with as much intensity as she was him. She hoped so.

From the very beginning there had been this connection between them. Even after college neither could contain it. She recalled how they would share breakfast together before classes and how they would study together most evenings and afternoons. When he graduated, she'd found Harvard lonely without him and he would come see her a lot on the weekends. The memories of their times together touched her heart because Devon never tried coming on too strong and he refused to take advantage of her in any way. He'd always been the perfect gentleman and she'd enjoyed being the temptress.

Playing that role now would probably send him running the other way.

The idea couldn't help but be appealing when he was standing there beneath the morning's sun. Other than when he wore casual clothes on the weekend, Devon had been strictly a designer-suits-and-expensive-ties man, and had been known as one of the most well-dressed men in town. He'd worn the clothes. The clothes hadn't worn him. And he'd worn them well. She studied him and thought that he still wore the clothes well. Even the jeans and T-shirt had her licking her lips in feminine appreciation.

Breaking eye contact with him, she looked up into the sky, wondering if the temperature was actually as hot as she felt or if the vibes emitting from Ray were the cause of a spike in her temperature.

When she looked back at him, she knew it was him. He was hot even while standing still.

Then he began walking toward her with that self-assured strut she knew so well. She figured it was so much a part of him he probably didn't realize he was doing it.

When he came to a stop in front of her, she forced her head to stop spinning from his closeness and his scent. He smelled all man. "Good morning, Ashley."

"Good morning, Ray. Did you have a good weekend?"

He smiled. "I did. Went fishing with Kaegan."

He had loved going fishing and she was glad he still did. "Did you catch anything?"

"Plenty. Most I threw back."

She came close to saying that some things never changed. He'd always caught more fish than she did whenever they went fishing. She would jokingly tell him that he was a man who could use his rod…in or out of the bedroom. She felt her cheeks tint and wondered how she could think of such a thing now.

Easy, she surmised. Whether she wanted to admit it or not, her husband still had an effect on her in the most sensuous way. More than anything, she had to remember that how she handled herself with him now could possibly determine if they had a future together. One wrong move on her part could end everything.

"Ready to get started?"

"Yes," she said, smiling up at him, trying not to feel off balance by his closeness. "I'm ready."

"You're used to being on a boat." Ray observed how easily Ashley moved around the vessel.

She quickly shifted her gaze from him to glance across the waters when the boat started to move. He wondered why she'd done that. Had his statement bothered her? "Ashley?"

She glanced back at him. "Yes. My husband and I owned a boat that was pretty similar to this one."

When she told him the model, he released an impressive whistle. "Wow, that boat is every man's dream."

"I know. At first I was upset with him when he suggested we buy it."

"Why? Don't you know all men love their toys?"

When she quickly glanced away again, he figured the conversation about her husband was bothering her. "I'm sorry. I should not have encouraged you to talk about your husband. That was insensitive of me."

She looked back at him and said, "Don't apologize. It's just what you said are the words he told me…about men and their toys. That's what made me cave. And the reason I got so upset with Devon was because we'd promised each other that for the first five years of our marriage we would make sacrifices. We would do without all those things we didn't particularly need until we became successful in our chosen professions. Then we would splurge, so to speak." She laughed. "I should have known he wouldn't be able to hold out."

He nodded, smiling at her. "But *you* did? Hold out?"

Ray watched a degree of sadness that touched her features. "Yes, I held out," she said softly.

For some reason Ray wanted to go to her, a woman he barely knew, and take her in his arms. Give her a shoulder to cry on if she needed one. It was obvious from the short time he'd known her that she'd loved her husband deeply. Losing him had been hard on her. It still was. He wondered about the type of man who could extract such a high degree of love and devotion from a woman. He wanted to believe the feelings were mutual and her husband had loved her and had been devoted to her just as much.

That made him wonder about the woman he'd been married to. What type of marriage had they shared? If it had been even close to the one he believed Ashley shared with her husband, then wouldn't he remember it? Was there a reason his memory refused to return?

Over the years he'd read up a lot on retrograde amnesia and one of the theories as to why a person's memory didn't quickly return was due to purely psychological reasons. Specifically, in trying to forget certain aspects of their life, the person's brain was forgetting it all and blocking the chance of their memory returning. Was that what was happening to him? There had to be a reason he had yet to get his memory back, although both Dr. Riggins and

Dr. Martin assured him that particular theory might not even apply to him. But still, he couldn't help but wonder at times if that was the case.

Deciding to treat Ashley just as he would any other cruiser, he began his tour narrative, telling her about the history of Catalina Cove as they moved through the waterways. He pointed out several areas such as the swamp and the bayous, making sure he provided the information about the wildlife that roamed the shores and swam the waters—namely, the raccoons, coyotes, gray wolves, beavers, otters and alligators. Then because of the swamp, there were mosquitoes that were almost as big as humans.

Saying that caused her to laugh. Ray much preferred seeing happiness in her eyes instead of sadness. She asked questions and seemed really interested in the different cultures living in Catalina Cove.

Since that seemed to hold her interest, he continued by delving more into the cove's history, telling her how people who braved the elements and lived on the bayou thought there was no place better to live. As part of his tour narrative he told her about the culture of those living on the bayou, a mixture of just about every influence from Spanish to French to German to African and Irish and Native American. There were those with predominantly French ancestry, some who still spoke the language and who made up the foundation of the Cajun culture.

"Vashti told me that Kaegan lives on the bayou and that he's part of the Pointe-au-Chien Native American tribe and that his family's ties to the cove and surrounding bayou go back generations, even before the first European settlers."

He nodded, smiling. "Yes, that's true. Kaegan is very proud of his heritage and the contributions his ancestors made to this area."

"You seem very knowledgeable about the area, Ray. Are you sure you didn't live here in another life or something?" she asked as a teasing glint appeared in her features.

He forced a smile, almost telling her that when it came to his past, he wasn't sure of anything. Instead he said, "I'm positive. When I moved here I wanted to learn as much as I could about the town and the people so dedicated to the cove and preserving the old ways. I read a lot. In fact, the library became my best friend."

There was no need to tell her the library also became his hiding place from the single women in town who were determined that he would be the catch of the day, the week, the month. It was hard for them to understand he'd just wanted to be left alone and liked the solitude.

It had taken a while but they'd finally redirected their attention to Sawyer, who'd been just as adamant as Ray about not becoming involved with anyone. It had been odd that none of the women tried coming on to Kaegan and it didn't take long for Ray to figure out why. Although no one talked about it, it seemed everyone knew of Kaegan and Bryce's history and figured why waste their time since sooner or later the two would come to their senses and get back together. Honestly, Ray didn't see such a thing happening, but...

"You handle this boat like a pro. Were you in the navy or something?"

He could let her assume, like most people in the cove did, that he used to be in the military, but for some reason he didn't want to knowingly lie to her. He shook his head. "No, I wasn't in the military." At least, as far as he knew he hadn't been. "I grew up around water and used to own a boat like this once."

Suddenly, he felt as if he'd been kicked in the chest and had to quickly grab hold of one of the posts to steady his balance. Why had he just told her that? And why did deep down he believe it to be true? Had he grown up around water and had he once owned a boat such as this one? Was that the reason why he felt so comfortable on the water and why he loved boats? And why he'd specifically wanted this one the moment he'd seen it?

"Ray? Are you all right?"

He glanced over at Ashley and saw a worried look on her face. Had he momentarily zoned out or something? The last thing he wanted was for her to question whether he was capable of returning them to shore or anything. "Yes, I'm fine. I just thought about something. No big deal. Now, let me show you all the other places around the cove."

ASHLEY HAD WATCHED Ray's face when he'd realized what he had said. He was right. He had grown up around water and he had once owned a boat like this one. In fact, it was the same model, just a tad bigger.

Had Dr. Riggins been right? Was being around her helping him to reclaim his memory? Were bits and pieces of people, things and events starting to float around in his head? The thought made her want to jump for joy, but she couldn't get too hopeful. A part of her couldn't help it. She couldn't help but feel positive that one day she would have her husband back.

But what if her husband didn't come back? What if he never got his memory back? Could she love him as Ray Sullivan when he was different from Devon? Ashley knew the answer to that. Yes, she could, and she knew that, although different, both men had qualities she admired.

Ray wasn't as power driven as Devon used to be. He was more laid-back. Making money wasn't a big priority for Ray. She realized Ray was in a way an older, more mature and confident version of Devon. A man who had learned hard lessons in life and who'd decided to take life one day at a time and enjoy smelling the roses along the way. There was no doubt in her mind that Ray still worked hard, but he didn't let work consume him.

Bottom line, she loved both the incredibly ambitious Devon and the laid-back Ray. They both brought something to the table that could satisfy her appetite. At that moment she knew that although she had loved the man Devon had been, she could also love and appreciate another version of him.

Ashley listened to what Ray was saying as his boat glided through the waters, showing her various parts of the cove, including a beautiful waterfall. Being out with him on this boat reminded her of other times they had gone out on their boat together. Seeing how expertly he was handling the boat gave her a sense of pride like she always had in his abilities. Gone was the Devon Ryan who prided himself on looking all suave, refined and debonair. He'd been replaced by Ray Sullivan, who stood on the bow looking every bit the sexy sea captain.

When he headed back to shore, she knew her two hours with him were almost up and she felt the regret deep in the pit of her stomach. "I enjoyed the tour of the cove, Ray."

He smiled. "I'm glad. And if you get the chance, please go on our website and write a nice review."

She couldn't help but chuckle. "I most certainly will."

Ashley shifted her gaze away from him, looked up into the sky and breathed in the scent of the ocean. She loved it out here on the water. Thanks to Devon, she had no choice. After losing him, she hadn't been able to bring herself to sell his boat. Instead she would take it out on occasion. Because her parents made such a fuss about her going out on the boat alone, she would get Emmie to go with her. Sometimes she would go by herself but didn't tell her parents because she hadn't wanted them to worry. It was those times when she'd been out on the waters by herself that she would feel close to Devon.

"Tell me about the place you found for the summer."

She turned her attention back to him. "It was the first place I saw." She told him where it was located and why she fell in love with it so much.

"That's a pretty secluded area. I thought you'd want to be in town."

She gave him a wide grin. "It's not too secluded and I could walk to town if I felt up to it. More than anything, I wanted something on the water, and that's what I got. I get to wake up to this, Ray," she said, spreading her arms wide.

"Lucky you," he said, grinning back at her.

"I guess that's something we have in common. Our love of the water."

He seemed to study her for a long moment, before saying, "Yes, it seems you're right. I'm glad nearly drowning didn't diminish your love for it."

"I'm glad, too, Ray. I'm glad, too."

CHAPTER FOURTEEN

RAY IGNORED THE conversation between Kaegan and Sawyer, too deep in his thoughts to do otherwise. It had been four days since he'd seen Ashley when she'd taken a tour on his boat. Even now the memories of that day still gripped him in ways he didn't understand.

He had thoroughly enjoyed her company, not as a paying customer but rather as a woman whose presence he wanted to be in. And then there had been that jarring moment, when he felt he might have recovered a part of his memory that had been lost to him. For some reason he truly believed what he'd told her about having grown up around water and owning a boat like the *Sunflower*.

He quickly brought his attention back to the conversation when he heard Ashley's name off Sawyer's lips. "What did you just say about Ashley Ryan?"

Sawyer glanced over at him. "I was just telling Kaegan, now that she's back, Vashti—"

"Back? She went somewhere?"

Sawyer nodded. "Yes. She went home to pack up more of her belongings. She's moving into Gertie Landers's place for the summer. Vashti and Bryce are helping her move today. Before leaving home this morning, Vashti asked that I stop by at some point today in case they needed muscle power. I told her I would, but that was before I remembered I'll be in court most of the day. That's why I just asked Kaegan to stop by in my place."

"Normally, I'd be able to have your back, man," Kaegan said, "but one of my men called in sick, so I have to go out on the boat today. Besides, with Bryce being there, it's better if I didn't show up anyway." He glanced over at Ray. "How's your schedule today?"

Ray knew he could tell Kaegan that he needed to be out on his own boat today as well, but he knew that would be a lie. Tyler was more than capable of handling things without him. Besides, he wanted to see Ashley again. He wasn't sure why she was slowly becoming an obsession with him, but she was. He would even admit to looking for her around the pier in the evenings when he got off work, hoping he would run into her again like he had that day and they'd end up sharing a meal together.

"Ray?"

"Yes?"

"Your schedule today?" Kaegan said, looking at him oddly.

Ray figured his friend was wondering what the hell was wrong with him today. "My schedule is flexible. I'm available if Vashti needs help with anything."

Sawyer smiled. "Thanks. I really appreciate it."

"HE'S HERE."

Ashley tried not to feel nervous from Vashti's words. It seemed Sawyer and Kaegan had deliberately arranged for Ray to come help them out. That had surprised her since she'd gotten the feeling that although they were rooting for Ray's memory to return, they weren't into playing matchmakers. Evidently they'd had a change of heart today.

"How do I look?" she asked Vashti quickly, pushing hair back from her face.

Vashti laughed. "Like a woman who's been busy yet still manages to look sexy as hell. Tell me, how do you do it?"

Ashley rolled her eyes. As far as she was concerned, Vashti was the real beauty with her soft brown eyes, long eyelashes, high cheekbones, shoulder-length dark brown hair and skin the color of rich mocha. She'd told her the first day they met that she was a mixture of several cultures—French, Spanish, African and Native American—and was proud of all four.

"I refuse to answer that question on the basis that I know you're just being kind," Ashley said, truly meaning it.

When there was a loud knock at the door, Vashti grinned and said, "Well, aren't you going to open it?"

"Yes." On nervous legs, Ashley headed for the door. Leaving Catalina Cove for those two days to return home had been hard knowing she was leaving Ray behind. Emmie, Suzanne and Kim had been at the airport waiting for her. She'd known Emmie would be there but hadn't expected Suzanne and Kim to fly in—she was glad they had. She had so much to share with them, and while she repacked, she'd covered everything.

She knew they were still in a daze at the thought that Devon was alive and they let her know they admired how she was handling things. More than once Suzanne had said that had it been her, she would not have been able to pull things off like Ashley was doing. In fact, her exact words had been, "After three years of horniness, I would have jumped his bones several times over by now."

Suzanne didn't know how many days and nights such thoughts had flowed through her mind. Just breathing the same air as her husband had a surreal effect on her.

Before opening the door, she glanced back over her shoulder and saw Vashti's encouraging smile. It gave her the courage she needed and she slowly opened the door.

And she fought the impulse to throw herself into her husband's arms.

He looked so good standing there in his jeans, muscle shirt and fisherman boots. This Devon was such a total turn-on. Sexy as sexy could be, and at that moment, it wouldn't bother her in the least if he never wore a suit again. The man standing before her seemed comfortable in his own skin... although he did appear almost as nervous as she was.

"Hello, Ashley."

She swallowed. "Hi, Ray."

"I understand you need help."

"Yes. Thanks for stopping by. Please come in. There are several boxes that are still in the car."

"Okay," he said, stepping inside the house. He smiled over at Vashti. "Hey, Vashti. You okay?"

She smiled back, nodding. "I'm okay but the baby's not. I think he's teething. I hate to run but I need to leave for a spell to go check on him."

Ashley knew that was nothing more than a made-up excuse. Granted, the baby might be teething, but there was no reason for Vashti to leave. "Thanks for all your help today, Vashti. I feel guilty keeping you from the inn."

Vashti waved off her words as she headed for the door. "You don't have to thank me for anything. I'm just glad you decided to stay through the summer. I'll see you guys later." And then she opened the door and was gone.

Ray looked around. "Where's Bryce?"

Ashley nervously licked her lips. "She left to go show some property in the area to a client."

"Oh. The boxes are in your car?"

"Yes."

He nodded. "I'll go and get them." He headed for the door.

"WHAT THE HELL am I doing here?" Ray muttered to himself as he grabbed one of the boxes off the back seat of Ashley's rental car. "Hell, the moment she opened that door and I saw her, I wanted to pull her into my arms and kiss her." No, dammit, what he'd really wanted to do was a lot more than kiss her.

Thoughts like that should not be in his head. He needed to remember why he hadn't gotten it on with a woman before now. Why he'd forbidden himself to even think about such a thing.

He reentered the house carrying the boxes but didn't see Ashley anywhere. So he called out to her.

"I'm in the master bedroom. You can bring the boxes in here, Ray."

Bedroom? It had been years...at least three, he knew...since he'd been in any woman's bedroom, no matter the reason. He drew in a deep breath and headed toward the direction of her voice.

He walked into the spacious bedroom and he could tell that already Ashley had added her touch. There were flowers and beautiful floral covers on the bed. And there were pillows, a lot of pillows, and a nice floral rug. But what caught his attention and held it more than anything was the bed. It was a huge oak bed that sat high off the floor and looked comfortable as hell. And it looked so damn inviting. For a quick moment he could envision Ashley in that bed.

"You can set the boxes over there. Thanks."

He just realized he'd been standing in one spot in the middle of the bedroom. "You're welcome." After placing the boxes down, he glanced around again. "This place came furnished, right?"

"Yes," she said, smiling. "But with just the basics. I decided to spruce it up a little."

Ray thought she was doing more than sprucing it up; she was making it a home. He found that odd for someone who only intended to stay for three months.

She came over to stand beside him to open one of the boxes and then glanced up at him. "You wouldn't happen to have a box cutter, would you?"

"No, but I have a pocketknife. That should work."

It did, and when he took a step back, he almost bumped into her. "Sorry. There's a couple more boxes I need to get out your car."

"Okay."

ASHLEY WATCHED RAY rush from the room like the devil himself was behind him. She could read her husband like a book and knew he was definitely attracted to her and was still trying to figure out why. She hoped the day would come when he put two and two together and got his memory back.

She was looking forward to her time in Catalina Cove. The one thing she knew about him was that he'd never been able to resist her for long. Nor could she resist him, so her willpower had to be just as strong as his. Even stronger.

"Do you also want these in here?" he asked, coming back into the room.

"You can set them here," she said, moving out of his way to stand by the window. She turned and looked out at the view. The cove was beautiful and today the water was the bluest green. There were a number of boaters out on the water and pelicans were flying close to shore in search of their catch for today. Just looking out the window was having such a calming effect on her, not at all like the man behind her, who had the ability to raise her temperature without even trying.

".Anything else?"

She glanced over her shoulder. "Yes. Come here for a minute. I want you to see the view I'll wake up to every morning."

RAY FELT A quiver up his spine and wished Ashley hadn't given him such a bright smile. He also wished he had more willpower to deny her request. What he should do was tell her if she didn't need any more help that he needed to leave. There were other things he could be doing…like remembering he had a company to run.

Instead he was moving his feet toward where she stood by the window, her entire body silhouetted in the glow of the noonday sun. Today she was wearing another cute pair of shorts and a diagonal print top. The prominent colors of yellow and blue seemed to enhance her skin tone, making her appear even more radiant.

With every step he took toward her, he tried convincing himself the only reason he was going to her was out of curiosity. He wanted to see the view. He tried forcing from his mind the image of her waking, stretching and getting out of bed wearing something soft, sexy and alluring that barely covered those legs.

If anyone would have told him even last month

that a woman would come to Catalina Cove who would get embedded deep in his skin, he would not have believed them. Yet here he was. Since the day he'd pulled her out of the water, this woman was constantly on his mind.

He wanted to stand beside her, but since she was in the middle of the window, it made more sense to stand directly behind her. He was tall enough to see over her head. But standing so close to her was causing all kinds of sensations to swamp him. He drew in a deep breath—a huge mistake when he took in her scent through his nostrils. Damn, she smelled good.

A long, sensual moment passed before he could finally say the word "beautiful." And he wasn't talking about the view out of her bedroom window. He was talking about her.

ASHLEY COULD FEEL her husband's heat as well as the warmth of his breath on her neck when he'd spoken. She momentarily closed her eyes, fighting the urge to lean back against him. She wished she didn't remember their very active sex life and what she'd gone without for the past three years. His touch. His kiss. His lovemaking…

She blinked open her eyes, drew in a deep breath, which included his masculine scent, and said, "Yes, I think the view is beautiful, too."

"I wasn't just talking about the view of the cove, Ashley."

His rough and sensuous voice made her draw in

another deep breath. She slowly turned. The moment she did, he reached out and brushed the back of his hand across her cheek. His touch made her heart beat fast in her chest.

For several tense seconds she just stood there and studied his features. Standing before her was the man she loved with every fiber of her being and he had no idea that every beat of her heart belonged to him. That for three years since receiving word of his death she'd been a woman grieving for her mate. A woman who knew that no other man could ever take his place. A woman who didn't care if he remembered her or not. A woman who cared even less if he was called Devon or Ray, because in her heart his name would forever be *Mine*.

"So what else were you talking about, Ray?"

He took a step closer and she could feel his erection press hard against her middle. Lordy, it had been three years too long, and although he might not remember her, this part of him did, and it was doing what it usually did when desire got the best of them— communicating with the area between her thighs, telling her exactly what it wanted. What it needed.

"I was talking about you," he said, staring down at her. "I don't understand."

She held his gaze and asked softly, "And what don't you understand, Ray?" Was it her imagination or was he lowering his head and his lips getting closer and closer to hers?

"Why I want you so much. I haven't wanted a woman this much in three years."

"Since your divorce?"

One of his eyebrows went up and then it lowered when he said, "Yes."

She swallowed and said, "And I haven't wanted a man as much as I want you in three years, too."

"Since your husband's death?"

"Yes," she said as his mouth got closer and closer.

"Then I guess this is about needs."

And then he sank his mouth into hers. Her eyes drifted shut as sensations she hadn't felt in three years, sensations she'd convinced herself she would never feel again, swept through her, capturing her in a maelstrom of passion, the strength of which she'd never felt before.

When he deepened the kiss, she moaned in a way that sent shudders all through her, feelings that only Devon could stir within her. Feelings he could not only initiate but take to unprecedented levels.

Like he was doing now.

The way he was taking her mouth was causing nerve endings inside of her to detonate. This kiss was bringing back detailed memories of nights and days spent in his arms, enjoying this delicious foreplay before they would strip off each other's clothes.

Devon had been a master kisser and she could definitely say he hadn't lost his touch. He had defined a whole new meaning of French kissing. He had his own special technique and had taught her just how to reciprocate or die trying.

She wished there was a way for this kiss to bring back memories for him like it was doing for her.

But for her it was doing more than rekindling memories. There was a distinctive heat spreading all over her, moving up her thighs and settling at the core between her legs. Now there was an insistent throb, a titillating ache. Her senses were being crushed under the onslaught of his masterful tongue.

She wrapped her arms around his neck to return the kiss the only way she knew how. The way he had taught her to do. From the sounds he was making, he still liked that way although he probably had no earthly idea why. He couldn't remember the many college nights they'd spent sharing heated kisses because he'd refused to take things further.

When he finally had and she'd gotten her first taste of deep-rooted desire and passion, she'd come apart. The reminder of that first time with him, three years without and what he was doing to her now, took over her mind and body, destroying the last remnants of her control.

Suddenly, it happened. Her arms tightened around his neck while sensuous spasms tore into her, and when the multitude of contractions became unbearable, she pulled back from his mouth and screamed, not caring if all of Catalina Cove could hear her. All that pent-up passion, sexual need and carnal hunger was being ripped out of her with unprecedented proficiency. Only Devon had the ability to do this to her. Devon who was now Ray.

He was still there, holding her in his arms and saying soothing passionate words while pressing soft kisses to her lips and running his hands over her backside, like he had every right to do so. He did.

In all honesty, she would not have been surprised if her loud screams had run him off. Devon had been used to her orgasms from kissing. She couldn't help but wonder what Ray thought of it.

Ashley closed her eyes as spasms continued to tear through her. She didn't even reopen them when she felt him sweep her off the floor to carry her across the room to the bed, placing her on it and lying down beside her.

She would forever recall his soothing words and the kisses he continued to nibble around her mouth. She wasn't sure how long they lay there, yet she still refused to open her eyes. She didn't want to see the look of lust instead of one of love in his eyes. The lack of recognition at this moment would break her heart.

As he continued to hold her, she felt the spasms begin to wane, and that was all she recalled before drifting off to sleep.

CHAPTER FIFTEEN

RAY EASED OFF the bed the moment he knew Ashley had drifted off to sleep. Shoving his hands in his pockets, he walked over to the window and looked out. Now he was seeing what Ashley had intended for him to see and she'd been right. The view was beautiful.

He turned and glanced at her sleeping in the bed. She was even more beautiful like this. When she had reached the pinnacle of sexual pleasure just from their kiss, he'd come pretty damn close to doing so himself.

He tossed his head back and looked up at the ceiling when regret began taking over his mind. He should never have kissed her. How in the world had he allowed such a thing to happen? It was as if the moment he'd gotten a taste of her mouth, something within him had snapped, propelling him with a greed he wasn't prepared for.

And it seemed as if a similar greed had propelled her to an orgasm she'd definitely needed. And like he'd said, it had been all about needs.

He understood how such a thing happened. She obviously had enjoyed a pretty active sex life with her husband. Ray had every reason to believe she hadn't been with a man since losing him and some women couldn't always depend on one of those pleasure toys to take care of business to the degree they might like. That kiss had given her a way to unleash all that sexual desire. He was glad in a way, but where did that leave him?

She had unknowingly lit a torch within him, a torch he had successfully kept dormant. But kissing her had blatantly reminded him that he was a man with needs he'd buried for three years. He had a feeling that now that the torch had been lit, it wouldn't be easy to snuff it out again. But he had to do so. He had no other choice. Needs or no needs.

The first thing he had to do was get away from here. As far as he could get and especially before she woke up. He couldn't handle any awkward moments between them and he knew there would be some.

Ray noticed a photo on the dresser. That of her and three other women. They were all smiling for the camera and you could tell the four were close. He glanced around and figured there would be a framed photo of her late husband someplace. When he didn't see one, he assumed she hadn't unpacked it yet. He cursed himself for being nosy.

When there was a movement on the bed, he glanced over and saw Ashley had shifted in sleep, making a portion of her shorts ride up her thighs. He felt his body get hard and begin throbbing. He had to get out of there and away from her.

Walking quickly, he moved toward the front door.

"How on earth am I going to face him again, Emmie?" Ashley asked, setting her wineglass down with a thud. It was night and she was sitting out on the screen patio that overlooked the ocean. It was beautiful how the moon, the only light that appeared in the sky, seemed to glow across the waters. Earlier that day she had awakened alone to remember just what had happened. There was no telling what Ray was thinking about her.

"Hey, don't beat yourself up over it. The way I see it, it was bound to happen. I'm surprised the two of you stopped at kissing. If you recall, you and Devon used to mate like rabbits."

Ashley did recall and wished she didn't. "That was then, and this is now. He is Ray."

"Yes, but Ray is still a man who, according to what you've said, has shunned women for three years. He's attracted to you, so the kiss was inevitable. You can't fault yourself for kissing him the way you've always done."

"But he doesn't know that. I'm not looking forward to seeing him anytime soon." But then, a part of her *was* looking forward to it. He was the reason she was here. The very reason she had rented the house for the summer.

"Get used to it. I have a feeling that kiss is only the beginning."

Emmie's words came back to her as she checked all the doors and climbed into bed that night. She had unpacked a lot of her belongings. Bryce and Vashti had returned with food since they figured she hadn't stopped to eat. She hadn't and appreciated their thoughtfulness. Vashti had brought the baby

with her and Ashley had thought he was a mini Sawyer. The little guy definitely was a cutie with all his
father's features.

Seeing him made her remember how much she'd
wanted a baby. Devon's baby. She wanted to believe there was still hope they would find their way
back together.

As she curled into bed, she couldn't help but
think of the kiss she'd shared with Ray. When she'd
awakened to find him gone, at first she'd felt a deep
rush of embarrassment, but talking to Emmie had
helped. Besides, although she'd been a willing par-
ticipant, she hadn't been the one to initiate the kiss.
To her that had been something.

And then for her it had meant everything to feel
her husband's lips possessively moving over hers
and making her remember how things used to be
between them. His kisses would always start off
sweet, then move to hot, scandalous and, finally,
all-consuming. He might not have his memory but
the mind-blowing technique was still there.

As she shifted positions a few times before settling comfortably in bed, there was no doubt in her
mind Ray would try avoiding her for a while, and
as hard as it would be, she had to let him. The next
move had to be his and she refused to consider the
possibility that he wouldn't make it.

"OUT LATE TONIGHT, aren't you, Ray?"

Ray lifted his head from drinking coffee as Sawyer
slid into the booth across from him. It was close to ten
at night, and instead of being home in bed as usual,

he was here, at Witherspoon Café, drinking coffee. "Yes, and I could say the same about you, Sheriff."

Sawyer grinned. "Trust me, there's nothing I'd rather be doing about now than be home with my wife and kids, but I'm covering for one of my guys tonight."

"Oh, I see."

Sawyer lifted a brow. "So what's your reason for being out so late? You rarely come back out once you go home."

Sawyer was right. But there was no way Ray would tell Sawyer he hadn't been able to sleep because the image of a certain woman wouldn't let him. Her image, along with memories of how she'd come apart in his arms, was too much to think about. So he had escaped here, needing a diversion.

But not before he'd driven by Ashley's place, convincing himself that he needed to make sure she was okay. Instead of going up to her door to find out, he'd parked under a cluster of trees in the lot adjacent to hers and sat there awhile, convincing himself it was concern and nothing else that had motivated him to be there. He'd known the moment her bedroom light had gone out.

"I couldn't sleep," he finally answered his friend truthfully.

"You're okay?"

He heard the concern in Sawyer's voice. Unlike Kaegan, who was closer in age to him, Sawyer was at least five years older and, to Ray's way of thinking, a little wiser. "I'm fine. Just restless."

Sawyer chuckled. "Usually when a man is restless it's because of a woman."

Ray didn't say anything and instead took another sip of his coffee. "You know my rule when it comes to women."

Sawyer nodded. "And you knew mine, which was pretty similar to yours. Then Vashti came to town and I threw the rule right out the damn window."

Ray shrugged. "That was easy for you to do."

"Hell no, it wasn't."

Ray couldn't help but grin. He recalled the time and thought Sawyer was right. It hadn't been easy. Like him, Sawyer hadn't dated any of the women in town either.

Getting involved with one was the last thing Ray needed or wanted. He had too much baggage and most women wanted a man who was ready to settle down. Hell, he couldn't settle down with one when he could very well belong to another somewhere.

"You want to talk about it?"

As much as he did, Ray knew there were some things that he had to figure out for himself. "No, I'm fine. No biggie."

Ray knew as soon as he said it that he hoped it was true, that this thing, this intense attraction he was feeling for Ashley, would eventually fizzle out. But then, after what had happened today between them, he wasn't sure that it would.

CHAPTER SIXTEEN

NEARLY TWO WEEKS went by and Ashley began questioning if the magnitude of the kiss she and Ray had shared had scared him off for good. She'd even been tempted to instigate a chance encounter with him outside of Lafitte Seafood House on the boardwalk like she'd done before, or to show up one morning at the café where he usually met for breakfast with his friends. She would talk herself out of it every time, wanting to believe this thing between them was something neither of them had the power to resist.

She knew from Vashti that July was the busiest month in Catalina Cove due to an increase in tourists. She had thoroughly enjoyed the Fourth of July parade and had hoped to see Ray but hadn't. In a couple of weeks the cove would kick off its shrimp festival. Ashley wanted to believe that the reason Ray hadn't come by was his busy schedule, but she knew she was only fooling herself.

She was sitting on the patio contemplating what her next move should be regarding Ray when her phone rang. She cringed, recognizing the ringtone. It was her mother. After drawing in a deep breath, she clicked on the phone. "Yes, Mom?"

"You're still in New Orleans?"

Ashley had decided to tell her mother that she was in New Orleans working on a job project instead of letting her know exactly where she was. Her mother was known to just pop up, regardless of the location. Ashley figured New Orleans was close enough to Catalina Cove. "Yes, Mom. I told you I'd be gone all summer."

"I know what you said but I want to know why. It's not like you're an employee, for heaven's sake. You own the company. Besides, it's not as if you have to work. With that deal he cinched before he died, Devon left you a wealthy woman. The only thing he didn't leave you with was a baby."

Ashley resented each time her mother said that. "Mom, is there a reason you called?"

"Of course there is a reason. Sam and I are your parents and we shouldn't have to worry about you, but we do."

Ashley rolled her eyes, tempted to tell her mother to keep her father out of this since he had long ago accepted she could take care of herself. Trying to keep control of her was her mother's doing. "Neither of you should be worrying about me. I'm fine."

"Well, we're back in Hardeeville and disappointed you're not here."

She was tempted to ask why they'd returned and why they hadn't remained in Kansas permanently. "Well, like I told you, I'm gone for the summer." And just in case her mother got any ideas of visiting, she added, "And I'll be busy the entire time."

"Elliott's been asking about you."

She refused to show any interest in the man her mother was still trying to shove down her throat at every opportunity. "That's nice, Mom. Now I need to go and finish up what I was doing."

"You're making a mistake, Ashley. I know how much you loved Devon, but you need to finally face the fact that he isn't coming back."

Ashley was tempted to tell her mother just how wrong she was about that. Instead she said, "I've really got to go, Mom. Give Dad my love. Goodbye."

She quickly clicked off the phone, not giving her mother time to say anything else. Gathering her wineglass and the book she'd been reading in her hands, she moved from the patio and into the house, deciding to finish reading in bed.

She was about to head for her bedroom when she heard the knock on her door. Her heart rate increased a notch. Drawing in a deep breath, she moved toward the door, hoping and wishing that it was Ray. When she glanced out the peephole and saw it was him, she fought back tears of happiness and joy.

Pulling herself together and knowing she shouldn't act as if she was overjoyed to see him, she swallowed before asking, "Who is it?"

She already knew, and glancing back through the peephole, she could tell from the expression on his face that he was aware she knew as well. The gaze holding hers in the peephole was causing shivers to race up and down her spine.

"It's Ray, Ashley."

His rough and sexy voice made her quiver even more. Her hands were shaking as she opened the door. And then he was standing there in jeans and an open collar shirt, looking as rough and handsome as she remembered with powerful, strong arms at his sides and staring at her with intense dark eyes. More than anything, she was tempted to throw herself into his arms, but she knew as much as she might want to do that, she couldn't. She had to retain her calm and composure.

"Ray." She didn't miss the fact that his gaze was taking in every inch of her body and she felt it like a caress.

"May I come in?"

She nodded. "Yes, you may." And she stepped aside.

IN A WAY Ray felt like a total ass, showing up at her place close to nine at night after deliberately avoiding her for almost two weeks. But tonight, he couldn't take it anymore. He refused to drive by just to make sure things looked okay and then go home and get into bed only to toss and turn with her on his mind.

And he refused to rack his brain anymore trying to figure out why, of all the women he'd met over the past three years, it was her and only her who had captured his interest. Not only had she captured his interest, she had him wishing for things he knew he couldn't have.

"Would you like something to drink, Ray?"

He glanced over at her, surprised she hadn't asked why the hell he'd shown up at her place at this hour. "Yes. I'll take a beer if you have it."

"I do. I'll be back in a minute."

He watched her stroll off and thought as he always did that she looked good wearing something as simple as a pair of shorts and a top. Shoving his hands into his pockets, he glanced around, thinking how neat the place was. Still, you got a feeling someone truly lived there.

The one thing he noticed was there wasn't a picture of her husband anywhere. He figured she'd probably placed one in her bedroom by now.

Why was he feeling a tinge of jealousy for a dead man? A man who'd undoubtedly enjoyed those kisses she'd showered Ray with the last time he was here. He'd never known such a passionate woman before. At least, in his limited scope of memory, he was sure he hadn't known one.

"Here you are."

Ray turned, and the moment their gazes collided, he drew in a sharp breath. He refused to believe coming here was a mistake. They had to talk. He had to get her to understand and accept that whatever this was between them had to be curtailed.

"Thanks," he said, taking the beer bottle from her hand and sensing her nervousness.

"Would you like to sit down, Ray?"

"Yes, thanks." He waited until she sat down on the sofa and then he took the seat opposite her. He

watched when she leaned back against the sofa
cushion and waited. Since he was the one who came
here invading her space, he should have something
to say. He did, but he wasn't quite ready to say it
yet. So instead he asked, "How have you been?"

She curled her legs beneath her. "I've been doing
okay. Finally settled in. Haven't been to town much."

He'd noticed. At least, he hadn't seen her around.
"Did you get the chance to go to the Fourth of July
parade?"

"Yes. It was nice," she said.

"It usually is."

"You didn't go?"

He shook his head. "Not this year." No need to
tell her that he hadn't gone to avoid seeing her. That
kiss they'd shared had rattled his brain in ways he
hadn't expected.

He tipped his head back and took a swig of beer.
He licked his lips and noticed her watching him
closely. Seeing the look made his breath stall. He
quickly recovered and asked, "You're not drinking anything?"

She shook her head. "No. I had a glass of wine
earlier. I usually do right before bed."

"I knew you usually go to bed around this time
and wanted to come before you did that."

Her brow lifted. "How would you know what
time I usually go to bed?"

Too late he realized just what he'd said, and his
mouth suddenly went dry. He took another swig of
beer and decided to level with her. "I've been driv-

ing by every night since you moved in. This place goes dark usually around the same time."

RAY'S WORDS GAVE Ashley pause. He'd been driving by here every night since she'd moved in? Why? It would have to be a conscious effort on his part since she didn't live on a main road. And if he'd taken the time to drive by, why hadn't he stopped in? She figured he was the only person who could answer that. But then, she already knew the answer.

"I want to apologize about what happened the last time you were here, Ray."

"You don't owe me an apology for that, Ashley. In a way I was honored."

"Honored?"

"Yes. I know how much you loved your husband. How much you still do. I'm glad you trusted me enough to let yourself go like that. To enjoy the moment. I should apologize to you for making you feel an apology was necessary. It's not."

"You left and didn't come back." There, she had called him out on it.

He nodded. "I'm going through some issues right now and one of the ways I'm dealing with those issues is by limiting my association with women. I've discovered a few things about you."

"Such as?"

"You're someone who is hard to resist, Ashley. I enjoy your company and deep down I know you're not a threat."

"A threat?"

"Yes. Like I said, I'm dealing with a few issues and I know what I can offer a woman and what I can't. I believe you're not a woman who would want more than I can give."

Ashley fell silent, knowing he was wrong about that. She wanted a lot more than he was willing to give, but she would settle on taking whatever she could. But for how long?

The answer came quickly. For as long as it took.

"I guess you can say I have issues of my own, Ray," she finally said. "I'm a woman who loves deeply."

He nodded. "I gathered as much, and I know you can only truly love one man."

What he said was true. "Yes, but then, I've never tried loving anyone else, and honestly, I've never wanted to. Devon and I met in college and he became my life. Don't get me wrong. We had our ups and downs like any married couple, but we refused to give in or give up. The one time we felt our marriage threatened, we sought counseling. I think it brought us closer together."

He took another swig of his beer and then said, "I think he was lucky to have had you."

"And I feel lucky to have had him." She paused a moment and then asked, "What about you and your marriage, Ray?" They'd been talking about her marriage and he might find it odd if she didn't at least inquire.

He studied his beer bottle and then met her eyes. "My past, which includes my marriage, is what I'm having issues with right now. Hopefully one day I'll be able to explain just what those issues are."

She mulled that over before she said, "Appears you're not over your wife any more than I'm over my husband." Ashley knew that wasn't the case but figured he needed to know what any other woman would assume.

Instead of correcting her on that assumption, he said, "You intrigue me, Ashley, and I want to spend time with you, but just as a friend."

She nodded and then deliberately threw out a challenge. "Typically, friends don't kiss, Ray. We did. You're the first man I've kissed since losing my husband, and I think it was quite obvious just how much I enjoyed it. So how are we supposed to handle this 'just as a friend' thing?"

CHAPTER SEVENTEEN

RAY BELIEVED ONE of the reasons he was so drawn to Ashley was her honesty. Although he didn't know her that well, there was something about her that made him feel she was a person he could trust. The only reason he hadn't told her about his memory loss was because it was something he wasn't ready to share with others yet. He'd finally gotten around to telling Bryce, whom he considered a good friend, a few weeks ago.

Perceptive as ever, Bryce claimed she had picked up on vibes between him and Ashley that day at the café when she and Ashley had been having lunch together. He didn't deny he was attracted to Ashley but shared the reason why that attraction couldn't go any further.

But even now, he would love for his hands to curl around Ashley instead of this beer bottle. She had every right to question him about his claim that friendship was all he wanted. He, of all people, knew better. The bottom line was that he had enjoyed kissing her, way too much. He had even gotten a masculine high when she'd climaxed in his arms from their kiss.

He finished off the last of his beer. Liquid courage, so to speak. But even that, he figured, wouldn't help much. Not when she was sitting there just a few feet from him looking more sexy and beautiful than any woman had a right to look. Her hair hung loose around her shoulders and her bangs nearly covered her eyes. Nearly but not completely. He could see the inquisitiveness in their dark depths. She was waiting on an answer.

"I don't plan on it happening again, Ashley," he finally said.

He could tell by the look on her face that his response surprised her. "Really? Is it anything we can stop?"

Every muscle in his body seemed to tighten with her question. "We can certainly try."

He tilted his head and studied her features and knew exactly what she was thinking. *Good luck on that happening.* Their gazes locked and he immediately felt it. That hot, irresistible attraction that had been there from the first. He knew her skepticism but would prove it could be done. He had to.

He watched as she slid her hair away from her eyes, as if to make sure she was seeing him and he was seeing her. He could feel the tension thrumming between them and knew even now those vibes Bryce had talked about were out in full force.

She straightened up in her seat. "Even with all our issues, Ray, I'm not sure we can just be friends. We like kissing each other. A lot. So I truly don't understand how that would be possible."

He leaned forward in his chair. "Because I would make it possible, Ashley. For starters, we could limit the time we spend together. I could call and check up on you if I had your phone number instead of stopping by." He wasn't sure why he'd said that when he would still want to stop by and see her.

"That's fine," she said, easing her cell phone from the pocket of her jeans. "What's your number?"

He rattled it off, and when his phone rang, he said, "Got it." Ray glanced at his watch. "It's time for me to go." He stood. "Thanks for the beer, Ashley."

She slid gracefully to her feet. "Thanks for dropping by to check on me. I'm glad you came." She paused a minute and then she said, "You know what I think, Ray?"

In a way he was almost too afraid to ask. "No. What do you think?"

"We can help each other with our issues."

He shook his head and smiled. "I'm not so sure about that."

She shrugged her shoulders and he watched her hair tumble around them. "Sooner or later, we'll both want to move on with our lives. The past can't control us forever, can it?"

Now he was the one to shrug his shoulders. "I guess not."

"I'll walk you to the door now. We both know what's liable to happen if you stay here any longer."

He didn't say anything as he followed her to the door. She opened it and turned to him. "Thanks again for stopping by."

Ray stared at her for a minute before saying, "I wish…"

She lifted a brow when he didn't finish his statement. "You wish what?"

He shook his head, reclaiming his senses. "Nothing. Good night." And then he was gone and he didn't look back.

THE MOMENT ASHLEY heard the sound of Ray's truck leaving, she leaned against the door and drew in a long breath. She had needed to be as straightforward with him as she could. Eventually they would sleep together and he needed to know it and own it. She wasn't playing games; she was playing for keeps.

Her goal was to make sure he played for keeps as well. She'd known that "just friends" thing wouldn't work the moment he'd said it. Even with a sincere smile indicating he was trying to do the right thing, he'd been looking at her in a way that had made her panties wet. He couldn't have it both ways and she needed to make sure he knew it.

So what now? She had to wait and see. There was more at stake than sex. She couldn't help but remember their kiss—the first she'd gotten from her husband in three years, a man supposedly dead. And whether he realized it or not, he'd put a lot of need, longing and desire into it and she'd reciprocated in kind. There was no way she could not, given their history.

Sighing deeply, Ashley went into the kitchen to dispose of the empty beer bottle. A few moments later she was headed toward her bedroom when there was a knock at her door. Her heart rate increased. For some reason she knew it was Ray. He had returned.

Moving toward the door, she looked out the peephole just to make sure it was him before opening the door. He stood there, his jaw clenching and unclenching. The look in his eyes was hot.

"You forget something, Ray?" she asked, fighting to remain calm while stepping aside to let him in.

"No, I didn't forget anything. But there's something I need to do," he said, entering and closing the door behind him.

She tilted her head up to look at him. "Oh? And what's that?"

He stood in front of her, feet braced apart with an air of determination surrounding him. Then he drew her into his arms and kissed her in a way that immediately made her swoon.

She gripped a pair of powerful shoulders as his mouth moved over hers. Then his tongue began mating with hers in a way that had her moaning. Devon or Ray, the man had the ability to make her aware of every single cell in her body. He could effortlessly set off an explosion of pleasure inside of her.

There was no way she could fight the emotions she was feeling, the sparks of heat engulfing her or the need she felt in the lower part of her belly that was taking over her senses. Her body's most primitive reaction was kicking in with a vengeance.

Then suddenly he released her. She was grateful he still had his arms around her waist or there was no doubt in her mind she would have fallen.

"Not kissing you is harder than I thought. Good night, Ashley."

And then he was gone.

RAY HAD DRIVEN less than a mile when he pulled to the shoulder of the road, not able to travel any farther. There was no way he could when intense heat was throbbing through his gut, filling him with more than just desire but a need the likes of which he'd never felt before. *How? Why?*

Going to her place had obviously been a mistake. He hadn't counted on confronting a sexual force so powerful that he could still feel it in every nerve of his body, with every pulse. There was something about Ashley Ryan he just couldn't put his finger on. To tell the truth, he'd rather put his hands on her instead. He definitely enjoyed kissing her and could see himself becoming addicted to her taste. So much for having that under control like he'd thought he would be able to do. For crying out loud, he'd been fine for three years, and then she came to town and it seemed his senses were in a tailspin.

He jumped when there was a tap on his window. It was Sawyer. Ray rolled the window down. "Evening, Sawyer."

"You okay, Ray? Truck trouble?" Sawyer asked him.

Ray wished that was it. Repairing his truck

would be easier than reining in his body's urgent demands. "Truck's fine. I just needed to sit a spell."

"On the side of the road? This time of night?" Sawyer asked, lifting a curious brow. "You live on the other side of town. What are you doing in this area?"

Ray sighed. When it came to Sawyer and Kaegan, he had no reason to lie. They knew as much about his history as he did. "I just left Ashley Ryan's place. I stopped by to check on her. To see how she was doing."

Sawyer nodded, eyeing him speculatively. "And how is she doing?"

"Okay. She's pretty much moved in. The place looks good."

"That's good. Well, glad to know your truck isn't broken, so there's no reason for you not to move on, right?"

Ray chuckled. It was just like his friend to keep it legal. "No reason at all. I'll see you at breakfast in the morning."

"Will do." Sawyer turned to walk off.

"Sawyer?"

Sawyer turned back around. "Yes?"

"For the longest time you swore not to get involved with anyone. Why Vashti? What made her different?"

Sawyer smiled and Ray knew that look. For a man who'd sworn off relationships, Sawyer had no problem letting anyone know he'd hit the jackpot with his wife. He leaned his elbow in the open truck window and said, "There was just something about

Vashti that touched me deeply. I didn't want it to happen but it did and I couldn't fight it. I saw in her something I wanted in my life. Something I had no idea that I needed until I met her."

Sawyer got quiet and then he looked Ray in the eye. "Is there any particular reason you're asking?"

Ray tipped his head back against the headrest. "Yes. It's Ashley Ryan. There's something about her I just can't figure out. I was doing fine and then she comes to town and…"

"Are you sure you were doing fine, Ray? Or were you just pretending to do fine? You didn't have a social life, and although you're friendly enough, you're only good friends with me, Kaegan, Vashti and Bryce. You might not want to hear this but Ashley Ryan might just be what you need."

"Dammit, Sawyer, I might have a wife somewhere."

"Yes, and it might be a wife that's doing what you're refusing to do, which is to move on with your life." Not waiting for Ray to respond, Sawyer straightened and said, "Good night, Ray. Think about what I said. I'll see you in the morning."

ASHLEY'S HAND TREMBLED as she traced her fingers across her lips. Lips that Ray had just thoroughly kissed. On shaky legs she made it to the sofa and sat down. Leaning back against the seat, she closed her eyes.

Oh, my God!

He couldn't keep kissing her with such greed

and hunger and then insist they be merely friends. If that was his plan, he might as well forget it because it wouldn't work. He was pushing her buttons whether he intended to or not. His willpower was definitely a lot stronger than hers because she didn't have the same reservations he had about them indulging in a relationship.

He was concerned about the woman in his past when, little did he know, she was that woman. More than anything, she wished she could level with him and let him know that. But Dr. Riggins had advised her of the possible repercussions if she did.

More than anything, she wanted Ray to fall in love with her all over again. No matter what it took, she intended to make new memories with him. She felt like she'd been given another chance with him and was determined for things to work in her favor. Their favor.

Knowing it was time to do something she hadn't thought she'd ever be ready to do, she slid off her wedding ring. She had met a man who'd charmed her into taking it off. Ironically, he was the same man who'd placed that ring on her finger eight years ago.

CHAPTER EIGHTEEN

TWO DAYS LATER Ray walked into the Witherspoon Café like he did most mornings to join Kaegan and Sawyer for breakfast. After he took his seat and greeted his friends, his attention was drawn to the woman sitting at a table on the other side of the room.

Ashley.

She was sitting alone and Bryce was placing a cup of coffee and a basket of muffins in front of her. She hadn't seen him yet; at least, he assumed she hadn't since she hadn't looked his way. His smile at seeing her came easy.

Ray had thought about her a lot over the past two days and had meant to call her but things had gotten busy. His last tour had been around five and then afterward he had assisted Kaegan on one of his boats on what they called a night raid. During certain times of the year, the middle of the night was the best time to drop the net for blue crabs. Last night they'd caught plenty.

Why was he trying to come up with excuses when there really weren't any? He had her phone number and could have called her. He'd come close to doing so but had talked himself out of it. Now seeing her was making him recall their kiss of two nights ago.

That kiss had energized him and memories of it had gotten him through the past two days. He had decided to call her today, no matter what. And now she was here. Even with the distance separating them, he thought she looked beautiful with an early morning glow to her face.

"Instead of sitting here staring, why don't you go join her?"

Ray glanced over at Kaegan. There was no need to pretend he had no idea what Kaegan was talking about. "She might prefer eating alone."

"You don't know that," Sawyer interjected, taking a sip of his coffee. "She might like some company."

Ray, unsure of that, asked, "You think so?"

"Although you didn't ask me what I think, I'm going to tell you anyway," Kaegan said. "I think that it's about time you start living your life, Ray."

Ray shifted his gaze from Kaegan to Sawyer, who smiled and said, "I didn't say a word."

Kaegan looked from Sawyer to Ray. "Say a word about what?"

"Nothing," Ray said quickly. He glanced back over at Ashley. "I think I will join her. I wonder what got her up so early."

"Not sure," Sawyer said, "but I'm sure you'll find out."

It took every ounce of control Ashley possessed not to glance over to the table where Ray was sitting.

She'd known the exact moment he had walked into the café. Her body had begun throbbing in places she hadn't been aware it could throb. When she hadn't seen him again for a couple of days, she decided to come to a place where she knew he would. Even if it meant being at the café at the crack of dawn to do it.

There were times when a woman had to do what a woman had to do. Ray was the most important person in her life. Always had been and always would be, whether he remembered that fact or not.

"Good morning, Ashley. May I join you?"

Ashley jerked her head up and looked into Ray's face. She hadn't realized he'd approached. Now he was standing beside her table. Her gaze swept over him and took in all the things so familiar and all the things so different. Namely, the beard. Devon hated facial hair of any kind but it seemed that had definitely changed. She liked it and thought his beard made him look even sexier.

Ashley met his gaze and her pulse began pounding. "Good morning, Ray, and, yes, you can join me."

"Thanks."

She watched as he pulled out the chair and settled his masculine frame into it. A sexual aura seemed to surround him. That was nothing new, but what made this unique was that, in her mind, this was no longer Devon but Ray. She was still trying to wrap her head around that.

"You're up early," he told her.

She smiled over at him. "Not too early. I thought I would go into New Orleans today." She bit into a muffin and she could feel his eyes on her. She looked up, and the instant their eyes locked, she felt a stirring in her stomach. The hot desire she saw in his dark gaze only intensified her desire for him.

No telling how long they would have just sat there if Bryce hadn't appeared. "Good morning, Ray," she said, placing a cup of coffee and another basket of blueberry muffins on the table.

Ashley glanced away but Ray looked up at Bryce, who was smiling at him. "Good morning, Bryce."

"About time you have a reason to break away from the pack," Bryce said before walking off smiling.

Ray shook his head before looking back at Ashley. "So you're going to New Orleans? Any special reason?"

"Shopping. Some of my favorite dress shops are there," she said, taking a sip of her coffee.

Over the rim of her cup, she watched Ray take a sip of his coffee before he said, "I would have called to see how you were doing but I've been busy."

She shrugged. "You don't owe me an explanation about anything, Ray."

"I believe that I do."

"You honestly don't."

He didn't say anything for a minute and she figured he'd decided to let it go. She looked over at him the moment he bit into one of the muffins. Her breath wobbled when he sank his teeth into the muffin filled with blueberries.

Memories he knew nothing about began to arouse her. There were times he used those same teeth to nibble a path up her naked thighs. Forcing the memories back, she said, "I take it you like the muffins here."

He smiled at her. "I do, and Bryce warmed them up just the way I like. They're good."

"Yes, they are," she agreed, taking another bite of her own muffin.

"How about dinner this evening, Ashley?"

His question caught her so by surprise that she nearly choked. She grabbed her glass of water to wash down the muffin.

"You okay?"

She nodded as she cleared her throat. "Yes, I'm fine." She took another gulp of water and asked, "Dinner?"

Their gazes held. "Yes. However, if you have other plans, I'll understand."

She shook her head. "No, I don't have other plans."

"Then is it okay to pick you up at seven?"

"Yes, seven is fine."

"I thought we'd go to Shanty's," he said. "Is that okay?"

Shanty's was one of the restaurants she'd heard was a popular dining place in town. Attire was dressy and she was glad she was going shopping today. "Yes, that's fine. I heard it's a nice place."

Their eyes locked again—a silent communication. She'd always been able to tell what Devon was thinking just by looking in his eyes. Reading him had become second nature. Whether he knew it or not, it still was. He wanted her. Just as much as she wanted him. He was fighting it.

"More coffee?"

They both looked up at Bryce, who unknowingly had interrupted something so intense it had Ashley nearly breathless.

As if Ray sensed her predicament, he said, "Yes, and you can leave the pot." His tone showed his annoyance at the interruption.

"Sure thing, Ray." Bryce set the pot in the middle of their table, and as if Ray's tone had amused her rather than irritated her, she walked off smiling again.

When he didn't say anything, Ashley said, "Bryce is a nice person. I like her."

Ray smiled. "Yes, she's a nice person and everybody likes her." He then chuckled. "Well, everybody except for Kaegan. Old history between them."

"So she said that the day we had lunch together here," Ashley said. Wanting to keep the conversation between them moving, she asked, "You have a full day with tours?"

"Not too much. I've mostly been helping Kaegan. He's been having huge orders this month for blue crabs and the best time to net them is at night.

I've been working with him during the evenings on his boats."

She took another sip of her coffee. She recalled during the tour that he'd told her that the blue crabs in the waters surrounding Catalina Cove were the largest anywhere in the United States. For that reason, they were always high in demand.

While he talked, explaining the process, she could envision him out on the boat, dressed in those jeans and snug T-shirt and pulling in the nets filled with crabs. "Sounds dangerous," she said, picturing how easy it would be for someone to fall overboard, especially at night.

"It could be but Kaegan hires men who know the importance of safety. To put your life in danger means putting the lives of others in danger as well."

A few moments later Ray glanced at his watch. "Time for me to head to the boat." He stood. "Don't worry about this," he said, grabbing the check off the table that Bryce had given to her earlier. "I got this and no argument about it this time."

She remembered what she'd told him the last time he'd tried paying for her meal. She chuckled, relenting. "Okay, no argument. Thanks."

He smiled back at her. "Is it so hard to give in?"

She shook her head. "Not for me. What about for you?"

He didn't say anything as he stared down at her and she could feel those vibes flare to life again.

"No, it's not hard for me. Not anymore." He paused a moment and then said, "I'll see you tonight at seven.

Enjoy your shopping and be safe on the roads." He turned to leave, pausing at the counter to pay for their meal before walking out the café.

She went stock-still and was glad Ray hadn't looked back. His words—*enjoy your shopping and be safe on the roads*—were what he would say every time she left home to go shopping.

"Are you okay, Ashley?"

She glanced up to find Sawyer standing by her table. "Yes, I'm okay."

"You had me worried there for a minute. I saw the look on your face when Ray walked off. Is everything okay?"

She nodded. "Yes. It's just that his parting words were what he would often say when I'd tell him I was going shopping. Do you think that means anything?" she asked, not able to downplay the hopefulness in her voice.

"Not sure, but I'd like to believe all the time he spends with you means something. It definitely can't hurt."

She nodded again. "He asked me out tonight. To dinner."

Sawyer smiled. "That's good. Vashti and I are hoping things work out for you and Ray."

"Thanks. I'm hoping that as well."

RAY PULLED INTO Ashley's yard and killed the engine to his truck. He glanced around the interior. At least he'd taken the time to clean it out earlier, but in a way he wished he had another vehicle for their date. And it was a date. He had finally accepted that. And it was one he was looking forward to. He had accepted that as well.

He knew there was a strong possibility he would never get his memory back, and after much soul-searching, he'd decided to move on with his life nonetheless. He didn't know what type of life he'd lived before his accident but he did know what type of life he was living now, and it was one he was proud of.

And then there was Ashley.

She was the woman whose existence was the catalyst behind the decisions he'd made. He hadn't known he'd been lonely, until her. He'd been able to control sexual needs, until her. And he'd thought he was perfectly satisfied with the way his life was going, until her. How Ashley had gotten under his skin, he still wasn't sure. All he knew was she was there.

And she was no longer wearing her ring.

That was one of the first things he'd noticed when he'd joined her for breakfast. He knew exactly what her removing her ring meant. She was ready to move on with her life and put the past behind her.

Funny, he'd decided to do the same thing. The words she'd spoken to him weeks ago had tumbled around in his mind all day. She wouldn't remove her ring until she had met a man who'd charmed her into doing so.

The thought that he'd had anything to do with that made him somewhat wary because he wasn't sure he was worthy. There was a lot about him that she didn't know and he was beginning to feel he was deceiving her into thinking he was someone he was not. There was only one way to remedy that. He would tell her the truth about himself. Tonight.

Hesitating before getting out of the truck, he leaned back in the seat and drew in a deep breath. If she decided she still wanted to see him after what he told her, it meant he would be starting a new chapter in his life. Was he ready?

He knew that was a silly question because he wouldn't be here if he wasn't.

Opening his truck door, he got out and looked down at himself. He had traded the jeans and T-shirt in for a pair of dark slacks, white collared shirt and dinner jacket. It was an outfit he'd purchased to wear to Sawyer and Vashti's wedding and hadn't worn it again. Until tonight. It was his first date as Ray Sullivan.

Strolling to the door, he knocked. She opened it and he immediately thought she looked amazing. She was wearing light makeup and her hair was curled at the ends and flowed loosely around her shoulders. He definitely liked her red shade of lipstick. The entire package was stunning.

She was wearing a pretty blue dress with a ruffled hem that hit right above the knees, complementing a gorgeous pair of legs. He recalled the first time he'd seen those legs and the effect they'd had on him. It had been that day he'd been inside

Smithy's Tackle Shop waiting in line. Minutes later he'd jumped in the ocean to save her.

"You look nice," he said as his gaze roamed over her.

"Thanks, and you look rather handsome yourself."

He chuckled. "Just a little something I threw together."

"And you did it so well. I'm ready if you are."

"I'm ready but there is something I want to talk to you about. After dinner."

She nodded. "Okay."

And then he did something that even surprised him. He took her hand as he led her out the door.

CHAPTER NINETEEN

"I LOVE THIS PLACE, Ray. Thanks for bringing me here."

Dinner had been great and Ashley had enjoyed his company. During the meal they'd made a lot of small talk, with him telling her more about his boat tours and with her telling him about the blog piece she was working on. She could tell he was proud of the business he'd started from the ground up, which didn't surprise her, as Devon had been just as proud of his first company.

But there was a sparkle in his eye, too, that said he was not only proud but that he genuinely enjoyed what he did for a living. Devon had been ambitious and fed off a good challenge, but she wasn't sure he'd been passionate about what he did. She was glad he'd found something to be passionate about as Ray.

They declined dessert but agreed on coffee. She'd noticed like before he kept the conversation more on her than on himself. Ashley had an idea what he wanted to talk to her about later and knew that no matter what he told her, she couldn't level with him as to her true role in his life. It was only until she was certain he had fallen in love with her a second time that she could reveal that.

"Ready to go?"

The sound of his deep, husky voice interrupted her thoughts. "Yes."

A short while later they were pulling into her yard. When he brought the truck to a stop, there was no need to ask if he wanted to come in because he'd already told her about the talk they needed to have.

"Thanks again for dinner, Ray."

"I'm glad you agreed to go out with me."

"There was no reason for me not to. I enjoy your company. I think you know that." And if there was any doubt in his mind of that, it would be gone by the time he left tonight.

Always the gentleman, he didn't say anything when he got out of the truck and came around to open the door for her. She knew the smile he gave her was meant to put her at ease but it didn't, not when she could see so much uncertainty in his face. She figured he thought what he had to tell her would basically end things between them before they could get started. But he was wrong about that.

When they reached her door and she opened her purse to retrieve her key, he said, "It's late. Maybe we could have that talk another time."

She had a feeling if they didn't have it tonight it would be something he would put off until no telling when. "It's not late, really. Besides, you have me curious." She was more than curious. She was downright antsy and wanted to get this done and over with so they could move on. Together.

He nodded and she opened the door and didn't look back when she entered and he closed the door behind him. "Would you like a beer or something?"

"No, I'm good."

It was on the tip of her tongue to agree with that assessment of himself. She put her purse aside and kicked off her shoes. Looking over her shoulder, she said, "You don't mind if I get comfortable, do you?"

"Not at all. This is your place."

Ashley wondered how he would react if she began removing her clothes. She decided not to pull such a stunt to find out. Moving over to the sofa, she sat down and deliberately crossed her legs and placed her hands on her knees. "So what do you want to talk to me about, Ray?"

RAY FELT A tightness in his chest as he watched Ashley. Whether she knew it or not, she was getting to him and in a big way. Moving toward the chair across from the sofa, he slid into the seat and tried to keep his concentration off her legs.

Clearing his throat, he said, "There's something about me that I think you need to know."

She lifted a brow. "And what's that?"

"I might be a married man."

She stared at him, and to his way of thinking, she seemed to take what he'd said rather calmly. To be sure she heard what he'd said, he repeated himself.

"I heard you, Ray, but I thought you were divorced. I don't understand."

He figured she wouldn't. Starting at the beginning, he began telling her about waking up from a coma, badly beaten and bruised and without any memory. She didn't say anything. Didn't even ask any questions. That was definitely different from when he'd told Bryce, who'd asked plenty of questions. If he didn't know better, he'd think she'd already known. But the people who did know about his condition would not have told a stranger his private business. "So there you have it. I have no memory of my past."

Ashley nodded. "I see."

He raked his hand over the top of his head, not understanding her easy acceptance. "You see?" he asked, feeling somewhat agitated. "How can you?"

She shifted in her seat, and damn, his attention was drawn to her legs when it should be on the question he'd asked her and what her response would be.

"I knew someone with amnesia once."

Ray drew in a breath as his agitation backed off. He hadn't thought he was the only person with memory loss but he hadn't known anyone who'd known someone else with amnesia. "You did?"

"Yes, while in college at Harvard. Carolyn was a member of my swim team. While home on spring break, she had jumped into a friend's pool and hit her head, resulting in memory loss. She missed an entire year of school. The team and I would visit her and she didn't know who we were. She didn't recognize anyone, not even her parents."

He was silent for a moment and then he asked, "Did she ever get her memory back?"

"Yes, but it was years later."

He inwardly admitted that was what he was truly afraid of now that he'd established this new life for himself. He wasn't sure he wanted his old life or to know anything about it now.

"And in a way that's what I'm afraid of," he said, speaking those fears aloud. "Of one day regaining knowledge of my past when I want so much to just put it behind me and move forward."

"And you can't?"

"No. For all I know, I could have a wife and kids somewhere. That's the main reason I refrained from getting involved with anyone. If my memory ever returns, things could get messy."

NOT IF YOUR past and present connect, Ashley wanted to say but couldn't. She had to remind herself that although Ray might be attracted to her, he didn't love her. In order for them to deal with him not knowing his past, emotions and not guilt needed to be involved. She didn't want him to feel guilty because he didn't love her but should. She wanted him to feel satisfied any issues regarding the woman in his past life, the woman he used to love, didn't matter because they would be one and the same.

For now she would play devil's advocate, giving him a reason to consider his choices. "Since moving here to the cove, what have you done to determine your true identity?"

"I had the papers in the area where I was found run the article again about me, and I had my information updated with missing persons. I figured someone had to be looking for me." He paused and then said, "I was disappointed to discover after six months that no one was."

His words tugged at her heart. At that moment she wanted to go to him and put her arms around him and tell him that the reason she hadn't looked for him was because she thought he'd died. There was no way had she known he was alive somewhere that she would not have searched for him.

The thought that he believed no one cared enough to look for him tore at her. It took every ounce of strength she had to hold back from telling him the truth. That she was his wife. The longer she kept the truth from him the worse it would be.

But remembering what Dr. Riggins said was what held her back. She had to believe if she kept to the plan that eventually Ray would develop feelings for her. She had to believe that.

"And if your memory never returns, then what, Ray? You're willing to live your life that way? Refusing to engage in a meaningful relationship ever?" she asked him.

He leaned forward. "Yes, meaningful or otherwise, I was willing to do those things. Until I met you. For some reason, from the first I was drawn to you in a way I couldn't ignore, no matter how much I tried. You made me begin questioning why I couldn't live a happy life like other men."

He paused a moment and then said, "I told myself you were safe because you were still grieving your husband. I enjoyed your company, and a friendship with you was all I wanted. And the good thing about it was I believed that's all you wanted, until a few days ago when you insinuated that a *friends only* relationship between us wouldn't work, and belatedly, I would have to agree."

He paused again before saying, "This morning I saw you'd removed your wedding ring. So now I need to ask you, Ashley, knowing how attracted we are to each other and the friends thing won't work, what is it that you want?"

It would be so easy to tell him that more than anything she wanted to be his again in every way. The woman he loved more than anything. The woman he desired. The woman who more than anything wanted his children and to live a long life with him. She wanted to be his sunflower again.

But for his sake, she couldn't take the easy way out. Rebuilding that kind of relationship with him again would be hard but not impossible. In fact, she was getting excited about the prospect of doing so. Devon always said she had the ability to literally blow his mind, and she wanted to blow his mind again, both in and out of the bedroom. Nothing she did would be taboo because the man sitting across from her was her husband. The one person she had vowed years ago to love, honor and cherish until death did them part. He had cheated death and she rejoiced in that fact.

Knowing he still probably thought of her as a grieving widow, with or without her ring, she had to convince him he would be doing her a tremendous favor if he helped her move on by engaging in an affair with her. Nothing permanent. Just during the time she was here in Catalina Cove. Or so he would think.

"What I want might seem a little selfish on my end, Ray," she finally said.

He lifted a brow. "Selfish in what way?"

She slowly stood and began pacing, intentionally giving him the impression she was nervous about giving him an answer. Truthfully, she was because the way she presented herself to him could be the turning point in their relationship. It could be success or failure. Not hers but theirs.

She stopped pacing and turned to him. No matter what, she had to make what she was about to tell him believable. She didn't miss the look in his eyes when she'd abruptly turned from pacing. He had been checking her out, something she'd noticed he did a lot. Hopefully, his intense attraction to her would overrule his resistance.

"You haven't been the only person who has refused to become involved in relationships. Meaningful or otherwise. After my husband died, I just could not fathom the thought of another man touching me, kissing me or just getting close to me, period. It seemed the desire to do any of those things was turned off. Until I met you."

She glanced down at the floor for a moment and then back at him. "I was attracted to you and it's escalated from there. I would go to bed thinking of you. And then when we kissed, I did something with you I hadn't ever done with a man other than my husband. I shared pleasure in a kiss that made me come. After that, it was your face I saw instead of Devon's in my dreams, Ray. I finally saw what was happening. I was finally able to desire someone other than Devon. For me it's a start and for now I don't want to lose it. I'm feeling like a woman again for the first time in years. For the first time since losing my husband."

He didn't say anything; he just continued to sit there and watch her. Then she added, "You asked what I want. I only have the rest of the summer here in the cove. By the end I hope to be a different person. A woman who will have accepted her fate and be able to handle just about anything. So what I'm asking you to consider, Ray, is to have an affair with me while I'm living here in Catalina Cove."

AT THAT INSTANT Ray's mouth literally went dry. Every muscle in his body felt in tune to Ashley in a way he'd never known for another woman before. And that was the kicker. He couldn't remember if the physical attraction he was experiencing was new or what he would normally experience with a woman. All he knew was that he wanted Ashley with a desperation that astounded him. But...

"It doesn't bother you I might be a married man?" She lifted her chin and held fast to his gaze when she said, "No. The man you used to be might have had a wife. However, the man you are now doesn't. I want to have an affair with the man you are now. Ray Sullivan."

Her words struck like lightning in his mind. Although he'd never analyzed his situation the way she had, what she said was true. He would never go back to being who he was if his memory didn't return. But he did have a grasp of the man he was now. What she'd said was what Dr. Martin had not only tried to get him to see but also to accept. And he hadn't until now.

He was Ray Sullivan, a single man who owned a touring company in Catalina Cove. That life began the day he'd walked out the hospital. He had survived. He was still surviving. And now the most gorgeous woman he knew wanted to have a summer fling with him.

"If you need more time to think about it, Ray, I understand."

Her words reclaimed his attention. He knew the eyes staring back at her were hot, dark and filled with a sexual need that he felt in his groin. He knew at that moment there was nothing to think about. For the past three years he'd thought so much on the subject it had become overkill. It had taken Ashley's one sentence to make him see reason.

Suddenly he felt not like a new man, but the man he should have been all along. A man no longer tormented by the past but a man who wanted to look forward to the future and whatever it held. He stood up from his chair and took the few steps to Ashley and watched her tilt her head back to look up at him. He thought she had a beautiful neck.

"I don't need time to think about anything, Ashley."

He could see the way her pulse was thumping in her throat and he was tempted to lick her neck. Resisting temptation, he took a step closer and said, "I accept your offer of a summer fling."

She nervously licked her lips and his guts tightened. "Starting when?" she asked him.

"Starting now." And then he lowered his mouth to hers.

CHAPTER TWENTY

THE MOMENT RAY's mouth began devouring hers, a little voice in Ashley's head whispered she'd gotten her husband back—at least half of the way. It would be up to her to make sure the other half would follow suit and their love was rekindled.

She turned her full concentration to their kiss and could feel all the emotions he was putting into it. Tonight he'd made a decision he hadn't planned on making. Now that he had, it seemed he was making up for lost time.

The same was true with her. This was her husband. The man she loved with all her heart. The man she thought she'd lost forever only to discover he was here, and she intended to claim him in any and every way she could. Even if it meant using her feminine wiles to entice him into lovemaking, which they used to enjoy doing so much. At this point, there was no shame in her game because she was fighting for the most important person in her life.

This kiss was different from any she'd gotten from Devon. And she knew. He was being driven by lust and not love. But knowing that wasn't a de-

terrent to the sensations he was stirring inside of
her. Sensations and needs she couldn't fight. And
she didn't want him to fight them either.

Her body was getting hotter with every stroke of
his tongue to hers. She could feel the hardness of his
erection pressed against her, practically molded to
the juncture of her thighs. And when he suddenly
deepened the kiss, her heart nearly missed a beat.
Whether he knew it or not, he was pushing her
over the edge. Too soon and she wanted to fight it.
When she experienced the big O again she wanted
him fully inside of her.

He suddenly pulled his mouth from hers and she
could see his massive chest labor with deep breaths.
She could sense every need and want in the dark
eyes staring at her.

"Oh, my God. Ashley," he said, slowly backing
up, taking steps away from her. "I don't know what
happened just now. I didn't mean to lose control
and kiss you like that. My desire for you is overwhelming. It's like something has been building up
inside of me for a while and tonight it demanded
to be freed."

And she wanted even more to come out. He had
no idea that she'd needed that type of kiss and wanted
more of anything and everything else he wanted to
share with her.

"I'm sorry."

His apology invaded her thoughts and she moved
forward, covering the distance separating them. "I
don't want you to be sorry, Ray. I wanted you to kiss

me that way. I needed for you to do it. Men aren't the only ones with needs."

"I know that, but…"

"But what?"

He leaned in and pressed his forehead against hers. "I don't want to hurt you. I can't promise you anything beyond fulfilling needs."

"You won't hurt me, Ray, and I'm not asking you for promises. I know what I'm doing. I know what I want, what I need and what I desire. You're all those things. Please don't deny me."

He pulled back and took hold of her hand. "Come on. Let's sit down and talk and—"

"No," she said, shaking her head and tugging her hand from his hold. "I don't want to sit down and talk. I want to make love with you."

She reached up and lightly ran her hand around the beard. She felt a scar and figured the beard was his way of hiding it. And because Devon never had facial scars, she could only conclude it was the result of what had happened to him. She pushed the thought of what he'd gone through to the back of her mind. Truthfully, whatever reason he'd chosen to wear a beard didn't matter. She liked the bearded look on him. The thick stubble covering his jaw made him appear sexier. Hotter. Just touching his face while he stared at her was heating her blood.

"I don't think you know how I feel when you touch me, Ashley."

She continued to stroke her hand along his face. "And how do you feel?"

"Lusty."

She decided to test his claim by easing the lower part of her body closer to feel his erection in his pants. It was throbbing hard against her. "And what do you intend to do with all that lust, Ray?"

"I shouldn't do anything with it, but I want you so damn much."

He was still fighting it, but she refused to let him. "I want you just as much." Leaning closer, she whispered against his mouth, "Make love to me, Ray. Please make love to me now."

RAY DREW IN a deep breath when she followed her words with a sweep of her tongue across his lips. Were all women this brazen? He couldn't remember. Had he always been a man who liked this type of aggressiveness in a woman? He wasn't sure of that either. All he knew was that he liked everything Ashley was doing to him. She wasn't waiting for him to comply with her request. Instead she'd practically taken charge. He was weak against her seductive strategies.

"You like that, Ray?" she whispered against his moist lips.

Hell yes, he liked it. He more than liked it. It made him wonder just what else she could do with her tongue. He shouldn't wonder about such a thing, but she was making it difficult for him not to. And then he knew the exact minute she lowered her hand to touch him. Right there at the crotch.

When she began fondling his hardness, he doubted

she had any idea what she was doing to him. He hadn't had sex for three years and at that moment he was feeling like a randy sailor who was back on land after having been at sea for years and ready to make up for lost time.

"I feel you, Ray."

Her words and touch were like kerosene thrown on an already blazing flame. He parted his lips to tell her that maybe they needed to slow down, but parting his lips ended up being the perfect opportunity for her to slide her tongue inside his mouth. He wasn't sure how long he'd be able to hang on before he lost the last shred of his control.

Ray knew he was a goner when she tried easing his zipper down. His erection made it difficult. She glanced up at him, clearly not happy. "I want this, Ray."

He knew exactly what she wanted, and it was the same thing he wanted her to have. "What do you want to do with it?" he asked, like he didn't know.

She leaned up and whispered close to his ear, "Put it in my mouth, for starters."

Oh, hell. He could barely breathe now. Maybe next time he'd give her the opportunity, but now he suddenly had some plans of his own. He wanted to show her that two could play her seduction game. "You're positive that you want to carry this further, Ashley? Are you sure you're ready?"

She whispered against his lips, "I'm past ready. It's time we both move on, don't you think?"

In all honesty, he couldn't think. He didn't want

to think. He just wanted to stand there and inhale her scent. Stand there and continue to hold her by the waist.

But he also wanted to do more. She was right. It was time they both moved on. He was Ray Sullivan and he refused to worry about a past he might never reclaim. Not when he could enjoy the present with Ashley.

The present but not a future.

He pushed that thought to the back of his mind because it was something he could accept just as easily as she could. They would live for the now, and when she left Catalina Cove at the end of the summer, he would have memories of their time together.

She had tried her hand at seduction long enough. Now it was his turn. With that thought in mind, he suddenly swept her off her feet and into his arms and quickly moved toward her bedroom.

After placing Ashley on the bed, Ray stepped back and gazed down at her. She looked simply beautiful staring back up at him. Her hair was all tumbled around her shoulders and her dress was twisted in ways that showed off her legs. Her chest, he noted, was heaving, taking in deep breaths. The same as him.

She watched as he removed his shirt and then went to the snap on his pants. He hadn't meant to give her a strip show, but since she was lying there seemingly transfixed with his every move, he thought, why not? He wondered when he had become so brazen. Was it an ingrained part of his character he didn't know about? It had to be. Why else would stripping off his clothes in front of her turn him on?

When she eased up on the bed and pulled her dress over her head and tossed it aside, he became the one mesmerized. Black lace. Both her bra and panties were made of black lace. Seeing it on her was a punch to the gut, something more than just lust. Had he been a lace man before?

He decided to stop trying to figure out why so much about what she was doing and what she was wearing was so arousing. He would accept all this was new to him because in a way it was. But it all came down to the fact that this was Ashley, a woman he wanted.

"What are you thinking, Ray?"

"Too much," he answered truthfully. He was thinking way too much instead of accepting his good fortune. Deciding to forgo removing the rest of his clothes for now, he moved toward the bed to finish removing hers.

ASHLEY WATCHED EVERY move Ray took toward her, remembering other times he'd done so with that same heated look in his eyes. A look that clearly told her what he wanted. She had deliberately worn black lace because Devon loved her in black lace and she always loved wearing it for him. She rarely purchased underthings that weren't made of lace for that reason.

When he pressed his knee on the bed, she fluffed

her bangs away from her face and moved toward him. Tonight was their night. More than anything, she wished what they did in this bed would trigger memories, but if they didn't, she wouldn't give up. They would build new ones.

"I love lace."

His words made her swallow. Was he remembering or merely making an observation? "Do you?"

"I believe so because seeing you in it is a total turn-on."

He was doing what Devon would do. Tell her how much she excited him and how he desired her. That part of him hadn't changed. "I hope that doesn't mean you don't plan to take it off me. I promise you might like what this lace is hiding."

"I am definitely sure that I will." And then with fingers that were just as deft as she remembered, he unhooked her bra and it slid off her.

"Beautiful," he said of her breasts, seemingly more to himself than to her. "So firm and full."

And ready for your mouth to devour them, she wanted to say, but didn't. She discovered she didn't have to when he lowered his mouth and sucked a nipple between his lips.

Lordy. She closed her eyes as sensations of having this mouth on her—Devon's mouth, Ray's mouth— sent her hormones skyrocketing and made her moan. And when he began sucking hard, she mumbled his name over and over, forcing herself to remember this was Ray and not Devon. That kind of slip would ruin everything, and she didn't intend to make it.

He quickly switched to the other breast to give that nipple the same torment. She wasn't sure how long he tortured her. But she knew she was seconds from going off the edge when he pulled back and began brushing kisses all over her body, nibbling gently, tasting and teasing. And when he slid his hands beneath the black lace of her panties, she moaned even more. Those same hands moved between her thighs and she knew he'd discovered she was wet and ready.

"These need to come off," he said, and she lifted her hips to accommodate him. He began easing her panties down her legs and suddenly went still.

Concerned, she asked, "Ray, what is it?"

She knew the answer when he ran the tip of his finger along the tattoo on the upper side of her hip. A sunflower. She drew in a sharp breath. She had forgotten about her tattoo.

He glanced up at her. "I didn't know you were into sunflowers."

She tried to retain her composure when she said, "It's my favorite flower."

He nodded as he continued to look at her. "I think it's mine as well."

She lifted a brow. "You think?"

"Yes. I have a tattoo of the word *sunflower* written on my back. Not sure why. It's one of those things I can't remember but I figure it must have meant something at some point."

"Yes, it must have."

"That's why I named my boat the *Sunflower*."

More than anything, she wished she could tell him the significance of their tattoos but couldn't. At least, not yet. Not when all he felt for her was lust.

She appreciated he let the matter drop, and after removing her panties and tossing them aside, he moved away from the bed to dispense with the rest of his clothing. The moment his penis was exposed, a sense of possessive familiarity raced through her. She quickly recalled that she had touched Ray and every part of his body before. Had tasted it as well. And to know he hadn't been involved with another woman sent desire racing all through her.

"I need to protect you," he said, and then he reached for his pants to retrieve a condom from his wallet. He held it up to read something on it and then looked at her. "Checking the date to make sure it's still good. I've been carrying it around in my wallet for almost three years now."

She decided not to tell him a part of her wished it wasn't effective. More than anything, she wanted his baby. A pregnancy from him would definitely be wanted.

After sheathing himself, he asked, "You sure about this, Ashley?"

She could tell from the sound of his voice that he was still unsure as to whether this was something she really wanted. "Yes. I am sure about this, Ray. In fact, I'm more sure of this than I've been of anything in my life."

She knew he thought what she said was merely words, but it was true. When she decided to move to Catalina Cove for the summer, she hadn't known if Ray would willingly reciprocate any interest. He had and now it came down to this and she intended for it to be something he wouldn't forget.

He came back to the bed, drew her into his arms. Their bodies rubbed against each other, causing heated friction to ignite. And when he began nibbling around her mouth, she tightened her arms around him, meshing their bodies even more.

Ray kissed her long and hard and in a way that made her stomach quiver and had desire humming through her veins. But the one thing that took over her mind and soul was love. She loved him more than life itself. When she thought she'd lost him, she'd been hurt and heartbroken beyond repair. Now he was back and was initiating foreplay in ways only he knew how to do. Her body was remembering, whether he did or not.

Without breaking the kiss, he lowered her down in the bed. Her naked hips flowed into his, their bodies perfectly aligned. The feel of his sculpted abdomen pressed against her sent every pulse in her body vibrating. And when he broke off the kiss, it left her panting for more.

Their gazes held as he moved his body over hers and heat curled inside her while at the same time her womb contracted with intense need.

"I want you so much, Ashley," he whispered softly. "I want to make it good for you."

She smiled up at him. "You will." He wouldn't know how true that was. The moment he slid inside of her body it would welcome him home. And she intended to give him the kind of homecoming he would think about for days. Devon had taught her just what he liked, and she was determined to make sure he got it tonight as Ray.

She moaned when she felt him easing inside of her, stretching her wide from months, years of inactivity. Her womanly muscles grabbed hold of his shaft the moment they felt him. She could tell from the look in his eyes that he was aware of it.

When she began milking him, the way he'd taught her to do, he went still, and for a second she thought he was remembering, but then he closed his eyes and whispered in a husky voice, "Jesus. That feels so good."

He began moving, thrusting hard in and out of her. Just the way she liked. His repeated strokes made her body's most primal reaction kick in with a vengeance. Her hips lifted off the bed with every one of his downward thrusts to meet him halfway.

Over and over, their mating sent heat flaring in every part of her body. She was fully aware of his every sensual movement and the sound of his low growls. Devon Ryan style. He could make love to her like nobody's business and was doing so now.

And when she felt deep arousal in her core where their bodies were connected, she released one hell of a scream at the same time he threw his head back, sucked in a long draw of air and began thrusting inside of her harder and faster. Suddenly, he hollered her name at the top of his voice.

His orgasm triggered another for her and she felt as if she was drowning. In his taste. In his scent. In everything about Ray Sullivan. Slipping an arm around his muscled back, she held on when he, too, went for another sensuous round. The air surrounding them shimmered with undeniable need. Needs being fulfilled.

The happiness of being reunited with her husband was so great Ashley could hardly stand it. Throbbing desire overtook them and once again they succumbed to the pleasures they'd found in each other's arms.

CHAPTER TWENTY-ONE

ASHLEY WOKE TO kisses being placed on the side of her face. She blinked when she saw Ray standing next to the bed fully dressed. Glancing at the clock, she saw it was close to 6:00 a.m. He had spent the night and she was over the moon about it.

"I need to go home and change for work."

She shifted to her back. "Okay."

He caressed the side of her face with the tip of his finger while staring down at her. "Can I stop by later?"

She smiled. "I was hoping you'd want to."

He smiled back at her. "I definitely want to. And we can eat out if you'd like."

She recalled last night at dinner they'd gotten a lot of attention from the locals who probably had known of Ray's no-dating rule and were surprised to see her out with him. A temporary newcomer.

"I have an even better idea."

"Which is?"

"Let me prepare something here."

He shook his head. "I don't want you to go to the trouble."

"No trouble and I'll prepare pork chops. You like pork chops."

He chuckled. "Yes, I do like pork chops. How did you know?"

Too late, Ashley realized her slip and quickly said, "I think you might have told me at some point."

"Oh." He straightened to his full height and then said, "In that case, I'd love to try your pork chops. I'll call before I come."

"All right."

He leaned back down and kissed her thoroughly. Straightening again, he said, "Enjoy your day."

She chuckled. "After a night like last night, there's no way I can't."

Ray gave her another huge smile before leaving.

When she heard the front door close behind him and then the sound of his truck leaving, she released a deep sigh, full of the happiness she felt. But that happiness hadn't come without hiccups. First was when he'd seen her tattoo and then just now with her slip about the pork chops. She would have to be careful in the future about the information she shared with him; otherwise he would get suspicious.

She lay looking up at the ceiling as she thought about last night. Oh, what a night. Ray said he'd been making up for lost time and so had she. Their time together had reminded her of how much they loved being in each other's arms, although Ray hadn't a clue of their past life together. He was still the expert lover and a man intent on satisfying her before seeking his own gratification.

Making love with him had been like coming home—at least, her body thought so. It had recognized Ray as the one person it had always wanted and needed. They had made love over and over last night, getting very little sleep. She wondered how he would manage at work. At least she had the luxury of sleeping late.

She shifted in bed and fluffed out her pillow, loving the familiar scent of Ray in the bed coverings. Last night had been just the beginning and she intended to do whatever it took to make sure things continued between them on a solid note.

Moments later she was about to doze back off to sleep when her phone rang. Recognizing the ringtone, she reached out and grabbed her phone off the nightstand. "Em, you're calling rather early. What's up?"

"Your mother."

Ashley frowned. "What's up with my mom?"

"She called last night wanting your address. She's determined to pay you a visit, saying she's worried there's a reason you're isolating yourself from everyone, and what you're doing isn't healthy. She accused me of enabling you and not helping you to move on in life."

Ashley nibbled at her bottom lip. "What did you tell her?"

"I told her what we agreed to tell her. That you were fine and were in New Orleans working on a very important piece for the company. She wasn't happy and wanted to know why it would take all summer. I came up with what I thought were good reasons, but your mother isn't buying it. She thinks the one thing you need in your life right now is another man. Namely, Elliott."

Ashley rolled her eyes. "I am not interested in Elliott."

"Of course, I know that. It seems that Elliott has a business trip to New Orleans next week and she wants him to surprise you."

Ashley released a frustrated sigh. "Anything else?"

"Yes. Just so you know, when she couldn't get any information out of me, she called Suzanne and Kim. They didn't tell her anything either. She told Kim she has a feeling something is going on with you and is going to talk to your dad about them going to New Orleans as well. She said she will turn that city inside out to find you and doesn't understand why you're being so secretive about where you're staying."

Ashley pulled herself up in bed. She wished she could call her dad and level with him and tell him exactly where she was and why but knew she couldn't. Under pressure from Imogene Hardwick, her father would cave in.

"I think you need to come home for a few days and assure them you're okay," Emmie said, breaking into her thoughts. "They weren't here when you came home to collect your things for the move to Catalina Cove for the summer. It's understandable for them to worry."

Ashley frowned. "First of all, Em, you know my dad is fine and the only person worrying needlessly is Mom. The only reason she's worried is because I'm not there for her to try to control my life. That's the reason she never got along with Devon. He refused to let her into our business."

She knew what she'd said was true. Devon's and her mother's personalities had clashed because both were such strong-willed individuals. Her mother liked to control, and Devon refused to fall in line. And he refused to let Ashley do so any longer. He'd gotten along great with her father but had to teach Ashley how to stand up to her mother's overpowering ways and not let Imogene make her feel as if she couldn't make any decisions without her.

When Ashley and Devon were married, her parents rarely visited, and when they did, it was for short periods. It was only after Devon's death that her mother assumed she could return to her domineering ways.

Ashley knew it was time to have a heart-to-heart talk with her parents. She wouldn't tell them anything about Ray but they needed to understand her life was her life and she would live it any way she wanted. She also knew such a conversation needed to be face-to-face, but now was the worst time for her to leave Catalina Cove. The last thing she needed was for Ray to feel she was being secretive about anything.

"You're right. I should come home for a few days and talk to Mom and Dad, although the timing is lousy. Last night Ray and I decided to become involved."

"You did? Oh, Ashley, I'm so happy for you."

Ashley smiled. "I'm happy, too. Everything about last night was beautiful, Em. The lovemaking better than ever. You don't know how great it felt being back in his arms after believing I'd lost him."

She felt herself getting emotional and couldn't help it. "But still, it's hard that he doesn't recognize me. It's hard knowing all last night was about lust for him and had nothing to do with love."

"But you can change that, Ash. I truly believe you can. Devon worshipped the ground you walked on and I refuse to believe that something about being with you won't trigger his memory."

"I hope so. I have to be careful what I say and doubly careful not to call him Devon instead of Ray. But there were two things that happened last night that needed quick thinking on my part."

"What?"

She told Emmie what had happened with the tattoo and pork chops. "Well, I know when he gets his memory back he will know why you did what you did."

"I'm hoping he'll be accepting before then. I'm not waiting for Ray to get his memory back, Em. Like I told you, I'm trying to entice him to fall in love with me a second time. The moment he tells me that he has, I will tell him the truth. At that point the past won't matter because he would have fallen in love with me a second time around, and all his anxieties of cheating on his first wife will be nonexistent."

"Well, Suzanne, Kim and I are rooting for you."

"Thanks. I owe you three because you guys are the reason I came to Catalina Cove in the first place. Had I not been here, my and Ray's paths would not have crossed."

"You think of him as Ray now?"

Ashley dwelled on Emmie's question for a moment and then said, "Yes. He has no memory of being Devon Ryan. That means I have to accept him as the person he is now."

"What about love, Ashley?"

She frowned. "What do you mean?"

"You loved yourself some Devon Ryan. His looks, his style, his personality, his debonair manner. From what you've been telling me, all that's changed. You might still find him handsome but what about the rest? Now you're describing him as some sort of rough and tough ship captain who doesn't have an elegant bone in his body. Can you accept that?"

"Yes, I can," Ashley said without thinking about it. "In fact, I have. Just like I want him to fall in love again with me, I'm finding myself falling in love again with him. Not as Devon but as Ray. There is so much I appreciate about the man he is now. In many ways they're the same person, but in others they're two different people, and I love them both."

Moments later after ending her phone conversation with Emmie, Ashley knew she needed to give her parents a call. The sooner the better.

"MORNING, KAEGAN," RAY SAID, sliding into the booth.

"Morning," Kaegan said, not bothering to glance over at Ray. His gaze was glued to Bryce, who was holding a conversation with two guys seated at a table on the other side of the café. Strangers in town.

"Where's Sawyer?" Ray asked.

It was only when Bryce left the men's table to seat new customers that Kaegan looked at Ray and answered his question. "I got a text that he and Vashti are taking Jade to that university in Nevada to check it out. It's hard to believe that she leaves for college in the fall. It seemed just yesterday when I came back to town and she was in junior high school. Time sure flies." He took a sip of his coffee and eyed Ray curiously. "You didn't stay home last night."

Ray lifted a brow. "And you know this how?"

Kaegan shrugged as he gave Ray a smile. "I couldn't sleep and thought I'd come bug you. Get you up to drink a beer with me."

"I told you I was taking Ashley to dinner."

"Yes, but this was later. Around eleven. Figured you'd be back home by then. I waited and you never showed up."

Ray leaned back. "What makes you think I didn't show up at all?"

Kaegan chuckled and took another sip of his coffee. "Because at some point I must have fallen asleep in my truck. When I woke up, it was close to five this morning."

Ray frowned, thinking of the humongous house that Kaegan owned on the bayou. "You slept in your truck in front of my house?"

"Yep."

Ray shook his head. "You could have gone inside, Kaegan. You have a key."

"Yes, but I didn't think you'd be gone all night."

At that moment Bryce appeared with Ray's coffee and a basket of blueberry muffins. "Good morning, Ray."

He smiled up at Bryce. "Good morning. Thanks."

"You're welcome." She cut her eyes over to Kaegan, which surprised Ray since she usually just ignored him. "Did you enjoy the movie last night, Kaegan?"

Ray switched his gaze to Kaegan and saw him glaring at Bryce. Nothing new there, but if looks could kill... "It was okay," Kaegan said. "You seemed to be enjoying yourself."

She smiled at him. "Of course. Any reason I wouldn't?"

"None that I know of."

Bryce walked off. Ray didn't say anything for a minute. Now he knew why Kaegan couldn't sleep. He'd gone somewhere and had seen Bryce. "You went to the movies last night?"

Kaegan was still glaring at Bryce as she waited on another table. "Yes. I didn't have anything better to do."

Ray nodded and took a sip of his coffee, expecting Kaegan to add more. When he didn't, he said, "I take it Bryce was there."

"Yes, with a damn date. Can you believe that?"

Yes, Ray could believe it. After all, Bryce was an attractive woman and she was single. However, Ray figured now was not a good time to remind Kaegan of that. If he wanted to be territorial toward a woman he swore most of the time he couldn't stand, then so be it.

"How was your date with Ashley?"

Since his friend knew he'd stayed out all night, that meant he had a good idea of how his date went with Ashley. But if conversing would get Kaegan's mind off Bryce, who'd wandered back over to the table where those two men were sitting, then Ray would accommodate him. "Good. Food was delicious, and I enjoyed her company."

"I'm glad. I like her."

Ray lifted a brow. "Why? You've only met her once or twice. You don't even know her."

"True, but she must not be all bad. She got you taking her out and not being antisocial anymore."

Ray smiled, thinking of the woman whose bed he had slept in last night. They hadn't done much sleeping, though. He hadn't lied when he'd told Kaegan that he had really enjoyed her company. What he hadn't elaborated on was that he'd enjoyed it both in and out of bed. It was as if once he'd gotten inside her body, he hadn't wanted to leave. And the kicker was she hadn't wanted him to either. She'd enjoyed their lovemaking as much as he had.

"No, she's not all bad. In fact, I think she's a special person." He paused a minute before adding, "So special that I told her about my memory loss."

Kaegan sat up straight. "You did? How did she react?"

"Not as shocked as I expected her to, but then she told me about this friend in college who'd lost her memory. Ashley did, however, say something that really got to me. Really made me think."

"What did she say?" Kaegan asked over the rim of his coffee cup.

Ray met his gaze. "I asked her if it bothered her that I might be a married man, and she said no, it didn't bother her, because the man I used to be might have had a wife—however, the man I am now doesn't."

Kaegan nodded. "That's a pretty damn logical and positive way of looking at it."

Ray thought so, too. "It is. Made me remember that when I'd been given a new identity I was told my life had started completely over. I was a new and different person starting then. I'd accepted that in some parts of my life but not in all."

He took a sip of his coffee and added, "Last night I discovered that Ashley and I have a lot in common. Hell, she even likes sunflowers."

"How do you know that?"

"She has a sunflower tattoo. Hers is the actual design of a flower, though."

"Oh, and where is hers?"

Kaegan's question made him recall not only

where it was but how he'd discovered it. "Where it's located isn't important."

Kaegan took a last swallow of his coffee. "If you say so. Sounds like you've gotten involved with a special woman you could have a nice future with."

"It's not like that."

Kaegan chuckled. "You didn't come home last night and you want me to think it's not like that."

Ray shrugged. "We enjoy each other's company and nothing more." No need to tell Kaegan he and Ashley had agreed on a summer fling. He would catch on to that fact soon enough.

"She's doing that deliberately," Kaegan suddenly burst out in irritation.

Ray's brows bunched. "Who is doing what deliberately?"

"Bryce. She knows I need a refill and she's deliberately making me wait."

Ray fought back a grin. "I'm sure she's just gotten a little busy, Kaegan. Here," he said, offering the basket of blueberry muffins to him. "Enjoy one of these while you wait."

CHAPTER TWENTY-TWO

ASHLEY'S CELL PHONE went off and she knew from the ringtone it was her mother. She had called earlier and Imogene claimed she was too busy to talk. Ashley hadn't even raised a brow at that. Her mother liked playing these "my time is not your time" games.

She clicked on the phone. "Yes, Mom?"

"I'm returning your call."

Ashley leaned back in her chair. "Thanks for doing that. I understand you're trying to find out my whereabouts. I told you."

"Yes, but you didn't give me a street address and New Orleans is a big place."

"Are you and Dad planning to visit?"

"No. However, Elliott will be in New Orleans next week and wants to see you."

Ashley rolled her eyes. "I have no desire to see him. Why can't you accept that?"

"Because I know what you're doing to yourself and I won't let you. Devon's dead and you need to get over it and start living again."

Her words lit Ashley's ire. "You have no right to tell me what I need to do. What you need to do is stay out of my business, Mom. I've repeatedly asked you to stop shoving Elliott down my throat. I have no interest in him."

"You would if you'd just go out with him. Do you know how many women want him?"

"Then they can have him. Honestly, I don't think a lot of him for allowing you to manipulate him this way. If I was looking for a man, he wouldn't be the kind I want."

"No, you'd prefer a man like Devon, who would disrespect your mother and come between us."

Ashley rolled her eyes again. "Devon did not come between us. He just refused to put up with your controlling attitude and I applaud him for standing up to you."

"How can you say something like that?"

"Easily. I love you, but I refuse to let you treat me like a child. I am a thirty-year-old adult."

Her mother didn't say anything for a minute and then she said, "You're allowing Devon to come between us even from the grave. I hadn't counted on that."

Ashley rubbed the bridge of her nose, feeling a gigantic headache coming on. "Look, Mom, I call you every week to see how you and Dad are doing and to let you know I'm fine. Most of the time you won't even take my calls. Yet you're calling around to my friends to find out where I am so you can send a man to see me. I prefer you not do that." Ashley knew what she was telling her mother was going in one ear and out the other.

"When will you come home?"

"In a few weeks but only for a short visit. When I get there, me, you and Dad are going to sit down and have a talk."

"Don't bother." Her mother hung up the phone.

BEFORE KNOCKING ON Ashley's door, Ray surveyed himself from head to toe. After getting off work, he had gone straight home to shower and change clothes, and now he was here. He had called her before leaving home to see if she needed him to make a stop anywhere. She'd thanked him for being thoughtful but assured him that she had everything she needed.

Thoughtful? He better not let that compliment go to his head. Too late. It was already there, although he was certain a thoughtful man would not have kept her up last night making love to her as many times as he had. He'd been horny, yes. Thoughtful? No.

He knocked on the door and glanced around the yard while he waited. This was the first time he'd really taken a good look at this place and he liked what he saw. A big yard. Lots of trees. Dead-end road that eliminated drive-through traffic. The bonus was having the ocean in the backyard.

Ashley would be here for only the summer and had mentioned Mrs. Landers's son was thinking about selling the place. Maybe this might be a good time to consider moving into a bigger place than what he had. His present property could become rental property and provide him with an income. Bryce was one of the top-notch Realtors in town. He would mention his interest to her the next time he saw her.

The door opened and Ashley stood there looking beautiful as ever. All day he'd pictured how she'd looked when he'd left her in bed that morning. Now here she was wearing a pair of jeans and a shirt that was cut off on the shoulders, showing a lot of skin. Skin he liked seeing. No matter when he saw her or how often, the sight of her managed to rev his motor.

"Hello, Ray."

"Ashley."

She moved aside to let him in. He walked across the threshold, closed the door behind him, turned and pulled her into his arms. He meant for the kiss to be long, greedy and intense. All the things that stirred his blood even more, and just like last night, she was returning it with a degree of passion that astounded him. That was another thing that had filled his mind today—all the kisses they'd shared last night. Was it normal for two people to be this in sync with each other this way? So well connected?

He pulled back from the kiss but continued to hold her in his arms, needing the feel of her there. Her heart, he noted, was racing just as fast as his. Tilting his head back, he looked at her and smiled.

"How was your day?"

"Okay. However, I didn't get much work done

for thinking about last night. You, Ray Sullivan, are something else."

He chuckled. "Works both ways, baby. I day-dreamed a lot today myself. I agree that last night was wonderful." He sniffed the air. "Hmm, something smells good."

She laughed. "And I hope it tastes as good as it smells."

"I'm sure it does."

"We'll see. If you want to go ahead and wash up, I'll put dinner on the table."

"Okay."

When he returned moments later and walked into her kitchen, he couldn't help but grin in pleasure. She had prepared a feast. "I'm impressed."

"Thanks. And just so you know, this Mid-Western turned Southern girl can cook."

"Who taught you?"

She met his gaze. "Devon. His grandmother taught him how to cook and he taught me."

"Good for him. Sadly, I can barely boil water."

"You're kidding, right?"

He chuckled. "I know it sounds pathetic but I kid you not. That's why I eat at the café so much. I'm sure I'd be able to cook if I put my mind to it, but I have no desire to do so. It's either the café or microwave dinners." When she looked at him as if that was the most god-awful thing she'd ever heard, he went over to her and kissed her lips. For some reason she looked so sad.

"Hey, I don't miss any meals. It's not that serious."

LITTLE DID HE know that for her it was that serious. The Devon she knew was a great cook. Funny how losing his memory had changed that. It was strange how he'd retained knowledge of some things, like the operating of a boat, but had forgotten how to do something else he'd loved just as equally.

"Well, whenever I'm around and in the mood to cook, I'm going to make sure you don't go hungry," she said, smiling up at him.

He chuckled. "I appreciate that."

They sat down at the table. In addition to the pork chops she'd promised, she'd also prepared mashed potatoes, mixed veggies, corn on the cob, mac and cheese and yeast rolls. "Everything looks good," he said.

"Thanks. Dig in."

He did. She couldn't help but watch him eat, knowing a lot of the dishes she'd prepared were personal recipes he'd shared with her over the years.

"Did you have many tours today?" she asked him.

"Quite a number. This is my busiest month with the shrimp festival in a couple of weeks. You plan on going, right?"

"Yes. I understand it's a three-day event that draws people from all over the United States."

"It does. There are water activities and fireworks every night. The good thing is that you'll have a real good view from your backyard."

They ate in silence for a moment, enjoying the meal.

"And just so you know, I'm thinking of buying this place if it ever goes on sale," Ray said.

She raised a brow. "This place here?"

"Yes. I like it and the view I saw this morning from your bedroom window was breathtaking."

"It is, isn't it?"

They talked about a number of other topics and he told her of his plans to go shrimping with Kaegan on Friday night to help make sure a number of restaurants in town were stocked up on shrimp for the festival. "I can feel the excitement in the air about the festival," she said when together they began clearing the table.

"Yes, there is. Hopefully by this time next year I'll have purchased an additional boat. I'm saving for it now. Business is good all year but especially so during this time."

Ashley didn't say anything. He was saving for it. It seemed his days of being an impulsive buyer were over. A least for now. Devon hadn't known the meaning of saving. She'd had to work hard to show him. "Will it be the same kind of boat?"

He shook his head as he helped her load the plates in the dishwasher. "No, a bigger one. I'd like to be able to take at least eight to ten people out at the same time. Now I'm limited to couples."

"Eight to ten people? Yes, that would definitely mean a larger boat," she said, grinning.

"Just think of how profitable that will be for my company. The first two years I kept expenses low. You're a business owner, so you know about tight times when you have to watch every penny."

She didn't say anything because since Devon's death she hadn't had to do that. In addition to the insurance proceeds, before his death Devon had cinched a huge deal that had made her a pretty wealthy woman. She had invested a lot of it with the help of Kim's husband, Jon Paul, who was sort of an investment genius. Thanks to him, she'd become even wealthier. Her mother liked reminding Ashley that she worked every day not because she had to, but because she wanted to.

"You've gotten quiet on me."

She glanced up at him and smiled. "I didn't mean to. I was just thinking. You have a lucrative business here and I'm always open to making money." Deciding to be honest, she said, "Devon's death left me in good financial shape and I'm always looking for ways to invest if you're interested." Ashley knew what she was really doing was giving Ray a chance to use his own money.

He looked at her for a moment. "Thanks for the offer, but I'm good for now. Kaegan loaned me the money to get started and I paid it back in a year. I try to do things on my own and not feel beholden to a lot of people. I guess you can say I like being my own man. That is important to me."

She turned from the sink to face him. "What else is important to you, Ray?"

He shrugged massive shoulders. "Like I told you, I have no recollection of my past, so I have no idea what type of man I was then or what I would have or would not have tolerated. Now I'm a private person who refuses to let a lot of people into my business. And those I do let in are there because I trust them deeply. So, I guess you can say friendship and trustworthiness are important to me."

Would Ray feel betrayed if he ever found out she was his wife and hadn't told him? Why would he if she explained why she'd done so? She had to believe that he would understand that everything she was doing was because she loved him and didn't want to set his condition back in any way.

She jumped when he snapped a finger in front of her face. "You drifted off to la-la land," he said, smiling. "You okay?"

She nodded. "Yes, I was just thinking about what you said. Friends and trust are important to me as well. I told you about my three close friends, Emmie, Suzanne and Kim. Suzanne and Kim and I grew up in Kansas and have been friends since grade school, whereas I met Emmie in college at Harvard. We still remain friends today. I trust them with my life."

He nodded. "I guess it's good to have people in your corner. For me, Sawyer and Kaegan have always been in mine and were the only people who knew about my memory loss. Vashti was added when she and Sawyer married. I couldn't expect him to keep something like that from her. And last month I decided to tell Bryce. I like and trust her. And last night I told you."

She met his gaze. "We've established the fact I'm not your friend, right?"

He moved to stand in front of her. Reached out his hand to slowly slide up the side of her body, settling on her waist. "Yes, you're more than that, Ashley."

She tilted her head to look closely at him. "Your lover, then?"

His smile appeared more heated than charming. "Do you think of yourself as my lover?"

She wanted to tell him that, no, she truly thought of herself as his wife. His one and only love, just like he was hers. However, she knew that was a position she had to work hard to reclaim. And she would.

"Right now I am whatever you want me to be, Ray...other than a mere friend."

He reached out and caressed the side of her face. "In that case, let's not define our relationship or worry about titles. It is what it is for now. All we have is the rest of the summer together. Then you'll leave and return to your world in South Carolina and I'll remain here in mine running my tour boat business."

When he lowered his mouth to hers and captured her lips, she wished more than anything that she could tell him he was wrong. They had more than just the summer. They had the same thing they'd pledged to have eight years ago at their wedding. They had the rest of their lives, and more than anything, she was determined to see that happen.

CHAPTER TWENTY-THREE

RAY GLANCED AT his wristwatch again. For the tenth time now? Ashley wasn't late, but damn, he was anxious to see her. The fact that he hadn't seen her in a couple of days might be the reason he was so eager to now.

"Hey, Ray."

He smiled and turned at the voice he recognized. "How are you, Bryce?"

She slid onto the bench next to him. "I'm okay. I'm surprised you're not out on your boat."

He chuckled. "I have to take time off sometime."

She nodded. "Looks like you're waiting on someone."

He lifted a brow. "What gave you that idea?"

Bryce grinned. "The way you keep looking at your watch makes it pretty obvious. Are you waiting for Ashley? I hear the two of you are an item now."

He wouldn't deny they were something but figured an item was stretching it a bit. She'd probably reached that conclusion because he and Ashley had been seen around the cove together on a number of occasions. "Not sure I'd say we're an item but we're good friends." He cringed when he said that. Hadn't he and Ashley decided they were more than friends?

"Whatever, Ray," Bryce said, giving him a knowing half smile as if she didn't believe him one bit. "I best move on. I'm meeting Mom near the Ferris wheel. See you later."

"Yeah, I'll see you later."

He watched her leave and then checked his watch again.

Moments later when he heard his name, he turned and saw the woman who'd called out to him. Deborah Chenille was a divorcée and the first woman to come on to him when he'd moved to the cove. She'd figured since they were both divorced that they had a lot in common. She'd been wrong about that. And when she began pursuing him with a vengeance, he'd had to take her aside and tell her flat out that he wasn't interested.

Deborah had stopped speaking to him for a while, which hadn't hurt his feelings any. He was glad when he'd heard she had gotten involved with some businessman living in Shreveport. However, rumor had it the relationship had ended and Ray wondered if that was why she was trying to get back to being friendly with him.

She waved her hand at him, and doing the neighborly thing, he waved back. He hoped she didn't take his friendliness as a sign of interest because it wasn't. The only woman he was interested in right now was Ashley.

He was still sort of amazed at how quickly she

had gotten under his skin and just how deep the obsession went. The more time they spent together, the more time he wanted to spend with her, which was the reason he'd decided to slow things down a bit, only seeing her two to three times a week. There had not been any more sleepovers at her place since that first night. He'd deliberately put an end to that. So much for doing that, because he'd only been miserable.

He liked her. Hell, he liked her a lot. However, there was no law that said just because they'd agreed to a summer fling they had to constantly be around each other. But that hadn't stopped him from thinking about her on those days that he didn't see her. Waking up in the middle of the night wanting her. Dreaming about her. He missed her tremendously, which was why he was looking at his watch again.

ASHLEY GLANCED AROUND as she walked. Vashti had tried warning her about the number of people who attended the Catalina Cove Shrimp Festival. People were everywhere, and according to Vashti, Friday wasn't the busiest day. More people attended on Saturday and just as many on Sunday as on Friday. She could see why all the merchants in the city were smiling. There was no doubt the festival was a boost to the cove's economy.

As she walked along the booths that had been set up, several people stopped and spoke to her, asking how she was doing. Most had been on the pier that day when she'd nearly drowned. She assured them she was fine and appreciated them for inquiring.

A lot had happened since she'd arrived in town. Two weeks ago she and Ray had first made love and agreed not to define their relationship. She couldn't even say over the past two weeks that they'd established a routine because they hadn't. There were some days she didn't see him at all, but at least he would call at night before she went to bed to see how she was doing. On those evenings he did drop by, they would either go out to dinner or she would whip them up something. Although they would end up making love, he made it a point to leave her house before midnight to return to his.

Ashley tried not to let it bother her that he had yet to invite her over to his place. Whenever the thought annoyed her, she quickly got over it, reminding herself that rebuilding a relationship with her husband was a process that couldn't be rushed. She needed to focus on the long-term and not the short-term. The goal was for him to get to know her and feel comfortable with her sharing his space. Men weren't as quick to do that as women.

At least he'd texted her and asked if she'd like to join him for lunch. She was going to meet him on the boardwalk near the ice cream shop. She knew exactly where that was since that shop had become one of her favorite spots in town.

She glanced at her watch and saw that she was ten minutes early and was glad because she didn't want to be late, especially since he was on his lunch hour. For a minute she'd thought she would be late when her father had called right before she'd left the house. He'd agreed with everything she'd told him about her mother's obsession with her dating Elliott. Ashley was smart enough to know that although her father might take her side now, it would be another story if her mother put any pressure on him.

Ashley had decided that the best thing to do was to fly home for a few days and spend some time with her parents. Although she wouldn't tell them about Ray, she would let them know she had met someone. Hopefully, the thought that she was getting over Devon enough to get interested in someone would get her mother off her back. There was no reason her parents needed to know just yet that the guy was Devon.

She smiled at the thought of how they would handle it when the day came and she told them the truth. Her father would be ecstatic. Her mother… umm, maybe not so much.

A short while later she reached the ice cream shop and saw Ray sitting on a bench, staring directly at her. She felt a deep stirring inside her the moment their gazes connected. She loved him so much and regretted she had to hold herself back from expressing just how deep that love went.

He stood and began moving toward her as she moved toward him. She wished more than anything that he saw her as the woman who should be in his life forever, but she knew that wasn't the case. She knew that look. It was one of desire and not love.

He was wearing a pair of khaki shorts and a T-shirt advertising his business and looked so hot she could barely stand it. She was only a few feet away when some woman, wearing a pair of hottie shorts and one of those midriff tops, approached Ray. The woman was all smiles and it didn't take a rocket scientist to see she was flirting with Ray. Ashley kept walking toward him and wondered how he would introduce her since the other woman was obviously someone he knew.

"Hi, Ray. I hope I'm not late," Ashley said, knowing she wasn't but wanting the woman to know he'd been waiting for her.

"No, you're right on time."

What Ashley hadn't expected was him reaching out and pulling her toward him and placing a kiss on her lips. He then said, "Ashley, I'd like you to meet Deborah. Deborah, this is Ashley."

"Hi, Deborah," Ashley said, noticing how the other woman was glaring at her.

Deborah barely shook her hand, which didn't bother Ashley any. Up close, the woman was beautiful; she had to give her that. It was a good thing Ray had made it pretty clear he had not been involved with any woman since losing his memory or Ashley would think maybe these two had once been an item from Deborah's territorial attitude.

"You're here just for the summer, right?" Deborah wanted to know. Ashley wondered where she'd gotten that information.

Ashley smiled. "Yes, that's right."

"Unless I can convince her to stay longer," Ray said, taking her hand in his.

"You can always try, Ray," Ashley said, smiling sweetly at him, appreciating whatever game he was playing for Deborah's benefit.

"I intend to," he replied, smiling back at her and rubbing his thumb across her hand. She doubted he knew it but that was what Devon used to do to her hand all the time. A little silent message to her. Rubbing her hand while holding it in just this way always meant he was horny and liable to jump her bones any minute.

"So, you've changed your mind about dating now, Ray?" Deborah asked, seemingly hopeful.

"Just when it comes to this woman right here," he said, smiling down at Ashley. "I guess you can say she wowed me."

"Did she?" Deborah said, giving Ashley a scowl.

"Yes. Now, if you will excuse us, we're on our way to lunch," Ray said, tightening his hold on Ashley's hand and leading her away.

They had walked a distance when she looked up at him. "So, what was that about?"

He glanced back down at her. "Nothing. It's not important." Then he said, "And just for the record, Ashley, you did wow me. So much, in fact, that I'm regretting the time when summer ends." He gave her a smile and added, "I might have to think of a way to get you to extend your time here."

She returned his smile, liking that thought. It

gave her hope. "Go ahead and think of something. Changing my mind might be easier than you think."

He threw his head back and laughed. "Don't tempt me."

When he led her away from the crowds toward the parking lot, she asked, "Where are we going?"

He came to a stop and faced her. "My place. I ordered lunch to be delivered. I hope that's all right."

Ashley couldn't stop her smile. That was better than all right. She would finally get to see the place Ray called home. "Yes, that's fine."

Still holding tight to her hand, Ray led her out to the parking lot and over to his truck. He opened the passenger door and helped her inside and snapped the seat belt across her. His closeness was playing havoc on her senses. Not only did he look good, he smelled good.

He closed the door and she watched him walk around the front of the truck to get in, sliding firm masculine thighs onto the driver's seat and fastening his seat belt. He turned the ignition in the truck and then backed out the parking space and headed toward the street.

Glancing over at her, he said, "You're quiet. What are you thinking about?"

She shrugged. "I missed seeing you the last couple of days." Although it was true, she regretted saying it the moment the words left her lips. The last thing she wanted was for him to feel she was putting him on the spot for not coming around.

When he brought the truck to a stop at a traffic

light, he said, "Although we talked every night, I wanted to see how long I could go without seeing you. Being with you. I discovered just how miserable I could be." He chuckled softly. "I won't be trying that again anytime soon."

She honestly didn't know what to think of that. What he said could be of a sexual nature since they did make love a lot whenever they were together, but she wasn't sure. Or was he insinuating that he'd begun developing feelings for her? Feelings he wasn't ready for. There was only one way to find out. "Why did you feel the need to do that, Ray? To see if you could go without seeing me?"

When he came to another traffic light, he said, "That's what I'm trying to figure out, Ashley."

She nodded, deciding not to say anything. Instead she looked out the window. Since moving to the cove, she'd driven around a bit exploring, and she recognized the area. Quaint historical homes lined both sides of the streets and most had long and winding driveways. They were a good ways from the water and she thought it odd since she knew how much he loved the ocean.

As if he read her mind, he said, "When I bought this place, it was all I could afford at the time. I liked it immediately because it's what I think a home should look like. My place is the last house on the road and I like my privacy. When I become successful, I plan to buy a bigger place on the water."

She chuckled. "Yes, I know, and you're eyeing the place I'm living in now."

He laughed. "Yes. You sold me on that view outside your bedroom window. You can't help but love it."

He pulled the truck into the driveway of a cute little house and for a minute Ashley just sat there and stared. The house bore a strong resemblance to Devon's grandmother's place in Hardeeville. The home he'd grown up in as a child. The place he'd refused to sell after his nana's death. Instead he'd rented it out to Mr. Rowman, an elderly man who'd been a member of Nana's church.

There was the small wraparound porch and the slanted roofline. The yard looked well cared for. Devon had never been a home-improvement type of man. At least, not to the point where he worked outside in the yard. They'd had one of the most immaculate lawns in the neighborhood because they'd hired a lawn service to make sure of it.

"Nice place," she said.

"Thanks. I think I timed it pretty good. The delivery service should be bringing our food in ten minutes. That will be enough time to show you around. Although this place lacks being on the water, it backs up against an apple grove."

"Apples? I guess I never thought of apples growing around here. I mostly think of blueberries."

He chuckled as he undid his seat belt. "That's our major fruit but we also grow apples, peaches, nectarines and muscadines. The cove even has a winery that you rarely hear about, but I understand it's pretty prosperous."

She smiled at him. "I'm learning something new about the cove every single day."

He broke eye contact with her to glance out the truck's windshield. "I love it here. I'm not saying it just because it's where I took up roots after losing my memory and there's no place in my mind to compare. I'm saying it because this is where I found peace and acceptance that I'd lost my memory. Instead of becoming depressed wondering what I'd lost with my memory, I got my therapist's help to start focusing on the things I'd gained."

Ashley didn't say anything. At that moment it hit her that there was a chance Ray might not ever get his memory back because in a way he didn't want it back. This was the life he lived now and he was content. That only made her wonder where that would leave her if he didn't want any part of his past, whether he remembered it or not.

CHAPTER TWENTY-FOUR

"READY TO GO INSIDE?" Ray asked after Ashley had gotten quiet on him. She smiled and that smile did something to him. Made him glad he'd come up with the idea of bringing her here for lunch.

"Yes, I'm ready."

Nodding, he got out the truck, walked around to open the truck door for her and leaned over to unbuckle her seat belt. He then impulsively swept her into his arms and carried her to the porch.

When he placed her on her feet, she laughed and said, "You didn't have to do that, so you better not complain if my weight causes your back to go out."

He laughed. "You're not heavy, trust me. And my back is good. Besides, the ground is unleveled and I wouldn't want you to miss a step."

He unlocked the front door and stood aside for her to enter. He went in behind her and closed the door, watching her look around. She looked good here in his home. Like she belonged.

Pushing that thought to the back of his mind, he said, "Let me show you around, although, honestly, there's not a lot to show. There're two bedrooms, and one I use as an office. A living room, dining room, kitchen and two bathrooms. What I fell in love with was the back porch. I love sitting out there in the evenings and drinking my beer. I thought we could sit out there for lunch."

"Okay."

He showed her around and she was quiet, but when they returned to the living room, she said, "I love it and it's obvious you're a neat freak. Nothing is out of place and your hardwood floors look so clean you can probably eat off them. Devon used to be a neat freak, too."

Ray thought about that for a moment and decided to address something that was beginning to bother him, although it shouldn't. "You do that a lot, Ashley."

She tilted her head to look up at him. "Do what?"

"Compare me to your dead husband."

The shocked look on her face said she was horrified. "I—I'm sorry. I hadn't realized I've been doing that."

He reached out and caressed the side of her face. "Hey, it's okay," he said, when deep down he knew it truly wasn't okay with him. "You loved him. You still do. The two of you had good years together, so it stands to reason you would do that." He was being logical about it now, but whenever she would do it he never thought logically. He would often get annoyed when he really shouldn't.

There was no reason to make her feel even worse by telling her that she'd even whispered her husband's name the last time they'd made love. That was when he began wondering if she was only seeing him as her dead husband's substitute. He'd needed the last two days to think about it. In the end, he'd missed her like crazy and couldn't wait to see her today.

"Come on. Let me show you out back."

He knew the moment she stepped on his back porch that she could see why he liked it so much. The apple grove was beautiful and the scent of fresh apples filled the air. "It's nice out here, Ray."

"Thanks. I had it screened in because of the mosquitoes. There are nights I even sleep out here," he said, explaining the reason for the daybed.

"I can see why," she said, glancing around. "I could lose myself out here."

"Even without the ocean view?"

She smiled at him. "Yes, even without the ocean view. You're right. It's so peaceful here."

At that moment the doorbell rang. "That's probably our lunch. You can use any of the bathrooms to wash your hands and I'll be back in a minute." He was about to walk off but then he pulled her into his arms.

"Welcome to my home, Ashley," he said, and then lowered his head to kiss her.

ASHLEY PRESSED HER body against Ray while he took her mouth with a hunger that she felt all the way to her toes. And she kissed him back because she needed this kiss.

She was bothered by what he'd said. About her

comparing him to Devon. She hadn't meant to do that but it had come naturally. She would have to be careful in the future. In building a new relationship with Ray, she didn't want him to think she was attracted to him because he was part of an old relationship with her husband.

But then, wasn't he? Wasn't she always looking for things about him that reminded her of Devon instead of fully accepting Ray for the person he was now?

He released her mouth and took a step back when the doorbell sounded again. "I better get that."

And then he was gone and she was left sighing deeply while licking her lips. She loved his taste. She loved him, period. Deciding to go wash her hands, she headed for one of the bathrooms. She recalled her reaction at seeing his bedroom.

His bed was large with one of those old iron bed frames. He told her most of the furniture had come with the house but over time he'd replaced all of it, except for the bed frame. The only thing it had needed was a new mattress and box spring and it had been good to go.

When she returned to the patio, he was placing two bags on a round table with two chairs. The aroma floated to her nostrils. "Something smells good."

He smiled at her, and seeing him standing there looking handsome and sexy had heat engulfing her, starting in the pit of her stomach. "I think you're going to like what I ordered. Takeout from Briggins."

Briggins Bar and Grill was another place he'd

introduced her to. She'd thought that she'd died and gone to heaven after tasting their hamburger and fries. "You, Ray Sullivan, have made my day."

He chuckled. "I'm glad. Can you take everything out the bags while I go wash my hands?"

"All right."

By the time he returned, she was all but licking her lips. He'd ordered hamburgers, french fries and onion rings. All the things she liked. "Come and sit down and let's dig in."

He rejoined her at the table and she said, "You're on lunch and have to return to work, right?"

"No, I'm off the rest of the day."

She lifted a brow as she sat down. "You are?"

"Yes. I always shut down half days during the festival."

"Doesn't that hurt business? I figured with this crowd you'd want to capitalize on that."

He shrugged. "I figure that making money all the time isn't everything. There are times when you have to just enjoy life."

"I agree," she said, her head spinning with the news that Ray didn't have to go back to work, which meant they would have more time to spend together today.

She recalled there was a time Devon had thought working was everything. For them to be success- ful was an obsession with him. It had gotten bad when she'd bought into his belief and they'd be- come power hungry. As a result, their marriage had suffered. Where other couples would had caved in and gotten a divorce, love had kept them together and had driven them to seek help from a marriage counselor.

She was beginning to like Ray's view on life more and more.

"So tell me," she said, smiling at him. "What things do you enjoy doing, other than being out on your boat?

He smiled back at her. "I like playing tennis. I'm pretty good at it, so I can only assume I played a lot at some point."

He had. Devon had been captain of the tennis team in college. "You play a lot here?"

"Not here as much as in New Orleans. The courts are better. A couple of years back, this big corporation wanted to build a tennis resort in the cove, but the zoning board wouldn't approve it."

"Why?"

"The cove wasn't ready for such a change. If you haven't noticed, there aren't any chain stores here."

"I did notice. However, I did see that Spencer's."

"Trust me, it's the only one and it's pretty new. Vashti will have to tell you how that came about."

"I'll be sure to ask her, and just so you know, I'm pretty good at tennis. Maybe we can play a game or two one day."

"No maybe about it. We need to add that to our schedule."

Tossing her bangs from her face, she said, "I ran into your assistant in the store yesterday. He's a nice guy."

"Yes, Tyler is nice and dependable. He told me this morning that he and his wife are expecting. I'm happy for them."

Ashley could tell from the sound of his voice that he was. "That's great."

"I think so. I'll become an honorary uncle again. I'm one to Sawyer and Vashti's son and Tyler said I'll be one to his kid. Can't wait."

She bit into a fry and gazed over at him. "You like kids?"

He glanced over at her like he thought she'd asked a dumb question. "Who doesn't?"

She shrugged. "There are some couples who don't want any and others who decide to wait till later."

He chuckled. "I can't see that being me. The waiting. It wouldn't bother me if I got my wife pregnant on our wedding night." He didn't say anything for a minute but a pensive look appeared on his face. "That's something that used to worry me."

"What?"

"Knowing how I feel about children and my desire to have them, maybe I did. And in addition to a wife, maybe I have a child or children somewhere. Not knowing is what pains me the most sometimes."

She wished she could take him out of his misery by letting him know he hadn't left behind any children. Just a wife who deeply loved him. Deciding to change the subject, she asked, "So, who owns the apple grove?"

RAY WAS WELL aware that Ashley had deliberately changed subjects. That was fine since he probably should not have said anything to her about how he felt about children anyway. It had been thoughtless of him. She had been married five years and she and her husband hadn't had any kids. Had they been one of those who might not want any like she'd mentioned?

If that was true, he would bet it had been her husband who'd been the reluctant one. He'd seen the way she held Sawyer and Vashti's son, Cutter, that day they'd run into them at dinner at Briggins. Vashti had to nearly pry the baby from Ashley's arms to get Cutter back. Her interaction with Cutter had touched him that day and he'd wondered then why she wasn't a mother.

"That apple grove is owned by Reid LaCroix, the wealthiest man in the cove."

She nodded. "He owns the blueberry plant as well, right?"

"Yes, and it employs a great number of people. He's an okay guy. I like him."

As they ate for a minute in silence, his chest tightened at the thought he might have bothered her with his comment about children. The last thing he wanted was to hurt her feelings about anything. "Ashley?"

She glanced up at him. "Yes?"

"I am sorry what I said about kids."

Her brow bunched. "Why would you be sorry?"

"I might have offended you. You and your husband didn't have kids and—"

"We wanted them," she cut in to say. "It was just a mutual decision to wait awhile. There were a number of things we wanted to accomplish before becoming parents." He saw the pained look in her eyes when she added, "We decided to wait and he died before we could start a family."

Ray nodded. "I'm sorry."

She bit into another fry and then said pensively, "So am I."

He bet she would have been a great mother. There was something about Ashley that was more than just her beauty and pleasing personality. There had been a connection between them from the start. A connection he was still trying to figure out.

"I heard there will be fireworks tonight."

He glanced over at her. "Yes, and you got one of the best views in town right here. Although I'm not close to the ocean, you can see the sky real good from here whenever there are fireworks."

She smiled. "Then I guess I need to drop by later."

He had news for her. He didn't intend for her to leave. At least, not for a while. He wanted to spend as much time with her today as he could. He realized now that there was a reason he had brought her to his home. He'd wanted to share with her a part of himself that he hadn't shared with any woman since becoming Ray Sullivan.

When they'd finished eating, together they gathered up the trash and disposed of it. "You want to take a walk?"

She glanced over at him. For some reason he liked how she looked in his kitchen. "A walk?"

"Yes, through the grove. Unless, of course, you need to get back home. If you do, I understand."

"No, I'm fine. I hadn't planned to get much writing done today anyway."

"Just so you know, I checked out one of your blogs."

"You did?" she asked excitedly.

"Yes. StayNTouch has a lot of followers."

"Yes, we do." She gave him a teasing smile. "So are you now one of StayNTouch's followers?"

"Not yet. Besides, the only person I want to stay in touch with is you."

He led her out the back door toward the grove. She wasn't saying much but he could tell from the look on her face what he'd just said had pleased her.

He'd discovered Ashley didn't ever talk just to be talking. She knew how to engage in what he considered wholesome conversation, which meant she only spoke when she had something meaningful to say. She was not a rambler.

For now he just liked her walking by his side. Probably too much. And he liked touching her, which was why he reached out and took her hand in his.

"Oh, Ray, this place is beautiful," she said in that awestruck voice he loved hearing. He'd first heard it when he'd taken her out for her tour and had shown her the Spike Waterfall that concealed the cave where the pirate Jean Lafitte hid his treasures.

"I think so, too. I'm glad Mr. LaCroix didn't fence it off from those living on this side. It backs up to the cove."

She glanced over at him. "You are close to the water."

He chuckled. "I don't consider it close since this grove sits on over eight hundred acres of land. If you take a mind to walk to the waterway from here, it's probably a good six miles that way."

"No, thank you. But it's a perfect place for a picnic, wouldn't you say?"

He smiled down at her. "I guess. I wouldn't know since I never had one there." Ray could see it as a possibility, though, with her. "I own one of those golf carts and got it for the purpose of riding through the groves. I made it all the way to the cove on it and it is beautiful where the grove ends and the cove begins. It might sound silly, but I consider it my special place where I go to think or just appreciate the beauty of nature while I eat a few apples."

"A few?"

He grinned. "Okay, a little more than a few. Delicious apples grow here." He stopped beside a tree and plucked one off a limb. He wiped it off on his shirt. "Here, taste it."

He handed her the apple and she took it and bit into it. The pleased smile that spread around her lips was priceless. "Thanks, Ray, for bringing me here."

They walked around a little more, and in deference to the sun's heat, they turned and headed back to his place. "What is your normal day like, Ray?"

"I go to work. Come home. Take a run either in the grove or around the neighborhood. Go back home and get a beer. At some point when I'm hungry I pop in a dinner in the microwave. Take a shower, write in my journal and then go to bed. Usually every morning I meet Sawyer and Kacgan for breakfast. But you know that part."

"You keep a journal?"

"Yes. My therapist suggested it. At first I thought it was crazy to write down what I did that day but now it's become sort of therapeutic. I like having it recorded somewhere just in case I…"

When he didn't finish, she said, "In case you lose your memory again?"

His hand tightened on hers. "Yes, in case I lose my memory again."

"Is that possible?"

They had reached his back patio. "I'm discovering anything is possible, Ashley. The doctors don't think it ever will, but I'm not taking any chances."

She nodded and then looked down at herself. "Now I feel hot and sticky."

He was about to tell her although that might be the case, she looked tempting as hell. Perspiration from their walk had caused the material of her outfit to cling to her in some pretty tantalizing places. "You can take a shower if you like and use my washer and dryer for your things."

She seemed to ponder his offer and then asked, "What will I wear while waiting for my clothes?"

He wanted to tell her she didn't have to have on anything but decided not to do that. Just because they'd shared a bed a number of times, he refused to assume anything when it came to Ashley. She wasn't the kind of woman a man could easily peg to be a certain way. "I have a number of T-shirts that would probably fit you like a dress," he said. He pushed the thought to the back of his mind that it would be more like a minidress.

"And just where will you be, Ray Sullivan, while I'm taking my shower?"

They were standing in the middle of his living room, still holding hands as they faced each other. He shrugged. "Not sure. I'll probably grab a beer, sit out on the patio and wait for you to finish. Why you ask? Do you need me for something?"

She nodded and then moistened her bottom lip with a swipe of her tongue. "Actually, I was thinking that maybe you could join me in that shower."

CHAPTER TWENTY-FIVE

ASHLEY WASN'T SURE what Ray's reaction would be to her proposal. All she knew was that she'd made the offer with a sexual need that was slowly consuming her. She forced herself to look everywhere but at him when he didn't say anything.

Then she felt his hand gently touch her chin, bringing her gaze back to connect to his. The look she saw in his eyes nearly made her weak in the knees. It caused an instant throbbing in her midsection. His pupils had darkened and naked desire was blatantly there for her to see. She did more than see it. She felt it in every pore, nerve and pulse in her body. And when he spoke, his tone was a seductive murmur that made moisture gather between her thighs.

"I would love to join you in that shower, Ashley. But be forewarned, a shower won't be all I'll be taking. I'll also be taking you."

Good God, she wanted him to take her. She was drowning in him and need was hammering her common senses, making them not so common, making them feel absolutely ravaged, which pushed her to ask, "How will you be taking me?"

He took a step closer to her and she sucked in a deep breath when she felt him. His large, hard erection was pressed against her. "If you want details, I can give them to you. However, I'd rather surprise you."

She moistened her lips again and watched his eyes darken even more with the movement of her tongue. "I like surprises."

Now his dark gaze looked turbulent. "In that case..." His mouth swooped down on hers in a long, deep kiss that immediately made her purr. It had her feeling out of control. She could actually feel a ball of sexual need burst to life at the center of her legs.

She barely recalled him sweeping her up into his arms, but she did recall the moment she buried her face in his chest, inhaling his masculine scent. A scent that was Ray's and not Devon's. Same body. Two different men. And she loved both.

He placed her on her feet and began stripping off her clothes followed by his. Then he swept her back into his arms. He moved toward his bathroom but stopped. Shifting her slightly in his arms, he opened the drawer to his nightstand to get protection. A whole handful of condom packets. At that moment, she didn't know whether she should be appreciative or petrified. She went for appreciative.

He went for her.

Even before turning on the water, he was backing her up against the shower wall, and the moment she opened her mouth to moan, his tongue slid inside and began feasting on her with a hunger that made her sex contract as if it was begging for what it had been denied for eight years.

Not today, but one day and with this man, she silently promised her womb. It would happen. Only with this man. He kissed her hard, exposing what she knew was deep, unquenchable lust. His skillful hands were everywhere, kneading her backside while she burned hot with desire.

He released her mouth and stared at her while reaching up to turn on the shower. A slow spray showered down on them, wetting their bodies, and the next thing she knew, he was using his hot and wet tongue to lick droplets of water from her shoulders down to her breasts. His hands had moved from her backside and were between her legs, stroking her.

"Ray…"

She called his name, wanting to tell him how his hands and mouth were making her feel. Instead his name was followed by a deep groan while he inserted a finger inside of her. When she whimpered his name again, his finger went deeper while his mouth was devouring her breasts, one nipple at a time.

And then he was lowering himself to the shower floor, getting on his knees as his tongue drew rings around her belly, cupping her thighs, holding them immobile. When she felt the powerful strokes of his finger inside her body, she was nearly pushed over the edge.

As if sensing her capitulation, he whispered, "Hold on for a little longer, baby."

Hold on? Did he think she honestly could?

As if to test her willpower further, he whispered, "I want to taste you when you come." Before she could react to his words, his mouth quickly replaced his finger.

"Ray…"

Her arms came down to grab hold of his shoulder. His tongue was deeply and thoroughly massaging her clit. It was too much. Way too much. She was trying to hold on, but the way he was using his mouth on her, implementing techniques that were both old and new to her, undeniably powerful and significant, pulverized what little control she had.

When he cupped her bottom, pushing her deeper into his mouth while his ardent tongue continued to work its magic, she couldn't hold back any longer and screamed out his name when a gigantic orgasm ripped through her.

RAY CONTINUED TO kiss Ashley deeply between the legs, loving the essence of her taste. He felt the spasms that raced through her body, and knowing he was giving her pleasure filled him with a kind of pride he didn't ever remember experiencing before.

Slowly standing to his feet, he pulled her into his arms and kissed her. Mingling his mouth with hers was something he would never get tired of doing. Breaking off the kiss, he reached for the soap and began lathering her body, touching her everywhere. He knew the moment she began to get aroused again. Not to be undone, she copied his actions and began lathering him all over as well.

Her touch was nearly too much and it occurred to him she was pretty damn good at what she was doing. He forced the thought from his mind, not understanding why he'd suddenly become jealous of a man he didn't know. A man whom Ashley would have had every right to make out with in the shower or anywhere else she chose.

When they'd both gotten lathered up, he kissed her again, but that didn't stop her hands from roaming all over him or his from roving over her. It was obvious that she was getting just as aroused from his touch as he was from hers.

Using the handheld showerhead, he began washing the foam off their bodies, alternating the action with a series of touches and intense kissing. And then there were the areas on her body where he deliberately sprayed the water. And from the darkening of her eyes, it was obvious a gush of water shot between her legs was causing the reaction he wanted.

"You're not playing fair, Ray Sullivan," she said, playfully manhandling him to take the showerhead from him. Now he was the one being sprayed and she immediately went for his manhood. The moment water hit, renewed sexual energy rocked him to the bone.

"Oh, baby, you're going to get it now," he threatened, reaching out to take the showerhead from her and placing it back but still allowing a shower of water to rain down on them.

"I hope I do get it, Ray, and now isn't soon enough." Ray would have thrown his head back to laugh if it had not been such a sensual moment. Reaching out, he pulled her wet body to his, capturing her mouth. Dear God, he liked kissing her and thought he could do it all day and all night to her mouth. It seemed to be made just for his.

He broke off the kiss, bent down to retrieve a condom and quickly sheathed himself. "You have no idea how much I want you, Ashley. I don't think you can even come close to knowing."

When he moved back toward her, she met him and wrapped her arms around his neck, cuddling intimately to him. "Then show me, Ray, so I'll know."

He intended to. It dawned on him at that moment that he had a reason for bringing her here and it hadn't been all about sex. He had a deep yearning to make her his. He wasn't sure where his possessive nature had come from all of a sudden. He would continue to live his life as Ray Sullivan and for now she would be the woman who shared it with him. He would deal with the end of the summer when it arrived. For now, he intended to take one day at a time.

He lifted her right leg and wrapped it around his waist. In that position he could feel her womanhood throb against his thigh. Damn, it felt good. Wet. Hot and burning with desire. "Are you sure you're ready for me, Ashley?" he asked, holding her gaze, moving his body so she could feel the hardness of his erection.

"Yes, I'm ready for you."

"And you want me?"

She nodded. "Yes, I want you. Stop toying with me, Ray."

He liked the sound of her no-nonsense voice. "Toying with you? I thought I was merely getting you ready."

"I'm already ready."

"Hmm, let's just see about that." He tilted her body slightly and thrust hard inside of her at the same moment he lowered his mouth to hers and took it in a ravishing kiss, filled with all the need he felt for her. Automatically, she tightened her leg around his waist at the same time she tightened her arms around his neck.

He began moving, stroking her from the inside out while thinking just how good it felt being inside of her. Each time he thrust harder, he went even deeper. To make sure she didn't feel any discomfort standing on one leg, he cupped her bare bottom as he continuously pumped into her, loving the feel of how her inner muscles were tightening around his erection, clenching it hard.

When he felt an orgasm about to slam into him, he broke off the kiss, threw his head back and released a deep, territorial growl. He continued to pump hard inside of her, determined not to let his release come until hers did, no matter how close to the edge he was.

And when she shouted his name, he knew she'd come again, and instinctively, his body followed her into another hemisphere.

AFTER GETTING OUT the shower, they toweled dry and he gave her one of his T-shirts to put on and showed her where his washer and dryer were located.

After loading her things in and starting the washer, she went looking for Ray and found him sitting out on the patio drinking a beer. The ceiling fans overhead were churning out air, which helped make it feel less hot. She could imagine him sitting out here at night alone, and in that moment she realized that although he had Kaegan and Sawyer as friends, basically Ray was alone. She intended to change things in that regard.

With more instinct than nerves, she crossed the patio and eased into his lap. From the look on his face, she could tell her bold move had surprised the hell out of him. And then to stun him even further, she reached for his beer bottle. "May I?"

Probably too stupefied to deny her anything at the moment, he nodded and released his beer to her. She took a swallow and handed it back to him. He didn't say anything as he watched her lick her lips. "Are you toying with me, Ashley?"

She smiled at him. "What makes you think that?"

As if he decided it might be best not to answer, he said, "No reason." Then he said, "Sorry I took you away from the festival."

"I'm not. I like being here with you, Ray."

He held her gaze. "Why?"

She shrugged. "Because I think you're a nice guy. A guy I'm finding that I like sharing my time with. And just for the record, it's not all about sex, although I think the sex is pretty good."

He chuckled. "You won't hear any complaints from me."

"I better not."

He shifted her in his lap so she could face him. "Kind of bossy, aren't you?"

She reached out and stroked his beard, loving the feel of it in her hand. "Yes, I suppose you can say that."

"Well, bossy lady, how about going boating with me on Sunday evening? Most of the tourists who came to town for the festival will have left by then."

Regret settled in her stomach. "Oh, Ray, I wish I could but I can't. I need to fly home Sunday."

"Oh."

She heard the disappointment in that single word and wanted to explain. She needed to explain so if he ever met her parents as Ray Sullivan, he would know what to expect. "It's showdown time with my parents."

He lifted a brow. "Your parents?"

"Yes." She realized she'd never discussed her parents with him, and doing so now would mean she was sharing more of herself with him. "By most standards, I have good parents. Dad and I get along great the majority of the time. But Mom and I clash a lot."

He chuckled. "Why? Is she bossy like you?"

Ashley smiled. "No, she's controlling. Not a little bit but a lot. She and Devon never got along, because he refused to let her control our lives."

"Good for him."

She was glad Ray felt that way. "Anyway, Mom thinks I'm taking too much time getting my life back together after Devon's death, so she's taken it upon herself to help me along by playing matchmaker."

"Matchmaker?" he asked, taking another sip of his beer.

"Yes. There's this guy she keeps shoving down my throat, although I told her I'm not ready to get seriously involved with anyone. I talked to her the other day and she wants Elliott to come see me and I refuse to let that happen."

"Good for you." His voice was hard and his jaw had clenched. Her heart skipped a beat. If she didn't know better, she'd think he was upset at the thought that another man was interested in her.

"Why is it a good thing, Ray?"

"Because you're a grown woman who knows her own mind and what she wants to do with it and who she wants or doesn't want in it. Your mother should respect that."

She couldn't help but smile. Now he sounded like Devon. "She doesn't and that's why I'm going home this weekend to make sure they understand. Unfortunately, Dad can't hold his own against Mom."

"In other words, he's a damn wimp."

Ashley hated her father being described that way but Ray's description was pretty darn accurate. "Yes."

Ray pulled her to him and rested his chin on the crown of her head. "Thanks for sharing that with me, Ashley. That deal about your parents."

Pulling back, she looked down at him. "I'll share anything with you, Ray. Anywhere and at any time."

Ashley figured an invitation couldn't get any more blatant than that.

He evidently thought so, too. Placing the beer bottle aside, he stood with her in his arms and headed back into the house. She didn't have to ask where they were going because she knew.

They were going to make love in his bed this time around.

CHAPTER TWENTY-SIX

"Morning, Ray. You're not joining us for breakfast?" Sawyer asked, glancing up at Ray over the rim of his coffee cup. Instead of sliding into the booth like he normally did, Ray stood there with what he knew was a satisfied smile on his face. Sawyer clearly recognized the smile and the meaning behind it.

"No, I'm getting it to go."

"To go? Why?" Kaegan asked, obviously hiding a grin. He might not be involved in a serious affair but Ray knew the man wasn't stupid.

"Maybe that's none of your business, Kaegan," Sawyer said, coming to Ray's defense.

"You're right, Sawyer," Ray said, grinning. "It's none of his business. You guys have a good day."

Leaving his friends, Ray moved toward the counter to order breakfast for him and Ashley. Waking up with her sleeping beside him had left him with a profound feeling of peace.

A short while later, he was placing the bags on his kitchen table. He went into the bedroom and found Ashley still sleeping. He stood there and stared at her for a moment before stripping off his clothes and getting back in bed.

Easing up close beside her, he inhaled her scent as he gently pulled her into his arms, trying hard not to wake her, and released a deep sigh when she continued to breathe evenly while he held her. He loved the feel of her naked flesh next to his. Loved the way even in sleep how he sensed her trusting nature, especially in knowing he was the first man she'd shared a bed with since losing her husband. He'd felt such pleasure when he had awakened in her bed and felt the same way now.

The only thing missing since the last time they'd spent the entire night together was a feeling of panic. The last time, he'd felt overwhelmed, not sure he was making the right move. Feeling like he was getting too attached to Ashley. Too obsessed.

Now he still felt those things. None of it bothered him. He'd tried putting distance between them. He'd convinced himself it was all about sex and fulfilling physical needs. But he knew that was a lie. Ashley was coming to mean something to him and he was no longer afraid of that realization.

What he was afraid of was that he wasn't coming to mean anything to her in the same way. There was no doubt in his mind that she liked him and enjoyed being with him. But what did it mean that for the first time in three years he was finally considering moving forward in his life, but unfortunately he'd hooked up with a woman who might not want to move on in hers?

Granted, she no longer wore her wedding ring and that was a beginning, but he had a feeling she was still stuck in the past, specifically on a husband who wouldn't be coming back. A man who was dead, yet whom she still refused to bury. At least she hadn't called Ray Devon like she'd done the last time they'd made love at her place.

Hearing her call him by another man's name had been disheartening and bothered him deeply to the point he'd stayed away for those two days to deal with it. But still, he knew that Ashley was starting to mean something to him. He didn't want that but didn't know any way to stop it.

He'd made love to her in this bed last night. A lot of times. Each time had driven him to want to do it again. And again. It was as if his bed, the sheets and all the bedcoverings had her name on them. As if they'd been waiting for her to slide between them, that one person, that one incredible woman who could make his life complete. He hadn't thought such a thing was possible. He'd been afraid to think such a thing was possible.

Fear of the unknown was what he still had to overcome. Fear that one day the other shoe would drop and he would get his memory back and discover the last three years had been a lie and that the life he'd remembered wouldn't be the life he wanted now.

Ray wasn't sure just how long he lay there holding Ashley, reveling in how a part of him wished things could have been different for them. That he was totally free to pursue her the way he'd like and not just settle for the summer. He closed his eyes, not wanting to think how he would feel when he would see her for the last time...on the day she packed up to return to South Carolina and the life she had there.

"Good morning, Ray."

He glanced down at her and saw she'd awakened. Damn, she looked beautiful. The sunlight that flowed in his bedroom window through the blinds seemed to highlight her features, giving them a stunning glow. "Good morning."

As if it was the most natural thing to do, he leaned in and kissed her with all the emotions he'd been feeling lately, especially those he'd encountered since returning from the café and rejoining her in bed. Emotions he found overwhelming but gloried in nonetheless.

When he released her mouth, he gazed down at her. "How do you feel this morning?"

"Great. Making love to you practically all night seems to have given me a new lease on life. Thank you for sharing your time yesterday and your bed." She didn't say anything for a moment and then she said, "It wasn't my plan to spend the night. I don't want you to think I'm clingy."

He reached out and brushed a few strands of hair back from her face. "I believe I'm the one who brought you here and I don't recall asking you to leave. In fact, I'm holding your clothes hostage."

She chuckled as she snuggled closer into his

arms. "That's right. You are, aren't you?" Her sigh was one of contentment. "It's Saturday. Don't you have something to do? It's day two of the festival."

"Nope. I don't have anything to do but enjoy the festivities like everyone else. I got up earlier and went out to get us breakfast. It's gotten cold by now, but I do own a microwave, so we're good."

She leaned up to brush a kiss across his lips. "Yes, we are good. In more ways than one, Ray."

He definitely agreed with that. "You're hungry?"

"Not yet."

"Good. I'm going to miss you all over again when you leave town on Sunday. When will you be back?"

"Thursday."

"That's a long time. I hope you know what that means." He pulled her into his arms to show her in case she didn't.

ABOUT AN HOUR after landing in Hilton Head, Ashley pulled into the parking lot of her parents' apartment complex. The flight hadn't been as bad as the one she'd taken the last time she'd come home. Or it could be that she had so many great new memories that even turbulence couldn't sidetrack her mind.

After breakfast Saturday, she'd gotten dressed and Ray had taken her back to her place, where she'd changed into a sundress, and together they left for the festival. They had spent the majority of the day taking in the sights and vendors and even a concert before grabbing a bite to eat and returning to her place. They watched a movie together and he didn't leave until this morning, kissing her long and hard before telling her to be safe and he would see her on Thursday.

She didn't want to get her hopes up about anything but the last couple of days with Ray had been idyllic. She only hoped things continued that way because every day she was falling deeper and deeper in love with her husband. The thought that he would never love her in return was too devastating a possibility to even consider.

Leaving her car, she walked up to the door. Her father knew she was coming. Her mother did not. She and her dad figured it would be best that way. The last time she'd talked to her mother and told her she was coming so they could talk, Imogene had said not to bother. Ashley knew that wasn't an option when Elliott had called her yesterday to say her mother suggested that he call her.

Ashley had been with Ray when she'd gotten the call. Although he hadn't said anything, she could tell by the tensing of his jaw that he hadn't appreciated Elliott calling during their time together. Now she was glad she'd told him the story about her mother and Elliott.

She rang the doorbell and the look on her mother's face told her she wasn't surprised to see her. That meant her father had caved as usual. "Hi, Mom."

Her mother was smiling and that wasn't a good sign. "Hello, Ashley. I'm glad you decided to come home to see your aging parents," Imogene said, and even leaned in to place a kiss on her cheek. Then she moved aside to let Ashley enter.

When Ashley walked inside, she knew the reason for her mother's good mood. Elliott was sitting on the sofa, grinning from ear to ear. "Your mother said you'd be coming home today and suggested I drop by to welcome you back."

Ashley's hand tightened on the strap of her purse. "There was no need for you to do that, Elliott." She looked at her mother. "Where is Dad?"

"He's out on the patio grilling. Since you were coming to town, I thought I'd invite Elliott over for dinner. Your dad volunteered to grill to give me a chance to get out of the kitchen."

Ashley knew her father never volunteered to grill. He hated doing it. "There was no need for either you or Dad to go to any trouble because I don't intend to stay. I'm here to meet with you and then to go to my place and rest up. I've already made plans for dinner with Emmie for later."

"Ashley," her mother said in her stern voice. "There's no way you're eating with Emmie when you came home to see us."

Her mother's authoritarian tone grated on Ashley's nerves. "I came home to speak with you, and I'd like to do it now, Mom, so I can leave."

"Leave? Ashley, don't be ridiculous."

"I'm not being ridiculous. Please let Dad know I want to talk with him now. And while you're doing that, I'll talk with Elliott."

Her mother must have seen the determined look

on her face and said, "Okay. I'll go get your dad while you entertain Elliott."

It didn't take Ashley any more than five minutes to entertain Elliott. She told him, like she'd told him several times before, that she wasn't interested in him. This time she went further and told him to lose her number, and if he tried to contact her, regardless of what her mother said, did or advised, she would consider it harassment and take legal action. That was enough to send Elliott quickly packing without looking back.

When her mother returned, she asked, "Where is Elliott?"

"He left."

"Left? Why? I ordered him to stay no matter what you said or did. I told him when the two of you get together, he would need a firm hand with you."

"And I made sure he knew we wouldn't be getting together at all."

"Can we all sit down and discuss this?" her father said, giving her an apologetic look, which she ignored.

"No, we can't. I'm here to get a few things straight with you two. I don't need you interfering in my life and please don't do it again."

"But you need someone," her mother implored. "Devon isn't coming back and you need to accept that."

Ashley wished she could tell her mother how wrong she was about that. Instead she said, "Look, Mom, I know you assume you know what's best for me, but you don't. I've told you countless times that neither you nor anyone else can control how long I grieve. You can't say how long it should last."

She paused a minute and then added, "Leaving town for a while was the best thing for me. I met someone."

Just like Ashley had expected, her mother's jaw dropped. "You met someone?" Imogene exclaimed. "Who? When?"

Ignoring her mother's questions, Ashley said, "All you need to know is that I really like him and we're talking." Of course, she and Ray were doing a lot more than talking, but her parents didn't need to know that.

"Well, I hope you're taking things slow. You can't rush into affairs these days."

So said the woman who'd been constantly trying to shove Elliott down her throat. "I ask that you stay out of my business, Mom. You've interfered long enough. Let me handle my own affairs."

"When will we get to meet him?" her father asked.

Ashley turned to her father. "When I think the time is right, Dad, and not before."

"We need to know when," her mother declared in a huff. "And we need to know his name."

Samuel turned to his wife. "We don't need to know anything, Genie. You heard what Ashley said. When she is ready to tell us anything, she will," he said in a firm voice. "For once you need to stay out of her business."

For the second time that day, her mother's jaw

dropped. "Don't take that tone of voice with me, Sam."

"I am taking it and meaning it as well," her father said loudly.

"You raised your voice to me," Imogene said in shock.

"Yes, I did, and I intend to do it more often. It's about time you let Ashley live her life, and I intend to start stepping up and make sure that you do," her father stated.

Ashley appreciated him at that moment and hoped he stuck to his guns. "I'm leaving now, but I'll be in town until Thursday. Suzanne and Kim are flying in tomorrow and we're all hanging out. If you want to plan dinner for Wednesday, Mom, then I'll be happy to come. Just call and let me know when. Bye."

She turned and left.

CHAPTER TWENTY-SEVEN

"WHEN DOES ASHLEY return to town?"

Ray glanced over at Sawyer. "How did you know she'd gone anywhere?"

Kaegan chuckled. "He's the sheriff, Ray. Sawyer knows everything that goes on in Catalina Cove."

Sawyer leaned back in his chair. "Not everything. However, I knew about Ashley because she mentioned it to Vashti. Was it supposed to be a secret?"

Ray took a sip of coffee. "No, it wasn't a secret."

"Well, I happen to know she was gone because you've been walking around with a sad face," Kaegan said, biting into a blueberry muffin.

Ray frowned. "I haven't had a sad face."

When both Sawyer and Kaegan merely grinned at him, Ray figured they might have been right about the sad face. He had been feeling pretty damn miserable for the past few days. "She'll be back on Thursday."

"Right in time for my party Friday night," Kaegan said. "Make sure you bring her."

Kaegan had given a party every year since he'd moved back to town. "I'll ask her."

Later in his office, Ray and Tyler had finished all the tours for that day. Since Ashley had been out of town, he'd worked late at the office every night catching up on paperwork. Before going home, he would swing by Ashley's place just to make sure everything looked okay. Then once he got home, he would fall into his regular routine.

He leaned back in his office chair, thinking just how much he missed Ashley. He hadn't figured he would miss her this deeply. Although he'd talked to her every night, he still missed her something crazy. He'd tried staying busy but found himself thinking of her and smiling when he remembered something she said or something they did together last weekend. Just yesterday he had caught Tyler looking at him as if he'd thought Ray had lost his mind. In a way, he had. He could finally admit he'd lost his mind over Ashley.

Ray rubbed his hand down his face in frustration. He should not have gotten attached to her when he knew they were only short-term.

"You're working late again tonight, Ray?"

He glanced up at Tyler. "Not too late. I thought you left."

"I decided to hang around and wait on Marie. She's meeting me at Lafitte's at seven."

Ray tossed a paper clip on his desk. "How's her pregnancy going?"

Tyler smiled. "So far, so good. She's feeling a lot better about it since she did that DNA test."

Ray lifted a brow. "What DNA test?"

Tyler eased down in the chair across from Ray's desk. "Marie was adopted and never knew her biological parents. One of her stepsisters, who was probably jealous of Marie being added to the household, used to tease her while growing up that Marie's mother had some sort of blood disease, which meant there was a good chance our baby would have it. Marie had decided never to have children, although she's been tested and all the results were negative. She refused to take any chances."

"What made her change her mind?"

"That DNA test. The results not only broke down her ethnicity but it also gives you a health profile. It turned out her stepsister had lied. There is no blood disease in either her father's or mother's families. The company also lets people opt in to being contacted by distant relatives, if they're open to it, but she didn't have any hits on that. Still, just knowing she didn't have to worry about any genetic disease has been such a relief."

Ray sat up in his chair. "But it's possible to sometimes track down relatives based on this DNA test?"

"Yes."

Ray began thinking. If he took that test, would it be possible for them to track down some of his relatives who might remember him? Did he truly want to know anything about his past now? Drawing in a deep breath, he knew that he did. He couldn't have the unknown always hanging over his head forever. Especially if he truly wanted to have a future with Ashley.

Future with Ashley?

Where on earth had that thought come from? He couldn't have a future with anyone if he was truly a married man. What if he found out he was?

At least he would know. Hell, it could be like Dr. Martin said and his wife could have moved on with her life. But if there were children, he would want to get to know them, regardless if he remembered them or not.

And if he discovered he was a free man, then he would ardently pursue Ashley like he wanted to. He would continue to give her time to get over her dead husband but he felt she was doing that now.

"Tyler, could you give me the name of the company that did this test for Marie?"

If Tyler found his request odd, he didn't show it. "Sure. I don't have it on me but I can call you with that information when I get home. It takes four to five weeks for the results to come back."

Ray nodded. That would be right before Ashley would be leaving at the end of the summer. It would be nice if he could discover something about his past before she left.

He didn't want to get his hopes up too much but the thought filled him with a type of joy he hadn't felt in a long time. "Thanks. I'd appreciate it."

ASHLEY PULLED HER luggage behind her as she entered her place back in Catalina Cove. Glad to be home. She smiled at how she thought of this place as

her home. While in Hardeeville, she had been antsy
to get back here because this was where Ray was.

She'd had a great time with Emmie, Suzanne
and Kim. They had wanted to know everything. Of
course, there were details that even her close friends
didn't need to know, and she'd deliberately skipped
over certain things. They kept saying again and again
how happy she looked. Even her parents had said
the same thing.

And speaking of her parents, it seemed that for
her father to finally get a backbone was the best
thing that could ever happen to her parents. After
Imogene's anger had worn off, it seemed she liked
the new Samuel. Ashley wondered if perhaps her
mother had deliberately been pushing her father over
the years into taking control because she was tired
of exerting hers. Ashley figured that was one thing
she'd never know.

All she knew was that when she'd dined with
them last night it had been the most pleasant experience she'd had with them in a long time. Even when
her father had announced their decision to move
back to Kansas permanently in about six months,
her mother hadn't protested. This time it had been
Ashley's jaw that had dropped.

She headed straight to her bedroom. The last time
she'd slept in this bed, Ray had been there with her.
All night. She still got sensuous quivers whenever
she remembered that night in vivid detail. She'd
missed him. It hadn't mattered that she'd talked to

him every night before getting in bed. She'd missed him just the same.

Deciding to unpack later, she moved to glance out the window and drew in a deep breath. She'd missed waking up to this view the last four days. She wondered if Ray was serious when he said he was interested in buying this place. She could envision him here and waking up in that bed without her.

No, she refused to see that. She had to believe he was beginning to feel for her what she already felt for him. She had to believe it was more than just two people sleeping together for him. She had to believe that.

Moving away from the window, she headed for the bathroom to take a shower. She had received a text message from Ray that morning before she'd left for the airport, inviting her to dinner. She'd texted him back that she would love to dine with him this evening. His response indicated he would pick her up at seven, but he hadn't said where they would be going. Honestly, it didn't matter as long as they were together. But knowing would have helped. Then she wouldn't have to wonder what to wear. She figured, when in doubt, wear a cute sundress and carry a jacket. That way she could dress it up or dress it down.

She had finished putting on her clothes and was about to apply lipstick when she heard the knock on her door. She glanced at the clock. It was seven exactly. Ray believed in being on time. Deciding to wait on the lipstick, she left her bedroom and headed toward the door, already feeling jolts of sexual energy rushing through her.

Taking a deep breath, she pressed to the door. "Who is it?"

"Ray."

She unlocked it and then said, "You can open it and come in." If she opened the door she would be tempted to throw herself in his arms the moment she saw him. Letting him do it would give her time to compose herself.

She took a step back and watched how the door slowly opened, first exposing a masculine thigh in gray dress slacks, and it only got better from there. By the time he stepped over the threshold, she was all but drooling. There was just something about a good-looking man, in good-looking clothes, who smelled good.

And good old Ray Sullivan was looking at her like he thought she was good, too. Good enough to eat. Naughty her, but she hoped he kept that thought.

He closed the door behind him and leaned against it with his hands shoved into the pockets of his slacks. She wondered if he knew that position made it quite obvious he wanted her. An erection didn't lie, especially not one the size of his.

"I missed you, Ashley."

She tilted her head to better look at him. "We talked every night."

"And?"

"Wasn't that enough?" she asked, wondering if they were actually going to leave here tonight. From the way they were looking at each other, there was a good chance they wouldn't.

"No, that wasn't enough. I could look at you every day and talk to you every hour and it still wouldn't be enough."

She wondered if he knew his words had a meaning she wasn't sure he wanted to make. But she knew in the bottom of her heart he had made them honestly. Deciding not to ask him to clarify, she asked, "What time is our dinner reservation and where are we going?"

He glanced at his watch. "Eight at Cagney Place. And you look gorgeous, by the way."

She smiled, pleased with his compliment. "And you look pretty dashing yourself."

"Do I?"

"Yes, Ray Sullivan, you do."

She watched as he slowly moved away from the door and started walking toward her. "I told myself I wouldn't kiss you."

"Why?"

"I might not be able to stop," he said easily. "Haven't you noticed that when it comes to kissing you, I don't have much control?"

Yes, she'd noticed, but she wasn't bothered by it since she hadn't any control while kissing him back. "Have I ever complained?"

"No, but we do need to make it to dinner on time," he pointed out.

"Ever heard of a quickie?" she asked boldly and then downplayed a blush. After all, this was her husband and she was free to do with him whatever she liked.

"Yes, I've heard of quickies. Not sure if I've ever participated in any."

He had. Numerous times. She could certainly attest to that. Most she'd orchestrated for not only his benefit but also for hers. "Then let me show you how it's done."

She reached up and wrapped her arms around his neck and lowered his mouth to hers.

THE MOMENT THEIR lips touched, Ray was a goner. Like kerosene being thrown on an already lit fire. Whatever she was doing with her tongue was driving him mad with desire. He took as much of her mouth torturing his as he could, then snatched his away.

Before he could draw in his next breath, she'd reached out, unzipped his pants and had his erected shaft in her hand. Swiftly maneuvering him against the closed door, she seemed to pounce on him like a cat and enfolded her legs around his waist. Instinctively, he cupped her bottom to balance her.

In a breathless whisper she said, "On birth control and safe. No reason to think you aren't, too."

That was all she said before tilting her body against his erection and sliding it inside of her. The mechanics of how she'd accomplished such a thing so easily without removing her panties vanished from his mind when, after arching her back, she began pummeling her body back and forth onto him, stopping just inches shy of disconnecting their bodies, before battering down on him again.

Her movements were precise and measured and he almost became weak in the knees. Hell, he'd never felt anything like this before, being skin to skin with her. The very thought that there wasn't a latex shield between them sent heat rushing to every part of him. He could feel her heat, her wetness, the way her inner muscles were clamping down hard on him. Right now she was the dominant one and he was at her mercy. Each time she thumped down, her chest would press against him, and he could feel her nipples through her dress.

Her eyes locked with his were hot and intense. He loved the way her hair hung to her shoulders, sweeping around her face with the movement of their bodies, almost in perfect sync. It was as if their bodies were dancing, the rhythm defined, the tempo indescribably sensual.

He felt himself get harder and harder inside of her. Bigger and bigger. Yet she was handling him a whole hell of a lot better than he was handling her. He started to tremble and released a guttural groan. "I can't hold on much longer."

"Then let go. I won't until you do," she said.

Her words were like a catalyst, and suddenly every muscle in his body seemed to explode, but what he concentrated on the most was the shaft buried deep inside of her. He felt the moment it detonated, and could imagine flooding her womb with his semen.

Jesus, it was too much when she began moving

faster and harder and then, precipitously, let out a scream as her body cascaded into a multitude of spasms. Her arms tightened around his neck and his grip tightened more on her bottom. She called his name over and over before lifting her head and crushing her mouth down on his. The moment her tongue slid inside his mouth, he captured it with his and began mating with it greedily. He loved the taste of her. Loved her scent. Loved every single thing about her. He loved...

He was snatched back to reality when she broke off the kiss. In a way he was glad. He didn't love her because he couldn't. He didn't have that right.

She stared at him and the most beautiful smile touched her lips. He was certain if he allowed it, Ashley would forever mess with his ever-loving mind.

"Did you enjoy that, Mr. Sullivan?" she asked when he slowly slid her down his body to stand back on her feet.

He watched her straighten her dress. Although he couldn't remember a thing from his past, he was certain he'd never done anything remotely this insane. "Yes, I definitely enjoyed it." Too damn much, he thought, tucking his manhood back inside and zipping his pants.

"Good. So now you know how it's done. I'm ready to leave for dinner now."

CHAPTER TWENTY-EIGHT

"WELCOME TO MY HOME, Ashley."

Ashley smiled up at Kaegan. "Thanks for inviting me."

"Hey, don't I get a welcome, too?" Ray asked, grinning.

"No, because your welcome is automatic. In fact, I'm depending on you to show her around. I've got cooking duties tonight."

Ray rolled his eyes. "It doesn't take a lot of time to boil seafood, Kaegan."

"No, but tonight I decided to grill as well. When you finish showing Ashley around, you know how to find your way to the party house."

When Kaegan walked off, Ashley glanced over at Ray. "The party house?"

Ray laughed. "Yes, one of the rooms on this floor is a corridor that leads to another building where he hosts his parties."

She nodded. "He gives a lot of them?"

"Not really. When he does entertain, it's mostly for his employees. He likes rewarding them when they break records, reach milestones or if the company gets a big deal."

"That's a good incentive," she said.

"Yes, it is. Don't get me wrong. He still gives good bonuses as well. If it weren't for his bonuses, I would never have saved up enough to start the boat touring company."

Ashley glanced around when they moved toward the staircase. "This house is humongous. You actually stayed here for six months before getting on your feet?" He'd told her how Kaegan had not only hired him but had given him a roof over his head when he first came to Catalina Cove.

"No. Kaegan hadn't built this house yet. We lived next door in his parents' home, which has since been torn down. It was much smaller with three bedrooms and two bathrooms. About the size of my place now and it's where Kaegan lived through his childhood. But all this is Chambray land. Land that Kaegan's ancestors lived on and took care of."

"Well, he certainly has a beautiful home here on the bayou. And I thought I had a beautiful view to wake up to every morning."

"You do have a beautiful view. Kaegan just has the bayou in his front yard."

Ashley knew what Ray meant. On the drive over, he'd shared that living on the bayou with Kaegan during that time had been a real adventure. He'd also told her how many cans of repellent he'd purchased over those six months because of the mosquitoes. That was why Kaegan had several lit mosquito torches lining the area.

As Ray showed her around, she thought Kaegan's home was beautiful. Ray mentioned that, due to the possibility of hurricanes, Kaegan had built a home that could withstand up to four-hundred-mile-an-hour winds and the tilt of the foundation, that wasn't even noticeable, was a deterrence to flooding.

She thought the place was huge for just one man but figured Kaegan was looking to the future when he would settle down and have a family. When she walked out on the huge screened-in patio, she was surprised to see Bryce. She figured Bryce would be the last person who would attend one of Kaegan's parties and said as much to Ray.

He smiled. "Kaegan invites her because she's Vashti's best friend and she shows up, I guess as a matter of principle. Then they ignore each other all night. Although I don't know what happened to break them up, they seem to have a love-hate relationship that neither will address. I think there is hurt on both sides."

Ashley couldn't help wondering what had torn Kaegan and Bryce apart. Why were they fighting hard to pretend neither existed when—if anyone watched them for any period of time—it was clearly obvious they couldn't keep their eyes off each other?

"There's Sawyer and Vashti," Ray said, leading her over to the couple, who stood talking to two men.

Vashti introduced the men as Isaac Elloran, a divorcé, and Vaughn Miller. Both had grown up in the cove and were classmates of Kaegan, Bryce and Vashti's. Isaac had moved back to town a couple of months ago, and Vaughn had moved back close to two years ago. Ashley thought Isaac and Vaughn were nice guys who seemed glad to be back living in the cove.

A few other people came to join them then, and Vashti made more introductions.

The food was good and there was plenty of it. Tents were set up outside where huge buckets of seafood—blue crabs, shrimp, crawfish and lobster—were being served, as well as grilled spare ribs. Ray and Ashley joined Sawyer and Vashti at a table with several other couples.

There was dancing and Ray took her hand and led her to the dance floor. Devon had always been a great dancer and it seemed Ray was as well. He admitted he didn't know why and figured he must have danced a lot in his other life because he liked doing it. He also admitted he hadn't danced in front of a group before now.

Ashley was glad Ray was shedding some of his inhibitions, and she wanted to believe she had something to do with it. Vashti certainly thought so. Twice, she'd pulled Ashley aside and said she was seeing a different Ray. One who was beginning to make peace with himself.

He had spent the night with her last night after bringing her home from dinner at Cagney Place. They'd made love all night, as if making up for the time they'd been apart. They'd even shared breakfast together that morning before he left to go home to get ready for work.

"Now that you're back, would you be interested in a boat ride this coming Sunday?" he asked as he took her around the dance floor for a slow number. She loved being held in his arms this way. Reminded her of old times.

"Yes, I'd love to. Thanks for inviting me."

He tightened his arms around her. "I can't think of any other woman I want to spend my time with, Ashley."

She pressed her face against his chest so he wouldn't see the tears forming in her eyes. She'd thought she would never hear such words from her husband again. Thinking she'd lost him forever had been the most tragic period in her life. No one could feel her pain, hurt and even at times her anger. Yes, anger. She'd felt Devon had been snatched from her too soon. She hadn't been prepared for the loss. And now he was back and she was here in his arms.

"Ready to leave?" Ray leaned down and whispered close to her ear. His warm breath bathed her skin, causing heat to slowly drum through her.

She lifted her head and met his gaze. "I am if you are."

"I am."

"Then I suggest we go tell everyone good-night."

RAY'S STOMACH DID somersaults on the drive back to Ashley's home. She tried engaging him in conversation but hearing her voice only made him want her that much more. He knew the degree of his desire for her was crazy, but there wasn't anything he could do about it. He needed her like yesterday and wanted her like right now.

When he'd arrived at her place she'd opened the door and stood there wearing jeans and a pink blouse that made her look feminine as hell. All he could think about was that quickie they'd had the day before. He was still thinking about it.

"You're quiet, Ray," Ashley said when he walked her to her door. "Are you okay?"

Did she want the honest-to-goodness truth? He wasn't sure but decided to give it to her anyway. "I've decided there's just something about that quickie yesterday."

She glanced up at him. "Oh, what about it?"

Besides liking it? he thought. "It made me want you even more."

"And you had me. Quite a bit, in fact. Last night when we returned from dinner, I could barely get inside the door."

He smiled at the memory. He had news for her. She'd barely get inside the door tonight either. He had been tempted to tell her about that DNA kit he'd done but decided not to do that. He hadn't told anyone about it, not even Kaegan and Sawyer. For him it was private and he wanted to keep it that way. He was hoping the results could perhaps add pieces to the puzzle of his memory.

"Ray?" She had pulled her key from her purse.

"Yes?"

"Is something bothering you?"

"I told you what's bothering me, Ashley."

"That's all?"

He smiled as he followed her inside. "Trust me. That's enough."

He closed the door behind them and pulled her into his arms.

CHAPTER TWENTY-NINE

RAY ENTERED HIS office and couldn't help the smile
that touched his lips. It was hard to believe it had
been almost four weeks since the night of Kaegan's
party. Clearly, waking up to a beautiful woman
every morning was pretty damn good for any man's
ego. However, when that woman was Ashley Ryan,
that was really putting a triple spread of icing on
the cake.

On top of that, he'd gotten an investor. The
wealthiest man in the cove had met with him today.
Over the past five years, Reid LaCroix had taken
it upon himself to help several small businesses
in town by offering low-interest loans. LaCroix
detested change and felt it was important to keep
local businesses in the cove thriving while keeping big corporations out. He saw assisting certain
small businesses he felt were on the climb to success as a way to do it. Both Kaegan and Vashti had
been recipients of LaCroix's generosity and now
so was Ray.

With the loan in place, his business could expand
the way he'd dreamed. He was pleased with how
both his business and his personal lives were going.

Ray thought about that time Ashley had offered to be his investor and he'd turned her down. At the time he hadn't wanted to mix business with pleasure. He didn't have that complication with Reid LaCroix. Their relationship was strictly one of business and he preferred it that way.

He and Ashley spent a lot of time together and had established a routine where she either stayed at his place at night or he stayed at hers. There were days when she would come to the marina and have lunch with him. He looked forward to them. They went to the movies, played video games together, and he'd even gone shopping with her in New Orleans a couple of times.

Then there were the times spent in bed. Each and every time they made love, he'd come close to telling her just how he felt, but he couldn't until he knew he could offer her a life with him.

After getting a cup of coffee, he settled down at his desk and switched on his computer. There were a lot of things he needed to do before the start of his workday. For starters, he was corresponding with the seller of a boat that had caught his eye.

Pulling up his email, he noticed one from the company that had done his DNA testing. His heart began beating hard as he clicked on it.

Hi, Ray,
Your DNA results are in and attached is your ethnicity breakdown.
Good news! We have located a DNA match. See

information below. We have made it convenient
to contact this person through us. If interested,
hit the contact button and an email will be sent to
your DNA match.

Ray studied the lone name: Kurtis Blaylock. He
frowned, trying to remember if the name rang a
bell, and it didn't. It indicated Blaylock was a top
match—first cousin.

He leaned back in his chair, knowing whatever
decision he made would change the rest of his life.
Kurtis Blaylock might very well be the only link
Ray had to his past. Was he ready to face whatever
this past included? What if he was married as he
assumed and was possibly a father? What about his
relationship with Ashley?

Ray knew that Ashley was the reason he'd done
the DNA test in the first place. If he was married,
there was no way he could stay married to a woman
he didn't remember. She would be a stranger to him.
Therefore, he'd decided if he was a married man,
he would ask for a divorce. If there were kids involved, he would want to be a part of their lives.
The only woman he could imagine ever being with
was Ashley.

He suddenly went still. He also knew the reason he felt that way. He had fallen in love with her.

There was no need to wonder how such a thing
had happened since Ashley was a woman any man
would love. It was just that simple. But then again,
nothing was simple, especially a serious relation-

326 FORGET ME NOT

ship with her. She deserved better, not a man without memory of his past and what was in it.

He wanted to find out. He needed to know. Sighing deeply, he sent Mr. Blaylock an email and hoped he got a response. He'd even included his phone number, in case the man was inclined to call him.

If Blaylock was a link to his past, he would deal with it. The problem was not knowing one way or the other.

"YOU LOOK HAPPY, ASHLEY."

Ashley smiled at Vashti, who'd invited her to lunch at Shelby by the Sea. It was a beautiful day and the view of the ocean was breathtaking from where they sat on the patio. "I am so happy, Vashti, that sometimes I have to pinch myself to make sure I'm not dreaming. And I believe Ray is happy as well."

Vashti chuckled. "I do, too. Kaegan and Sawyer certainly think so. They've never seen him so carefree and laid-back. We're all rooting for you and Ray, you know."

Yes, she did know. The three were Ray's friends, but over the past months they'd also become hers.

And she and Ray were developing a close relationship. Ray enjoyed reading and was well versed on a number of topics. He liked museums and they'd gone to plenty together, doing overnight trips to Shreveport and Little Rock. The only thing they hadn't talked about was her leaving Catalina Cove. Her lease ran out in two weeks. Their summer fling would be over and she was to return to South Carolina.

She tried not to think about it, although she knew he was just as aware of the time as she was. What if he hadn't fallen in love with her by then? Had she been wrong to assume he would just because of how they'd met years ago?

She recalled the night he'd shared with her the pain he felt at knowing he hadn't been reported missing by anyone. She could tell by the tone of his voice he was hurt and disappointed. Keeping that truth from him only made her dilemma more difficult because she knew the reason she hadn't looked for him.

She felt antsy about revealing the truth if he ever did get his memory back. And if he didn't or if he didn't fall in love with her, it would mean lying to him forever. She was walking a fine line. She was damned if she did and damned if she didn't.

"Ashley?"

She stopped studying the food on her plate. "Sorry, did you say something?"

Vashti gave her a supportive smile and reached out and touched her arm. "For what this is worth, although Ray might not have expressed how he feels, I do believe he's fallen in love with you. I've always seen the way you look at him, but now I'm seeing the way he looks at you. I believe he has decisions to make. Big ones. He has this fear of building a future with you only to have it destroyed if his memory returns. Of course, that's not going to happen, since you are one and the same, but he doesn't know that."

"And I plan to tell him when I'm sure he loves

me because then it won't matter. I need for him to tell me how he feels."

"I believe he will. You have two weeks and anything can happen by then."

Ashley nodded. Vashti was right. Anything could happen and she hoped when it did it leaned in her favor.

CHAPTER THIRTY

RAY PULLED INTO Ashley's driveway a little disappointed. It had been three days and he guessed it had been too much to hope that Kurtis Blaylock would have returned his call by now. Refusing to twiddle his thumbs while he waited, Ray had tried researching the guy on the internet by looking at several social media accounts, but nothing came up for his name.

Getting out of the truck, he headed for Ashley's door. At least he had a little bit of good news heading into the weekend. Already he had bought the boat he needed and it would be delivered to him this weekend.

He had come here straight from work, which was now the norm. He wouldn't say he had just as many clothes at Ashley's place as he did at his own, but he had enough things here to shower, change and take her out. And he loved taking her out. Loved being seen with her. Sharing a meal. And for a man who a few months ago preferred his solitude, that said a lot.

It was all Ashley's doing. She had walked into his life and it had changed tremendously. Well, she hadn't actually walked in, but still, the way they'd met was remarkable. He would lie beside her and remember that day. The day he could have lost her before realizing just what a jewel she was. Before realizing what she would come to mean to him. And a part of him wanted to believe that he meant something to her as well. He would often notice her looking at him, studying him when she thought his concentration was elsewhere. Little did she know, his concentration, whether obvious or not, was always on her.

As he got closer to the door, he could hear music coming from the inside. She loved playing soft jazz. It was her favorite. It was his favorite, too.

Suddenly, he stopped walking.

It was his, too…

Was it? Yes, he enjoyed listening to it but only because he had no other choice with her around. Right? Now he wasn't sure. And why did the names of popular jazz singers flow through his mind when he assumed he'd never been a fan of jazz?

He began walking again. That was another thing he needed to put into his journal. Since he never knew whose place he would spend the night at, he now kept his journal in the truck. That way he could still jot down things before going to bed. It still wasn't easy not knowing his real name, where he was from, his birthday, practically anything and everything from his past, but he could make a life for himself and try to forge ahead anyway.

The question he needed to ask himself was, had he truly forged ahead? What if Blaylock never called?

What if he was still left in the dark about his past? Would he walk out of the shadows and into the light with Ashley regardless? In two weeks she would be leaving Catalina Cove. Then what? Right now, he couldn't imagine how his life would be without her here. But did he have a right to ask her to stay when he couldn't offer her a future?

He paused when he reached her door. He *could* offer her a future. According to the law, he was legally free to build a new life for himself, including remarrying. He'd always known it but had never considered taking advantage of it, until Ashley. The big question was whether or not she would enter into such an arrangement.

Was marriage something she'd want after losing her husband the way she had? Or was she satisfied with things the way they were between them?

There was only one way to find out. He would give Kurtis Blaylock another week. If Ray didn't hear from him by then, he would tell Ashley just how he felt and hope she felt or could feel the same way about him.

Using the key she'd given him last week, he let himself in and then stopped dead in his tracks. "Whoa!"

She stood in the middle of her living room dressed in a very revealing, almost transparent nightie. Nightie? It was still daylight outside. His gaze roamed up and down her and he felt himself get hard.

"Hello, Ray," she said, taking a few steps toward him.

He closed the door behind him, feeling weak in

the knees. All he could do was stand there, lean back against the door for support and look at her. Desire became a pulsing, throbbing need, and it took a while before he could speak.

"What's going on, Ashley?"

That was a stupid question when he could clearly see what was going on. He could definitely *clearly* see. Every single inch of her incredible silky-looking brown skin. Every exotic curve on her body. This thing she was wearing would be the perfect attire for any man's X-rated fantasies. She was standing there sexiness personified. And what had she done with her hair? It had that Meghan Markle look. He'd heard some refer to it as messy but he thought of it as sexy.

As he watched her, getting more turned on by the second, she used her tongue to stroke her bottom lip with a sensual lick, making his erection throb even more. Even her toes were painted a different color than they had been this morning. They had been a hot red. Now they were an ocean blue.

"I thought I'd seduce you today, Ray."

Hell, it couldn't get any plainer than that. He'd wanted to take her out but he was just as fine with staying in. Especially when her outfit held so many promises. Her entire appearance reflected more than primal attraction. It spoke of a need that went straight to his bone.

"And in case you're wondering, I've prepared dinner. We can eat afterward."

No need to ask after what. "I need to shower," he said, feeling a deep lump in his throat.

"I know. I have the water going already. Just follow me."

She turned and he watched the sinfully erotic movement of her hips as she moved toward the bedroom. Licking his lips, he couldn't do anything but follow behind her while his erection ached against his jeans.

When he got to the bedroom, he noticed the bed was already turned down. And candles around, ready to be lit. Hell, he could get used to this. Coming home to a half-naked woman every evening. Making love to her every night. Waking up to her every morning.

He stood there nearly drowning in her. Her scent. Everything about her. "All this and dinner? You've been busy."

She shrugged barely covered shoulders. "You think?"

He could see evidence of her work. "I know."

She smiled. "Your bath awaits and I plan to sit in that chair right there until you come back. Everything you need is ready for you. When you finish, I'll be ready for you out here."

Ready for him? A rush of anticipation clawed his insides. A seductive promise. One he knew she would keep.

ASHLEY SAT DOWN and waited like she told Ray she would do. They had only ten more days together. Then he expected her to pack up and return to South Carolina. There was no way she could do that when her heart was here. No way she could live in Hardeeville when the one man she'd mourned for the past three years was living here in Catalina Cove.

It mattered not that even after spending time with him for nearly three months he still didn't know her. Nor did it matter that she wasn't sure if during that time he was falling in love with her. What mattered now more than anything was that she loved him, had enough love to sustain them forever if she needed to.

What she needed to do was make sure he wanted her to stay in the cove. She would leave in two weeks but had every plan to return. She even contemplated selling the house in Hardeeville because she could never live there when he was here.

The big question of the hour was, how would he feel about her deciding to stay? Had she miscalculated and he was ready for their affair to end? Had she read the signs wrong? She had honestly thought something would have broken through his memory by now.

So far, nothing had. Not their lovemaking. Not any of the truthful information about her past life she'd shared with him. And not their kisses, which was something that had always been one of their favorite pastimes. Was his memory so locked back in his mind that he would never regain it?

She'd known there was that possibility, so she'd hoped he would fall in love with her as Ashley Ryan, a woman he did not know. He was almost there;

she could feel it. Her plan was to push him more. If not toward the finish line, then at least give him something that would make him want her to stay in Catalina Cove.

If she did, and Ray never regained his memories, things would become more complicated. Her parents would eventually want to come and visit her. They would want to meet Ray and would know immediately who he was. Her father might be able to play along for Ray's benefit but her mother could not.

But for now that didn't matter. That was the least of her problems. It was time to finally tell her parents the truth that Devon was alive. She would do so when she returned home. Hopefully, after hearing the complete story, they would understand why she needed more time with Devon, without their interference. Again, she could see her father understanding, but her mother, not so much. It would take her father to handle Imogene, and it seemed her father was still doing so. Ashley was glad of that.

More than anything, Ashley was a woman intent on fighting for what she remembered, even if Ray didn't, as a love and romance of a lifetime.

The sound of the shower being turned off reached her ears. Moments later the door opened and there her husband stood, naked. He hadn't even taken the time to wrap a towel around his waist. He stood there unashamed, straight, tall and masculine, in all his glorious splendor. For a moment, seeing him made her feel light-headed with love.

He said nothing as he stood there and looked at

her and all kinds of sensations curled her stomach, with potent need lapping close behind. She was certain if he touched her right now, she would incinerate. On the other hand, if he didn't, she was liable to die right here and now.

He began walking toward her with that Devon Ryan strut that Ray Sullivan now owned so well. It had to be the sexiest walk ever made by a man. Definitely the sexiest one she'd ever seen. Hands down. He came to a stop in front of her, his knees touching hers, causing shivers to pass through her.

He reached out his hand to her and she took it. Meeting his gaze, she cleared her throat. "Dinner is ready if you want to eat first."

He shook his head and said in a deep, husky voice, "Dinner can wait. I'd rather make love to you now."

And she wanted to make love to him. "All right."

He tugged on her hand and pulled her from the chair. Because he didn't step back, her body was pressed against him. She could feel every fine muscle on his body. Every hard plane. And she could definitely feel his erection pressing hard against her middle. Right there at the juncture of her thighs.

She beamed at him and that was as far as she got. He swept her off her feet and into his arms to carry her over to the bed. He placed her on it and joined her there, taking her mouth with an urgency she felt all through her body.

Ashley was convinced there was something about making love with Ray that made her want to extend herself, be open to all sorts of ideas. Although some were things she'd tried with Devon, thanks to Ray's loss of memory, he had no recollection of them. Like the use of her mouth on his body. Tonight she wanted to concentrate on his taste.

He whipped her nightie off in a flash and she rose up on her knees to grip powerful shoulders, needing to mate her mouth with his. He was a great kisser, and in return, she was using her tongue to show him how much she enjoyed having his inside her mouth.

Whenever they made love, the union was intense and left her needing more and wanting to give more. There was only so much she could take, and when she pulled back from the kiss, he wouldn't let up. Now he was trailing hot, wet kisses along the side of her neck and licking her skin in a way that had her moaning his name.

Then she did something she knew he didn't expect; she pushed him on his back and hovered over him. Before he could switch their positions, her mouth was there, on his chest, licking her way down toward his belly. She didn't have to look up to see the deep, hot intensity in his eyes. She felt it and her breathing quickened.

She knew what she wanted and where her mouth was headed. Parts of her felt thrilled at the prospect. She and Devon had long ago decided that their bedroom was their sanctuary, a place to worship each other's bodies and stimulate each other's minds. Each time she and Ray made love, she hoped he was getting more and more comfortable with the thought that with her nothing was taboo if the couple agreed on it.

It had been like that with the quickies they'd engaged in whenever the mood hit, which seemed quite a bit. Or the orgasms during their kisses when pushed over the edge. She'd tried exposing him to her sexual greed in moderation, and it wasn't long before she'd discovered that, just like Devon, Ray was a generous bed partner, one open to new ideas. They had tried new positions for their pleasure, thrilling them both.

But she had yet to taste him as Ray Sullivan.

Her mouth had known every inch of Devon's body, was well familiar with the taste of his skin, and she wanted the same with Ray. A shiver of anticipation raced through her.

Still licking his chest, she reached down and took his engorged hardness in her hand, immediately liked the way it felt. His moans reached her ears and she knew he liked her touching him there. Her mouth traveled lower and she licked around his navel a few times.

Slowly, she lifted her head up and looked into his eyes before she captured his manhood with her mouth.

He moaned when her tongue glided over him, loving the texture of his skin and his manly aroma. And she loved running her fingers through the thatch of curls that encased his erection. He was perfect in every way and he was hers.

She felt his hands in her hair while her mouth

worked him. For her, this intimate act was just a way to let him know she craved every inch of him.

When his hand tightened on her head, she tried locking her mouth down on him, but he wouldn't let her. He jerked her up, and in a quick-fire move, now she was the one on her back with him staring down at her. The look in his eyes was hot and blazing.

So he'd know what to expect, she whispered, "Next time I want the entire shebang and not just a sample taste."

Instead of saying anything, he held her hands over her head in a tight grip as he angled himself in the perfect position above her. Then he eased down and their gazes held as his erection slid between her womanly folds that were already wet for his entry.

"Ray…"

He continued to stare down at her and she found herself becoming lost in the depth of his dark eyes. He kept going, pressing hard, sinking deeper, and her body was reacting to him being so fully embedded inside of her.

Then he began thrusting, pulling almost out and then plunging hard into her again and again. Over and over he continued, establishing a rhythm she quickly adjusted to. She deliberately flexed her inner muscles, intent on pulling everything she could out of him. He increased the pace, quickly driving her over the edge.

He threw his head back as he continued to ride her as if his very life depended on it. Whether he realized it or not, he was surrendering his all to her each time they made love and her body accepted his capitulation with all the love in her heart.

When his body jerked into an orgasm, hers followed. He released a loud groan at the same time she did and she could feel the heat of his semen filling her core and plunging her deeper and deeper into earth-shattering climax.

The scent of sex filled the air, and as her body released her from what seemed to be never-ending spasms, he lowered his face toward hers and took her mouth in a hunger that pushed her into another orgasm.

And she pushed him, and once again, they experienced another explosion together, knowing before daybreak, there would be many more. She had three years to make up for.

CHAPTER THIRTY-ONE

RAY'S CELL PHONE rang the moment he walked inside his house. He'd only intended to be here for a minute, just long enough to use the clippers to shape up his beard. He and Ashley had plans to join Sawyer and Vashti for dinner.

Pulling the phone off his belt, he glanced at the number and didn't recognize the caller but decided to answer it anyway. With LaCroix as a solid investor, he had the funds to lease more dock space. There was a chance the caller was someone from a company he needed to talk to.

"Ray Sullivan."

Although Ray could hear breathing on the other end, the caller didn't say anything. He repeated, "This is Ray Sullivan."

"Yes, this is Kurtis Blaylock. I got your message through Your Legacy. Sorry for the delay. I've been out of the country."

Ray nodded. It had been close to a week and he'd figured the man wouldn't be calling. "I appreciate you getting back with me."

"No problem, but there must be some mistake because I don't have any living relatives. I paid for the full package, but really I only wanted my DNA results for my ethnicity breakdown and nothing more. I wasn't looking for long-lost relatives because I don't have any."

Ray sat down at the kitchen table. "What makes you think you don't have any living relatives?"

"Because I don't. My parents died a few years back. My father didn't have any siblings, nor did he have any other children. My mother had one younger brother. He and his wife had a son who was killed about three years ago. He was my only cousin."

About three years ago? Ray's breath began coming out rapidly and he quickly fought to even it out. "What happened?"

"Car accident."

Ray swallowed. "And there was a body?"

Kurtis Blaylock didn't answer for a minute. "Why do you need to know that?"

It was obvious the man was suspicious of his motives, so he knew the best way to handle things to get the answers he sought was to be honest. "I woke up in the hospital almost three years ago badly beaten and with amnesia. I couldn't remember anything, including my name. I know that might sound farfetched, but I'm telling the truth. If I need to, I can put you in touch with the doctor who treated me when I finally came out of my coma in Chicago."

"Chicago? Coma?"

"Yes, I was in a coma for three weeks. I'm told I was airlifted from a place called Tulip, Indiana, to

Chicago because they had a better medical facility there to treat me."

"Wow, I'm sorry about that, man." Then as if Kurtis Blaylock wanted to believe him, he said, "No, there wasn't a body because the car went off the bridge into the Ohio River. Neither the car or a body was recovered. The family saw the accident on traffic videos. Devon had been speeding."

"Devon?"

"Yes, Devon."

He'd never thought the name Devon was common but evidently it was since that was the name of Ashley's dead husband...who'd also been killed in a car accident when his car had gone off the bridge and into the Ohio River.

Ray's heart began pounding in his chest painfully hard. The hairs on his arms rose. "Did he have a wife or children?"

Kurtis Blaylock didn't say anything. Then as if he didn't like where the lines of questions were leading, he said, "Look, man, I've told you all you need to know. There was a mix-up. I'm sure of it. You aren't my cousin and I'm sorry Your Legacy made a mistake about there being a strong connection in our DNA. I wish you the best." And then there was a click in Ray's ear.

Ray wasn't surprised. Even with his offer to put Blaylock in contact with his doctor, the man hadn't felt comfortable telling him anything else when he inquired as to whether there had been a wife and children.

Ray honestly didn't know what to make of what he'd been told. Should he disregard what Blaylock had said? Just believe that he didn't know any more than he had before he'd received the call? Blaylock was convinced Your Legacy had made a mistake. Had they really?

And from the conversation he'd just had, Blaylock's cousin, whose name was Devon, had been killed in a car accident. Just like Ashley's husband. And then there was the mention of the Ohio River.

Ray wanted to believe there was no way there was a connection, but those facts just seemed too coincidental. Why was he suddenly seeing red flags? This would be something for someone with a cop's mind to figure out. Someone like Sawyer.

Had he been hanging around Sawyer for so long that now he'd developed a suspicious mind? "Get real, Sullivan," he muttered as he headed toward the bedroom to get his clippers. "You're pulling at straws that are making you think crazy stuff. There's no way any of this could be connected to Ashley and her not telling you if it was. Coincidences do happen and this is just one of those times."

But still. There was the three-year time frame. The name Devon. The car going into the Ohio River. For some reason, those were three things he just couldn't overlook. Instead of entering his bedroom, he made a right turn into his home office.

Sitting down at his desk, he turned on the computer. He searched Ashley's name. Automatically, several Ashley Ryans came up with photos. He recognized his Ashley immediately.

His Ashley?

Telling himself it was curiosity and nothing more that pushed him to find out more about Ashley's deceased husband, he checked for a Facebook and Twitter account for Devon Ryan and found nothing.

Remembering she'd once told him her husband was a staunchly professional businessman, Ray decided to try LinkedIn. He still didn't find anything and concluded after three years if there had been any sites belonging to the man on social media, they would have been taken down by now.

He went to the website for StayNTouch. Most of the information he read he already knew because Ashley had shared it with him and he'd visited the site before. There were nice photographs of Ashley, the woman she'd told him about who was her partner and good friend, Emmie Givens, and members of her staff.

Ray leaned back in his chair, questioning what he was doing sitting here trying to research information about Ashley's husband when nothing about the man had made him curious before. But no matter how hard he tried, he could not dismiss the goose bumps still rippling along his arms.

There was a link beneath one of Ashley's photos that led to her bio. He clicked on it and read it. Again there was nothing printed that she hadn't told him about. She was born in Kansas, graduated with a degree from Harvard, got married a year after graduation and was married five years to Devon Ryan. He read about the foundation she had established in her husband's memory. The Devon Ryan Foundation. Now, that was something he hadn't known about. Probably only because the topic never came up.

He searched for newspaper articles about Devon Ryan's death, and within seconds an article from the *Hardeeville Today* appeared and with it was a photograph of Devon Ryan.

Ray suddenly felt the blood drain from his face at the same time his heart began pounding painfully hard in his chest. The photo staring back at him shared his likeness.

It was absolute. Unless Ray had a twin somewhere, he and Devon Ryan were the same man.

His guts suddenly clenched at what that meant and he suddenly recoiled at the thought of Ashley's duplicity. For a minute he couldn't move his fingers to click on the link to Devon Ryan's obituary. It was as if Ray's hands were frozen from shock.

For a minute it felt as if he couldn't breathe and he fought to draw in a deep breath. His mind became jumbled with all kinds of questions. There was no way Ashley hadn't recognized him, although he hadn't remembered her. Why hadn't she been truthful to him? Why had she played this getting-to-know-you game with him?

Anger, the intensity he'd never felt before for anyone, coiled in the pit of his stomach and he nearly knocked his chair over. He suddenly felt those earlier goose bumps replaced by sweat that ran cold and fast down his armpits. Anger was a new sensation with him. He'd gotten upset before but never filled with a degree of anger that quickly slipped into rage.

Ashley had lied to him. The first woman he'd allowed himself to fully trust in three years, a woman he'd fallen in love with, had played him. For what purpose, he didn't know, but as he stormed out the room, out the house and to his truck, he was determined to find out.

CHAPTER THIRTY-TWO

ASHLEY STOOD AT the mirror in her bedroom as she finished styling her hair. She was excited about tonight because it was the first time she and Ray would be joining another couple for dinner. Namely, Sawyer and Vashti.

Tonight they would be dining at the Lighthouse. The cove's lighthouse turned restaurant was the place to dine but you had to make reservations weeks, sometimes months, in advance to get a table. Using his connections, Sawyer had managed to get their reservation for tonight.

She was excited. She and Vashti had become good friends and she knew how close Ray and Sawyer's friendship was. Another reason she was excited was because of the conversation she'd had today with Dr. Riggins. She'd told him she felt that although Ray hadn't committed to her in any way, she truly wanted to come clean and tell him the truth. At this stage of their relationship, she felt that he would be able to handle the truth without any setbacks.

Surprisingly, Dr. Riggins agreed, but only if she felt as strongly as she did that Ray had developed feelings for her, although he hadn't stated them. Like

Vashti had suggested, the reason he hadn't committed might very well be the unknown wife. Removing that factor might be what Ray needed. More than anything, she wanted to believe that. She had selected a sexy dress for tonight, and then for later, she'd chosen an even sexier negligee.

When her phone rang, she recognized the ringtone. It was Devon's cousin, Kurtis. Although there had been a four-year difference in their ages, Devon and Kurtis had always been close. Kurt had been best man at their wedding and had considered Devon more a younger brother than a cousin.

Kurt owned an international retail business and traveled a lot. More often than not, he spent more time at his place in Paris than he did in the States. He was probably calling to let her know he was back in the country. She hadn't talked to him in about six months. He had been her pillar of strength after Devon's death and had taken losing his cousin hard.

She clicked on the phone. "Hello, Kurt."

"Ashley, how are you?"

"I'm fine. What about you?"

"Doing well. You're still in Louisiana?"

"Yes, I'm still in Louisiana." She'd texted him months ago to let him know she needed time to herself but hadn't elaborated as to why. Nor had she told him where exactly in Louisiana she'd gone to. Nobody knew that other than her three closest friends. Had she told Kurt that Devon was alive, there was no way she could have kept him from returning to the States immediately.

"I just had a strange conversation with a guy a short while ago, Ash. A conversation you need to know about."

Ashley lifted her brow. "Oh? What was it about?"

"A man called because of the results of a DNA test he'd taken. Because we'd used the same company, he was sent my name as a close match. He sent a message through the company we used, asking me to contact him. At first I disregarded his request since I know I don't have any cousins. But out of curiosity, I called him back today."

Ashley moved to sit on the edge of the bed. She understood, since as far as they knew, Devon was his only cousin. "And?"

"And the minute he answered the phone I was taken aback. He actually sounded like Devon. But since I knew that was impossible, I regrouped. He wanted to ask about the test results to see how the two of us were related. I told him there must be some mistake because I didn't have a living cousin, and that my only cousin, on either of my parents' side, had been killed in an automobile accident three years ago."

Ashley nervously nibbled on her bottom lip. The hairs on the back of her neck stood up. "Was he satisfied with that?"

"I'm not sure. Not certain if what he told me next is true or not but he claimed he'd been in some kind of an accident three years ago and had woken up in the hospital without his memory."

Ashley jumped up, certain blood had drained

from her face. "Did he give you his name?" she asked, nearly frantic.

"Yes, and calm down, Ash. I figured the call wasn't on the up-and-up when he asked if Devon had a wife and children. That's when I ended the call."

"What was his name, Kurt?" she asked, hearing the edge of hysteria in her voice and certain Kurt heard it, too. "I need to know his name."

"Ashley, are you okay?"

"What's his name, Kurt?" she repeated again, agitated. Needing desperately to know.

"He said his name was Ray Sullivan."

"Oh, my God!" She forced back the urge to scream.

"Ashley? Are you all right?"

"No. Yes. Look, Kurt. I need to go." She needed to get to Ray. What if he put two and two together? The information might cause a setback with him finding out that way.

"Ashley, what's going on?"

"I can't tell you now, but I promise to call you back later, Kurt, and tell you everything. Bye." She quickly clicked off the phone, grabbed her purse off the bed and headed for the door.

Ray had said he was going straight home after work before coming to her place. Chances were he was home, and she hoped what he'd discovered, if he'd figured out anything, hadn't—

At that moment her front door flew open in a way that nearly rocked it off the hinges. Ray slammed it behind him and he stood there looking madder than hell. His legs were braced apart with arms folded across his chest. And if looks could kill, she would be dead.

When he spoke, his voice trembled in rage. "Why didn't you tell me I was your supposedly dead husband?"

CHAPTER THIRTY-THREE

"I CAN EXPLAIN, RAY."

Ray honestly doubted she could. They'd spent practically the entire summer together and she hadn't explained then. What he wanted was answers. "So? Am I your husband? The one you claimed was dead?"

She was nervous. He could tell. Her lies had caught up with her. She should be proud of herself since she had played him well. What had been her motive for keeping quiet? Did it have anything to do with insurance money? What?

"Yes, you're my Devon."

Her words made something within him snap. He moved from the door to come stand in front of her, boiling in rage to the point where he could feel a vein pulse at the base of his throat. "I am not your anything. You lied to me. You used me. Played me. You could have told me the truth at any time, yet you didn't. I trusted you."

"Don't you think I had a reason for not telling you? You didn't know me and telling you could have caused you to have a setback. Could have made it even more difficult for your memories to ever return."

"So you lied to me?"

"I didn't lie to you. Everything I told you about Devon and my marriage was the truth."

"You lied by omission, Ashley. You told me what you wanted me to know."

"I talked to your doctor and he—"

More anger poured through him. "My doctor? You don't even know my doctor."

"I got in touch with him through Kaegan and—"

"Kaegan? Kaegan knows who you are?" he roared as crimson haze practically covered his vision.

"Yes. Sawyer and Vashti know as well. They've known from the first when I told them who you were."

At that moment a shimmering wave of fury clouded every word she'd said. Black rage consumed his every thought. "You got to my friends? My *only* friends? The only people I trusted? You somehow convinced them to lie to me? To go along with your sick plan?"

"It wasn't that way at all. I—"

"No! I don't want to hear anything you have to say. You are not the woman I thought you were and I don't want any part of you and I hope you leave town. If you think you have a claim on me, you're wrong. If I am married to you, then I'm getting a divorce. I don't and won't have anything to do with you. Ever."

And then he stormed out the house, slamming the door behind him.

"RAY!" ASHLEY RACED to the door, calling after him, but he refused to look back. He got into his truck and took off like the devil himself was after him.

She closed the door as tears she couldn't hold back rolled unheeded down her face.

Why hadn't Ray let her explain? Why had he refused to listen to anything she had to say? Now he believed she had deliberated played him for a fool. And because of her he thought his friends had betrayed him.

That gave her pause. That was the last thing he needed to believe.

She pulled her phone out of her purse to call Sawyer. He answered on the first ring. "Ray found out, Sawyer. He found out my true identity and now he hates me. And he's hurt that you guys knew and didn't tell him."

She could hear Sawyer mutter a curse through the phone. "Where is he?"

"I don't know. He just left here and he's mad. I'm worried about him."

"I'll contact Kaegan. We'll find him and talk some sense into him. I'll call you later." He clicked off the phone.

Placing her phone aside, Ashley swiped at the tears that were beginning to fall again. At that moment she wasn't sure anyone would be able to talk any sense into Ray.

RAY KNEW HE should pull over to the side of the road and let the fury roll off of him, but he couldn't. He kept driving. He felt like going somewhere and ramming his fist in a door, kicking a hole in a wall or something. How could he have allowed himself to be taken in?

Not wanting to go home, he kept driving toward the marina. He needed to go out on his boat. Right now he wanted to find solace out on the waters. He needed to be out on the ocean.

He continued driving until he saw the pier. He turned his car into the crowded parking lot. It looked like a party was going on at one of the bar and grills. Then he remembered. The New Orleans Saints had a preseason game tomorrow and the town was celebrating a win before it happened.

After parking his truck he got out and walked down the long pier toward his boat. It was hard to ignore the loud noise coming from inside the establishment. At least some people had a reason to be happy and celebrate. His jaw hardened with every step he took. This was where he needed to be.

And alone.

THE RINGING OF her cell phone had Ashley pulling herself up in bed and wiping at the tears she couldn't stop from falling. She'd found Devon only to lose him all over again. The caller ID indicated it was Vashti. She quickly clicked on the phone.

"Vashti? Did Sawyer find Ray?"

"No. Both he and Kaegan are still looking for him. Ray didn't go home after leaving your place. That's the first place they checked. That means he's probably on his boat, so they're headed for the docks. I want to know how you're doing."

"Oh, Vashti. Ray actually believed I had an ulterior motive for keeping my identity from him. He wouldn't let me explain."

"He's upset, Ashley. Ray is a rational man. Once he calms down and thinks things through, he'll see just how wrong he is. Men are stubborn creatures. Trust me, I know."

"I want to believe he'll think things through, but—"

"Believe, Ashley. Keep the faith. Since we're not going out to eat, I'm going to have the chef prepare something here at the inn if you want to join me."

"Thanks but I'm fine. Besides, I can't eat a thing until I know Ray is okay. He wants me to leave town."

"Are you?"

Ashley shook her head. "No. I can't."

"And you shouldn't. I'll call you back if I hear anything from Sawyer."

"Thanks." She clicked off the phone. Easing off the bed, she went into the bathroom to wash her face, then changed out of the outfit she'd planned to wear for dinner and replaced it with a caftan.

Returning to the bedroom, she picked up her phone. It was time to call Kurt and tell him everything.

CHAPTER THIRTY-FOUR

"COMING ABOARD, RAY," Kaegan said, stepping onto Ray's boat.

Ray didn't bother to glance up. He was out in the middle of the ocean and he'd heard another boat approach from behind, but he hadn't checked to see who it was. He preferred just sitting there while nursing a bottle of beer and staring at the water.

"And what if I don't want you here?" he said, frowning. Finally turning around, he wasn't surprised to see Sawyer as well.

"That's just tough," Sawyer said, dropping down on one of the benches. "I'm missing a good meal at the Lighthouse because of you, Ray."

Ray narrowed his gaze at him. "And you think I give a damn about that. I thought you guys were my friends. Men I could trust, and in the end, you—"

"Cared enough to want what was best for you," Kaegan said, just as angry.

"What was best for me? You didn't even know her. For all you knew, her falling into the ocean might have been a setup just to get close to me."

Sawyer crossed his arms over his chest. "You ought to know me better than that. I'm a suspicious bastard by nature and don't take anything at face value. I had her checked out. And what I discovered was a woman who for the past three years has been grieving hard over the loss of her husband. A woman who came here to try to get on with her life and found the husband she thought was dead for three years, walking around like he didn't have a damn care in the world. A world that didn't include her."

"Are you blaming me for not knowing who she was?"

"No. And a part of me understands why you're upset. At least until she explains things. But you didn't let her do that, Ray. You didn't give her the chance," Sawyer said.

"If you had," Kaegan said, sliding on the bench beside Sawyer, "you would have learned that it was Dr. Riggins's suggestion that she not tell you."

"And you believed that because she said it?" Ray bit out.

"No, we believed it because we heard it. We were with her when she spoke to Dennis. I called him myself only after I was certain she was who she claimed to be. Hell, she still had your wedding pictures in her phone to prove it," Kaegan said.

Ray stared at Sawyer and Kaegan. "She should have told me the truth."

"Like Kaegan said, your doctor suggested she didn't. He said when people try to force someone with amnesia to remember, it can make things worse, make it even more unlikely those memories will ever return. It was his idea that she give you the chance to get to know her. The perfect plan would be for you to fall in love with her a second time.

"She took a chance on you, Ray, not knowing how things would turn out. She moved here to be near you, to be a part of your life, to get to know you as Ray Sullivan and not Devon Ryan. Because she loved you that much." Sawyer leaned against the back of the bench.

When Ray didn't say anything, Kaegan said, "And you did fall in love with her." He reached for a beer out the cooler and added, "Any fool can see that. So what's the problem? Not everyone can fall in love with the same woman twice." He cleared his throat. "Hell, let's just say that most men wouldn't want to, but Ashley's different."

Ray still didn't say anything, just took a long swig of his beer. "Are the two of you through?" he finally asked.

"No, but for now yes," Sawyer said. "I hope we gave you something to think about. We believe that you will. Otherwise, you will lose the best thing that has happened to you since you became Ray Sullivan. Like Kaegan, I believe you've fallen in love with her. If you accept the woman Ashley is, the woman who truly loves you, you'll see just what a special person she is."

Sawyer stood. "Kaegan and I are leaving."

Kaegan stood as well. "You can stay out here and feel sorry for yourself, Ray, or you can thank your lucky stars for Ashley and do something to make sure you can keep her. Hell, she might be ready to get rid of you after this. Think you weren't worth the effort and trouble and that she wasted three years mourning for an ungrateful ass."

Neither man said anything else as they climbed back into their boat and left. Ray remained sitting in the same spot, drinking his beer while thinking about everything Kaegan and Sawyer had said.

Finishing off his beer, he stood and crossed to where the makeshift bed was and lay looking up at the sky. It was getting dark and the stars were coming out. He needed to go back but wasn't ready yet.

Instead he lay there, replaying in his mind all the time he'd spent with Ashley since her near drowning. He shook his head. All the times he thought he'd been competing against Ashley's dead husband he'd only been competing against himself. She'd still been wearing her ring—her wedding ring—from him.

He didn't remember a life with her but he could see how he would have had one with her. He rubbed a hand down his face. Why couldn't he remember falling in love with her the first time around? Why couldn't he remember his past life with her? No wonder she'd called him Devon when they'd made love that time.

Sawyer and Kaegan were right. He did love her and right now he was letting his anger hijack his common sense. Now he knew why he'd gotten so angry at the thought she had betrayed him. It was because he loved her so much. If he hadn't loved her so much, he wouldn't care.

Now he had to decide what he was going to do about it. He lay there for no telling how long. Possibly an hour or two. It was completely dark now.

He eased to his feet and moved to the controls of the boat, ready to go back to shore. He needed to see Ashley.

ASHLEY CHECKED THE clock on the nightstand again. It was close to ten at night. Vashti, who'd been worried about her not eating, had been kind enough to bring her a plate from the inn. She'd told her that Sawyer and Kaegan had found Ray out on the ocean in his boat. Whether they'd been able to talk some sense into him, they weren't sure. They had tried but Ray could be stubborn at times. That had been four hours ago.

She knew and understood Ray's anger. She just needed him to hear her out. Recalling her conversation with Kurt, she couldn't help but feel full with emotions. Devon's tough-as-nails older cousin had cried over the phone at the news that Devon was alive. She warned Kurt about coming here because Devon's memory still hadn't returned.

When she heard the knock on the door, she quickly eased out of bed and slipped into her robe. Was it Ray? Why would he knock when he had a key? What if it wasn't him but Sawyer or Kaegan telling her something had happened? It couldn't be safe for him to be out there in the middle of the ocean alone at night.

When she looked out the peephole, she saw it was Ray and opened the door. "Ray."

"May I come in, Ashley?"

She nodded and stepped back. "Yes."

Entering, he closed the door behind him. "I owe you an apology for how I acted and what I said. Kaegan and Sawyer took me to task about it."

She lifted her chin. "That's why you're here? Because they took you to task?"

"No. I needed time to think, Ashley. I can't remember my life with you as Devon Ryan."

"I don't recall asking you to remember," she said, crossing her arms over her chest. "The reason I stayed was to know you as Ray and to give you a chance to know me. You don't know the hell I've been going through. And for me to come here, see you, talk to you, kiss you and make love to you, knowing to you I was nothing more than any other woman, it hurt, but I did it because there is no other man I could ever love but you. If you can't believe that, then I truly don't know what to say."

She felt like she had bled out her emotions to him. Forcing back tears, she refused to cry. "I loved you as Devon and love you even more as Ray."

He seemed nervous, which was a lot different from when he'd stormed in hours ago, full of anger. He cleared his throat. "I'm sorry. I'm truly sorry. When I came here earlier, I'd been only thinking of myself, Ashley. I was both angry and afraid."

She lifted a brow. She understood the angry part but... "What were you afraid of?"

He looked down at his feet a second before glancing back at her. Then she saw it. There was vulnerability in his eyes she hadn't detected before. She watched how he drew in a deep breath before crossing the room to stand in front of her.

"I had fallen in love with you, Ashley, weeks ago. And I had made decisions but I couldn't ask for a future with you until I could put my past to rest. Namely, if there was a former wife out there. I couldn't do that to you."

He paused a moment and then said, "I discovered there was and it was you. I felt the only possible reason for you not to tell me the truth was that my worst fears had been confirmed."

"Which were?" she asked, dropping her arms to her sides.

"That I'd been a lousy husband. I'd hurt you and mistreated you in some way. If that was true it meant I would be the last person you'd want to hook up with again. That also meant you did what you did for revenge or greed. Hell, I don't know. I didn't want to think that but I did and I'm sorry. I am truly sorry. I also had this fear that now that you'd found me you would want me to go back to being Devon, a man I don't know and who I doubt I'd ever be again even if I regained my memory. I didn't know how you'd feel about that."

Ashley tried calming her mind from reeling at his words of love to her. He'd just admitted to falling in love with her. That was what she'd wanted. Had hoped for. Had prayed for.

Reaching out, she took hold of his arms. "You weren't a lousy husband, Ray. You were the best. You and I had a good marriage. Everything I told you about us was the truth. The one time there were problems in our marriage, we dealt with it together. Our love kept us strong. I would not have worked so hard to regain a place in your life, in your heart, had you not been worthy of my love and affection. I would not have worn your ring so long after losing you if I had bad memories of the time we shared together."

She smiled through the tears she couldn't hold back any longer. She knew what she said next would be important to him. It would be important to him as much as it would be to her because she knew what it meant.

"I fell in love with you all over again as Ray Sullivan. I know and accept there is a possibility you might never get your memory back. You're different from Devon but I accept you as the man you are. You were a good man as Devon. I got to know you as Ray and I love you, but I still love Devon, too. It doesn't matter what you call yourself—I will still love you and call you my husband."

"Oh, baby, and I love you." Pulling her into his arms, he lowered his mouth and kissed her in a hot, deep mating of their mouths.

She slid her arms around his neck, deepening the kiss even more and totally aware of his scent of the sea, the heat of the arms holding her and the magnitude of the desire they were feeling for each other.

When they broke the kiss, they just stood there, wrapped in each other's arms, trying to catch their breaths while her head rested on his chest. She'd meant what she'd told him. It didn't matter what he called himself. He was still hers. Her husband.

She lifted her head to look up at him. "I am claiming you as mine, Ray."

He used his hand to softly brush against the side of her face. "And I am claiming you as mine."

He swept her off her feet and carried her into the bedroom.

HE COULD HAVE lost her. That thought was racing through Ray's mind as he put Ashley on her feet near the bed. At that moment he promised himself he would never do that again. Even when he hadn't truly known and understood, she had been his rock. And from this day forward he would always love her and cherish her.

Ray quickly removed her caftan and then removed his own clothes before carrying her to the chair. He sat and at the same time she straddled him, bringing her body down on his hard erection.

He wanted to look into her face with every stroke he made into her body. He wanted to see her every expression, hear each one of her groans. He began moving at the same time she did. He clutched tight to her hips, and they rode each other hard while staring into each other's eyes.

"I love you," he said, his words somewhat choppy from the quick intake of breath.

She smiled and whispered, "And I love you."

He doubted he would ever tire of hearing her say that to him. He felt his stomach knotting just seconds before his guts began shivering. The erection buried deep inside of her began throbbing to an intensity he'd never felt before—for the first time he was making love to his wife and the woman he intended to make his wife again.

"Ray!"

She called his name and threw her head back. He leaned in and placed a kiss at the middle of her neck. She was moving her body so fast that he had to hold on tight to her. Otherwise they would tumble out the chair. They didn't. But they shared one hell of an orgasm that seemed to last forever.

When the spasms for both of them subsided, he kissed her deeply and stood with her in his arms. "Now for the bed."

And as he stared deep into her eyes, he gave her a silent promise for what would be one hell of a night.

ASHLEY WOKE AND panicked when she found the place beside her empty. Glancing around the room, she spotted a naked Ray standing at her bedroom window, admiring the view at daybreak. Usually she was up by now, but thanks to him, she'd had a late and a very vigorous night.

Wondering what he was thinking, she eased out of bed and joined him at the window. "Beautiful view, isn't it?"

He glanced down at her nakedness and smiled. "I like the one I'm looking at now better."

She couldn't help but grin at that. "I won't complain if you think that way."

He took her hand in his. "There are so many questions I want to ask you. Although I don't remember, I'd like to try to piece together what might have happened that day, three years ago. Will you tell me?"

She lifted a brow. "Now?"

He chuckled. "No, not now but later."

"Yes, I'll tell you."

He nodded. "For now I need to know why the hell I got the word *sunflower* written across my back."

She laughed as she eased closer to his side and placed his arms around her. "We met in college on a blind date set up by your roommate who was in one of my classes. That first date, you gave me a sunflower because you'd somehow found out it was my favorite flower. From that night on, you would give me sunflowers often just because. On our honeymoon, we decided to mark each other. It was my choice for it to be a sunflower." She chuckled. "You flatly refused to have a flower on your back, so you opted for the word."

He nodded, grinning. "I figured it meant something. Now I know."

"Any more questions?" she asked him.

"Yes. How did I get so lucky to end up with the same woman twice?"

She smiled. "I guess you can say it's been one of those forget-me-not situations. It was meant for our paths to cross a second time and to fall in love all over again."

He turned toward her. "Yes, I think so, too. What about getting married all over again? Do you think that's possible, Ashley? Will you marry me and become Ashley Sullivan?"

"Ray," she said as happiness filled her to the brim. "Yes, I will marry you and become Ashley Sullivan and live here in Catalina Cove with you. I love it here."

"Then I guess you'd be glad to hear that as of yesterday, I put a deposit down on this place. The owners decided to sell. I was able to get this and the house next door."

"The house next door?"

"Yes. Bryce found out they were about to list it and told me about it. We made them a good offer for it before they did. I sweetened the deal by offering a cash payment."

"Cash?"

"Yes. I was able to use the money I was saving for that boat."

"But didn't you use it for the boat? I saw it and it's beautiful."

"No, I didn't have to." He then told her about Reid LaCroix and how he'd come in as an investor.

"Oh, Ray, that's wonderful!"

"I think so, too. And just so you know why I took him on as an investor when you also offered to be one, it's because I didn't want to mix business with pleasure. For me, you were my pleasure."

He paused a moment and then he said, "In a way it worked out for the best because this house is an investment opportunity. For us. It's one where both business and pleasure are welcomed. We'll be a team. We can live here starting out, and when we begin having children, we can do what Kaegan did and demolish the houses and build our dream home. One big enough for us and our family. I meant what I said about wanting kids, Ashley."

"And I meant what I said as well. And since we're both wide awake, now is as good a time as any to tell you the details of the day of your accident."

They got back in bed, and while he held her, she told him everything she knew. What happened after their last conversation would always be a missing block until he remembered. She also told him of Devon's relationship with her parents—namely, her mother—and of his close relation to his cousin, Kurt, and how Kurt had called her not long after talking to him. She also told him about just how wealthy he'd left her and they discussed how they would handle him "coming back from the dead" with their family and friends.

"I wonder who was driving your rental car that day when it went off the bridge. That person might have family somewhere looking for him as well," she said.

"Considering how I ended up in the hospital, forgive me for not really giving a damn."

"The hardest part of rekindling a relationship with you was trying hard not to call you Devon."

He chuckled. "You did once, while we were making love."

She was shocked. "I did?"

"Yes."

"Oops. I tried not to, honestly."

"Now I understand," he said, placing a kiss on her lips. "However, at the time, it did rub me the wrong way. I had been trying to impress you with my bedroom skills and for you to call out your dead husband's name left a sore spot. But I'd recovered by the next time I saw you."

"I'm glad," she said, cuddling up closer to him.

She knew this was just the beginning for them. There was a chance his memory might never return and if that happened she was okay with it. He could relive those memories through her if and when he wanted to. She was happy that they had a wedding to plan and she had a feeling being married to this man would be just as wonderful the second time around.

EPILOGUE

The first week in December

RAY GLANCED AROUND the backyard of Shelby by the Sea. Finally, his wedding day, and it hadn't come soon enough to suit him. However, he wouldn't complain and would admit the three months prior had been interesting and eventful.

He'd discovered just what a likable guy Devon Ryan had been. One who'd definitely shot straight from the hip and that was what everyone had respected about him. Ray got reacquainted with family and friends he didn't remember, and it seemed everyone had a "Devon" story to tell.

And if he hadn't gotten along with his mother-in-law before, he was certainly getting along with her now. According to Ashley, they had her father to thank for that. He'd met Ashley's three friends, Emmie, Suzanne and Kim, and liked them as well.

"You don't seem nervous," Kaegan leaned over and whispered.

He smiled. "I'm not. I'm ready to get this over with so the honeymoon can begin."

Sawyer leaned close to say, "This is a great spot and a fantastic day. The weather is cooperating."

Ray had to agree. They were standing under a huge gazebo that had been beautifully decorated with the ocean as a backdrop. Shelby by the Sea had hosted a lot of weddings in this very spot, including Sawyer and Vashti's, but Ray was convinced today would be the best one because it was his.

When the music began playing, Ray knew it was time, and his two best friends took their place beside him with the minister. Ashley would walk down the aisle on her father's arm and he couldn't wait to see her. They were treating this as a first-time wedding for the both of them with plans to honeymoon in Hawaii.

He hadn't been nervous before but he was nervous now. To him, this was his first wedding, and he couldn't wait to see his bride. Bryce, Vashti and Ashley's three best friends had deliberately kept her out of his sight for the last twenty-four hours and he'd been miserable as heck.

He swallowed deeply when he finally saw her walking down the aisle with her father toward him. The moment he looked into her face, saw her smile, felt her happiness, he suddenly staggered backward.

"Hey, you okay?" Kaegan leaned over to ask him.

He glanced at his friend. "Yes, I'm fine. She looks stunning," he said, glad everyone's attention was focused on the bride and not on him.

His attention was riveted on the bride as well, and the closer she got to him the more love he had for her. Deep love. Never-ending love. A love for always.

When she reached him, her father placed her hand in his and together they turned to the minister to say the words that would bind their lives together forever.

ASHLEY LET OUT a deep moan when Ray kissed her the moment he placed her on her feet after carrying her over the threshold of their hotel room. Both the wedding and reception had been beautiful and they'd left for the airport right before the reception ended.

It had been a long flight and she'd slept all the way, deciding to get her rest then. She was certain once they reached their destination they had other things to do besides sleep.

When he released her mouth, all she could say was "Wow!"

He chuckled. They had changed out of their wedding attire into comfortable clothing before leaving the cove.

"This room is beautiful," she said, smiling up at him. Of course they'd gotten an ocean view.

"Yes, it is. Let's go out on the balcony."

Taking her hand, he led them to the balcony and opened the set of French doors. The weather was wonderful and the ocean was a beautiful blue-green. He pulled her to his side. "I must say I'm a little disappointed," he said.

She glanced up at him, frowning. "About what?"

"I told you to tell me everything about our marriage when I was Devon."

She looked at him, puzzled. "I did."

He raised their joined hands to his lips and kissed her knuckles. "You didn't tell me about that promise I made to you on our wedding night, which is the reason we were waiting to have kids."

"Oh, that," she said, shrugging her shoulders. "That was a long time ago. And it doesn't matter because you want kids now and we've agreed to start trying in a year."

He shook his head. "No, I think we should start now. A promise is a promise."

She frowned. "Who told you about that promise? It was my mother, wasn't it?" Before he could answer, she said, "She promised not to tell you. That was a promise I made with Devon and not with you. Mom had no right to tell you anything."

He turned her toward him and leaned down and kissed her lips. "Your mother didn't tell me."

Her frown deepened. She didn't want to believe her father would have said anything or her close friends. Maybe it had been Kurt. He'd known about the promise. She hadn't told him not to say anything because she figured such a thing would never come up in one of Kurt and Ray's conversations.

"Well, if Mom didn't tell you, who did?"

He reached out and wrapped his arms around her waist. Looking into her eyes, he said, "I remembered."

She blinked. "You what?"

"I remembered. My memory returned just like that, when I saw you walking down the aisle on your father's arm. I suddenly remembered another time you did that same thing. If you recall, as Devon I'd always said seeing you coming down the aisle to me, looking so beautiful on our wedding day, was one of my most cherished moments in my life. It was the same again today and that's what sparked my memory. I remember everything. Including how I landed in the hospital but I don't want to talk about it now. I just want to celebrate what would have been our five-year wedding anniversary and now our marriage. And just like I intended three years ago, I want to make a baby."

Sweeping her into his arms, he carried her back inside and headed straight for the bedroom.

She looked forward to a wonderful future with the man whose heart she'd somehow managed to capture a second time around, and she was looking forward to their future together in Catalina Cove.

* * * * *

Fall in love with Catalina Cove all over again in Finding Home Again, *the story of Kaegan and Bryce, from* New York Times *bestselling author Brenda Jackson and HQN Books.*

READERS CAN'T GET ENOUGH OF KATE MESSNER!

EYE OF THE STORM

A BANK STREET BEST CHILDREN'S BOOKS OF THE YEAR BOOK

AN INDIE NEXT LIST PICK

"A great addition to any collection." —*LMC*

"Plenty of action. . . . These heart-pounding scenes
will be a hit." —*School Library Journal*

"This fast-paced read will sweep readers along
to its powerful . . . conclusion." —*VOYA*

Wake Up Missing

AN INDIE NEXT LIST PICK

"Combines a fascinating concept with page-turning
suspense. . . . A wild roller-coaster ride through the
Florida swamps." —Margaret Peterson Haddix, author of
The Missing series and the Shadow Children series

"Loved it! Mystery, intrigue, danger, and creepy futuristic science
set in today's world? Yes, please!" —Lisa McMann, *New York
Times* bestselling author of *Wake* and *The Unwanteds*

"A winner." —Bruce Coville, author of The Unicorn
Chronicles and *My Teacher Is an Alien*

Sugar and Ice

The Brilliant Fall of Gianna Z.

Books by Kate Messner

The Brilliant Fall of Gianna Z.
Sugar and Ice
Eye of the Storm
Wake Up Missing

EYE OF THE STORM

KATE MESSNER

WALKER BOOKS FOR YOUNG READERS
AN IMPRINT OF BLOOMSBURY
NEW YORK   LONDON   NEW DELHI   SYDNEY

First published in the United States of America in March 2012
by Walker Books for Young Readers, an imprint of Bloomsbury Publishing, Inc.
Paperback edition published in April 2014
www.bloomsbury.com

Bloomsbury is a registered trademark of Bloomsbury Publishing Plc

For information about permission to reproduce selections from this book, write to
Permissions, Walker BFYR, 1385 Broadway, New York, New York 10018
Bloomsbury books may be purchased for business or promotional use. For information on bulk purchases
please contact Macmillan Corporate and Premium Sales Department at specialmarkets@macmillan.com

"Geometry" from *The Yellow House on the Corner*, Carnegie Mellon University Press, Pittsburgh, PA.
© 1980 by Rita Dove. Reprinted by permission of the author.

The Library of Congress has cataloged the hardcover edition as follows:
Messner, Kate.
Eye of the storm / by Kate Messner. — 1st U.S. ed.
p.   cm.
Summary: Jaden's summer visit with her meteorologist father, who has just returned from spending four years
in Russia conducting weather experiments not permitted in the United States, fills her with apprehension and
fear as she discovers that living at her father's planned community, Placid Meadows, is anything but placid.
ISBN 978-0-8027-2313-0 (hardcover)
[1. Fathers and daughters—Fiction. 2. Storms—Fiction. 3. Weather—Fiction.
4. Climatology—Fiction. 5. Mystery and detective stories.] I. Title.
PZ7.M5615Ey 2012   [Fic]—dc22   2011006393

ISBN 978-0-8027-3435-8 (paperback)

Book design by Nicole Gastonguay
Typeset by Westchester Book Composition
Printed and bound in the U.S.A. by Thomson-Shore Inc., Dexter, Michigan
2 4 6 8 10 9 7 5 3

All papers used by Bloomsbury Publishing, Inc., are natural, recyclable products
made from wood grown in well-managed forests. The manufacturing processes
conform to the environmental regulations of the country of origin.

For my aunt, Maureen Lahue,
and for all librarians
fighting the good fight
for books and knowledge

Chapter 1

There are no words to describe this sound.

In the old days, they said tornadoes sounded like freight trains. I've seen video archives of survivors being interviewed, all out of breath. They describe an approaching rumble and then a roar. Wind pouring out of the sky. Buildings shaking. And finally, the train rumbling off, fading away as the storm lumbers on.

But that was then.

There are no words for the sound of what is happening now.

A thick, dark shadow is snaking down from the cloud that followed us from the airport. It's wider and stronger than anything those people in the video archives had ever seen. Bigger than anything they could have imagined.

It is headed straight for us.

"No worries, Jaden," Dad says, but both our DataSlates are wailing with high-pitched storm alerts. His eyes dart to the rearview mirror as he pulls the HV into a safety lot.

I've heard about these huge roadside shelters, but we don't have them at home in Vermont. The one time Mom and I got caught out with a storm coming, we just knocked on somebody's door. It goes without saying in New England: on storm days, you let anybody who needs help into your safe room.

But in this part of Oklahoma, there are fewer houses now, hardly any doors to knock on. This huge concrete structure is the first building we've seen for miles. It's almost full, but Dad maneuvers into one of the last spaces. "We'll be fine here."

"Good timing, I guess." My voice shakes, even though I try to pretend it's no big deal; Mom warned me the storms would be more frequent here, but I never thought I'd see one before we even got to Dad's house.

"That good timing's no accident." Dad leans back in his seat and picks up his DataSlate. The glow of the screen lights his face an eerie blue, even as the sky outside grows darker. "When StormSafe got the government contract to build these lots, we put one every fifteen miles on major roads so you'd never be more than a few minutes from safety."

"That's how much warning you get when a storm's coming?"

"Give or take."

They're like the Revolutionary War—era taverns I learned about in my online history course, spaced fifteen miles apart because that's how far a traveler could ride in a day. Here we are, 275 years later, driving hydrogen vehicles instead of horses, and we're back to needing shelter every fifteen miles.

Lightning flashes outside. I tug my backpack from the floor into my lap and run the strap between my fingers, over and over, so I can concentrate on that instead of the pounding in my chest. I can't freak out. Not on my first day with Dad in four years. He lives for storms like this.

A plastic chair tumbles, legs over arms over legs, past the entrance we came in.

"This is turning into a good one." Dad cranks the volume on his DataSlate so we can hear the regional news feed over the screaming wind. If they mention the storm, we'll know it's big. Normally, they send out the DataSlate alerts that replaced the old tornado sirens and leave it at that. Mom said when she was growing up, her town got on national news once when a tornado wiped out half a mobile home park. *National* news!

Now the news feeds only report the biggest of the big, the true monsters. It sounds like this could be one of them.

"The National Storm Center confirms a tornado warning for all of eastern Logan County," the voice on the DataSlate says. "NSC meteorologists say the system that developed this afternoon has spawned three separate tornadoes—the latest, a possible NF-6. Residents are advised to get to safe rooms immediately."

"NF-6?" I swallow hard. We have our share of storms back home—who doesn't?—but the worst I've seen was the NF-4 that ripped the roof off Mom's environmental science lab at the University of Vermont.

"Could be." Dad leans to see past me, out the shelter door. The tornado doesn't even have its funnel shape anymore; the thick, jerking rope has swelled into a churning blur of brown-black wind.

"It's rain-wrapped!" Dad shouts over the roaring. "Tough to see how big it's grown. But at least it's not a Niner!" That's weather-geek slang for an NF-9, the second highest rating on the new scale they developed a decade ago when it became clear the storms had outgrown the old Enhanced Fujita Scale that went from one to five. When I was a baby, EF-5 was the worst a tornado could be. The New Fujita Scale goes up to ten, though nobody's ever seen a ten touch down. What would they call it? A Tenner?

The lights flicker, and I grip the door handle.

"Relax, Jaden." Dad punches me lightly on the arm, and it sets something off inside me. All the swallowed-up storm jitters rise in my throat, and I want to scream. Instead, I swallow that, too, and my eyes fill with tears.

I've been on the ground all of two hours, and I'm not used to it here. None of it feels like home.

Not the desolate brown flatness of the land.

Not the stark concrete gray of the shelters.

And not the storms. Especially not storms like this.

Dad should know that.

Maybe he'd understand how I feel, understand *me*, if he hadn't spent the past four years in Russia, doing weather experiments that weren't allowed in the United States. Maybe he'd ask how I'm doing now that—

"Jaden, look!" He holds up his DataSlate and turns the radar screen my way. "This hook echo is incredible!"

He points to the blob on the screen. It's churning, growing, hungry enough to swallow half of Oklahoma. A curled-up green extension sticks out one side of the storm, like a witch's finger calling us in.

I know what he wants me to say. He wants me to *ooh* and *ahh* and talk about the rotation like we used to when I was little and I'd sit on his lap, and he'd laugh because I knew how to read a satellite map before I was five. He wants me to be WeatherGirl, the nickname he gave me before he left, before he and Mom split up, before the storms got this bad, before everything. He wants me to say how awesome it is, how fantastic and powerful. How amazing.

But it's not. It is terrifying and loud, pounding the concrete shelter we're hiding in with uprooted hackberry shrubs and tree trunks and God knows what else. I grab the door and hold on.

"Relax, Jaden. This is no big deal around here. You're safe. I designed this shelter model myself. StormSafe tested these things under conditions that were far more—"

He's trying to comfort me, but he is screaming, *screaming* over the storm he says is no big deal. So I scream back.

"Dad, *stop!*" I put my head down on the dashboard and press my hands into my eyes, but I still can't escape from the sound. Forget the passing freight train. This is like being *inside* the engine of the train, inside the throat of some ancient Greek monster that's roared down out of the sky. It's throwing recycling bins and branches, torn-off roof tiles so frantic and flapping they look like huge tortured birds, all flying past the entrance to the lot. I scream again, "Just stop! Stop!" And I don't know if I'm screaming at Dad or the storm or both. But neither responds.

Finally, I sit up and open my eyes. Dad is ignoring the weather outside, staring at me. He closes the radar image—the storm looks even bigger in the glimpse I catch before it's sucked into a folder on his screen—and pulls up his StormSafe corporate log-in page. He turns the slate away from me as if I'd be able to see or remember his stupid password in the middle of this and pokes at the onscreen keys. "Relax," he says. "It's weakening now."

I squeeze my eyes closed against the pounding, against the attack from the wind and debris, and I don't answer him. But as if by magic, the roar of that monster-from-the-sky fades back into something more like an old-fashioned freight train and then dissolves altogether.

I don't open my eyes.

I sit, listening to the train rumble off. I squeeze my eyes shut tighter and think.

This was not a storm. It was a monster.

This is not home.

And this is not the same father I used to have, the one who tucked me into bed, singing songs about the wind.

That father took me out for ice cream on a summer night four years ago. He ordered rainbow sprinkles on his cone, right along with me, and he told me why he had to go on another trip. Why he wasn't coming home anytime soon. Why he needed to open a new StormSafe headquarters in a country that would allow him to do his research. And he left.

This father who has come back to me . . . I open one eye a crack. His fingers fly over the DataSlate. His eyes focus on the scrolling columns of numbers, laser-intense. Fierce.

He feels like someone I don't even know.

Chapter 2

No matter how bad things get in Logan County, no matter how the clouds swirl, how the radar screens light up, I'll be safe in Placid Meadows.

Perfectly, one hundred percent safe.

That's what Dad promised Mom, how he convinced her to send me here, to the heart of the storm belt, for the summer. And his new, self-sufficient StormSafe community does sound impressive. Safety. Higher water and kilowatt allowances, thanks to Placid Meadows' private solar and wind energy reserves. Eye on Tomorrow Science Camp, the state-of-the-art program Dad's corporation runs for "the best and brightest young minds" in the world. Dad said it went without saying that I was one of them and sent me admissions papers, but I still wanted to take the official entrance exam. When I answered the last question on my DataSlate and pressed the SUBMIT button, the score that appeared on the screen put me in the top five percent of applicants. I couldn't argue that I didn't belong there.

Plus Mom had her own research project waiting in the shadow

of an active Costa Rican volcano. Not to be outdone by my father's adoration of storms, Mom's had her own love affair . . . with frogs. While Dad's been studying the effects of global warming on storm formation, she's been researching its impact on wildlife in sensitive ecosystems, particularly rain forest amphibians like the poison dart frog. Mom's wanted to take this trip for years but had nobody I could stay with until now.

"This must be WeatherGirl!" As we pull up to the Placid Meadows gate, a beanpole of a man leans down into the HV window.

Dad nods in my direction. "This is indeed my daughter Jaden, the infamous WeatherGirl." My stomach's still tangled from the storm, but I smile; nobody's called me that in four years, and even though I'm a total science geek, I'm surprised Dad still thinks about me that way. Surprised, and I guess a little pleased.

"Hi, Jaden. I'm Lou." He points to the shiny silver name tag on his navy blue uniform. There's a StormSafe emblem above his name. Does everybody here work for Dad? "Any update on the expansion, Dr. Meggs?"

"Unfortunately, no," Dad says. "Looks like Phase Two is going to be delayed a bit."

"What's Phase Two?" I ask.

"Phase One of Placid Meadows is full, and we have two dozen families waitlisted, so we're going to expand the development. *If* we can get the land we need."

Lou chuckles. "Those farmers getting you down?"

Dad isn't smiling anymore. "Honestly, why someone would be crazy enough to stay here to run a dying farm is beyond me. And why *anybody* would turn down an offer that's five times what the property is worth . . ." Dad shakes his head, then looks at the dashboard clock. "I'd better get Jaden home." He lifts two fingers from the steering wheel in a wave.

When he drives through the Placid Meadows gate, it's like driving from Kansas into the Land of Oz.

From the minute I stepped off the plane, Oklahoma has been a place of charcoal skies and yellow-gray clouds. It's like Florida when the hurricanes started getting bigger; no one lives here anymore unless they're too attached to family farms or they can't afford to leave. The oil wells were abandoned a decade ago when the international fossil fuels ban took effect. The sprawling cattle ranches are ghost towns. It's a state abandoned, except for a few farms, storm-torn mobile home parks, and corrections department energy farms, where convicted criminals ride generator-cycles outside in the daytime and sleep in StormSafe bunkers at night. It's a black-and-white world, with shades of brown.

But Placid Meadows blooms in full, all-of-a-sudden color.

A billowing garden of bright flowers divides the street. In the middle is a fat boulder with a bronze plaque affixed to it. WELCOME TO PLACID MEADOWS, A STORMSAFE COMMUNITY, it says in calm, loopy cursive. All around, the garden bursts with reds and pinks and fuchsias. Tall purples tip their heads, and spreading silver blues creep along the curb.

"It's beautiful." I lower my window to breathe in all that brightness, and for the first time since I said good-bye to Mom at the airport in Burlington, I almost feel calm.

Dad pulls over and smiles, and his face relaxes into something I almost recognize from the Dad I had before. "Isn't it the most gorgeous garden you've ever seen?"

I nod, but this new glimpse of Dad is more interesting than the plants now. The DataSlate man from the car seems to have been sucked into a folder deep inside him. Now he looks like someone who might order rainbow sprinkles on an ice cream cone again someday. Between that and the flowers, I feel my heart lift. Maybe this summer will be all right.

"The flowers are so perfect." I lean out my window.

"Of course they are. Everything we plant is DNA-ture; it's the best." He puts the HV back in gear. "We better go. Mirielle's making an early dinner."

Mirielle. The stepmom I've only seen on my DataSlate videophone, and always with my new half sister, Remi, in her arms.

Dad pulls away from the garden, farther into the development.

The street is lined with StormSafe houses, concrete structures tinted mauve, slate blue, and sea green. They have windows, which surprises me a little; they must be made of glass that's engineered not to shatter under pressure. And there are bigger buildings, without windows.

"Are those houses, too?" I ask.

"Nope—that one's the community warehouse." Dad nods toward a big brick-colored structure as we pass. "DNA-ture delivers food orders once a week so we don't need to go out to the regional grocery store."

No wonder the farms Dad mentioned to Lou aren't doing so well.

Dad points out my window. "Here's the entertainment dome."

He slows down as we pass a building that looks like the big skating rink at home. The electronic sign outside has a schedule of showings. Movies. Sporting events. Ballet and theater streamed in live from the National Arts Center in New York. And something called Museum Night, with Natural History: Jurassic Period on Tuesday and American History 1900–2050 on Thursday.

"What's Museum Night?" I ask as Dad pulls away.

He smiles a little. "Do you remember when you were really small—I think you were three—when we took you to closing ceremonies for the American Museum of Natural History in New York City?"

"Kind of." I remember walking through a room with huge dinosaurs and another one with all kinds of rocks and gems. And Mom was crying. "Mostly, I remember Mom being sad."

Dad nods. "It broke her heart when the government decided most of the major museums needed to close so artifacts could be protected in underground bunkers until the storm crisis is resolved. But this place"—he looks in the rearview mirror—"is the museum of the future. It's all holograms, so it changes every night. What did it say for this week?"

"Jurassic and American History."

"Great shows; you should go," Dad says. "You walk a path through the dome, and you'll see dinosaurs approaching. The T-Rex looks like it's about to eat you for dinner." He chuckles. "They're just holograms, so they don't bite, but they're realistic. American History is fascinating, too. You meet history makers of the twentieth and twenty-first centuries—Martin Luther King, Steve Jobs, Al Gore—and former presidents, too. I think they have Barack Obama and Grace Farley in this show."

"Interesting," I say, and it is. But then I have another flash of memory from the museum's closing night—the feel of a cool, rough dinosaur tail under my hand when I ducked under the velvet rope to touch it, even though the signs said not to. It felt real, like it might come alive and roar any second. A hologram could never feel like that.

We turn a corner, and Dad slows down. "That's Risha Patel, the girl I told you about on our video-call last week."

The girl looks about my age. Her long black hair has a bright green streak along one side. She must have a BeatBud in her ear because she's bobbing her head back and forth to something fast and playing imaginary drums in the air, right above the handlebars of her bicycle as she rides along, hands-free.

Dad speeds up again, but I turn in my seat and stare.

She is riding a bike.

Nobody rides bikes anymore at home. The storms churn up so fast, there's not a kid in our neighborhood who's allowed to ride more than halfway down the block, so why bother? Amelia was the last of my friends to give hers up. She held out right through last summer and never cared how ridiculous she looked riding up and down the street, back and forth, alone. When we laughed, she told us that in her mind, she was going all over town, through the woods past the big tree house where our moms used to camp out when they were little, branches brushing her cheeks as she flew down the trails. But at the end of the summer, we got our StormSafe Mall and Teen Center, and even Amelia figured that was better than imaginary trails. The recycling crew picked up her bike at the beginning of October.

Was this girl imagining faraway places, too?

"Does she live right around here?" I ask Dad.

He shakes his head. "The Patels live on the other side of the development. Closer to the Eye on Tomorrow campus."

"Wow." I scan the horizon. The storm we just saw has already barreled off, but there are more clouds churning in the west. "She's far from home for a storm day."

Dad laughs. "I see it's going to take you a while to get used to being a StormSafe kid." He slows down and pulls into the driveway of an adobe-colored concrete box. "It's different here." He presses a button on the dashboard, and a dome-shaped mouth yawns open on one wall. He pulls the HV forward into what must be the Storm-Safe version of a garage. Three bicycles are lined up inside, one in my favorite color, electric blue.

"We ride bikes all over the place here. In fact," he says, nodding to the fleet along the wall, "it was supposed to be a surprise, but the blue one's yours. You'll love having that freedom again."

"But . . . how can that be safe? I know the *houses* are safer here, but if you're outside . . . I mean, the storms are even worse than at home, so—"

"How many times do I have to tell you?" Dad shakes his head, smiling. "While you are inside the gates of Placid Meadows, you are safe. Totally and completely safe."

He presses another button on the dashboard. The garage door rumbles again, and behind us, the mouth on this safe, safe house slides shut.

Chapter 3

When Dad opens the kitchen door, French disco music bursts out to meet us. Mirielle is twirling around the room barefoot in a long flowered skirt and lemon-yellow tank top. Remi is six months old now and swaddled in a big, every-colored scarf slung around Mirielle's neck like she is part of the outfit.

Mirielle presses a button to send the potatoes down for peeling and—"Oh!"—almost twirls into me on her way back for the carrots. "Jaden, you're here!" She leans in to kiss my cheek. I smell Remi's head—soap and baby. Mirielle turns to Dad. "Did you get caught in the storm? I hate when you have to go out there." She says it as if "out there" and "in here" are totally different planets.

"I know, love." Dad steps up to the biometric panel on the refrigerator. He presses a finger to the reflective glass and taps impatiently, waiting for it to identify him by his print. "We spent about ten minutes in a safety lot. No problem." For some reason, relief cools my face when the fridge sends Dad out a glass of iced tea. He still drinks it with lemon, and at this point, anything that hasn't changed is welcome.

KATE MESSNER

"You want something to drink?" Dad asks.

"No thanks." I look past him and wonder where my room is.

Mirielle catches me peering into the living room. "Would you like to see the rest of the house?"

"Go ahead." Dad steps up and rests his finger on another bio-metric panel just outside a steel door on the wall opposite the kitchen appliances. "I'm going to check in with headquarters before dinner."

I stand by the door for a second and see a bank of computers inside before I realize Dad's office won't be part of my tour. Then I follow Mirielle out of the kitchen and up a spiral staircase to a sleeping loft. It's bigger than mine at home, but it has a bedspread of the same bright blue. I wonder if they did this on purpose, tried to make my room look like home so I wouldn't miss Mom so much.

But then Mirielle pulls open the little drawer on my nightstand, and what I see inside makes me miss Mom even more.

It's a book. The hardcover kind with pages you turn by catching the corner with your fingertip. We have this one at home, but I didn't bring any paper books; Dad says reading paper books is like driving on square, stone wheels. He's been reading exclusively on his DataSlate since before I was born.

This book is by Rita Dove, an American poet who loves math as much as she loves words. In the photograph on the book jacket, she's beautiful and maybe around Mom's age, but she must be in her nineties now. I sit down on the bed and flip through the pages to find my favorite, "Geometry." It's about what she feels like when she proves a mathematical theorem.

. . . the house expands:
the windows jerk free to hover near the ceiling,
the ceiling floats away with a sigh.

When I first read this poem, the ceiling part freaked me out a little. Then Mom told me it was written way back in 1980, before most people knew what it was like to have the roof blow off your house for real.

I run my hand over the raised letters on the book's cover. "Did my mom send this?"

Mirielle smiles and sits next to me. "She thought you might miss your books, so she had your great-aunt Linda pick up a copy at the antique shop and drop it off when your father wasn't home." Mirielle glances toward the door. "She suggested I tuck it away for you."

"Aunt Linda? Really?" Even though she's technically my great-aunt, I've always known her as Aunt Linda. I haven't seen her in years, though. She paints and gardens, and I'm not surprised she likes poetry, too. She took care of Dad when he was little, pretty much raised him. I put the book down next to me. "How close does she live?"

"About twenty miles. But she and your father don't really talk."

"How come? Won't I get to see her? It's been a long time."

Mirielle's pretty green eyes cloud over. "Your father thought Linda should move to Placid Meadows, but she'd have no part of it. He was furious, and so no . . . she doesn't drop in for dinner."

My disappointment must show on my face. Mirielle reaches out and touches my arm. "But she is your relative, too, no? Maybe we will have a visit one day while your father is at work." She stands up, tucks the book back in the nightstand, and gently closes the drawer. She smiles like we're sharing a secret, and I realize we are. We both know Dad wouldn't want paper books cluttering up his house.

Besides, it's poetry. Dad always says a world like ours needs science to save it, that pretty words never protected anybody from a storm.

Which reminds me. "How do I get to the safe room from here?"

"There is no one safe room," Mirielle says. "Everywhere is safe."

The ugly concrete designs make perfect sense now, and so does Dad's promise to Mom. The whole *house* must be a giant safe room.

"I will show you the living room instead, yes?"

On the way downstairs, we pass the bathroom, and I peek inside. It's enormous, and there's no liter-meter on the wall, like at home. Could the Placid Meadows water rations be so much higher that we don't even have to keep track? I add longer showers to the list of good things about living here for the summer.

"Here we are." Mirielle steps into the living room. One whole wall is an entertainment window. There are plush black chairs, an antique rocker, a leather sofa, and bookcases like ours at home. But no books. Here, the shelves are full of digital frames. Most are storm shots, black-gray blurs of tornadoes from Dad's research trips all over the world, but the two frames on the end have a slideshow of family photos.

I stand next to Mirielle and watch the images change.

Mirielle and Dad at their wedding in Russia two years ago.

Eating cake.

Dancing.

Photos of Remi as a newborn.

Then pictures of me.

There are a bunch of photos taken in the first house Mom and Dad owned. I'm three years old, pushing a toy lawn mower in the yard. It's the old-fashioned kind that needed a person to steer it. There's me in a high chair with jam smeared all over my face.

Then I am four. Dressed for my first day of school. The tornadoes were spreading north then. I'd been so excited for school but so scared that a storm would sweep away the house while I was gone.

There are school photos for the next three years. I am five, then six, then seven. My backpack goes from purple, to pink, to red with blue stripes, to bright orange.

When the picture changes again, I am eight. The counter is torn up behind me—they must have been installing the SmartKitchen—and books are spread out on the table. That was the year before they built the StormSafe schools and shelters, and we all home-schooled with classes streamed to our computers. Mom created most of her own lessons, though, and I loved staying home. It was just before Dad left for Russia, too, the last year we were whole.

The frame flashes again, and suddenly, my face looks older—last year's school picture. Mom must have beamed it here.

"We need a new photograph of you," Mirielle says. "Your hair is longer now."

"Yeah, a little."

I step closer to the shelves to look at the other frame with family photos, the smaller one. One of the pictures looks like an old-fashioned portrait of my father.

"Is that Dad?"

Mirielle has been humming softly to Remi. "Hmm?" She stops and leans toward the frame. "Oh, no, that's your *grand-père*; these are your father's parents, Enam and Athena, when they were young. You have seen photos of them before, yes?"

I have, but never one that looks so real. There is something fierce in my grandmother's eyes. An intensity that looks like it should have burned out the camera's lens. "She reminds me a little of Dad," I say, and wonder how much Mirielle knows about the woman who would have been her mother-in-law.

I never met Grandma Athena. She died way before I was born, and it was Mom, not Dad, who told me about her. Like Dad, she had an amazing mind. She studied with a ferocity that made people afraid of her. She met Grandpa in graduate school, married him four months later, and had Dad right after they graduated. When the September 11th terrorist attacks happened in 2001 and the United States went to war with Afghanistan, Grandpa enlisted in the military and Grandma went to work for some secret government science program. It was all classified—like the scientists who developed the atomic bomb during World War II—so nobody knew exactly what she was doing.

When Dad was twelve, Grandpa was killed in Afghanistan, Grandma died in a car accident, and Dad had to go live with Aunt Linda, all within a few weeks. Mom says that's everything she knows; Dad never talked about it and still doesn't. I've always known not to ask.

Before today, I'd only seen one picture of Grandma Athena, faded on paper. It made her look old and brittle, too. But this photo feels alive, as if I might catch her blinking, and I have trouble looking away until Mirielle breaks the spell. "You must be hungry."

"Kind of." I follow her back to the kitchen. "Want me to hold the baby?"

Mirielle unsnuggles Remi from the scarf. She fusses for a minute but then gets a handful of my brown hair wrapped around her fist and curls up against me.

I turn back to the living room for one more look at Grandma Athena, but the picture has already changed.

Chapter 4

"Did you try the broccoli?" Dad raises his eyebrows at the perfectly formed trees piled on one side of my plate. "It's DNA-ture's bestselling vegetable for a reason, you know."

"I know." I've seen the pop-up ad on my DataSlate so many times I can quote it. *"DNA-ture: Vegetables Even Kids Will Love. Our foods have the undesirable qualities bioengineered right out of them."*

"It's true." Dad picks up a stalk from my plate. "No bitterness. No mushiness."

"Still the same old broccoli." I stand to take my plate to the auto-clean bin.

"Still the same old Jaden. Stubborn as usual." He frowns and pops the broccoli into his mouth.

I should have known better than to knock DNA-ture, the bio-botanicals company he runs along with StormSafe—but as I open my mouth to apologize, I see him smiling. "I'm going back to my office. There are still some storms around to deal with." I'm about to ask Dad how he'll "deal with" them when the doorbell rings.

"Would you answer that for me?" Mirielle asks, leaning down to pick up Remi.

The air-drumming girl with the green-streaked hair, Risha, is about to push the doorbell again when I answer. "Oh!" she says, jumping back a little. She brushes hair from her eyes, and two gold bangles, patterned with zeros and ones, clang together on her wrist. "You're here! Yay! I mean, hi!"

"Hi to you, too! I'm Jaden."

"I know." She bounces on the toes of her pink high tops. ". . . and my mom told me you're almost thirteen like me and you're going to Eye on Tomorrow, too. I'm Risha. Want to go for a bike ride?"

"What a good idea!" Mirielle joins us at the door. "Risha can show you around."

"Okay." The clouds are dark, but they're still a ways off, and Mirielle doesn't seem worried. "Let me get my bike."

I head for the garage, thinking how weird it feels to say that again.

My bike.

Riding a bicycle was something I thought was gone forever. Something future kids would hear about in stories from the old times, before the earth's average temperature grew so warm, before the atmosphere became so unstable, so friendly to huge storms. I thought bikes were gone, like hikes in the woods and picnics that aren't in the backyard. Somehow, Dad's company has found a way to give those things back to people.

"Come on!" Risha coasts by me, pedaling backward as fast as

she can, her sneakers a hot-pink blur. "We'll go by my house and then campus."

We ride around a corner, and Risha waves to two girls jogging on the sidewalk. "Hey, Tess! Ava!"

They wave back as we zip past them.

"Will they be at camp?" I ask, pumping harder to catch up with Risha.

"The Beekman twins? Of course." She lets out a snort that sounds more like a rhinoceros than a skinny girl with a delicate nose. "They moved into Placid Meadows a couple years ago, so they were in all my classes at school. Their father owns the British company that produced the first successful HV model. The storms in Britain have gotten bad, too, so he brought the family here and *paid* their way in."

Her tone of voice makes me glad I insisted on taking the test, even though Dad was ready to enroll me without it. "Is the camp mostly Placid Meadows kids?" I ask.

"It depends." Risha pedals up a small hill. "A few really high scorers moved here with their families, all expenses paid. Some guys who live around here like Alex and Tomas—I'll introduce you, but I have dibs on Tomas—come for free, too. My mom says it was part of the tax deal your dad's company got. They have to provide opportunities for local kids." She crests the top of the hill and starts coasting. I follow her down and over a bridge that crosses a little creek. Just on the other side, she squeezes her hand brakes and stops so abruptly I almost bump her rear tire.

"Here's my house," she says.

It looks like Dad's, right down to the gobble-up-your-car garage door, only this one is pale blue instead of adobe colored. "It's pretty," I say.

"Not really." She laughs. "But it's bigger than our apartment in New York, and safer. Plus it's close to school." She points to a concrete and steel building halfway down the block. It looks brand new. "And not far from the Entertainment Dome."

"Do you go there a lot?"

Risha shrugs. "Not really. Once you know when the T-Rex is going to pop out, it's not that exciting. And the American History show just makes me mad. Can you believe they spent so long arguing before the courts decided that people can marry whoever they want? Maybe if they'd worried more about carbon emissions back then and less about bossing everybody around, we'd still have real museums with real stuff in them, you know?"

Risha lets out a huff and starts pedaling straight ahead, but the clouds off to our left catch my attention. They're closer. And darker.

"Hey, Risha, do you want to head home?"

"Why? Don't you want to see the campus?" She keeps riding.

The wind whips up dirt from the empty lot, and it stings my cheeks. "Risha, shouldn't we go? It looks bad over there."

She hollers something over her shoulder but I can't hear what, and then she turns—an abrupt right down a driveway I would have missed—and stops. Looming ahead of us is a building twenty times the size of the houses. It's behind a fancy, locked wrought-iron gate.

"Whoa!" I pull my bike up next to her. "What's this?"

"Eye on Tomorrow." Risha leans on her handlebars and rests

her chin on her hands, grinning at the building. "Where the brightest minds of today prepare to lead us into the future. And that's just the reception building. You'll see the rest in the morning."

The reception building gleams, all steel and windows. There are another half dozen shining buildings behind it, built around a grassy quad. The largest has a huge white dome—five times the size of the Entertainment Dome—growing out of the center. Dad told me this place was impressive, but I thought he was exaggerating. This summer camp for schoolkids looks more high-tech than Mom's university.

It makes sense, though. StormSafe created Eye on Tomorrow four years ago as a model for the government's new Surge Ahead program to create leaders in math and science. The United States had been behind other countries in those areas when the storms intensified. Now, it's like everybody suddenly figured out science is important, so they're building facilities for gifted students around the country. Eye on Tomorrow was the first—and is apparently still the best.

"Were you here last summer?" I ask Risha.

She nods. "Once you test in, you get to come every summer. The idea is for campers to keep coming back and then work for StormSafe and its sister companies once they get out of school. Doesn't your dad tell you anything?" She looks at her watch. "Come on, it's almost eight o'clock, and I want to show you one more thing if you can keep a secret because my parents would kill me if they found out, and yours probably would, too. You can keep a secret, right?" She looks at me over her shoulder.

"Sure, I guess."

She leads the way down another hidden path through some brush. A branch tugs at my hair, and I have a pang of missing Amelia. She'd love this bike ride, with real trees and trails that aren't just in her imagination.

"Well, look who made it," a deep, older-than-us boy voice calls out, and again, I almost bump Risha's back tire because she stops so fast. In front of her, a chain-link fence rises up from the dusty ground to way over our heads. This must be the edge of Placid Meadows; the fence stretches out in both directions. The only opening is where the barrier is interrupted by a big old oak tree whose trunk and branches apparently ignored the fence and kept right on growing, twisting the wires and pulling open a gap that looks just big enough to squeeze through.

On the other side of the fence, two boys stand back a few steps, straddling bicycles of their own. Theirs are older and rusted, like they've been out in a storm or two.

"Sorry I'm late." Risha shrugs at the taller of the two boys. She jumps off her bike, climbs through the gap in the fence, and motions for me to come, too.

"We thought you stood us up."

"Never." She gestures toward me as I'm pulling a twig out of my hair. "This is my friend Jaden."

"Hey." The tall boy smiles one of those lazy, movie-star smiles with his eyes half closed. He must be the one she has dibs on.

"Jaden Meggs, meet Tomas Hazen and Alex Carillo."

"Hi." I nod to Tomas and wave past him to Alex, who's shorter, about my height, with dark skin like Risha's and black hair that curls around his ears.

"Hey." His brown eyes are asking questions, and he tips his head. "Meggs?"

"Jaden," I say. "I just moved in—"

"With your dad? *The* Stephen Meggs?" He looks at Risha and raises his eyebrows.

"Yes, her dad is Dr. Meggs, Alex. Get over it." Risha glares at him. "She's visiting for the summer because she qualified for Eye on Tomorrow." She turns to me. "*Somebody*'s a little touchy about DNA-ture because his parents don't believe in factory-made foods. They're part of the organic farming collective that still grows stuff in fields."

"Yeah, well, somebody else can't seem to take no for an answer when a piece of property's *not* for sale." Alex folds his arms in front of him.

"Well, maybe *somebody* shouldn't have accepted the camp scholarship if he thought Jaden's dad was so horrible. But I bet you'll be there tomorrow." Risha walks off toward the riverbank with Tomas.

I'm left here with Alex. "I don't know much about my dad's work," I squeak out.

"Sorry," Alex says, looking down. Risha's argument seems to have taken the wind out of him. "I'm kind of defensive about the farm." He scuffs his work boots in the dust. "You must know your dad wants to build more houses, right?"

I wish I didn't. But I remember his conversation with Lou about Phase Two. "I kind of heard about it. He's offered to buy your farm?"

"Yeah . . . about ten times." Alex puts down the kickstand, climbs off his bike, and stands looking out over the field. "Most everybody's selling. Mom keeps telling Dad we should take the money, but he won't. Every time your dad sends somebody with another offer, they fight. Selling this place would kill my dad. I know it would." He shrugs. "This is what we do."

"Well, it's not like you *have* to sell. He's just asking," I say. But I remember the frustration in my father's voice when he talked about the land. I bet he's been pushing hard.

"I know. And she's right, too." Alex nods reluctantly toward Risha, who's tossing stones into the river with Tomas. "What I said before was dumb. You're not your dad."

"I don't even know if my dad is my dad anymore." The words slip out before I can filter what I'm saying to this boy I just met. They hang in the air like dust, and Alex looks at me. I bend down to pluck a blade of grass and arrange it between my thumbs to make a whistle. Amelia used to do it all the time and finally taught me how. I lift my hands to my mouth and blow. It sounds like a crow.

"You have some impressive skills there," Alex says, smiling a little.

"Thanks." I try to do it again, but the grass slips from my hands and flutters back to the ground. "Unfortunately, it's not a very useful skill. Do you think they have grass-whistling at Eye on Tomorrow?"

Alex frowns. "Hmm . . . you could study how the force of your breath and the width of the grass affect the rate of vibration. . . ."

"I think I'll stick to meteorology."

"Yeah?" Alex says. "That's what I studied last summer. What's your focus going to be?"

"Honestly?" I haven't told anyone this yet, not even Dad. "What I've always wanted to do is work on storm dissipation. You know . . . the theory that you can actually stop a tornado from forming if you change the conditions in the storm so—"

"I know what storm dissipation is." Alex looks at me as if he's seeing me for the first time, as if we just arrived at the fence. "How'd you get interested in that?"

"I don't know." I lean against the fence next to him, watching Risha and Tomas trying to balance on a log at the edge of the river. They're laughing, and it makes me think of Mom's tree house in the woods from when she was young. She took me there once, on a day when that seemed safe. I climbed up and watched the sun peeking in and out of the leaves. I never wanted to leave. "My mom tells stories about when she was little, before it got like this. I always kind of wish I could have lived back then. Without the storms being part of everybody's lives."

A gust of wind whips the tree branches back and forth over our heads, and a few leaves fly past. One gets stuck in a diamond in the fence. I reach out for it, just as Alex does the same. But he pulls his hand back and looks up at the swirling gray sky. The dark wall cloud in the west is looming closer.

"Hey, Tomas!" he calls. "We gotta get going."

"But we just got here." Risha pouts for a second, but then she's smiling again. "See you in the morning, bright and early!"

"Too early." Tomas grins. "See ya."

Alex waves, and they get on their bikes and ride away.

"Risha, we should go, too. It's getting bad."

We climb back through the fence and head for our bikes. Risha looks back and sighs. "He is so cute."

For a second, Alex's dark eyes flash in my mind, but I know she's talking about Tomas. I climb on my bike and put up the kickstand. "He seems nice. Kind of quiet, huh?"

"He's usually more fun. His mom's been sick, having all these tests, and they just figured out it's pancreatic cancer."

"They can get her treatment, can't they?" Pancreatic cancer was one of the last kinds to be totally cured, but there've been treatment centers around for at least five years now.

"Yeah, but not here. Probably New York—Tomas's brother is in college there—but his dad's worried about the farm and where they'll stay and money and everything. They'll figure it out; it's just on his mind is all."

Wind shakes the trees, and suddenly the weather's on my mind. It's getting darker. "Risha, come on. We need to go."

She looks at me as if I've suggested she bring an umbrella out on a perfectly sunny day. She's not even on her bike yet. "We're fine, Jaden. It's not like it's coming *here*."

But then thunder rumbles, and I don't wait to find out. I start pedaling, and once we're back on the main road, I see the storm *is* closer—way closer. The sky has turned a gray-green color that makes my stomach churn. I don't know if Risha's following, and I don't look up. I remember the turns, back over the bridge, past Risha's house, and back to Dad and Mirielle's place.

I stop in the driveway, gasping for breath.

Risha skids up next to me. "Now what?"

I turn to her, ready to tell her how crazy she is, but over her shoulder, I see the wall cloud, the heart of the storm, moving away from us.

I can only stare.

"It's going the other way," I say finally.

"They always do." Risha tips her head and looks at me. "Let me get this right, Jay-girl. Your father runs the company that built this place. And he didn't bother to let you know you're safe from the tornadoes here?"

"Well, he did, but . . ." I remember his words in the car. His promise to Mom. To me.

Inside the gate, you are completely, one hundred percent safe.

"I figured it just had safer . . . safe rooms or something." I can't stop staring at the cloud that seemed to bounce off our neighborhood as if the chain-link fence extended all the way to the heavens. As if steel wires could keep out the weather.

Risha rolls her eyes. "It's not only the houses. It's *all* of Placid Meadows. That's the whole deal with a StormSafe community; technology keeps the entire property safe."

"How?"

"Well, I don't know exactly." Risha frowns a little. "I always assumed the storms got . . . like . . . zapped at the perimeter somehow. But whatever it is, it works. They *never* hit us. It's even in the contracts."

"In the contracts?" Since when did nature make contracts with anybody?

"When you buy a house. Right there with the number of bedrooms and deeded rights to the playground and whatever. That's why people are willing to pay so much to live in such ugly houses, I guess." She laughs a little and looks at her watch. "I'm going to head home. Grandma's making chicken tandoori." She rides off in the direction of the storm clouds that are barreling off toward someone else's home.

Not ours.

Never ours.

It's in the contract.

Chapter 5

"You won't need that," Dad says as I'm sliding my DataSlate into my backpack Monday morning. "Eye on Tomorrow supplies everything except the brainpower."

"Seriously?" Back home, nobody leaves the house without a DataSlate; how else would you get an alert when a storm's coming? But Dad reminds me.

"You're in Placid Meadows now. You don't need the storm alert." He smiles. "We don't allow DataSlates at camp anyway, until everyone's settled and understands the rules about keeping research confidential."

"Okay." I pull my DataSlate out of my backpack and run my finger around the cool, smooth edge.

"See you this afternoon." Dad goes to his office. A few notes of Mozart drift out before the door slides shut behind him.

I put my DataSlate back in my bag—I'll feel too weird without it—toss the whole thing over my shoulder on the way to the garage, and take off on my bike.

When I get to camp, the wrought-iron gate is wide open, and

Risha's inside, riding her bike around the drop-off driveway with some other kids. There's a boy with a brush cut pacing back and forth on the sidewalk. Maybe he's new, like me. Tess and Ava Beekman, those twins from Britain, are sitting on the grass talking with a couple of boys.

"Hey, Jaden!" Risha waves and almost swerves into a dented green pickup idling by the reception building.

I gasp, first because I think Risha's going to crash, and second, because somebody's driving a gas-powered vehicle. They've been illegal for ten years. How could somebody still be driving one around? Are the rules here that different?

"Easy, genius!" Alex climbs out of the truck, waves to the woman driving, and brushes dried grass from his faded jeans. "Don't run me over on the first day."

Risha doesn't let a second go by. "Where's Tomas?"

"He had to help his mom; I guess she's been feeling pretty crummy. He'll be here later." Alex turns to me and smiles. "You up for this?"

"Of course." But looking up at the tower beyond the reception building, the billowing white dome next to it, the sprawling campus, I wonder if I really am.

Alex turns to say hi to another boy getting dropped off, and Risha and I start toward the reception building. I lean close to her as we walk. "What's up with the truck?"

She makes a scared face. "Oh my gosh, you're not a spy with the International Climate Commission, are you?"

"No, but—"

Risha laughs. "I'm kidding. You didn't really think it was gas-powered, did you? Nobody's that dumb. A bunch of the farmers around here have rigged up old trucks to run on vegetable oil. Kind of messy, but it's cheaper than a new HV." She pulls open the door to the lobby.

"Welcome, welcome." The man waving us inside has a reddish-brown ponytail and a face full of freckles that run together in splotches over his nose. He looks young enough to be a camper, but his badge says VAN GARDNER, EYE ON TOMORROW STAFF.

He steps up to me and smiles. "First summer here?"

I nod.

"I'm Van, camp director." He shakes my hand, then turns to Alex. "Good to have you back, my man." He nods at Risha. "Planning more work in bio-botanicals?"

She shakes her head. "I'd rather be in the cloning lab this summer if I can. Tomas was telling me about it, and it sounds interesting."

While Risha talks with Van, I reach over my shoulder to get my DataSlate from my backpack. I want to see if Mom answered the message I sent after dinner last night. Reception in the jungle's probably too spotty for videophone to work, but she should at least have text messaging.

"They're going to take that," Alex says. "No outside technology in the beginning."

"Really?" I pretend to be surprised.

"Got a drive you can put your stuff on so you don't lose too much when they destroy it?"

"Destroy it?"

Alex raises his eyebrows. "Last kid who brought a DataSlate had to watch while they took it out back and ran over it with the Eye on Tomorrow field trip vehicle. They tried to run him over, too, but he was fast." A smile creeps onto his face.

"Very funny."

"I'm just messing with you. They *will* take it for now, though. You can get it at the end of the day."

Sure enough, Van steps up and holds out his hand. "Sorry, Alex speaks the truth."

I give it to him, and he points us toward the auditorium. "Let's head into orientation and get this show on the road."

I end up sitting between Alex and Risha, but all her attention turns toward Tomas when he arrives. "You're doing cloning again, right? Because that's what I'm requesting."

"So, Jaden," Alex says. "You and I kind of have the same area of interest."

"Yeah, I've always liked weather," is all I can think to say. My fingers are itching for the DataSlate Van took away. Even if I can't connect with Mom, having it makes me feel like she's not so far away.

"All right, campers! Good morning!" Van bounds down the wide steps to the podium at the front of the auditorium. "I'm going to help you get your bearings. These first few days, we'll walk through the facilities and review rules and regulations."

Van presses a button on the podium, and legs grow up from out of the floor in front of us, materializing from the shiny black shoes on up. I know it's only a holo-sim, but it still startles me. Within a few seconds, the figure has a torso, arms, a neck. And finally, a face.

My father's face.

And my father's voice.

"Good morning, Eye on Tomorrow campers."

Dad's American StormSafe employees opened Eye on Tomorrow four years ago, right after he left for Russia, but it doesn't surprise me that it's his face and voice greeting the campers. Even from overseas, Dad would have made sure his vision played out the way he wanted.

"We are so very glad that you're here," the holo-sim says.

It's just a computer-generated projection, but it makes my hands go cold, as if this picture made of light has Dad's real eyes and mind. Does it know I brought my DataSlate even though he said not to? That it was confiscated?

I look up, but the eyes on the holo-sim look like they're focused on something in the back of the auditorium. No one else seems fazed by Dad's appearance. Tomas is watching Risha doodle on her notebook, zeros and ones like those on her bracelets. I watch, too, for a second, until Dad's voice starts up again.

"As you know, Eye on Tomorrow is a special place. Here, you'll be provided with the most exclusive data sets, the most advanced technology, the most elite instructors . . ."

I glance over at Van and catch him mouthing the words that holo-Dad must deliver to every new summer crew.

"Along with that privilege comes responsibility. Here at Eye on Tomorrow, we expect campers to arrive on time each morning. Bring nothing but yourselves for now; we supply everything except the brainpower. And leave with nothing. No equipment, data files, or documents may be taken from the campus at the end of the day, and photography is prohibited, to protect the unique learning environment we've worked so hard to build."

"Now let's all keep an Eye on Tomorrow." The holo-sim winks. "And always do your best, because we'll have our eye on you." Then it vanishes from the top of Dad's head down to the last shiny black toe of his shoe, as if someone took an eraser to the air and rubbed him out, atom by atom.

Van steps forward. "Ready to take a walk?"

Alex taps my shoulder. "So are you requesting meteorology for a focus area? Some people work in teams."

Is he asking if I want to work with him? This is the same kid who didn't like my last name yesterday. "Haven't really thought about it yet."

"Well sure, there's no rush," he says, and looks down at his hands resting on the seat in front of us.

"You coming?" Risha calls from the door, and I realize we're holding up the line.

I leave Alex's not-quite-an-invitation alone for now and hurry to the door. When we step outside, sunlight burns my eyes, and warm, wet outdoor air wraps around me. Risha and Tomas have gone ahead, so I walk with Alex.

"This way." Van points us toward the next building over, the one with the white dome, a giant golf ball perched on top of a short, thick column of glass. "Might as well start with the best we have to offer."

The best the camp has to offer? I look over, and Alex answers the question before I even ask it out loud.

"Storm Sim Dome."

"What's in there?"

"Computers," he says as we step up to the huge building, waiting for Van to scan his fingerprint and open the door. "Turbo-fans. Storm simulators. Storm pool and plumbing."

I stare up at the dome, processing what he's just said. "Are you telling me there's real wind and rain and everything in there?" It's shiny, almost too big and bright to look at up close.

Van holds the door open. "File in." The air inside is cold and clean, and the main chamber of the dome is cavernous. It reminds me of the story Aunt Linda told me once about her family's trip to that old amusement park, Epcot Center, when she was little. It's gone now, wiped out years ago in one of the first inland hurricanes like the rest of Disney's Florida empire, but Aunt Linda said it was magical, like being inside a giant globe, the heart of the whole world.

My eyes drift down from the dome's ceiling, and I see what looks like the heart of this building—an enclosed safety-glass box housing the mainframe computer system that must control everything.

A model city surrounds the console. It looks like Oklahoma City used to look forty years ago, full of offices and shopping areas, parks and schools, homes, and barns on the outskirts, all built to scale. About half the city is in perfect condition; the rest of the buildings are as battered as the ones *outside* Placid Meadows are now.

The cement floor is still damp. Van gestures down at it. "Watch the puddles; we had a test run earlier."

I look around, wondering how it all works. The precipitation must come from the water heads mounted on the ceiling and the hoses that snake out from the walls every few meters. It even smells like a storm in here. Does that rain-ruined smell just happen, or is it pumped in with the wind, through the enormous fans that hang from the ceiling and walls?

"Why do they do all this?" I whisper to Alex. "Wouldn't computer simulations be easier?"

"They used to do that, but there were too many variables. Van says you need real buildings, real towns, to see what a real storm can do."

The last few campers file in. It's quiet, but then a motor clicks on, and the fans begin to hum quietly, almost as if they're whispering promises about what they can do.

Tomas is the first to speak up. "You gonna run this thing for us?"

Van shakes his head. "Later in the week, maybe. It doesn't mean much if you don't understand what you're seeing, but this is where our meteorology program is based. It's all exclusive, patented technology—one of a kind. Well, three of a kind, actually. There's one up at the StormSafe complex and one at the company's property in Russia. Just wanted you to have a look at it for today."

He walks us out of the dome, back into the bright light and sunshine air.

The rest of the morning is a parade of in and outs, more rooms filled with elaborate equipment. This is what I imagined Dad's

StormSafe headquarters might look like. If they provide this stuff at a camp for teenagers, what must he have at work?

After lunch, we're back in the orientation center to talk about areas of study.

This time, there's no holo-sim of Dad. Instead, a three-dimensional globe of light drops from the ceiling as classical music starts to play.

Alex leans over. "Mozart," he whispers. "They did some study that shows classical music helps to develop synapses between the hemispheres of the brain and makes us better problem solvers."

It's also Dad's favorite, but I don't mention that. Alex probably wouldn't like Mozart anymore.

Dad's voice rises over the violins. "Welcome back, Eye on Tomorrow campers. This afternoon, we'll take a look at the problems our world is facing today . . . and tomorrow. And we'll ask you to make a commitment to one of those challenges for the summer."

The globe at the center of the room spins and then explodes into a million bits of light that shoot out toward the walls, and in its place now is a spinning cloud. It's just light, just a holo-image, but somehow the air feels wetter, heavier than it did a few seconds ago. Dad's voice describes the first challenge, the one we all know about already—the storms.

"Warmer global temperatures have led to increased instances of tornadic storms, not only in the traditional storm belt, but worldwide. Through the careful planning and vigilance of the

International Climate Committee, we've managed to reverse the planetary warming trend. However, as you know, campers, it will be two more years before greenhouse gases are reduced to a level that will have a positive impact on weather patterns. Our goal at StormSafe and here at Eye on Tomorrow is to bridge the gap—to find solutions that will keep people safe until then."

It's not only the tornadoes, Dad says, but also hurricanes of greater intensity and size, tropical cyclones around the globe, droughts and heat waves, that need to be controlled. "When we master our climate," Dad's voice promises, "we'll be the masters of our planet."

He goes on to describe three more challenges: the bio-botanicals program that he promises will revolutionize the world's food supply and end hunger through an expansion of DNA-ture bioengineering and factory-grown food practices; the robotics research that will automate the world's industries and services, from motorcycles to medicine, within thirty years; and the cellular generation and human cloning center, where scholars have already begun developing successful technology to create, through DNA-based cloning, any part of the human body for transplant or other use.

When the human figure representing the last area of study fades and sinks into the floor, the lights come on and Van is back in front of us, bouncing on his sneakers. "Ready to solve the world's problems? We'll see you back here, first thing in the morning, to get started."

Chapter 6

The rest of the week flies past in a blur of computer screens, robotics, radar and satellite panels, stainless steel counters, test tubes, and greenhouses with more monitoring equipment than I could have imagined. Each day, Van leads us through a different research center on campus. Sometimes we do lab experiments and try out equipment. Van asks us questions along the way to see who might be best suited to each area of study.

I figured kids who have spent two and three summers here would be way ahead of me, but I can actually answer most of Van's questions. Especially when it comes to meteorology.

"You're doing great," Risha whispers to me as we walk between buildings.

"Thanks. I'm surprised I'm not further behind everybody who's been here before."

"You're not behind at all," Risha says, pulling open the door to the bio-botanicals building. "The program this year is way more intense than what we did last summer."

Even so, Risha knows the answer to almost every question in the bio-botanicals lab, where she spent last summer.

"Are you sure you want to switch to cloning?" I whisper.

She glances sideways at Tomas, smiles and shrugs at me, and answers another question. Her bracelets clink together whenever she raises her hand, and finally, when Van turns to explain some new kind of lower-carb sweet corn, I reach for her wrist. "What are the numbers supposed to be?"

She slips a bracelet off her hand and passes it to me. "It's binary code, the sequence of ones and zeros they used to represent processing instructions for a computer."

I run my finger along waves of numbers etched in the gold. "So what will this tell a computer to do?"

"Nothing." She wiggles the other two off her wrist. "This is just regular text." She points to the first line of numbers on one bracelet. "See this sequence?"

I read it aloud. "01011001."

"That's *y*."

"That's all one letter?"

"And then here . . ." She points to the second set of eight numbers, 01101111. ". . . is an *o*. It spells out, 'You must be the change you wish to see in the world.' It's a saying from some old Indian guy, Gandhi. My grandmother's always quoting him and trying to get me to read about him." She waves at the air with her green-and-black-striped fingernails. "She figured if she translated it into in a language I like, I might actually pay attention, so she had these made for me."

"Your grandmother sounds awesome." I try to imagine what Grandma Athena would be like if she were alive. What would she talk to me about? Risha slides the bracelets back onto her wrist as Van leads us down a hall toward the next lab.

"Is the code on your notebook a quote from the same guy?" I ask Risha.

"No . . ." She pulls me off to the side, tips her head toward Tomas, and whispers, "It's his name. In binary code."

That makes me laugh. I should have guessed. "Now I understand why you like it, even if it isn't really used anymore."

She shrugs. "Not everything has to be useful."

I think about the book of poems in my nightstand. "Don't let my dad hear you say that. You'll be tossed out of this place faster than you can blink."

She laughs and pulls me along to catch up with the boys.

On our second visit to the Storm Sim Dome, Van skips the quiz and sits us down on a row of long benches along one wall. "Instead of asking you questions here to check on your knowledge, we're going to try something else."

He pulls a box of DataSlates from under the bench and starts passing them out. "These are preloaded with the same software we have on the core system in the dome. You've all been asking me when you'll get to see the Sim Dome in action, and the answer is now. Show me what you'd do if I turned this entire dome over to you for one simulation." He hands the last DataSlate to Tomas.

"What are we doing with these?" Risha asks.

"You're formulating a theory about the effect that a given variable has on storm formation. Then I'd like you to design a simulation to test it."

Tess Beekman squints at him. "I don't get it."

Van sighs. "There's a simulation program loaded on each of these DataSlates. It will ask you for a theory. You need an if-then statement. For example, if you think that raising the temperature in the atmosphere will cause a storm to move more quickly, you select that theory. *If* the temperature is raised x degrees, *then* this will happen. Then you design a simulation. Don't worry—the software will walk you through the steps. Essentially, you'll be telling the Sim Dome what conditions to create in the atmosphere above our model town, and then you'll see what effect that has on the storms." He looks around. "At least some of you will. We're only going to run the most promising simulations in the dome." He looks back at Tess. "Understand now?"

She shrugs. "Kind of."

"Okay then. Get to it." He looks at his watch. "You have one hour." He heads for the staff computer in the corner of the room.

The DataSlate suddenly feels heavy in my hands. This isn't a quick question I can raise my hand to answer or a click-the-right-response exam. It's an actual problem with no solution in sight, and I'm supposed to come up with one.

Risha sits next to me on the bench, her fingers already flying over her DataSlate, words pouring onto her screen. I look down the row of DataSlates in laps. Everyone else is inputting text.

My heart feels like it's thumping out that frantic stream of num-bers from Risha's bracelets, but I open the Sim Dome software and stare at the blank text box with "Theory" written at the top.

The only sound is the hum of fans and the tapping of fingers, reminding me that Eye on Tomorrow is in a different league. This is a place for people with theories.

I stare at the empty box and panic. I may have a head full of ideas, but none of them are my own. My parents are the scientists; I'm the kid who loves to read, who can always get a hundred on the test when the answers are supplied ahead of time. But here, we are starting from nothing.

I look down the row. The anxious boy with the brush cut types a few words. Looks at his watch. Types a few more. Rubs his finger under his lower lip. Looks at his watch again. Just being near him makes me nervous.

There must be something. Some theory I can test.

If. Then.

If. Then.

If something, then . . . what?

I close my eyes and imagine the storm from my first night here. The one that never touched Placid Meadows.

If a housing contract promises storm-free living, then the tor-nadoes stay away.

If a company builds a magic fence around a neighborhood, then the residents live happily ever after.

None of it makes sense. What's keeping the storms at bay? Where do they go when they turn away from the fence?

If. Then.

Where could the storms go that wouldn't hurt anyone?

Not away. But up.

Back into the sky.

If. Then.

What makes a tornado go away?

I close my eyes. The DataSlate is still cool in my hands, but the rest of me breathes in the memory of hot, humid air. An August night, five, maybe six years ago, watching a storm in the distance with Dad. It loomed, big and dark, over the Adirondacks, heading east across the lake to Vermont. We creaked back and forth on the porch swing as the thunder grew louder.

We watched that storm swell bigger, watched it uncurl a long, dark arm that wrapped around the sky and started spinning. It dropped down from the cloud, then stretched into a longer, skinnier funnel as if some potter's hands were shaping it, all the while spinning the wheel faster and faster.

"Dad, should we go downstairs?" I felt like we should. The storm was getting closer, and tree branches were starting to scratch against the porch roof in the wind.

"Soon." Dad stared at the storm, mesmerized. Then he squinted off to the west. "Or maybe not."

Another cloud was approaching, a big brother to the first, taller, with broader shoulders. When they met, it was like the younger brother flinched. The tornado lifted up from the ground and never caught its breath again. We watched, creaking back and forth as it rose slowly back up into the cloud.

Then we sat and listened to the rain.

Later, when Dad tucked me into bed, I asked where the tornado had gone. Most fathers would have made up a story for a kid my age, maybe something about God pulling on the rope, tugging it back to the heavens, away from us. A cozy-under-the-sheets, sleep-tight story. Mine gave a meteorology lesson.

"Sometimes, Jaden, a cold outflow of wind from a storm system can cause a tornado to dissipate."

"You mean go away?"

"Yes. And in this case, it was that second thunderstorm that came and wrapped up the first one in its outflow." He tucked the cool sheets around me. "Bet you can't spin around now either."

I wiggled, and giggled, and Dad kissed me on the head. "Night, WeatherGirl."

"Twenty-five minutes left." Van's voice snaps me back to now. I open my eyes and stare at the blank box on my screen.

I have an idea. It's an old one from a hot summer night that feels like a lifetime ago, but it's all I have, so I start typing.

IF a tornado-producing storm collides with a second, larger storm . . .

That's a good start. There will be data from different-size storms loaded in the simulator. I can choose two that should work.

THEN . . . Then what?

I fly through the procedural steps, and I'm thinking how to state the outcome when Van calls time, so I simply type:

PROJECTED OUTCOME: Tornado dies.

—just as he steps down the row, takes the DataSlate from my hands, and adds it to the stack teetering in his arms.

"Well, now," he says, lining them up on the counter outside the safety box that encloses the real control panel. "This is an interesting collection of theories." He picks up the first few and sets them back down without saying anything. "I can see we'll need to work on experiment design. Some of these aren't even in a format that could be entered into our dome software."

He moves on to the next DataSlate, which he reads and tucks under his arm, nodding. He goes through the rest of the slates and picks up the last one, too.

He holds those up and turns to us. "We have two theories that are developed enough—not perfect, mind you—but developed *enough* to run on the simulator. Mr. Carillo?"

Alex stands up.

"Come on into the control chamber with me. Miss Meggs? You, too. The rest of you head over to the observation area behind the glass. We'll explain each simulation on the microphone so you know what you're seeing. Let's find out if either theory holds up in the Dome."

Chapter 7

"Can everyone hear me?" Van's voice booms out of the speakers, and on the other side of the room, behind the safety glass, the rest of the campers nod. He turns back to Alex and me. "Who's first?"

I look at Alex. Is his stomach churning like mine?

"I'll go first," he says. Van stands up, and Alex slides into the chair in front of the control panels. "Do you want me to explain what I wrote?"

"Of course." Van adjusts the microphone.

"My theory involves storm dissipation," Alex says. His voice echoes through the dome.

Van leans in toward the microphone, glancing back at me. "Actually, both theories do. That's why this is a particularly interesting pairing."

"Okay." Alex takes a breath. "Current theory holds that tornadoes form when the hot updraft within a supercell meets a cold rainy downdraft. So here's my idea." Alex reads from his DataSlate. His fingers have dirt and grass stains as if he came right from working on the farm this morning, but his hands aren't shaking like mine.

"*If* the cold downdraft of a tornado-forming supercell is heated with microwave energy from an orbiting satellite, *then* an essential ingredient for tornado formation will be absent, and the storm will dissipate."

He looks at Van, who nods. "Similar to the research you were doing last summer, no?"

"It is, but I've been tweaking it," Alex says. "Should I just . . . run it now?"

"Go for it. The Dome has simulated satellites built into the ceiling. Adjust the level for how much energy they'll be giving off. Choose one of the preloaded historical tornado models—any one of those should work—give it a few seconds to form, and then run your simulation. We'll see if it dissipates." He almost sounds bored, but my heart is pumping, and it's not even my turn yet.

Some of the confidence has drained out of Alex's face, but his hands are steady as he connects his DataSlate to the main system, transfers his data, and presses the button to start the Sim Dome re-creation.

The lights go down, and immediately, water vapor hisses out of ducts in the ceiling and on the upper walls. Like magic, clouds form over the model city. The synthetic fabric that makes up the tree foliage rustles and then whips in the wind generated by the fans that surround the community on all sides. When the cloud darkens and gives birth to the beginning of a swirling, charcoal-colored funnel, Van nudges Alex. "Go ahead."

Alex's finger hovers over the INTRODUCE VARIABLE button. He takes a breath and then taps it lightly.

A panel slides open on the ceiling, exposing a model satellite that lowers slowly, a foot or so. Under the clouds, the tornado stretches lower, lower, until it touches down inches from the first building—a small red barn next to a white farmhouse outside the city.

A sharp ray of light streaks down from the satellite. I can't look away from the light, the storm, the clouds, the funnel, to see how Alex is reacting, but I feel his body tensing next to me. Will this blast of energy warm the tornado away?

The tornado licks at the edges of the barn. "Come on," Alex whispers, and I tear my eyes from the storm to look at his face.

His eyes travel down the beam from the satellite, as if he could strengthen it by pure will, all the way to the heart of the cloud, where that blast of energy *should* be warming the downdraft, *should* be stopping the storm's rotation.

"Come on, come on!"

The storm explodes then, with a sharp burst of lightning, and even Van jumps in surprise. Blinding light fills the dome and seems to feed the tornado. It swells up bigger, darker. It devours the barn, the house, and then races from the farm to the first simulated neighborhood. Houses. A school. In pieces. A church steeple flies off into the vortex. The rest of the building follows. A playground. Slides. Swings. A tumbling jumble of monkey bars all sucked into the storm.

Alex's fist pounds down on the counter, and Van reaches forward to press a red button on the control panel.

The lights flicker, then come on overhead.

The rain stops pounding. Leftover drips from the ceiling plunk down onto the rubble as the clouds are sucked into the ventilation system in the walls.

When they clear, I stare out at half a town, perfect and painted with trees still standing, plastic people still posed on porches.

The other half is flattened.

Alex's jaw is tense, his fist still clenched on the counter where it landed.

"That's why we have the Sim Dome, my friend." Van puts a hand on Alex's shoulder. "Sometimes, things work on paper; they work fine in your mind, but the real deal turns out very different. That's why we don't do this all digitally anymore. Until you're dealing with real wind, meeting real buildings, you don't know what'll happen." He turns to me. "You're next, Miss Meggs. Let's see what you do with the half a city that survived your colleague's experiment."

Alex stands and steps back so I can sit down, and I feel his eyes on me as I'm opening my file. I glance over my shoulder, expecting . . . I don't know. Maybe that he'll want me to fail, too, not to show him up. But even though his eyes are still intense, frustrated, he gives me the smallest nod. Encouragement?

I make the connection and feed my data to the mainframe computer.

"Which storm's going to be your subject?" Van leans over my shoulder and taps the screen, and a list of model storms appears. I choose an NF-3 that hit Germany eight years ago. And then I'll need to introduce a larger supercell to serve as the second storm in my experiment. My hands shake so much I can barely control my finger to point to the right model. Some of the shaking is nerves—Van standing over me, Alex's eyes on me, the wall of faces behind the glass, all staring from the other side of the room—but some of it is excitement, too. Could this actually work?

"Go ahead." Van flicks his hand toward the button that will dim the lights and start the clouds building.

I swallow hard and tap the command: BEGIN SIMULATION.

Clouds swirl out of the walls and down from the ceiling, like they did with Alex's storm, and this time, I'm ready when the wind starts to whip the trees and the rain pounds down on the roofs that are left in the model city. I watch the bottom edge of the wall cloud, holding my breath, until the funnel cloud takes shape and touches down.

The ground explodes in a whirl of dust, and Van points to the words INTRODUCE VARIABLE on the screen. "Do it now."

I press the button and hold my breath.

The tornado is already on the ground as the second storm begins to form off to the left. The vapor is still gathering when the first storm hits the model town's business district. It's not as strong as Alex's tornado, so the buildings aren't flattened, but roofs tear away from shops, and debris flies.

"Come on," I whisper, and I hear the echo of Alex's hopes as I watch the new funnel finish forming, watch it darken and advance toward the first. "Come on. Go. *Go.*"

The first tornado strengthens. It tosses cars that were parked on Main Street, hurls them through store windows, and the sound of shattering sim-glass—how do they make it so loud?—crashes over the wind.

My second storm closes in on the first. "Come on," I whisper. "Knock it down. Do it."

And I hear Alex's voice, quiet behind me. "Come on, work."

For a second, the tornado stops in its path, churning up dirt, frozen in time as the two storms finally touch.

Then it goes wild.

The big brother cloud, the one that was supposed to wrap around the first storm and settle it down, does something else. It opens up its arms, sucks the first storm inside, and squeezes, until the whole thing turns into a darker, angrier, super-charged monster.

"No!" I scream. I can't help it. Because a second tornado drops down from the cloud like an angry whip. And a third. Both stronger than the first. They barrel down streets, through downtown, and the office buildings implode and feed the storm until the whole city is gone.

Van's arm blurs in front of me and presses the button to shut down the dome. Only then do I feel my face is wet with tears. I swipe at them with my sleeve.

Van smirks. "Well, scholars. We have some rebuilding to do, don't we?"

I feel a hand on my shoulder. Alex.

I brush it away, stand up, and head for the door, but Van puts up a hand to stop me. "Those were good efforts from both of you. But you've got a long road of research ahead before you can produce something that works in this world as well as that one." He nods down at the DataSlate in my hand. I'd forgotten it wasn't mine.

Mine's at home in the drawer with my poetry book. I haven't brought it back since that first day.

I set the DataSlate on the counter, but Van shakes his head. "Keep that one over the weekend. Play with some new ideas. Bring it back on Monday. I'm going to recommend you two for the meteorology team." He opens the door, and we head out into the humid air of the Dome to meet up with the others, filing out of the observation room.

"All right, campers, let's call it a day. I've seen what I need to see. On Monday, I'd like you to tell me what you'd like to study and whether you'll work alone or with a partner."

We leave the Dome and start back toward the welcome building, but there's none of the usual in-between-buildings banter. I get the feeling that even the campers who were around last summer have never seen anything in the Sim Dome quite like this.

"Whatcha doing for lunch?" Risha finally asks when we get back to our bikes.

I shrug. "I'm not too hungry. That was just so . . . intense."

"I think we need a picnic!" Risha stands up on the pedals of her bike and pulls the front wheel off the ground to spin around.

It's such a crazy idea, I laugh, which I'm sure was her whole goal. Picnics are like bike riding back home. But it figures there'd be a StormSafe picnic shelter, too. "Where do you have picnics?"

"I know a place," she says, "but I'll have to blindfold you to take you there; it's top-secret-super-classified."

I laugh again, and my stomach grumbles.

"You guys have to come, too, okay?" She makes her top-secret-super-classified picnic eyes at Alex and Tomas.

"I guess." Tomas gives her the lazy smile. "As long as Alex and geek girl put their killer DataSlates away."

Risha laughs, but Alex doesn't. "I'll come," he says, and puts the DataSlate into his backpack.

I reach over my shoulder to unzip mine, and a warm hand catches my fingers.

"Got it." Alex lets go of my hand and unzips the bag so I can slip the DataSlate inside. He gives the strap a light tug, and I turn around. "Sounds like we're going to be in the met program together." He takes a deep breath. "Maybe we can talk about being partners?"

I can't help smiling a little. I wasn't crazy that day in the auditorium. It was an invitation after all.

I nod and get on my bike. "Sure. We can talk."

Chapter 8

"Your top-secret picnic location looks kind of familiar, Rish." Tomas weaves through trees to the fence, holding a cooler full of food from Risha's house out in front of him.

I scan the horizon for clouds, but the sky's all blue. My DataSlate in my backpack is quiet—no weather alerts for now—and the afternoon sun feels good after a morning of air-conditioned camp.

We climb through the gap in the fence, balance beam our way across a fallen tree stretching over the river, and follow Risha, who's run ahead through the trees, bracelets clinking on her wrist.

"Here we go." Tomas steps into a field with neatly planted rows of grain, and we head for the gazebo on the other side. Its white paint is peeling, but Risha flies up the steps and perches herself on the fence as if it's her fairy-tale castle, and she's been waiting all day for the prince to get home.

"It's beautiful." It's like I've fallen into one of the olden-days books Mom used to read to me.

"Yeah," Tomas says. He looks a little sad.

"How long have you lived around here?"

"Since I was born. It's getting hard to take care of the farm, though, with my brother gone. My dad's not sure . . ."

"You can't sell, man," Alex says. "No way."

"Yeah, I know. Dad's all talk. I don't think he'll ever leave this place." He lifts the cooler onto the picnic table.

"Jaden, sit by me!" Risha pats a spot next to her on the splintery bench.

I sit down and get a sandwich from the cooler. I'm starving, and for the first time since we left Eye on Tomorrow, I feel relaxed enough to talk about the Sim Dome. "Sure is nice to see blue sky after this morning."

"I know!" Risha takes a big bite of her sandwich and goes on talking through the lettuce. "That sim was crazy-real."

Alex sits down across from me. "Have you ever . . ." He pauses. "Never mind."

I take a bite of my DNA-ture apple and look up at Alex. "Have I ever what?"

"Well . . . have you seen the equipment your dad has at work? I mean, you probably can't talk about it if it's classified and stuff, but I wonder if it's the same."

I shake my head. "Never even been there."

"It feels like . . ." Alex unwraps his sandwich but doesn't eat. He turns it over and over in his hands, as if the bread and turkey and cheese layers hold the answer to some puzzle. "We have so much equipment at Eye on Tomorrow—and I'm sure your dad has even better stuff up there." He nods toward the StormSafe compound in the distance. The sun is reflecting off its steel and safety-glass walls, making it glow. "It feels like we should be able to figure this out."

I nod and look to the west, where the sky's clouding up. I know exactly what he means. How could we know everything we know, have everything we have, and not be able to live in a world where you can go for a walk without watching the clouds?

"I'm going to pick flowers." Risha tips her head off toward the meadow. Before she goes, she bends down by the picnic table and plucks a dandelion that's gone to seed. "Make a wish!" She blows on it, and silver stars swirl all around our heads as she runs off. Tomas picks up the bag of *nankhatai*, the Indian tea cookies Risha's grandmother made, and follows her.

Alex looks toward the clouds on the horizon. "They better not go far. This isn't Placid Meadows."

His voice has an edge.

"What's wrong with Placid Meadows?"

He shakes his head. "Nothing. I'd imagine it's great if you can afford to live there. But you must know what those places cost."

I shrug, rather than admit that I don't. I wonder if our picnic spot is part of the land Dad's trying to buy for his Phase Two.

There's a rustling in the weeds then, and a golden retriever bounds out of the brush and up the steps to our table. It puts a paw up on Alex's lap and tips its head.

"Hey, Newton." Alex scratches the dog behind an ear, then carefully untangles a burr stuck in its long reddish fur.

"Sorry," he says, looking up. "I didn't mean to make you feel crummy. It's just hard to take sometimes. But what Risha said before is right. If it weren't for your dad, I'd be right here—and only here—this summer, pulling weeds and picking worms off tomato plants and running for the storm shelter every other day instead of spending half of it in a huge science complex."

We sit for a long time, watching the clouds. Alex feeds Newton scraps of turkey from his sandwich, and I listen to Risha laughing with Tomas.

When Alex finally speaks, it's so quiet I barely hear him. "I'm frustrated, I guess. I thought I'd figured out how to stop them all together."

"The storms?"

He nods and starts picking at the weathered wood of the picnic table.

"I'm starting to think it's impossible. My dad's been working on this forever. He's got some exclusive agreement with the government for his weather manipulation research. Anyway, Mom told me they were sure they had the formulas this winter, but when they did the simulation, it failed."

"Did you see the formulas?" He leans forward.

"No. I probably wouldn't have understood them anyway. This stuff is out of our league."

"No, it's not. Last summer at Eye on Tomorrow, I had a formula drawn up, based on the same theory, and it *worked*. At least on paper."

"Did you run it through the Sim Dome?"

He sighs. "That didn't work, and I don't know why. It should have." He jerks his hand back from the table. "Ow! Splinter."

He pulls it out, and blood seeps out from under his thumbnail. He stands and shoves his hand into his pocket. "Look, I just . . . I feel like I'm out of ideas. That's why I was kind of hoping we could work together." He doesn't look at me and doesn't wait for an answer. He starts gathering sandwich wrappers and picks up the rest of my apple. "Are you going to finish this?"

I shake my head. He looks down at the DNA-ture sticker and grimaces. "Is this stuff all you ever eat?"

"It's not bad. I'm not in the mood for fruit right now."

"Oh no?" His dark eyes smile a little. "Come with me." He takes off across the field with Newton at his side.

I look over my shoulder for Risha, who's plopped down in the weeds, showing Tomas how to weave daisies together into a chain. Behind them, the clouds are growing, but they're still a long way off.

There's time before our weather alerts go off, so I catch up with Alex as he reaches the barn. It smells like old paint and hay. A twisted copper weathervane with a rooster on top leans against the side.

"That's an old one, huh?" I run my finger along the W for West.

"It was already here when my grandpa bought this place way back," Alex says. He looks up at the barn's sloped roof. "Came flying off in the wind Friday night."

"That storm we saw coming from the fence?"

He nods. "Just missed us. We were lucky. Tomas says their

neighbors two places down lost their barn and almost their whole herd of Scottish Highland cattle."

"That you, Alex?" a deep voice calls from the barn, and a man in a faded blue shirt steps out, brushing dust off his hands. His face looks like he's spent a lot of time working in the sun, and he has warm brown eyes surrounded by the kind of wrinkles you get from laughing. "You take care of the chickens yet?" he asks Alex. Then he sees me.

"Dad, this is my friend Jaden I told you about. From camp."

His father nods at me and reaches out to shake my hand. His is warm and rough with calluses. "Very nice to meet you," he says. But he doesn't smile. He looks back at Alex and raises his eyebrows. "Don't forget we have a farm to run." And heads back into the barn.

"Sorry," Alex says, turning to me. "He's . . . not thrilled with us being friends."

"Oh."

Goats or sheep bleat from inside the barn, and there's the sound of feed pouring into a trough. Alex looks at the barn door as if he can see through it. "He's really not cold like that. He's just—I made the mistake of telling him who your dad is, so . . ."

"So he figures I'm here to make another offer on your farm?" My face flushes hot, and I turn away from the barn. "I . . . I should be getting home anyway. It's—"

"Jaden, wait." He puts a hand on my shoulder. It's tentative, barely there, but it keeps me from walking away. "I want to show you something." He steps onto a low stone wall that runs along the barn. "Follow me."

I hesitate.

"Please?"

I climb up and follow him to a patch of garden on the south side of the barn. Mounds of green grow out of straw-covered soil, and ripening red spots peek out from each plant.

"You *grow* strawberries?" I've never seen strawberries growing outside, as far as I can remember. They were one of the first DNA-ture products. Dad used to bring home cartons full of fat, smooth, seedless berries. "These are so much smaller than real ones."

Alex laughs. "These *are* real ones." He squats down, gently brushes aside some leaves with one hand, reaches deep into the heart of the plant with the other, and pulls out a perfect red berry.

No. It's not perfect.

The berry is asymmetrical. One ripe, red side bulges higher than the other, and raggedy green leaves stick out the top in every direction, like some crazy puppet hat. The dimple at the base of the fruit looks a little like the one on Alex's chin.

He holds it up. "*This* is a *real* strawberry. Look."

"It looks great," I say.

"No. *Really* look." He rests one hand on my shoulder and with the other, holds the strawberry out about a foot in front of my face. "Tell me what you see." I try to ignore the warmth spreading down my arm and look, really look.

"It's red." But even as I say it, I know it's more than that. It's not red like the strawberries in Mirielle's refrigerator at the house. Not the perfect, crayon-box red, the same on every side. This one is a million shades of red, from the deep rich color of new blood to the blush that must be creeping up my cheeks. "It's a lot of different promises of red."

"What else?" He turns the strawberry slowly, but doesn't move his hand from my shoulder.

"The seeds are different colors, too." I can't compare them to the seeds on DNA-ture strawberries because they've been engineered out—people who took the "build-a-better-fruit" surveys complained they got stuck in their teeth—so they're gone now. The skin is perfectly soft and smooth. But this strawberry has tiny hairs that catch the sun and raindrop-shaped seeds spilling down the sides, around all of its uneven curves. "Gold and pink and brownish."

"Now." Alex smiles a little. "Close your eyes."

I look at him.

"Don't worry." He laughs a little and takes his hand off my shoulder. "I want you to taste this. *Really* taste it."

I close my eyes. I can still feel the warmth of his hand on my shoulder, or maybe it's the sun getting warmer.

"Ready? Open your mouth."

I do.

The soft-rough seeds brush my lips first. Then that same surface—alive, I think—settles on my tongue, along with the warmth. It feels like this berry still holds the heat of the sun inside it.

I am almost afraid to bite down, but Alex's hand rests on my shoulder again, and I am painfully self-conscious of what I must look like standing here with my mouth around a strawberry, so I take a bite.

And I taste the sun.

All of the warmth, the sweetness, this imperfect outdoor berry has collected explodes in my mouth. And eyes still closed, suddenly, I am three years old, sitting cross-legged in a garden or field—I don't know where exactly—but I am picking berries with Aunt Linda. Dropping them into a big wicker basket in the dirt between us, and my hands are stained red, and my chin is sticky with sweet red juice, and Aunt Linda is laughing in the sun.

I had forgotten what strawberries felt like until now.

I open my eyes. Alex has dropped his hand from my shoulder again, and the one that held the strawberry hangs at his side, still pinching a clump of leaves and a bit of berry with my teeth marks.

"Now are you in mood for fruit?" he asks.

I would answer, but I'm afraid it would come out a million kinds of stupid. So I nod, and bend down to pick another berry. It's rough and imperfect, and perfectly warm, in my hand.

Chapter 9

You *have* to partner with him at camp. You guys look so cute together!" Risha's cheeks are flushed as we hurry back to the fence, and I'm not sure if it's because we're rushing now that the clouds are rumbling closer or because she was having her own picnic moment with Tomas and the daisy chain.

"Aw, cut it out." I climb through the gap in the silver wires. "He did ask if I wanted to work together, though. And we're interested in the same theories of weather manipulation, so maybe . . ."

Risha strikes a professor pose, with serious eyes and hands pressed together. "We're interested in the same theories," she mimics, and laughs. "I think you're interested in more than his theories, Jaden."

When we reach the end of the dirt path, she looks up and down the street, hands on her hips. "What do you want to do? They're running Animals of Yesterday at the Entertainment Dome. You get to walk along a trail with a bunch of extinct wildlife—woolly mammoths and polar bears and stuff."

"No, I think I want to go home." I wonder how Mom's doing in

Costa Rica. I hope her endangered frogs don't become part of the Animals of Yesterday show anytime soon. I wish she'd get in touch.

Our DataSlate weather alerts go off, and I jump about a mile. Risha laughs.

The storm is close enough now that people outside Placid Meadows will be heading for safe rooms. Even here, the high-pitched alert makes me want to walk faster, but Risha veers off toward the park. "Relax, we're inside now. Let's hang at the playground a while."

I follow her toward the slide. "Has it been like this since you moved in?"

"Like what?" She climbs the ladder and slides down.

I wait at the bottom. "Like this . . . where you just *know* the tornadoes won't touch down here?"

Risha dusts off her shorts and heads for the monkey bars. "Yeah, I told you, it was in the contracts."

"But how can they promise that? Did the contract say *how* they do it?"

"Nope." She shrugs. "Most people moved here from places where it's gotten so bad that no one cares *why* they're safe. I mean, people ask, sure, but your dad obviously can't be giving away all his company's secrets, and really everybody's just happy to be able to go outside again, you know?" Two little kids are on the swings, daring each other to go higher, while their moms sit on a bench by the carousel talking.

"But my dad's storm dissipation project failed—that's what

· · 70 · ·

Mom said. It can't be that technology. And if it's not that, then what is it? Some kind of force field around the neighborhood?" I climb up to the top of the jungle gym and sit down on one of the crossbars, dangling my feet down through the middle.

"I guess." Risha scampers up after me and hangs upside down from her knees a few bars over. "Does it matter what it is, as long as it works?" Thunder rumbles in the distance, and tree branches rustle as the wind picks up. The moms on the bench don't even miss a beat in their conversation.

"S'cuse me, lady!" One of the kids from the swing set climbs up the other side of the jungle gym and runs into our Jaden-and-Risha roadblock here at the top.

"Sorry." I lower myself to the ground, and Risha climbs down the other side.

"Let's go swing!" She takes off and is swinging six feet off the ground by the time I even get started, but pretty soon I'm flying beside her. I can't remember the last time I was on a swing outside. Our underground play centers at home have great swing sets— huge ones—but the air on your face is still indoor air. Stale and safe. Here, it's real wind, carrying the smell of the storm.

"You know," Risha says, her hair flying around her face, "if you swing back and forth a hundred times with your eyes closed and then open them at the very top, then the first boy you see from up there will be the one you marry. Think I can see Tomas from up here?"

"Doubt it." I swing forward, so high that the chain goes slack and for a second I feel like I'm hanging there, attached to nothing. Then the chain catches, and I swing back with Risha at my side. "Besides, they must be in a safe room by now. That storm's growing. Hey, how's his mom?"

Risha stops pumping her legs and just swings. "She needs to get into a treatment center, but Tomas says there's a waiting list for most of the good ones. We didn't talk about it much—and don't you dare tell Alex because he doesn't know this yet, but Tomas said they might even move."

"*Move?* What about the farm?"

Risha smiles a sad smile. "Well, they know they won't have trouble selling it." She waves her hand through the air as if that idea is a bug she can swat away. "But they've talked about other things, too, like his mom staying with his brother in New York if she can get into that clinic. I'm sure it'll be okay."

"Mama, look! Look! It's almost to the fence. Let's do the rhyme!" The two kids from the jungle gym run toward the bench, pointing to the cloud. I stop swinging and listen.

Twister, twister, go away,
Don't you bother us today.
Take your rain and winds that blow,
Turn around now, I say, GO!

They point and giggle, and make shooing motions with their hands.

I stare at them, these kids who have no memories of a place

where storms come into the neighborhood. Here, it is nothing but a game. It's like that "Ring Around the Rosy" chant Mom told me about. The rhyme was all about symptoms of the plague—rosy cheeks, sweet-smelling breath, falling down dead—and kids chanted it, laughing while they jumped rope, without ever realizing where it came from.

I look up at the monster cloud and try to imagine what it would be like never to have been afraid of it. A funnel is creeping down from it, but the storm doesn't seem to be getting any closer. It looks like the system is stalling on the other side of the fence.

Just like Dad's contracts promise.

"Better do it one more time," one of the moms says, smiling.

"I'm standing up on the bench this time," the little girl says, climbing up. "So it'll hear me better."

Twister, twister, go away,
Don't you bother us today.
Take your rain and winds that blow,
Turn around now, I say, GO!

She points fiercely toward the storm cloud, which is indeed moving away from the fence now, still churning, still blowing, but most definitely going.

"Yay!" The little girl jumps down and cheers again. "I made it go away!"

"Good job." Her mother pulls her in and kisses her above her ponytail. "Now get your jacket, and let's go make Daddy some supper."

I scuff my sneakers in the dirt under my swing and watch them leave. The mothers, the kids, the storm. All leaving.

Risha's been swinging this whole time. She jumps off and flies into the brown grass in front of me, tumbling into a somersault and laughing like the kids. "Clearly, I am the champion of the swing set," she says. "How come you stopped?"

I shake my head. "No reason. You ready to head home now?"

She shrugs. "Sure."

We make small talk on the way home, but I can't stop watching the storm as it moves away. It isn't dissipating. If anything, it looks like it's still growing.

And leaving.

As if someone steered it away, with a magic chant.

Or maybe with a bank of computers, in a home office, behind a shiny steel door?

Chapter 10

Jaden, what would you like? More oatmeal?" Mirielle is dancing around the kitchen clearing breakfast dishes and cooing to Remi, cradled in a blue and green scarf this time. She must feel like she's riding around on an ocean wave, the way Mirielle swoops and turns.

Mirielle's DataSlate reader is open next to her empty cup of tea; she must have been reading at breakfast. I'm surprised when I lean over to read the title on the screen: *Quantum Reality: The Physics of Consciousness in a Post-Romantic World*. Mirielle was one of Dad's interns in Russia; she was studying physics when they met, but she's so busy with Remi it didn't occur to me she'd still have time for science.

She sees me looking at the reader. "Would you like me to send you a copy?"

"That's okay." I look at her, spinning away with the orange juice glasses. "I didn't know you were still interested in stuff like this."

"Oh, I am interested in many things. Too busy to read about them all sometimes. Just like I'm too busy to dance anywhere but in my own kitchen these days." She tickles Remi's chin.

"Where did you used to dance?"

"In Paris, of course!" She stops spinning and smiles. "And Moscow after I moved there. I danced professionally for six years. Your father never told you?"

"No. Why'd you stop?"

"Busy with my studies at first, and then as the storms spread, there just weren't opportunities." She looks up at the kitchen lights as if she's remembering brighter lights on a stage. "And of course here in the U.S., there's only the National Ballet performed for cameras. It wouldn't be the same without a real audience." She pushes my bowl of fruit closer. "You can't be full. At least have more fruit."

"I'm fine, thanks." I poke at a strawberry with my fork and puncture two little holes in its perfectness. I can't help but think of Alex and his father, and their farm. "Do you ever get organic fruit?" I ask Mirielle.

"Oh, *mon dieu*, no!" She glances quickly at Dad's office door as if it might slide open and eat us at the very suggestion. "We eat only DNA-ture. Always. The deliveries are so convenient; I never have to go out to the market," she says as if she's in a DNA-ture advertisement. She looks at the door again, then leans in closer to me. "But your aunt Linda?" She lowers her voice. "She grows berries the old way, and vegetables, too. She gave me some raspberries when she dropped off your book. They were a bit overripe, some of them, but oh, they were so sweet!"

That makes me smile. And it makes me like Aunt Linda even more. "Can we go see her soon?"

Mirielle nods. "I think we can figure something out. Maybe later this—"

She stops at the sound of Dad's office door humming open. He's just inside the room, holding something small and round—is it a compass?—in one hand and his DataSlate in the other. He's on a video call. "No, Mom. I'm certainly not going to—" He sees us standing there and turns away, lowering his voice. All I hear after that is the word "later."

Did I hear right? He almost always called Mom by her first name, Rebekah, but sometimes he'd call her Mom if I was around. Was that Mom on the phone in Costa Rica? And if it was, why didn't he let me talk?

He steps out and presses his thumb to the fridge panel.

"Who was that?" I blurt out.

"What?" He squints at me.

"On the phone? Was that Mom in Costa Rica?"

"Oh, no. No. It was . . ." He looks at Mirielle. "Your mother. She wants you to call her later." She nods, and Dad reaches for the Bio-Wake Cola the refrigerator sent out. He's still holding the compass thing. It's made of wood and looks old.

"What's that?" I ask.

"This?" He looks down as if he'd forgotten it was in his hand. "It's an antique barometer I keep in the office. I use it as a paper-weight, picked it up while I was talking, I guess." He slips it into his pocket. "Listen, I need to head into work. I've called a meeting for noon at headquarters. We have to reevaluate the perimeter because some debris blew up against the fence. There was never any danger, but we had a few complaints."

"Was that the storm from dinnertime last night?" I take my fruit salad to the counter. "I . . . saw it turn away from Placid Meadows," I say quietly.

"Of course it turned away, and in plenty of time, too. Nothing's hit since the fence went up, and if that's not—"

"How does it work?" I'd stayed up until midnight waiting for him to come out of his office so I could ask about the storms, where they went, and what made them go. But he must have worked all night.

He takes a gulp of soda, then holds in a belch. "What do you mean? You know about my research."

"But Mom told me your project didn't work. And that was about dissipating tornadoes, anyway, wasn't it? The storm last night didn't stop rotating. It looked like it was getting bigger. If you're not destroying the storms, then what . . . what *are* you doing?"

Mirielle's DataSlate chirps on the counter. "Oh! It's my sister." She jostles Remi, who's starting to fuss a little.

"Here, I'll take her," Dad says, and carefully lifts her from the scarf. The baby wiggles a little, as if she can't quite get comfortable against Dad's bony shoulder. Dad strokes her soft fluff of hair until she settles. Then he takes a deep breath and looks at me. "You're right, Jaden. I'm not dissipating the storms." The muscles around his eyes tighten. "That was my research, and that was my intent, but as I'm sure Mom told you, after all our years of research, the simulation failed. I've been over it a thousand times. It works on paper, but not in real life."

"Have you *tried* it in real life? Maybe it does work."

He shakes his head. "We can't. What if something went wrong and we made a storm more powerful? You can't test theories with people's lives. That's why StormSafe is so far out ahead with weather modification research. We have the patent on the Sim Dome, so we can actually test our theories."

"And this one always fails when you try it as a simulation?"

He nods. "We have the very best Sim Dome money can buy up at headquarters. More advanced than yours at camp, and that's nothing to laugh at. It's failed every time." He chugs down the rest of his soda, feeds the can into the recycler, and settles into a counter chair with Remi snuggled against him. "But I had already made a promise to all these people." He nods to the hallway, where Mirielle is chatting into her DataSlate. "We *will* get it right one of these days. We will. But for the moment, the best I can do is keep my family, and a handful of other families like ours, safe another way."

"Which is?"

"An electromagnetic storm shield that we *were* able to test successfully."

"What's that do? Send the tornadoes away?"

Dad nods. "Deflects them, yes." I watch him stroking Remi's hair as she sleeps. His hands are soft, but his face is hard, eyebrows furrowed.

"So the field sends the storm . . . ?"

"Away from the most populated areas. Away from her." Dad kisses the top of Remi's head. "Away from you. Away from here, and that's the best I can do for now. At least it's something."

He says it like it's a success but still looks like someone who thinks he's a failure, and it makes me sad for him, after all his work.

"Well, it's a start anyway, right?"

He doesn't smile, but he nods.

I stand up and take a banana from the counter. "Do you think I could see StormSafe soon? Like a tour?"

"Sure. How come?"

"We're getting assignments at camp, and I may work with this other kid in weather manipulation. I . . . uh . . ." I decide to say it. "I'm interested in the dissipation technology."

"Hold on a minute then; I have something you might like to see." He disappears into his office, comes back out with his DataSlate. "Got yours?" I hand it to him, and he starts copying his file called "Effects of Microwave Radiation on Supercell Downdrafts and Vortex Formation."

"Is this your research?"

"It's the summary." The file finishes transferring. Mirielle's done talking with her sister, so Dad hands Remi over, heads for his office, and holds his thumb to the panel. "Read it," he tells me. "You'll see in the last section how the simulation failed, sent us back to square one. But maybe you'll have better luck." He steps inside, and the door slides shut.

Chapter 11

Alex is in his usual seat at camp Monday morning. He looks up from his DataSlate when I sit down next to him. "Hey."

I gasp. "What happened to you?" Even in the dim light, I can see the angry red scrape on his forehead.

"Aw, nothing." He shrugs. "It was dumb. Newton went chasing after a groundhog when you guys left. It was right as that storm turned and started heading up our way. I went after him and caught a tree branch in the head. Stupid." He touches it as if to show me it's no big deal, but he winces.

"All right, scholars!" Van jogs down the aisle holding a remote, aiming it toward the front of the room as if it's a laser gun. "Today, we face down the problems of the future." He presses a button on the remote, and Dad's holo-sim appears.

"Welcome back, campers. Today, you'll learn the concentration for your studies at Eye on Tomorrow. Please look at the screen behind me for your assignments."

A map of the campus appears on screen, with the different

buildings labeled by specialty. Then, campers' photographs start appearing next to buildings, while Dad announces who will be where. "Risha Patel, cellular generation and human cloning center." Risha's face breaks into a smile when Tomas is assigned to cloning as well.

The Beekman twins high-five one another when they both end up in robotics and artificial intelligence. The two boys they hang around with are assigned to bio-botanicals.

I already know from what Van said that I'll be in meteorology, but still, a shiver of excitement runs through me when my face appears on screen next to the Sim Dome. Alex is there, too.

Finally, the last camper's photograph appears. The brush-cut boy, whose name is Randall Harrington, is headed to cloning, and I can't help imagining an army of anxious brush-cut kids checking their watches. Then the screen goes black and it's just Dad looking out at us. "Today is the start of your life as a scientist," he says. "Make us proud. And always keep your eye on tomorrow."

Alex turns to face me when the lights come up. "So, will you work with me? Two brains are better than one."

"Depends on who the brains belong to." I smile as the door opens, and sunlight streams in. "But in this case, yeah. I think two are better."

Alex grins. "Want to start in the library? We can go over what we already know and build on that. Hopefully, Van will give us another shot at the Sim Dome soon."

"Sure." I turn to Risha. "Want to work in the library with us?"

"Not now, thanks. I'm off to the cloning lab."

"With *Tomas*?" I tease her. "I can't believe you switched from bio-botanicals just to hang out with him."

"I'm interested in *all* of it." She laughs. "So I might as well be interested *and* work with him." She gives me a shove toward the door. "Go on, weather geek. Get studying. I'll catch up with you later."

I walk with Alex across the grassy quad. "Ready to get to work?" He pulls open the library door. "Hey, Ms. Walpole." The librarian, a tall, slender woman with brown-gray dreadlocks, red-framed glasses, and dangling turquoise earrings, is twisted around a computer, apparently trying to fix something. She looks up, smiles, and waves as we step inside.

"Wow." The smell of paper books surprises me. "I thought it would be all computers."

"Over my dead body." The librarian stands there with a data cable dangling from one hand. "People ought to be able to get their information however they like best." She nods and goes back to wrestling with the computer.

"You tell 'em, Ms. Walpole." Alex laughs and heads for one of the tables. "She's awesome." He nods back over his shoulder as we sit down. "She's been here since the place started, from what I hear. She was one of the people whose property they needed to make room for the campus, but she wouldn't sell unless she got to be in charge of Eye on Tomorrow's library and education program for the little kids. Then she drafted up this list of conditions: it has to be open to the whole community—she was big on that since the town library shut down—and it has to have books in paper, too. I guess your dad agreed." Alex grins and gestures around a room full of floor-to-ceiling bookshelves, in addition to the row of computers up front. "Besides that, she brings us oatmeal raisin cookies sometimes when we're working. That's my kind of librarian."

"Me too," I say. I wonder if Ms. Walpole has paper poetry books at home, too. I bet she does. "Should we get some books?"

"There's a lot on supercell formation over in the five hundreds if you want to go look. I'll find my notes from last year."

"Okay." I head for the stacks, running my hands along the bumps of book spines as I go. A ton's been written about our topic. *Supercell, Superstorm* and *Planet Earth: The New Storm Belt* chronicle the shift from climate norms to the new weather patterns that have developed over the past fifty years, since the climate's warmed and grown so conducive to storms. *Seeds of Disaster: Foundations of Tornadogenesis* is probably the best-known text on the actual structure of tornadoes and why some supercells give rise to funnel clouds while others don't. *In the Eye of the Storm: Five Researchers on the Cutting Edge of Weather Modification* looks at the wave of scientists who worked on weather modification in the years before Dad and his colleagues.

I'm surprised to see a copy of *Playing God: The Case Against Meteorological Manipulation*; it flies in the face of everything Dad believes in, but I pull the book and add it to the teetering pile in my arms.

"You call that a few books?" Alex meets me on my way to the table, in time to keep the pile from toppling. We spread the books on the big table.

"Where should we start?" I ask.

"We're not exactly starting. I did a lot last summer." He pulls out his DataSlate. Van gave us clearance to bring them, now that we're settled in our concentrations of study. When Alex turns his on, there's a photograph of his family on the screen. There's Alex smiling at the camera in a white shirt and jeans. His mom, looking neater and less frazzled than she does when she's dropping him off. His dad, actually smiling. And a little girl hugging Newton.

"You have a little sister?"

"Julia just turned seven." He touches the DataSlate screen, and a document opens. "Here's the formula I came up with last year. It's based on some stuff from the Sim Dome computer. You know the basic premise, right? The one I tried in the dome? It's the same thing your dad is working from."

I nod. "Heat the downdraft." Dad used to talk about it all the time at dinner, back when there were still Meggs family dinners. He believed you could find the spot where a storm is beginning to rotate and stop a tornado from forming. It was like any recipe, he told me one night in between bites of chocolate cake. If you didn't have flour and cocoa and butter and all the other ingredients, you couldn't make cake. Tornadoes have ingredients, too—the rotation begins when a warmer updraft comes up against a cold, rainy downdraft. So what if you heated the air to get rid of that cold rainy downdraft? No ingredients—no tornado.

Alex turns to a sketch screen on his DataSlate, and there's a diagram like the one Dad used to draw on his napkins. He taps the center of the partially formed funnel cloud. "Right here is the spot we'd need to blast."

"Microwaves?"

"Yep. From satellites."

"Powered how?"

"Solar." He swipes the screen with his finger, and the next page appears—a sketch of a satellite with solar panels mounted on top. Yellow sketch lines representing microwave energy beam down to the bottom of the screen. "This is all in place already. They've had satellites collecting solar energy and beaming it down to storage facilities for almost ten years. It would just be a matter of amping it up and redirecting it into the heart of the storm."

"But that's what nobody can quite figure out, right? How much do you amp it up?"

"Right. Last summer, I played around with a formula for the amount of microwave energy you'd need, depending on the size and energy of the storm." He swipes to another page. "And every time I ran the numbers, it made perfect sense. But when I got time in the Sim Dome, I couldn't get it to work. It always . . . well, you saw what happened when I tried last week."

"That's what happened to my dad." I turn on my DataSlate and find the file he copied for me. "He gave me the summary."

Alex leans in, and his dark eyes scan line after line of numbers, explanations of what should have happened, but didn't.

Alex nods slowly. "Where did he do the simulation, do you know?"

"Up at StormSafe."

"Shoot." Alex sighs and tips back in his chair. "I was hoping it might have been a glitch with the Sim Dome here at Eye on Tomorrow, but if he used StormSafe equipment, that stuff's gotta be right. That means the data must be off." He stares off into a corner of the library, then nods toward my DataSlate.

"Did he use data from a real storm for the simulation?"

"I'm not sure." I skim through the document again. There's a link at the end. I click on it, and video from an online archive fills the screen. "This must be it." It's amateur storm footage from 2008, the kind people used to get when they went driving around in trucks, chasing tornadoes, back when you had to go looking for them to see one.

"Man," Alex says, breathing out. "It's a big one for back then."

Shaky video, shot through a car windshield, shows a funnel cloud forming and then touching down. It's nothing I haven't seen before, but the reaction to it—the way the guys in the car are acting—makes my stomach clench.

"We got debris! We got debris!" one of them shouts, as if he's won a new HV.

"Look at that thing!" the other one screams. "Dude, look! Can we get closer?"

They drive closer.

"Idiots," Alex whispers under his breath. But he doesn't turn away. There is something mesmerizing about watching these people sitting in the line of a tornado as if it's some kind of old-fashioned video game.

"Come on, baby," the camera guy's voice says. "Come on. Keep going." Like he's coaxing an animal out of a cave.

"Oh my God!" one of the guys yells. "Reverse! Put it in reverse!"

The tornado comes straight at them, and they're cursing and the video is shaking everywhere as they fly backward down the long stretch of road until the tornado gains on them and gains on them and they stop driving.

"Duck down! Get down!" one of them screams, and wind whips the car, pelts it with branches and dirt and rain until finally, the storm passes.

A few seconds of quiet. Then whooping, cheering. "Man, we were all over that thing! That was awesome! That was just—"

Alex presses the STOP button, and there is silence.

I realize I've been holding my breath. I breathe out and turn to him. He is shaking his head.

"It's surreal, isn't it?" he says. "That they'd put themselves in the path? That anyone could think this was entertaining?"

I stare at the frozen images, the men in their baseball caps, laughing, high-fiving each other. They must be in their twenties in this video. They're old men now. If they've survived. "They didn't know," I say. "It was fun for them. Exciting and fun. They didn't know what was about to happen with the climate, the storms."

"Stupid," Alex mutters, opening a book.

But I can't stop looking at their frozen faces amid the dust. They had no idea what was coming. Are we like that today? Is there something worse on the way that will make our storms seem like nothing at all?

"Come on," Alex says. "Let's work."

I turn the pages of the *Seeds of Disaster* book. The theories about tornado formation here are the best and latest, but there's still a big mystery about why the storms form some times and not others, when almost the exact same conditions are present.

I flip through the weather text, but in my mind, I'm turning pages in the poetry book on my nightstand, and I remember that one, "Geometry."

> ... *the house expands:*
> *the windows jerk free to hover near the ceiling,*
> *the ceiling floats away with a sigh.*

I stare up at the library ceiling, gleaming golden wood with dark brown knots, and I imagine it lifting up, up over our heads and drifting off. The idea of solving a problem, feeling everything open up with possibility and with more problems to solve, too, fills me like a kite filling with wind.

Alex's shoulder brushes mine, and I jump.

"Sorry, I was looking at what you were reading." He nods down at the book. "You finding anything good?"

"Not yet. Just thinking."

"Me, too."

He lowers his head, and I watch him swiping through pages and pages of numbers, numbers that should have been the magic formula to make the winds stop blowing, to keep the weathervane on his family's barn where it belongs, to let Newton chase groundhogs in the afternoon. But the deeper his frown gets, the more I start to believe there will never be a magic formula to make everything okay.

"It's about time to call it a day, kids." Ms. Walpole steps up to our table, a stack of books in her arms. She smells like the vanilla candles my mom likes. "Did you find everything?"

"Not exactly." Alex tips back in his chair and sighs.

"Put your chair down. You'll crack your head open," she says. When his chair legs are back on the ground, she nods. "Now, what is it that you need?"

"Data," Alex and I say together, and that makes us laugh a little, even though it's been a frustrating afternoon.

"Solid tornado formation data that will work in a simulation," Alex adds. "Nothing you can help with, unfortunately."

Ms. Walpole frowns and puts down her pile of books. "The data you have isn't working?" she asks.

Alex shakes his head. "Nope. Even though it should."

"You've checked it and rechecked it?" She clicks her tongue against the roof of her mouth.

"Yep."

Ms. Walpole raises her eyebrows. "Then that's an easy one. Collect new data."

Alex lets out half a laugh. "Sure. Do you happen to know where there's a high-tech weather balloon or something we can borrow?"

She crosses her arms in front of her and looks over her glasses at us. "As a matter of fact, I do."

Chapter 12

This wasn't on our orientation tour," I say as Ms. Walpole unlocks the warehouse tucked behind the Sim Dome. It's such an unremarkable building—dull aluminum paneling, nestled among all the shiny steel and glass—that I didn't even notice when we walked past it before.

"Hmph." She presses her finger to a biometric panel alongside a garage door, and it slides open. "That's because Van Gardner's so caught up in his shiny new toys that he forgets everything else."

We step inside a room that's bigger than any airplane hangar—huge and basic.

"This place is simply to hold equipment—acres and acres of equipment that somebody thought was too old to keep using," Ms. Walpole says as we start down one of the long rows of floor-to-ceiling storage racks, and right away, I can see that people here have strange ideas about what's old.

There's a whole fleet of four-wheel-drive vehicles that look like they've been converted from gasoline to hydrogen, each one outfitted with some fancy gizmo on top. "What's sticking up from the trucks?" I ask.

"That's a mobile meso-net unit—a multipurpose measuring machine made up of steel rods and twirling computer weather sensors that record things like barometric pressure and wind speed," Ms. Walpole says.

I nod; I read about them in one of Dad's old journals. In the early days of tornado research, scientists used to drive these things close to the storms and drop off probes in the path, hoping for a direct hit. They wanted to see inside the heart of the tornado. That's how they learned a lot about storm formation, how vertical wind shear can turn an ordinary thunderstorm into something stronger.

"And they don't use these anymore?"

"Oh, they still use them. They just have better ones now." Ms. Walpole leads us around a corner and down another long row of shelves. These are loaded with computers that can't be more than a year or two old—not state of the art like the ones in the Sim Dome, but still plenty powerful.

"Hey," Alex says. "Aren't these the ones from the camp lab last summer?"

Ms. Walpole nods. "They've been replaced. They may bring these out for the Tomorrow Kids program we run during school vacations."

"Is that for younger kids?" I ask.

Alex nods. "It's open to anybody, and really, they just do fun stuff, but they're always looking for future campers. That's how I got in; two weeks after my first vacation camp, they invited my folks to get me tested. Tomas, too."

"If they'd only known what they were getting into." Ms. Walpole smiles. "How's Mrs. Hazen doing, have you heard?"

"Not that good. Tomas doesn't like to talk about it." Alex shrugs. "She needs to go to New York or somewhere for treatment."

Ms. Walpole nods. "I thought I heard him say something like that to Van this week. I hope they're not thinking of giving up the farm."

"They're not," Alex says quickly, and I bite my lip to keep from telling him what Risha said.

"Right down here," Ms. Walpole says. At the far end of the warehouse there's a tall rack filled with bins of rain gear, and one of the old National Weather Service trucks is parked behind it. In the back of the pickup is a sleek model airplane with a five- or six-foot wingspan.

Alex's eyes get huge. I step closer and see this is no toy; it's one of the original DataDrones—the indestructible, remote-operated planes that helped scientists make some of their first real breakthroughs in figuring out how tornadoes are born.

Alex runs his hand along one of the wings. "Graphene, right?"

Ms. Walpole nods. "It was the strongest substance in the world when this was developed."

And it wasn't that long ago. Five or six years, maybe? I remember Dad talking about how amazing the drones were. "They're not using it anymore?" I ask.

"This showed up a few weeks ago," Ms. Walpole says. "I guess the new ones have more efficient radar built in."

Alex reaches into the back of the truck and picks up the

remote-control device that must run the plane. It has regular remote buttons and levers with some kind of computer screen below them. "So . . ." He sounds like he's trying not to get too excited, but his eyes give him away. "This still works?"

Ms. Walpole gives a sharp nod. "I'm sure it does. Contrary to popular opinion around this place, just because something is a little older doesn't mean it's not useful." She pushes her glasses up on her nose.

Alex looks down at the control panel in his hands. "Can we . . . uh . . . borrow it?"

"Well, it's not doing anyone any good sitting in the back of a van, is it?" Behind the glasses, Ms. Walpole's green eyes have a glint of mischief in them, and I smile, imagining Dad trying to negotiate with her. "I'm certainly not going to stop you from making use of the tools you need to carry out your research. I'm here to help, after all."

"Should we check with Van or something?" I ask.

She purses her lips. "I'm not sure I would recommend that. It's often easier to be forgiven than it is to get permission in situations such as this." She pauses. "But of course, I never said that." She looks at her watch, silver and obviously antique. "I'd better get back to the library. I'm afraid I often forget to lock up when I leave a building, so you two will need to do that on your way out, all right?"

Alex grins. "You got it. And thanks."

She walks briskly back down the aisle, then turns back to us. "You'll want to leave promptly, and use the main entrance. The other staff members are all in a meeting in the auditorium for another hour. I'd best join them now."

I can't quite believe what we're about to do, so I just stand, listening to her footsteps fade all the way to the door. It thunks closed, and Alex turns to me. "Ready to borrow an airplane?"

Chapter 13

How long can you stay?" Alex leans against the bottom of the playground slide at the park near campus, frowning down at his DataSlate. A storm is forming west of us, but there's no way to tell yet if it will spawn tornadoes. Just in case, we set up the drone so it's ready to take off from the open space where kids play kickball.

"I can stay a while, I guess." Dad never mentioned a curfew, and Mirielle usually makes dinner pretty late. "So . . . if we do get a storm, the idea here is to fly the plane into it and gather data so . . ." I was so bowled over by the very idea of "borrowing" a weather drone, so nervous as we carried it silently out the Eye on Tomorrow gate and lugged it here, that I never actually processed what we're trying to do. Gather data about a storm, sure. Then what?

"Well, I figure the numbers I'm using in my project must be off. I tried the simulation with two different storms last summer and got the same results, which means maybe all the storm data in the system at camp is wrong."

"So if we have a brand new storm . . . and collect our own brand new data . . ." This kind of problem-solving is so different from the

Eye on Tomorrow entrance exam, this starting-from-scratch thinking, but I'm getting it. "Then the simulation should work?"

"Well, hopefully," Alex says. "Or if not, we'll know the data wasn't
the problem and the whole theory's a bust." He sighs and looks
down at the DataSlate. "Oh!" He jumps up and climbs the ladder to
the top of the slide, facing west. "I think we're in business. Come up
and see!"

There's not much room on the platform at the top of the slide,
so we crowd together, and Alex points to the horizon. "See that
rotation?"

The rotation I notice first is in my stomach, which is kind of
flipping out being so close to him up here, but I force myself to focus
on the clouds. "Yeah. That looks like it's going to produce a funnel
cloud."

Before I've finished my sentence, he's climbing down the ladder
and heading for the remote control we left by the kickball field. The
storm is moving fast; the sky is darkening, and the wind is already
picking up. I can't believe we're actually going to fly this thing. It
feels too adult-scientist, too serious, too *real* to be happening to a
couple of kids at science camp. But Alex hands me the remote.

"Hold this while I check the sensors, okay?"

My hands shake, even though Alex swears he's flown remote
control planes before and this is no different. All we have to do is fly
it into the storm; once we punch through the wall, the drone will
be swept up into the tornado and sensors can gather data. The wireless system is set up to send information directly to my DataSlate,
so we'll get readings right away. Then we'll recover the full set of

data from the hard drive when the drone lands. Or crashes. I'm picturing us returning the plane to the storage building in pieces, explaining to Van or, worse, my father, what we were thinking, when Alex shouts, "Press the red button! Now!"

I press it, and the drone's engine hums to life. "I thought you were going to fly it!"

"I want to make sure the sensors are working," he says, waving over his shoulder at me as he squints down at the plane. "You'll be fine—just start it going forward and then throttle up to lift off, and I'll take over from there!"

Throttle up? The controls feel like some kids' video game in my hand, but I know this is real, with real consequences. If something happens to this plane and we have to—

"Jaden, start it! The storm's coming and if it turns away before we get there, we're not going to make it!"

I force my thumb to push the lever, and the plane jerks forward on the ground.

"Good!" Alex yells. "Good! Now speed up! Go!"

I push the lever all the way forward, and the plane bounces along, speeding up, bumping over the dusty kickball field where second base would be.

"Now throttle up! Now!" Alex shouts as he grabs the DataSlate from the grass and runs to my side.

I press the button to throttle up, and the plane rises off the ground, just missing a shrub at the edge of the park. It wavers, headed for the fence, and I can't imagine how we're going to keep it steady in the wind. "Here!" I shove the controls into Alex's hands,

· · 98 · ·

take my DataSlate, and call up the program that will receive the drone's data.

The page comes up blank but immediately starts filling with numbers. Columns and columns of numbers. Wind speeds. Temperatures. Barometric pressures. They're mostly the same numbers, over and over, as Alex maneuvers the plane over the fence, outside Placid Meadows and closer to the storm.

The rotation we spotted from the top of the slide is swirling faster, and already a thick, dark rope is forming, stretching down from the cloud. Alex takes his eyes off the plane to watch the storm and lets out a whoop. "We got it!" He sounds like one of those storm chasers on the video, and I wonder if we're as stupid as they were, playing with fire, with something we don't understand.

"Here we go . . . getting close now . . . Watch!" He means to watch the plane or the storm, or maybe the data, but I watch Alex, his eyes as intense as anyone's I've ever seen. He bites his lip in concentration, and the tendons in his hands tense as he clutches the remote and drives the plane full throttle—faster, faster, faster—until it surges through the gray wall of wind into the heart of the storm.

"It's in! Watch the data, Jaden! What are we getting?"

I look down at the numbers flying over the screen in my hands. Flying faster than the wind, but my eyes start to see patterns. Changes. Wind speeds rising. Temperatures rising. Barometric pressure dropping like mad. This is what it's like to be inside a storm.

"Okay, it's turning. The storm's turning. I'm going to try to keep the drone inside. Tell me what you see!" I sneak another glance at

Alex, but his eyes don't move from the handheld controls. The computer screen below the control panel shows a blinking blue dot, swirling, flying, inside the storm.

The numbers on the DataSlate hold steady. Soon, I should see . . . what? If there's a field at the edge of Placid Meadows that dissipates storms or deflects them, the numbers should start to show it weakening.

But they don't.

"I'm not sure how long before it's thrown clear. Are you getting stuff?" Alex's voice is tense with concentration. "Jaden, talk to me! We've got maybe another ten seconds. I'm losing the signal. What are you seeing?"

I can't answer. Because I can't begin to process the numbers flying past my eyes.

"I . . . It's going too fast for me to see." But that's a lie. I can see the numbers, and I know what they mean. As the storm pulls away from Placid Meadows, the wind speeds are increasing. The temperatures are getting higher. And the barometric pressure has plunged to a level I've never even seen before.

I understand, but I can't make myself say it out loud.

This storm didn't weaken when it hit the Placid Meadows perimeter. It turned away, toward someone else's home. And got stronger.

Chapter 14

The brave thing would be to ask Dad more about his failed project tonight. Ask him why he thinks his simulation went wrong, why all the number crunching wasn't enough, and what he's doing about it now. Ask him what really happens to storms when they leave Placid Meadows. And maybe that would start to answer the questions swirling in my head since Alex and I flew the drone this afternoon, since I lied to Alex. I told Alex it all went by too quickly, that my DataSlate's battery died before I could process the numbers. I told him we'd need to recover data from the hard drive to see what really happened. I couldn't tell him the truth. Not without asking my father some questions first.

But Dad's eyes are angrier than the clouds as he bursts into the kitchen, and Mirielle's delicate spinach salad just about wilts when he slams his briefcase on the table.

"Stephen, what is it?" She sets down her wineglass and rushes over to press a hand to his cheek.

He brushes it away, pops open his briefcase, pulls out his

DataSlate, and drops it onto the granite counter with a clatter. "We're losing support for Phase Two. Look!"

He turns on the DataSlate—I'm surprised the screen doesn't shatter under his glare—and jabs at it until the document appears. "This is from our investors' group. Sixty days to acquire the rest of the property we need, or we lose our funding. And I've got two hold-outs who *will not* sell."

My stomach twists. I'm pretty sure I'm working with one of the holdouts' kids. And Risha's in love with the other one.

"Can you not offer more money for the farmland?" Mirielle asks, setting a place for Dad at dinner. "It seems to me that—"

"Do you have any idea what we've offered? Ten *times* the market value of their property, but *noooo* . . . these are *family farms*. Well, they can take their worm-bitten apples and their lumpy, seedy strawberries and kiss my—"

"Stephen!" Mirielle is back in her seat at the table, but her eyes shoot lasers over the roast chicken and gravy, and Dad stops. Mirielle puts a gentle hand on Remi's head and looks my way, too. "You are scaring the children."

As much as I don't like being called a child, her words take the electricity out of Dad's anger at the farmers, and I'm thankful. No wonder Mirielle keeps Aunt Linda's berries a secret.

"Sit down." Mirielle motions to the chair next to her, and Dad sinks into it like a scarecrow that's lost its straw. She pours him a glass of Scotch.

Dad presses his hands against his eyes. "How am I going to pull this off in sixty days?"

"Isn't there somewhere else you could build? I mean, you can't very well make somebody sell land if they don't want to, right?" When Dad turns to look at me, I wish I could pull the words back, but like Risha's dandelion fluff, blown into the wind at our picnic, they're swirling all around our heads, impossible to catch.

The voice that follows his glare isn't angry; it's measured and calm, like Dad sounds in his holo-talks. "The planned expansion of Placid Meadows will allow another fifty families to live within the secure environment of a StormSafe community. This is about people's lives, Jaden—not about some silly family tradition."

"I know." I nod. But I think of Alex and the strawberries his family grows in the sun. A wad of spinach sticks in my throat. "What are you going to do?"

"I'll tell you what I'm not going to do." Dad takes a drink, then thumps his glass down, hard, on the wood table. "I am *not* losing this project."

As soon as Mirielle leaves to put Remi to bed, the storm clouds settle back in Dad's eyes, and he doesn't say another word to me. I sink into the old wooden rocking chair in the living room—perfect except that Grandma Athena's creepy photo always stares at it—and read through the files that Alex beamed to my DataSlate. I can't help keeping one eye on Dad, though, pacing back and forth from his office to the kitchen. He's in and out all night. A few times, he blusters out to the porch and stands there, muttering and looking off to the west. The last time the screen door slams, he comes back smiling.

"Jaden, you're still up?"

"I'm reading through some data my camp partner shared with me from last summer." I hesitate, afraid that talking to him at all will somehow give away what I did this afternoon at the park, who I'm working with, what I saw. "We're working together on the storm dissipation project."

Dad nods. "Good challenge, that one. You read that abstract I gave you?"

"Yeah. My partner had the same problem when he ran the simulation on his data last summer." This is where I should ask him more. Instead, I wait to see if he'll offer up details without my having to ask.

"Well, some things aren't meant to be." He yawns.

"I guess not." His office door is open, so I expect him to go back there like he usually does, to lift a tired hand to the sensor and make the steel door slide shut so he can work into the night.

But he doesn't. He stretches his arms up so high that his fingertips brush the ceiling and then heads for his bedroom. "Don't stay up too late."

I say good night.

I listen to the lock click, hear the water in the bathroom, the toilet flushing.

I hear the snap of the white noise machine turning on, the smooth, soothing whoosh that he says clears his mind of all the numbers and formulas so he can rest.

I page through Alex's files one more time, until I'm sure Dad must be asleep.

I start to stand, and the rocking chair creaks.

I freeze.

But no one's watching except Grandma Athena, trapped in her frame.

I turn away from her and head for the open office door.

Chapter 15

The room is dark.

Only the tiniest bit of kitchen light creeps in, and even with the door open, all the sounds from outside get swallowed up by this space.

I set my DataSlate on the edge of the huge mahogany desk and look out to the kitchen clock. It's midnight, and I don't know when Remi usually wakes to nurse. Will Mirielle bring her to the kitchen? Just in case, I press a button—no need for a fingerprint scan on the inside—and watch the cold steel door slide closed. The kitchen light snuffs out, but a power switch glows next to the door.

I flick it on. Overhead lights glimmer, and flat screens flicker to life on every wall.

The screen to my left shows real-time images of a row of satellites. Eight of them. I step closer. Are those solar panels attached? Underneath each image is a display panel with numbers, all gradually climbing. They are labeled in kilowatts. I reach out to touch one of the panels, and a new window emerges from the center of the screen.

It's full of constantly changing numbers. Some look like the data that whizzed past on my DataSlate while the drone was flying in the storm. Wind speeds, barometric pressure readings, and temperatures. Some look like kilowatt levels, measures of energy. Others appear to be geographic coordinates, latitude and longitude. What do they all mean?

What does any of it mean? Maybe I read the data wrong this afternoon. Maybe it's not what it looks like and I'll never have to talk to Alex about what I think I saw.

I cross the room to Dad's desk and turn on the computer.

It hums to life, flashing a blue background at me while the system loads. Over the desk is a screen showing live radar images of the region, from north of the airport, all along the river. A second big storm looks like it just missed us around the time Dad went to bed. It was close to Alex's house, from the look of this track.

I hope Newton was in for the night.

I hope they're safe.

The computer login screen appears. Dad's username, SMeggs, is already in the login box, but it's asking for a fingerprint scan or password.

I have the wrong prints, so I ignore the biometric panel and set my fingers on the keys, hoping for inspiration.

I try the obvious first. What he loves most.

stormsafe. dna-ture. I try it with the hyphen and without. No.

Then I try mirielle. And remi. jaden.

The message flashes again: incorrect password.

I sink back in the chair. I should have known I wouldn't be able

to just pop onto his computer. The desk has a single drawer, and I
slide it open looking for a list or scrap of paper, even though deep
down I know Dad's too smart to leave his passwords lying around.
Of course he is. The only thing in the drawer is a jumble of computer and DataSlate wires, a couple of storage drives, a bottle of
BioWake pills, and the barometer he had in his hand the other day.

It fills my palm when I pick it up, a perfect ring of dark, polished
wood with the barometer mechanism showing through a quarter-
size glass window. Around the window is a yellowed ring of barometric pressure markings and five weather patterns written in fancy
old script.

Stormy.
Rain.
Change.
Fair.
Very Dry.

Why would Dad, with his walls of satellite maps and live radar
screens, keep something like this around? Dad, whose motto is
"Science will save us," who won't even read a paper book anymore,
is hanging on to an old weather instrument that has words like *fair*
instead of data? It's not even in great shape for an antique. It doesn't
seem to work at all, and the wood finish is worn away at the bottom
and on the sides, as if it's spent a lot of time being held in someone's hand.

I put it back in the drawer and look back at the log-in box on the computer screen.

barometer.

Incorrect password.

I try combinations of all the words that have already failed. remijaden. placidstorm. I even try Mom's name, rebekah, in case his password is left over from a long time ago. Nothing works.

And then as if the walls suddenly dissolved, I sense Grandma's eyes staring out from her photo in the living room. Grandma, who loved science as much as Dad does.

I type athena.

The desktop appears.

I pull up a search box and type in latitude and longitude coordinates from the screen across the room.

35° 24' N 97° 36' W

A map appears on the screen with a marker pointing to the center. I click to zoom in on the satellite image of that spot, but I already recognize enough of the streets and the bend of the river to know what I will see.

The fence. The river and the trees. The daisy and dandelion meadows, and the field with the gazebo.

The barn with the battered weathervane. And the strawberries.

The Carillo farm, where Alex's family works and lives. Why is Dad's satellite focused here?

My breathing quickens, though I still don't know what it all means. I swivel Dad's chair around—I feel too small in it, swallowed up by black leather and his smell of work, sweat, and Scotch—and face the satellite wall again.

Current output: 00:00

PowerBank: 327.9 MW

35° 24' N 97° 36' W

I stare at the numbers and wait for them to arrange themselves into something that makes sense. I wait for the windows to jerk free and hover near the ceiling, like in the poem.

They don't.

But the more I stare, the more two letters stand out.

MW. The abbreviation for megawatts. Energy.

Energy mixed with geographic coordinates.

Is someone blasting energy—microwave energy—down from the satellites?

Is this the technology that didn't work in the simulations? It didn't work in Alex's trial, and it didn't work in Dad's. The whole concept of blasting energy at a tornado to stop the rotation was deemed too risky, too dangerous for the real world. So what's going on here?

Is Dad testing it anyway? Without government approval? Do the other scientists at StormSafe even know what he's doing?

My brain is churning. I swing the chair back around to face the radar screen. The storm is getting smaller now. What happened before? Did something go wrong when Dad tried to dissipate the storms today? Did he make them bigger by accident? Is that why the numbers from the drone's data readings looked the way they did?

I look down at the computer screen and start scanning the file names. Most of them have only project numbers: RL7421, 139Q, SS451.

Meaningless. And the more I stare at the numbers, the more I want to scream. I take a deep breath and look up at the ceiling that will never float away with a sigh.

When I look back at the computer, a file called Family Photos catches my eye. I click on it and find the same collection of photos running on the Data Frame in the living room. I'm about to close the folder and go back to the numbers when I notice that one of the files in that folder isn't an image. It's text, and it's labeled AGM.

Those are Grandma's initials.

Athena Grace Meggs.

As I click to open the folder, there's a faint sound from the other side of the door. Footsteps on the kitchen floor.

I freeze.

My father's voice drifts in, muffled. "No, honey, I'm fine. Go back to bed. Couldn't sleep, so I'm going to get some work done."

My heart freezes, and my hands are shaking so much it's all I can do to close out the folder and log out.

The fingerprint sensor beeps.

The lock mechanism clicks.

The door will slide open in seconds, and no matter how wildly I look around the room, there is nowhere to hide in this sparse electronic workspace.

I race to the power switch, hit it, and the room goes dark. In the blackness, I dive under Dad's desk just before the door hums open and he turns the lights back on.

He's wearing dress shoes with his pajama bottoms. They click on the floor and echo off the walls and make my heart pound harder.

He steps right up to the desk and pauses in front of his computer. If he sits down, will he notice that his chair is warm?

The dust under here tickles my throat. I swallow a cough, eyes watering.

What am I doing? Why am I hiding from my own father in the house that's supposed to be my home?

I should come out; he'd probably laugh. But something in the click of his shoes, something in the faces I've already seen him wear this week, tells me to stay still. And quiet.

Dad doesn't sit. He walks to the satellite wall and touches the panel under the screen. He's facing away from me, and I let my eyes move around the room again. At least I got logged out of his computer. At least there's nothing to—

My heart bolts up into my throat, and I almost choke on it. Because right there, its corner hanging over the edge of Dad's desk above me, is my DataSlate.

I can't let him see it.

I take a deep breath and inch forward on the floor.

Dad turns, and I freeze. He stands still for a second—is he looking at the radar screen above the desk?—and then turns back to the satellite wall.

I stretch my arm up slowly, silently.

I can't reach it.

I slide one knee forward, then the other, and reach again. My fingers close around the edge of the DataSlate just as Dad's Data-Slate chimes.

I startle, and it falls from the edge of the desk and almost through my fingers, but I make a last mad grab and catch it.

"There you are! It's about time," Dad says quietly.

"That's a fine way to say hello, Stephen." A woman's voice. I lean out the tiniest bit, but the screen is facing away from me, so I can't see her face.

"Shh . . . hold on, let me plug in my earpiece so we don't wake the whole house."

Under the desk, I pull my DataSlate back into the shadows and try to slow my breathing while Dad talks. I can hear only his side of the conversation now.

"I know," he says into the DataSlate's camera. His shiny black shoes click back and forth, louder and fainter, over and over. When he walks away, I breathe.

"Yes, good timing." He laughs a little. "It was a monster. They won't be able to find their roof in the morning. And maybe they'll decide they don't love that farmland as much as they thought. We'll have the bulldozers here before you know it."

Dad walks away again, but I keep holding my breath. My father is *laughing* at the storm that just came through.

"Yep. Listen, I need to get some work done, but I'll see you tomorrow. . . . Love you, too. Good night."

I gasp, then hold my breath, afraid he's heard. His shoes click closer again, and I tense as he sinks into the leather office chair.

Above, there are clicks on the keyboard. I calm my breathing, but my brain feels like it's about to explode.

Love you, too? Who *was* that? He was talking like she knew all about the storm and the lawsuit. It must be someone he works with. *Love you, too.* No wonder he spends so much time at StormSafe. My heart sinks, thinking of Mirielle, so understanding while Dad's at work all the time.

"Hm." Dad's heel lifts off the floor and he starts bouncing his knee, something he's always done when he's thinking hard.

More clicks.

A sigh.

Then the chair pushes back from the desk. Shoes click all the way to the entrance, then out and through the kitchen until the door slides shut and I am alone in the office again.

I don't come out.

Not yet.

I wait with my itchy nose in the dust for what must be another ten minutes until I'm sure he won't be back until morning.

Finally, I unfold my cramped legs, climb out, and slide into the leather chair.

I log in, go straight to the AGM folder, and start reading data files.

The numbers look almost exactly like what Alex shared with me, right down to the formulas, the projected kilowatts necessary to warm a downdraft enough to stop rotation within a storm.

I read through file after file, willing my eyes to stay open.

This data should work. It all makes sense, just the way Alex explained it. The simulation should have worked, too.

I go back to the beginning and start reading again. There must be something here I'm missing. Something that will give me that understanding, that vision of how it all fits together.

But the numbers blur.

They start to spin and mix with dust and broken glass and tree limbs. I look harder. There has to be a pattern, but everything is moving so fast it's blurry.

Then the whole screen swells and darkens, and there is a monster tornado coming. I'm riding my bike, and someone is behind me—sometimes it's Risha, sometimes Alex, and sometimes Amelia from home. The voice keeps changing but it always shouts the same thing, "Go! Faster! Hurry!" But no matter how fast I try to go, how hard I push down on the pedals, they just spin effortlessly, and I go nowhere. I can see the house—not Dad's concrete block but our house back in Vermont—and I keep pedaling, pedaling, as the storm gets closer and closer. The drone flies back and forth, back and forth. Roof tiles start flying off the house. Windows shatter, and in one of the gaping empty windowpanes, I see Mom's face for a split second before the blackness swallows her up.

"NO!!"

I wake up with a jerk. My hands are sweating, despite the air-conditioning in Dad's office. And the computer clock says 4:30 AM.

How could I have let myself fall asleep? What if Dad had come back?

I take a last look at the computer screen, the folder full of swirling file names, and this time, one file stands out. Not numbers, but initials and words.

AGM-FAKEABSTRACT

Was it even here before? How could I have missed it? I shiver and click on the file.

I have read this document before. Dad put a copy on my DataSlate. It is the file that summarized his research on storm dissipation and its failure. That's what he told me.

With my heart racing, I search the folder, looking for another document, but there is nothing else labeled abstract or summary or AGM.

Nothing.

I open up each of the remaining documents. Only more data.

Now the computer clock reads 4:52. And I know that no matter how late Dad stays up, his alarm goes off at 5.

I need to get out of here.

But I can't.

I have to know.

I run a full hard-drive search.

Find: AGM

The list that scrolls down must be a hundred documents long, and it looks like all of them are in the folder I just finished reading through.

I scroll to the bottom.

All but one.

A file named AGM-AB buried five folders deep in a file called 2048 TAXES.

The digital clock reads 4:57.

I double click the file and realize I've been holding my breath.

It starts out like the other summary. I suck in words as if they're oxygen until I get to the spot in the document where it diverges from the one I've already read.

The rest of this summary is nothing like the one on my DataSlate.

The simulation did not fail.

Dad's experiment worked.

The computer clock turns to 4:58, and there is no time for questions. No time to ask why he gave me a phony summary, why he wanted the world to think he failed. I grab my DataSlate, click out the data-transfer stick, plug it into the back of Dad's drive, and drag the file over. I go back to the original folder with the data and copy that, too.

4:59.

The progress bar can't move quickly enough, and it makes me want to pound the computer. *Faster! Transfer! Go!*

The last file copies as the clock turns.

Forcing myself to keep breathing, I unplug from Dad's computer, log out, and press the button to make the steel door slide open.

Dad's alarm is beeping in the bedroom.

The SmartKitchen is brewing his coffee.

As the office door begins to slide closed behind me, I look back at the wall of satellites, the wall of radar images, of storms, and dissipation data and secrets, wondering . . . what really goes on in this room?

Chapter 16

Alex isn't at camp. When we left the park yesterday, his plan was to recover the drone and then head home. Did he find it? Has he seen the data it collected? What if that second storm hit before he made it home?

I sit through Van's morning directions with my DataSlate in my hands, half expecting him to snatch it away, even though I have permission to have it. It's off, but I can feel its weight, its danger, practically burning my hands with what I learned last night. Part of me is dying to talk to Alex about our results from the drone flight now, to show him this new data and see what he makes of it. But there's also a knot in my stomach. What if he sees something awful?

The holo-sim turns on, and Dad rises out of the floor. In today's lecture, he's talking about responsibility, integrity of data, and cooperation. My chest feels tighter with every word.

Responsibility? Integrity?

He lied. He lied about everything. Why?

I need to talk to Alex, but at the same time, I'm terrified. I've started the conversation with him in my head a thousand times, and I've thought about never telling him at all. But he needs to know that his research was solid. I want to give him that.

. "Hey." I know it's Alex behind me from his whisper as he leans forward.

"You're here!" I turn in my seat to see him. "I need to—"

Even in the dim light, the sight of his face steals my words. He's hurt again. And the scrape on his temple from the other night is nothing compared to this. There's a gash across his right cheek, butter-flied together with a steri-strip. Another over his left eye still bleeds under its bandage. His chin is scraped raw.

"What happened?" I whisper.

But even as the words leave my mouth, I know it was the storm I saw on the radar.

The storm that made my father smile before he went to bed.

The one he laughed about in his office with his *love-you-too* woman on the video call.

"I'm okay. And I got the drone."

"But you're not okay. Where—"

"Shhh . . . we'll talk later. Turn around now, or Van's going to get on your case," Alex whispers, so I turn back to face my father. His holo-image talks over my head, smiles at the back of the auditorium. How can he do this? How can he *laugh* at someone's farm being hit, someone's body being beaten like this? How can he have the power to stop these storms and not use it? I want to throw myself at him, pound him with my fists.

But he's untouchable.

I'd fly right through him to the floor.

"Now that you have your partners and your focus, we'll skip the lectures and go straight to morning research. This is the last day you'll see me for a while," holo-Dad says.

Unless you happen to live in my house, I think.

Dad's image disappears, and I shiver. Knowing what I know about Dad's research, what he found and isn't telling anyone, makes me wonder about camp.

The high-tech equipment. The library. The top-of-the-line computers. Why is education such a big part of his company's mission? Why spend so much money on—

"You coming?" The lights are back on, and Alex is standing halfway down the row of seats, waiting for me.

I tuck my DataSlate in my backpack as Van comes walking up the aisle. "What happened to you?" Van pauses next to Alex and raises his eyebrows. "Get in a fight with your girlfriend here?"

Alex laughs a little. "Got caught out during the storm last night."

"Be more careful, my man. We're counting on you here." Van frowns at the bandage on Alex's forehead. "Stop by the first aid station before you get to work today. Marcy'll fix you up."

"I'll come, too," I say. "I need to talk to you . . . about stuff."

Van tips his head in a question, but I don't answer. He shrugs, says "You go easy on him today," and heads out the back door.

Alex and I walk down a long hall to the first aid station, tucked into a bright room near the entrance. Every time I turn to say something, the bandages on his face feel like accusations. Dad knew how to stop the storm that did this. He chose not to.

I finally find words. "So that weather hit while you were out looking for the drone?"

Alex shakes his head. "Not really." He turns toward me and says quietly, "I got the drone, and it's fine; it's back at the house, but I haven't downloaded the data yet because that storm . . ." He shakes his head. "It came out of nowhere."

"Why weren't you in a safe room?"

"Never got the alert."

My face falls. "Was your DataSlate out of power, or—"

"There *was* no alert. You didn't get an alarm on yours last night, did you?"

I shake my head. I'd had it right in my lap, going over and over that data. The alarm that should have sounded on every data device within a ten-mile radius never went off.

"We had no clue until the wind kicked up. Thought we had time to get the chickens in, but debris started flying before I got back to the barn."

Alex pulls open the door to the first aid station, and we step inside. The room is full of sunlight, and the white walls are so bright they make me squint. A bouncy young woman in scrubs—she must be Marcy—is scrolling through records on a DataSlate. She lifts her head, takes one look at Alex, and says, "Well, I don't need to guess which one of you is my customer, do I?" She starts rummaging in a drawer full of bandages and ointment.

Alex hops onto one of the stools near the window and motions me closer. "What'd you want to talk about?"

"I . . . can talk to you later." I glance over at Marcy, who seems nice enough, but I'm not ready to tell anyone else about this. I'm not even sure I'm ready to tell Alex. But I have to.

"Here we go." Marcy swoops over Alex and eases off his old bandage. "Ooh, that's a good one. Let's clean it and get you patched up." She raises a UV wand, gives the wound a quick zap to sterilize it, and is reaching for a new bandage when the door opens.

It's Tomas. "Oh, hey, guys." He waits until Marcy looks up. "Van sent me to get him something for a headache?"

"In the meds kit right there on the counter." She starts unwrapping a bandage, but the door bangs open again, and one of the Beekman twins—I can't tell them apart—is holding her arm.

"I tripped on Ava's robot. I think I sprained something," she whines.

Marcy sighs, hands me the bandage—"Can you finish up here?"—and reaches into the freezer for an ice pack.

While she's having Tess try to move her arm in different ways, I finish unwrapping the bandage. "When you were flying the drone yesterday," I whisper, leaning in toward Alex, "I . . . I did see some of the numbers." I cover his cut gently with the clean gauze and take a deep breath. "I wasn't sure I was reading them right, but . . . I think I was."

His eyes light up. "And?"

"I'll be right back; I'm going to take her to the main office to file an accident report." Marcy hustles out of the room with Tess, and we're alone with Tomas, still shuffling through the bottles of pain reliever.

He looks over at us, then picks up one of the bottles and grins. "Better get these to Van before he gets grumpy." He leaves, and I turn back to Alex.

I have to force myself to say the words. He'll see for himself when we download the data anyway. "The storm wasn't dissipating at the fence."

"But it turned away at the perimeter."

"And kept going, remember? Whatever happened at the fence didn't weaken it, Alex. Wait until you see the numbers."

"You saw the numbers?"

I nod. "I saw enough."

He stares up at me from the stool, and I watch his eyes shift from a look of confusion to shocked understanding. "It left . . . and got stronger?"

I nod. "And then last night, my dad left his office open." I take my DataSlate from my backpack on the floor and pull up another stool next to him. "I went onto his computer and looked up his results from his dissipation research, from the simulation he did that was like yours."

"And? It failed, right? You told me that before."

"That's what I thought." I click into the folder I copied and turn the screen so he can see the full list of files. "Remember the abstract he printed up for me? The one that summarized his failed simulation?"

"Yeah."

"This is it." I point to the document.

AGM-FAKEABSTRACT

His eyebrows knit together, and the new bandage tugs at his skin. He raises a slow hand to it. "It . . . wasn't real?"

"This is the real one." I click the other document open, hand him the DataSlate, and hold my breath.

Alex reads. His eyes grow wider with every word. Finally, he shakes his head. "Why?" He turns to me, as if I'm a stranger. "Why would he hide this? This information . . ." He taps the DataSlate screen, and his voice gets louder. "This is gold. This is going to solve everything. With proof of the simulation's success, they could have gotten government clearance to do an actual storm-trial using the satellites that are already up." He's talking faster now. "I mean, I don't know if they're totally equipped to send down the right amounts of energy or if the accuracy is what it would need to be yet, given it's not the reason they were origi-nally built, but still . . ." He shakes his head again and looks at me, angry. "What's your dad thinking?"

My mouth goes dry. "I don't know." I'm afraid to tell him more. About the wall of satellites, about the digital kilowatt readings fluctuating during last night's storm.

And I cannot bring myself to tell him the detail that haunts me, that makes my stomach hurt the most. That when the whirling cloud of dust and debris swept across the river last night, my father was happy. As happy as he had been all day.

Without warning, Alex springs up. His stool clatters against the counter and almost tips over. "We need to rerun this simulation." He waves the DataSlate at me. "We can use your dad's original numbers . . . and then try our new data from the drone, too. Let's see if there's availability this morning. It's early in the project, so most people haven't had time to get their sims set up yet."

I follow him to the door, and when he pushes it open, Tomas jumps back to avoid being smacked in the face.

"Oh!" He holds up the bottle of headache meds—"Got the wrong kind. See you guys later on"—and hurries past us back into the first aid room.

Alex walks down the hallway, out the door, and across campus so fast I can barely keep up.

Van's working on the main computer when we get to the Sim Dome. "Hey, champ," he says to Alex.

"Do you think we could run that simulation once more?" Alex blurts out, waving his DataSlate.

"Seriously, my friend?" Van folds his arms in front of him.

"I know it failed before, but I'm positive I have the numbers right now." He turns to me. "We know that—"

"That sometimes a minor input error can throw off a whole experiment," I interrupt. Was he actually going to *tell* Van that I *stole* my father's data? My eyes flash a warning at Alex before I turn back to Van. "We have two sets of numbers we want to double-check."

Van chuckles and shakes his head, but he walks to the access panel and slips in the key card that provides access to the simulation computer. "You found a kindred spirit, Alex. She's as stubborn as you are." He winks at Alex as the door slides open. "Go for it, but this is the last time I can let you run this one. It's a waste of resources."

"Okay, thanks." We step into the control room, just as Tomas arrives, hopefully with the right meds this time. We need Van in a good mood.

Alex plugs his DataSlate into the mainframe and feeds in the numbers. The same numbers my father used for the successful simulation he ran up at StormSafe. The one that worked.

The computer beeps, and a red button appears with the words **BEGIN SIMULATION**. Alex looks over at Van, who's huddled close to Tomas, talking. Finally, he glances up and gives us a sharp nod. Alex takes a deep breath, clicks the button, and leans back in his chair to watch.

A new button appears on the computer screen—INITIATE VARIABLE—but Alex's eyes are on the charcoal clouds forming high up in the dome to his left. They darken and swirl as they cross the river, and right before they reach the model city laid out on the grid in front of us, a funnel cloud drops down.

"Okay," Alex whispers. "Here we go." He watches, intent as the funnel widens and stretches toward the field of faux grass and synthetic trees, and just as it looks ready to touch down, he triggers the variable, presses the button that tells the computer-generated tornado that three hundred virtual kilowatts of microwave energy are blasting into its heart, heating the air in the downdraft. He's told the tornado to imagine the exact circumstances that would lead to its death.

I hold my breath and watch.

There is a spark from the vortex of the storm, and it seems to pause as if it's considering the new variable. Then the funnel cloud swells and pushes forward into the model city. It devours the library, the fire station, the school, four-five-six-seven houses, and grows fat with debris, heading for the business district.

Then the computer screen goes blank. The wind stops blowing, the clouds disappear, and the swirling-whirling-flying debris clatters to the floor. The lights in the dome flicker and go out.

When they come back on, Van and Tomas are stepping out of the observation room. Tomas leaves the dome without waving or even looking at us. "Sorry," Van radios into our cube, "I don't see the point in continuing. You're done."

Alex slides open the door, steps into the main dome, and throws his hands up in the air. "I don't understand how—"

"What you don't seem to understand is that it's time to give up on this one." Van ushers us toward the door.

"Van, wait. We have another set of numbers, different data." Alex doesn't say where the new data came from, thank God, and Van doesn't ask.

Alex starts to turn back to the control panel. "Couldn't we—"

"No," Van snaps. "At some point, you need to accept when a theory isn't working." He opens the door for us to leave, and a rush of warm air flows in. "Go back to the drawing board and consider some other ideas. You've tried the heat-the-downdraft approach, and it failed. Look into wind shear or another theory. But it's time to let this one go."

Alex's hands are clenched into fists. "But I know this should work." He looks back into the dome as if there might be someone else who will give him permission to run the other numbers. But there's just Van blocking the way.

"Has the Sim Dome been checked over since last year?" Alex asks. "Has it been recalibrated to make sure the storms react in line with the data? And the software's up to date and everything?"

Van's face relaxes into a little smile. "It stinks to be wrong, doesn't it? I wish I could tell you it wasn't you, my friend, but this Sim Dome is as up-to-date and fine-tuned as they come. It was checked over, top to bottom, and recalibrated over the weekend."

Alex sighs. "Well, couldn't the guy have made a mistake?"

"I doubt that very much." Van walks us to the door, smirking. "The guy was Dr. Meggs himself."

Chapter 17

Alex doesn't say a word as we walk across the quad. He doesn't hold open the library door.

"So now what are we going to do?" I ask Alex.

He wheels around, eyes burning. "*We?*" He looks at me hard, then lets out an incredulous little laugh. "*We* aren't going to do anything because *we* just got completely shut down. I'd say this one's in *your* court now."

"Alex, why are you mad at *me*? What's wrong?"

"What's wrong? Your father did the maintenance on the Sim Dome himself. He could calibrate that system in his sleep. Do you think for one second it's an accident our simulation didn't work?"

"Well, maybe . . . ," I begin. The thought had already crept into my brain—no, into my gut, in an awful twisting way—before we even left the observation cube. But part of me needs to believe that the dad who used to sing to me at night might still have something good inside.

Alex doesn't wait for me to finish my sentence. He plows into the library and stomps toward the table where we were working.

"I know what it looks like," I whisper, "but maybe we could talk to him about this. There might be a reason. Maybe he has, I don't know, some other information that . . ."

Alex's eyes burn the rest of my words into ashes. "Listen to you." He leans back against a bookshelf and stares at me as if I'm someone he's never met before, someone he wouldn't want to know. "This isn't a computer game." His voice trembles, and his hand shakes as he raises his arm and gestures back in the direction of the Sim Dome. "This is about people's lives. About my family. What your father is doing here is—"

"You don't *know* what he's doing."

"Yes I do, and so do you. It doesn't take a genius, Jaden. And unless you do something about it—"

"Unless *I do something about it?*"

Ms. Walpole pokes her head around the corner. "Is everything okay?"

"Fine, yeah." Alex pulls a book from the shelf and starts flipping through it.

She frowns and steps up beside us. "Shall I ask about the 'library materials' I loaned you yesterday? Or shall I presume you've returned them already?"

Alex looks up at her. "The plane is fine, but it's—"

"Mr. Carillo, the book that I loaned you is a rare volume, and I trust it will be returned in good shape when you're finished." Ms. Walpole raises her eyebrows at him and raises a finger to her lips.

I look around, but we're the only ones in the library that I can see. Is she suggesting that the place is bugged? That someone's listening in? What kind of camp *is* this?

Alex nods slowly. "The book has been very useful. Thanks. It's at my house, and I'll return it soon."

"Perfect." She walks back to her desk, picks up her book, and starts reading.

Alex goes back to flipping pages in the book he's holding, but I put out a hand to stop him. "You say you want me to *do something?* What am I supposed to do?" I whisper, and my thoughts are swirling so much I hardly care who's listening.

He looks up from the book, and says in a voice too low for anyone listening in to hear, so quiet I can barely make out the words myself, "Get yourself into the dome at his company somehow," he whispers. "Run the numbers there." His eyes are urgent, pleading. But I'm already shaking my head.

"I can't." I remember the feeling of hiding under his desk. What would he have done if he'd caught me? "It's too much of a risk. I can't."

The light in Alex's eyes clicks off. "Then you're not the person I thought you were." He looks more sad than angry as he pushes the book back onto the shelf and walks out the door.

In the morning, I sit in my usual auditorium seat and wait for a hand on my arm or a whisper in my ear. When Van finishes a quick morning update, Risha runs to meet Tomas, and I walk to the library alone.

I upload four new meteorology and climatology texts to my DataSlate and spend the next three days reading, bookmarking, and trying to get used to being a team of one.

Ms. Walpole drops a little paper bag on my table as she walks by on one of her book-shelving missions. Oatmeal raisin cookies.

"Thanks," I whisper when she comes by again.

She stops next to my chair. "Where's our boy?"

"He's . . . not happy with me," is all I can muster.

"Well, he'll get over it. Have a cookie," she says, as if it's some ordinary boy-girl thing like him having a crush on somebody else. If only. "And tell him he needs to return that rare book before people start asking questions." She raises her eyebrows at the ceiling, and I wonder again who's listening.

I keep watching the library door after she leaves, but Alex never walks through it.

He won't even look at me the rest of the week.

Saturday's too hot to go outside, so I spend the afternoon in my room, reading.

I try writing to Mom, but it bounces back again, so I call Amelia for a video-chat instead. It's good to see her face and great to hear what everyone's doing at home, but when she asks how things are going here, I don't have much to offer. I try to explain the projects at camp, but she makes a face, and I feel like I've moved away to another planet where the language isn't even the same as it is on Earth.

Sunday morning, Dad leaves for StormSafe before it's light, and when I come downstairs, Mirielle is packing the diaper bag. "Good morning!" She winks at me. "I thought we girls might go on a little adventure today."

"What kind of adventure?"

"Your aunt Linda invited us to visit." She hums a light, breezy song that seems to match the lilacs on her sleeveless blouse. I watch her tickling Remi in her bouncy chair, setting the timer to make sure Dad's dinner will be ready later, and my chest tightens.

Who was that woman on the phone? Does Mirielle have any idea what Dad's whispering to somebody else in his office late at night?

Mirielle pauses with a bottle of juice in her hand and tips her head at me. "Are you all right? I thought you'd be pleased."

I realize my whole face is clenched up, and I force myself to relax. "Yes, it's great. Thanks."

As we drive out of town, past the beat-up trailer parks, past the Corrections Department energy farm and an underground play center that's seen better days, I lower my window. The country roads are lined with big old maple and pine trees that have somehow survived the storms. The fields are strewn with wildflowers. I take a deep breath and sigh. "I know it's not as safe out here, but it feels . . . I don't know . . . fresher. Cleaner, somehow."

"It's safe enough for right now. We have two DataSlates. We'll get alerts if anything changes." Mirielle glances over at me and smiles a little. "And I know what you mean about the air. Sometimes, Remi and I go for drives when your father is at work." She glances in the rearview mirror. "Only when the weather's quiet, of course."

We drive through a long stretch of woods—even the trees smell different out here—and then out into a more open stretch where the trees are smaller, planted in rows.

"Are these fruit trees?" I ask.

"Mmm-hmm." Mirielle reaches behind her to tickle Remi's foot. "Peaches mostly. Linda grows them, too."

Around a curve, the orchards end, and finally, there's a white farmhouse. It's old, the kind you'd expect to have lots of long hallways and closets. There's a porch with big pillars and rocking chairs out front. Behind the house is an old red barn, half falling down, and a brown horse wandering around outside a stable. Next to the barn, there's a tiny farm stand that looks like someone might have nailed it together out of old barn pieces this morning. A hand-painted sign leaning against it reads:

SWEET RASPBERRIES: $12/PINT
FRESH PEACHES: $2 EACH
COMPLIMENTS: FREE

Mirielle pulls into the driveway, and I smile. This place feels like everything I remember about Aunt Linda. She comes running from the house in a flowered blouse and blue jeans and pulls me into a hug the second I'm out of the car.

"My great stars, Jaden! It's been years." She holds me back so she can look at me. "You are your mother's daughter, aren't you?"

"Most people say I look like Dad."

Aunt Linda's smile flickers like a lightbulb with a loose wire, but then it's back. "Well, I suppose you look like Jaden," she says.

The horse whinnies outside the barn, and I turn.

"That Nutmeg . . . always looking for a treat." She digs into her pocket and pulls out a few sugar cubes. "Do you want to go say hello to her before we go inside?"

"Sure."

Aunt Linda leans in to talk quietly to Remi as I clunk down the wooden porch steps and across the grass. It's hard to imagine a person as gentle and relaxed as Aunt Linda raising someone as intense as my father. But I guess part of who you are is genetics, and when I think of Grandma Athena's fiery eyes staring out from her frame, it's easy to see her spirit alive in Dad.

The sugar cubes are rough and sticky in my palm as I step up to the split-rail fence. Nutmeg ambles over, and I climb onto the first rung to pet her on the nose.

"Hold the sugar flat on your palm," Aunt Linda calls to me, "so she doesn't get your fingers."

I do, and Nutmeg's warm, snuffly lips scarf it up.

I feed her my last three cubes. She sniffs my pocket, decides I'm of no more use to her, and wanders away.

"She's beautiful," I say, joining Aunt Linda and Mirielle back on the porch.

"She's been with me a long time." Aunt Linda holds open the door to the kitchen, and we walk into a bright yellow room with a wooden chopping block in the middle and, above it, a rack of copper pots and pans. The wall over the sink has old wallpaper with tiny apples all in rows.

Aunt Linda serves up lemonade and peach pie, and we sit at the big wooden table, talking about camp and Mom's trip and Remi sitting up all by herself. When I finish my pie, I get up to look at the dishes displayed over the sink, all painted in bright colors.

"That's my wall of fame," Aunt Linda says, laughing. She pulls down a coffee mug with an old guy's face painted on it. On the other side there's a short poem called "Fire and Ice."

"Robert Frost." She nods up at the shelf. "And there's Emily Dickinson and Walt Whitman. All my favorite poets. I paint their portraits on one side and a poem on the other."

Rita Dove's not there, but the poet mugs remind me of her. "Thank you for the book."

"You are most welcome." Aunt Linda pulls me into a hug and looks at Mirielle. "Can you stay a while?"

Way in the distance, thunder rumbles, as if it's answering for Mirielle. *No, time to head home.*

Mirielle smiles but shakes her head. "We'd better go. But we'll find time for another visit soon. I'll get Remi changed, and then we'll be off." She picks up the diaper bag and carries Remi into the living room.

"Thanks for today," I tell Aunt Linda, and she has no idea how much I mean it, how much I needed some plain old family love. "I wish you lived closer."

She grins and raises her mug. "Placid Meadows is not my cup of tea, my dear. But I would love for you to visit often."

"Me too," I say, "but there's Dad . . ."

"Oh, I know. He's not too fond of me these days."

"He's not too fond of anybody. Except Mirielle and Remi some-times." I hadn't said it before, but that's how I feel. "It's kind of like he's not *my* dad anymore."

Aunt Linda puts a warm arm around my shoulders. "Oh, sweet Jaden," she says. "He loves you. But you can't count on him showing it in any of the usual ways, I'm afraid. Lord knows I loved that boy when he was growing up—still do—but he wanted his mother all those years and could never have her. Not even before she died, which is the saddest thing of all. She loved her work so much, and it was always urgent-urgent-urgent. She thought she'd have plenty of time for your dad later." She shakes her head.

In the other room, Mirielle sings to Remi, something soft in French.

"So now Dad does the same thing," I say, "to me."

Aunt Linda looks like she wants to argue, but she can't. She gives me a squeeze.

"All set?" Mirielle carries Remi back into the kitchen. "We'll be back soon, I promise." I hug Aunt Linda one more time and hope Mirielle means it.

Nutmeg is at the fence when we step off the porch, probably hoping for more sugar. "Bye, girl," I tell her, and I pat her nose. It feels like velvet in the sun, soft and warm and good.

The clouds are already closer when we pull out of the drive-way. Mirielle catches me sneaking glances out the rear window.

"Not to worry," she says. "We will be home soon. Safe and sound."

We will be, I think. But what about Aunt Linda? What about Nutmeg, who's not protected by anything other than weathered timber once she's in the barn? How long will it be before one of these storms makes a direct hit?

Chapter 18

The storm comes just as we're pulling into Placid Meadows and passes quickly. It's small, so I don't worry about Aunt Linda—this time.

With the sun blazing again, it's steaming hot, so after lunch we collapse on the couch with iced tea while Remi naps in her bouncy seat.

Mirielle turns on the entertainment window. "Oh good! There's ballet streaming from the National Arts Center." Two men and two women twirl and leap through a routine in the underground theater hundreds of miles away.

Mirielle watches the dancers. And I watch Mirielle. Her face flickers between happy and sad, and I wonder if she's remembering performances of her own, back when there were real audiences all over the world.

"Do other countries do this now, too?" I ask.

She startles as if she'd been far away. With the dancers, maybe. "Do they do what?"

"Have a national arts feed instead of live performances."

KATE MESSNER

She nods sadly. "Most do. My sister in Paris says they're building a new theater there, with a safe room directly underneath.
Around here, there are only tiny local dance groups. They perform
in church basements mostly, community safe rooms. Your father
has never wanted to go, but I'd love to see them." Her eyes drift
back to the entertainment window, where one of the men is lifting
the woman high over his head. In her gleaming white dress, she
looks like a seagull soaring. Mirielle sighs. "They aren't profession-
als, of course, but it would be lovely to see real live people dancing
again."

Watching Mirielle's eyes mist makes me clench my jaw. Dad was
probably too busy at work, too busy with whoever he was talking to
on the videophone, for some stupid ballet. "I'd go with you some
time," I blurt out.

She smiles. "I'd love·that. I'll see what I can find."

"Maybe Aunt Linda could come," I say. Somehow, I miss her
already. I bet she'd like the dancing, too.

She nods slowly. "On some night when your father is busy." Her
green eyes dart over to his office door for a second. "We will tell
him we are doing some shopping, perhaps."

The doorbell rings then. "I'll get it." I step carefully around Remi
in her bouncy chair and go to the door, where Risha's lifting her
hand to ring again.

"Where've you been all weekend?" She pulls her BeatBuds out
of her ears, steps past me into the kitchen, and paws through the fruit
bowl on the counter. Her hair is tied back in a gauzy purple scarf
that flows down her back. "You have to come on a bike ride with

me or I'm going to die of boredom." She polishes an apple on her purple-and-red-striped T-shirt and takes a big bite.

"It's too hot."

"Jaden, pleeease? Just to the park for a while."

If I say no, Risha will want to know what's wrong, and I don't want to talk about Alex, so I call good-bye to Mirielle and get my bike.

The air is heavy as soup-steam, but it still feels good to pedal.

"Hey," I say as Risha takes a turn toward the fence. "Aren't we going to the park?"

"Change of plans." She glances back at me, eyes twinkling. She's made plans with the boys, I can tell, and my stomach twists at the thought of seeing Alex now.

"Not today, Risha." Besides, the clouds are starting to build again, and just because the first storm today was mild doesn't mean the next one will be. "You said you wanted to go to the park for a while. I'm not going outside the fence. There's weather coming."

"Not even for a little while? Tomas has hardly talked to me all week. He's been acting all weird, and I know he's worried about his mom. I just want to see him."

She keeps riding toward the fence, and I follow her, thinking I'll stay back while she goes to see the boys.

But when Risha jumps off her bike and climbs through the gap without looking back, something in me can't let her go alone with the clouds swirling. "Fine," I say. "This better be fast."

"Yay!" She's already on the other side, and I have to scramble through to catch her.

Risha winds her way toward the gazebo where we had our picnic—it's empty—and then races to the Carillos' barn and pulls open the door. Two chocolate-brown goats nuzzle each other in one stall. In another, a fat black pig is sleeping. Some chickens are wandering around, too. One wall is lined with bales of hay or straw. Another has dozens of tools—pitchforks, shovels, and axes—hanging from cast-iron hooks. "Hellooo?" Risha looks around. "Shoot," she says, turning back to me. "They probably figured we weren't coming."

I try not to look too happy. "They probably figured they should head for a safe room." The sky looks grayer and greener, more menacing than it did a few minutes ago.

"Well, boo," she says. Then she grabs my hand. "That's okay. I still want to show you something." She ducks between two vintage tractors with steering wheels for actual people who'd drive them and ride around on them. Then she bends down and tugs at a big metal ring sticking up from the floor. "Help me with this, will you?"

I wrap my hand around the cool metal, too, and pull. A creaky panel of wood lifts up from the floor—a trapdoor.

"Check this out." Risha climbs down a metal-runged ladder and fades into the dark.

I wait for her to pop up again, but she doesn't.

"Are you coming back?" I call, squatting by the swung-open door. My voice sounds echoey and cold. The skies have opened up now, and rain is pelting the roof like a mad drummer. The wind blows a flurry of wet, battered leaves through the open door, and I shiver, even though the air is still warm. "Risha, I want to go home."

She doesn't answer.

I stand up, shake out my knees, and head for the barn door. I'm about to step out into the rain when a colossal bolt of lightning cracks through the sky, close enough that the tiny hairs on the back of my neck tingle. Thunder follows half a second later—a sharp, deep crack that shakes the whole barn.

Wind rattles the windows, and outside, tree branches are starting to snap. The sky is dark. Too dark.

Don't let this happen now. Not with us out here.

There's no way I can leave now. I turn away from the pounding rain and call again, "Risha?"

Something knocks on the barn roof. Again. And then two knocks turn into frantic pounding, beating on the roof, and outside, hailstones the size of my fist pummel the dirt.

The sky explodes in light and thunder again. Vibrations shake the barn.

And then there's another sound.

A growing roar that rumbles through my body.

I run for the trapdoor.

I don't know what's down there, but I know what's coming, and I can't be in this room full of sharp metal tools when it hits.

I step onto the ladder, cling to the cool metal rungs, and lower myself, step by trembling step. Above me, where the trapdoor is flopped open, the square of light flashes with lightning. The whole foundation of the building seems to shudder, and the wind blows through the door, through gaps in the beams, with a high-pitched whine that makes me shiver.

Without stopping to think, I climb back up the ladder rungs

into the barn and tug on the handle of the trapdoor. It's solid wood, and I can barely move it, but throwing all my weight against it, I'm able to lug it up from the barn floor, ease back down onto the ladder, and let the door thump shut over my head.

I know I am on the ladder with three, maybe four rungs to climb down, but the darkness feels too thick to move through. Even with the heavy wooden door closed over my head, I can hear the wind roar.

"Risha!" I call, but her name echoes back at me off the floor.

I take a shuddery breath and blink hard, but my eyes don't adjust, so still swallowed in the dark, I start climbing down again.

The rusty metal scratches my palms. I hold on tight, concentrating on that as I lower myself one rung at a time.

Down, down, down, until I see a sliver of light off to one side. I follow it down a long hallway with cool stone walls, and the roar of the wind grows muffled. The light brightens, and finally, I get to the source, a room at the end of the long hall. I push the heavy, half-shut door until it swings open.

"You came down!" Risha is lounging on a daybed. Rock music plays from speakers mounted on the walls. She pats the seat next to her. "Isn't this so perfect?"

I step into the room, and the door swings shut behind me with a thick, wooden thud that makes me jump. *Perfect?* She's bouncing lightly on the daybed, grinning, while the storm rages outside. I can't hear it way down here, but I know it's still there.

She reaches for a bottle of water—there are cases of them, rows of canned goods and packages of all kinds of food. Might as well be comfortable if you're stuck in a tiny room, pretending everything's all right.

"Jaden, we're fine here. What's wrong?"

What's wrong? I open my mouth to answer her, but nothing comes out. This. This is wrong, I think. This world where people have to run for shelter nearly every afternoon, where most people live in fear that this storm—this one—might be the one that destroys every-thing. This world, where a handful of people are so used to being safe, so used to living inside StormSafe's little bubble, that they never worry at all.

"What is this?" I finally ask. "It doesn't look like a regular safe room."

"It's an old bomb shelter from the 1960s. Isn't it the best? It's just like a safe room, really—concrete walls, reinforced with steel. I think this must be what the StormSafe houses were based on." She grabs a package of chocolate sandwich cookies from the shelf above her, tears it open, and shoves a whole one in her mouth.

"Want one?" She holds the package out to me. Cookies. In the middle of a storm that looks like it could devour us whole. My stomach twists, and I shake my head.

I strain my ears for the sounds of the storm, but I can't sort any-thing out anymore. The fluorescent light overhead flickers. What's going on up there?

"Sure you don't want one?" she asks.

"How can you sit there eating cookies?" I blurt out.

She swallows. "We hang out here all the time. It's fine. Tomas and Alex and I kind of took this place over, so we always—"

The music stops and the lights go out, and it feels like the blackness swallows up Risha, too, because she never finishes her sentence. The roar whooshes louder, and the wind isn't low, loud static anymore. It's growling, hissing, popping over our heads.

I reach out for Risha in the blackness, where I hope her hand might be. It's cool and damp. An edge of her fingernail scratches my palm.

"Has this ever happened when you were here before?" I whisper.

"No." She squeezes my hand. "But Alex told me he rode out a storm here once. We'll be okay." But her voice is quiet. Not so confident. Not so Risha.

I don't let go of her hand.

It sounds like the storm is chewing its way through the building over our heads, spitting out mouthfuls of metal, crunching wood into splinters.

I close my eyes and open them again. It looks exactly the same. Black and terrifying and loud.

When I was little, afraid of the dark, Mom used to tell me that nothing could ever be as scary as the monsters in my imagination, that all my nightmares would vanish when she turned on the light. But this time, I already know that's not true. I am imagining a monster upstairs, and I'm afraid—so afraid—that reality will be a million times worse.

I squeeze Risha's hand and hear her ragged breath. I lean closer, and she rests her head against my shoulder, the smell of chocolate cookies on her breath mixing with something else. Sweat. Or fear.

The monster roars louder. How long can the barn hold out?

Glass shatters over our heads. Something splinters, crackle by sharp crackle by groan. Is it the support beam right above us? The barn roof? A wall? Whatever it is creaks, moans a long final moan, and then CRACKS.

Is it broken? Gone?

The wind doesn't answer; it only screams and roars.

Until finally, the sounds fade.

I don't know how long we sit. Long enough for chaos to turn to distant rumbling and then silence.

Long enough for our pounding hearts to sound like cannons in the dark.

We huddle together without moving, without speaking a word, and somewhere inside, I begin to understand what has happened. Even Risha, with all her StormSafe confidence, knows this was no everyday storm. It was bad. But we sit in the dark, still holding hands, both under the spell of the same fairy tale lie.

If you don't look, it won't hurt.

It you don't turn on the lights, you'll never see the monster.

If we stay here in the blackness, if we never go up to see what happened, then maybe it never happened at all.

But then come the sounds.

Quiet at first.

Uneven. Stopping and starting footsteps.

Creaking. Lifting. Wood sliding-against-wood.

A voice so faint I can't tell whose it is or what it's saying. But the tone is unmistakable. The raw edge, the desperation. Someone needs help.

"Risha?" I start to pull my hand away from her, but she holds on. I wiggle my hand free and stand.

I still can't see, but I hear the daybed creak and know she's standing to follow me. I slide a hand against the cool dampness of the wall until I feel the doorframe and take a step out into the hall.

"I'm scared," Risha whispers, and admitting that is so not-Risha that a wave of cold terror races through me. What's waiting for us out there?

"Me, too." We feel our way down the still-night-black hallway, scuffing our feet all the way to the end. The toe of my sneaker bumps something that makes a dull metal clang.

The ladder.

"Ready to go up?"

I wait until I feel her closer to me, feel her shoulder brushing against mine. I take hold of a cold metal rung and start climbing.

Risha's right behind me; her hand brushes my ankle every couple of rungs.

At the top, I keep one hand clutched around a ladder rung. With the other, I reach over my head to push on the spot where the trap-door should open.

It doesn't budge.

"Can you steady me?"

"Hold on." I feel one of Risha's arms wrap around my calves to help me stay balanced on the rung. I let go of the ladder and use both hands to push up as hard as I can, until I'm sure my face is bursting red.

There is nothing at first—as if the door's been sealed. I give it another big push, and then, a crack of light appears.

I bend my knees and push harder. Something slides off the tilting door onto the floor, and the crack grows wider, until the light opens up into a bright, narrow beam of sun. The trapdoor swings wide, thuds down on the barn floor, and there is light. Bright, blinding yellow-white light, like we've flopped open the door to heaven.

I step up another rung and see I am wrong. So wrong.

This is as far from heaven as a world can be.

The light is so bright because there is nothing between us and the sky.

The barn is gone.

Gone, except for half a wall whose skeleton teeters, creaking as if it's in pain. A splintered wooden rod sticks out from the middle of the wall—it wasn't there before—and somehow in the midst of this chaos, I am fixated on it.

I crawl up out of the hole in the floor, my knees scraping over splintered wood, and rise, shaking, to my feet.

I climb over twisted metal, boards, and beams, through wood splinters and feathers and dust—up to the wall where the wooden rod sticks straight out.

It is the pitchfork I'd seen hanging from a hook on the other wall, part of the tidy row of tools, all lined up before the storm.

I wrap my hands around the handle and pull. I hang on it with all my body weight.

It doesn't move.

I breathe, hoarse and deep, and rest my hand on a ragged beam. It feels as if it's the only thing holding me up. I hold on as if the winds might return any second and blow me away, and slowly, I turn away from this piece of wall.

Around it, beams lay scattered over one another like pickup sticks tossed by a giant.

An ax is embedded in what must have been one of the main support beams. Shreds of roofing litter the foundation like bits of paper torn to shreds.

The tractor is gone. Way down near the driveway, I make out a mass of twisted red metal wrapped around a tree.

Risha is frozen halfway up the ladder, clutching the trapdoor frame so hard I worry the metal edge will cut her hand.

"Rish?" I call. But she won't come up. She's in shock.

"Risha?"

She stares. Blinks hard. Squeezes her eyes closed. Opens them again.

I know what she is trying to do.

It doesn't work.

It's all still here.

And then the voice returns, clearer this time, but ragged and choked.

"Newton! Newton!"

I turn toward the farmhouse, or where the farmhouse would have been, and suck in my breath. The concrete safe room is all that's left, but I can breathe after I count the figures coming out of it. Alex's parents. His little sister, Julia. Tomas.

Alex climbs over the debris, and even from here, I see his tear-stained face.

"Newton! Newton, come on, boy!"

"Alex!" I call from the barn, and he whirls around as if I'm a ghost or another storm. I don't care; I start running, tripping over twisted metal tools and clambering over splintered boards until I reach him. I want to throw my arms around him.

But I don't.

"I . . . let me help you," I say.

"Where were you?"

"In that room under the barn. With Risha."

"Where is she?"

"She's okay." I turn to the barn where finally, Risha is rising up from the shelter, ladder rung by ladder rung.

When I turn back to Alex, his face is twisted in pain. "I could hear him barking," he whispers. "But we had to close the door." He turns and heads toward a high pile of debris that looks like it might have been the garage once. "Newton!"

He is flinging boards, and tears burn my eyes. If Newton is under there . . .

"Alex . . ." His father's quiet voice cuts through the clattering wood. He stands at the edge of the heap of house pieces, shakes his head, and holds out his arms. Alex collapses into them, sobbing.

"Is there anything we can do?" whispers Risha, who's made her way over to the safe room that still stands.

Alex's mom is leaning against the concrete wall, holding a first aid kit. It looks small and pathetic in her hand. She shakes her head. "Maybe . . . maybe tomorrow." She looks out over the farm, at debris that's scattered all the way out to the main road. What can we possibly do to help tomorrow? Or any day? What can anyone do?

Risha tugs my sleeve, then slides her hand down to hold mine again. Tight. "We should probably go," she says.

But I can't. I can't move from this place, watching Alex's shoulders heave under his father's arm. His dad waits until the sobs slow and finally stop. He doesn't say a word. What can he say? That everything will be all right? It won't.

"Hold on," I tell Risha. I make my way to Alex and put a hand tentatively on his back. I expect him to whirl around and push my hand away, but he doesn't. Alex's dad gives his shoulder one last squeeze and leaves us alone.

"I'm sorry," I whisper.

He doesn't answer. He stares at that one wall left of the barn with empty eyes.

The sky is so quiet now it's hard to believe what has happened. How can something vanish so quickly and leave so much brokenness behind?

"Alex, please just know that—"

"Shh!" He holds up both hands and squints his eyes shut tight, and I'm sure it's because he can't even stand the sound of my voice. But then I hear it, too.

A whimper.

"It's coming from over there!" Alex pushes past me back toward the one wall that's left of the barn. He steps over boards and twisted metal.

"Newton!"

He starts to step over another pile of rubble—did it used to be the goat pen?—but stops and collapses to the barn floor.

I run, tripping through the debris, until I reach him.

And then I stop.

Newton is splayed in the dust, panting with shallow breaths. His head is bleeding between his ears. A patch of fur is gone, and the rest is matted with blood and dust. One of his legs is twisted at a sick angle, bleeding, too. My breath catches, and my stomach twists, and I have to look away.

"Get some water," Alex's father says quietly behind me. I run back to the shelter because it's the one thing I can do instead of crumbling. I climb down the ladder, stumble down the hallway into the blackness. I crack my shin on the daybed frame, fall forward, and feel the shelf. I flail my arms around until they connect with cool smooth plastic. I take two water bottles and find my way back up into the light.

"Here." I kneel down next to Alex and unscrew the cap from one bottle. He takes it from me and pours it first over the open break in Newton's leg, then over the cut on his head. The bleeding has slowed, but Newton's breaths are coming fast and shallow.

"Shhh . . . it's okay, boy." I put a hand to Newton's shoulder and feel his heartbeat, rapid. Scared.

"We need . . ." Alex is choking back sobs. He squeezes his eyes shut, then opens them again. "I gotta have a bandage or . . . or something."

Risha slips the scarf from her hair and hands it to him. She walks off and sits down in the grass next to Tomas, still in shock.

"Wrap it around the leg just enough to secure it," Alex's father says, leaning over us. "We'll try to get him into town to the vet. Maybe . . ." But his voice trails off.

Alex wraps the scarf around Newton's leg, careful to avoid hurting him even more. He swipes at his eyes with his shirtsleeve and stands, staring over the debris of the barn. Not far from the trapdoor he finds a long piece of board and drags it back next to Newton. Together, we ease the dog onto it.

"Careful," Alex whispers. It must hurt, and I'm expecting Newton to snap at me, but he never does. He just keeps panting, looking up at Alex with big dog eyes that seem to say a million things at once. *How could you let this happen to me?* But also, *I trust you. Please help.*

"I'll get the truck," Alex's dad says quietly. Somehow, it survived the storm, parked at the edge of a field not fifty yards from the barn, as if the tornado couldn't be bothered with it. Alex's mom has already gone back to the safe room with Julia. She doesn't need to see all this.

Alex kneels next to Newton, rubbing behind his ear. His hand is caked with blood.

"I'm sorry," I whisper.

He doesn't look up.

"I am." The words are choked, but I force them out. "About Newton and the farm, and about not doing anything. This is awful, Alex, your family and Newton . . ." And Aunt Linda and Nutmeg, I think. Did this storm hit them, too?

"Alex, I was wrong. It *is* worth the risk. Stopping this is worth almost anything." Hot tears streak down my cheeks. "I'll do it. Okay? I'm going to go up there. I promise."

He turns to me and shrugs. The pickup rumbles up, and he stands to help his father lift Newton into the back.

I watch as Alex climbs in next to his dog, holding him close as the truck pulls away.

Chapter 19

It's a full week before I can make good on my promise.

A full week of watching and waiting. Of making weather small talk with Dad, chitchatting with Mirielle, and playing peek-a-boo with Remi.

A full week of camp, going through the motions without Alex.

A full week of wondering when he'll be back. Wondering if Newton is going to be okay.

Finally, on Monday morning, Dad finishes breakfast and heads to his office. Mirielle is out shopping, so there's no one to swoop in and clear the counter. I watch the door close, grab what I need, and call Risha. "I got it."

She's been amazing since the storm. I told her everything when we got back home that night, about Alex, our argument, and what I promised him I'd do. I confessed my plan to somehow get into my father's work office and access his computers. Instead of telling me how crazy I am, Risha asked about the security systems at Storm-Safe. When I told her it was probably a fingerprint scan, she smiled.

"That'll be the easy part then," she said. "You just need the right fingerprints."

And now I have them.

I meet Risha and we ride as fast as we can to camp; we get there half an hour before it starts.

Risha scans her print and ushers me into the Finger Factory, the nickname she and Tomas gave Eye on Tomorrow's cloning center.

We step into what amounts to a coatroom, with hooks on the walls and a row of lockers. Risha opens one and hands me a lab coat, hair cover, and latex gloves. "Put these on, okay? We don't want any cross contamination or it'll mess everything up."

Once we're outfitted, she scans her print again, and the door to the actual laboratory slides open. Humming with high-powered computer servers and packed with DNA extraction equipment, this is every bit as impressive as the Sim Dome.

The entire room shines with stainless steel. Every countertop gleams; most are covered with trays of test tubes in perfect lines. There are incubators—some quietly warming genetic stews, some turning in slow rotation.

Risha leads me to a workstation along the wall and nods toward a white petri dish on the counter. Something pinkish gray is floating in it. "We've been trying to grow an ear," she says. "It seems to be working, but Van says it'll be another couple weeks before we can find out if it has all the parts it'll need to hear."

"Well, good luck."

"What?" she says.

"Good luck."

"What?" She holds her hand up to her ear—her real ear—and I realize she's making a joke. I laugh a little, and it takes away some of the fear racing through me. It's not that we're not allowed to be here. Van gave Risha permission for early work sessions a while ago, and if anyone asks, she'll just say she's giving me a tour. But if anyone here found out what was in my bag—Dad's coffee mug from this morning, with his fingerprints on it—that would be another story.

"All right, let's get moving." Risha walks down the long counter to a larger, more high-tech workstation and climbs up onto a high stool.

"This is it," she says, and motions for me to take a seat next to her. In front of us is a device that looks like some combination of an electron microscope, an incubator, and a petri dish. Risha pulls clear goggles down over her eyes, picks up a pair of stainless steel forceps, and bends down over the dish, squinting. She holds her breath and pokes with steady hands at the fleshy something in the fluid.

"This turned out perfectly . . ." Slowly and smoothly, she lifts the tip of the forceps from the petri dish. Hanging from the end is a crumpled, yellowish clear membrane. "Here it is." She takes a second pair of forceps and uses it to grab the other edge so it hangs in a thin oval strip. "Got the cup?"

I pull the coffee mug from my bag and point to the clearest print.

"Perfect." Risha carefully maneuvers the tissue into place over the print and presses down on it with a gloved finger for a few seconds. She peels it back off the mug with the forceps and holds the tissue up to the light. "Beautiful." She lowers it back into the solution in the petri dish, and it floats delicately on top. "Let's give it the rest of the day for the pattern to grow. But I'd say you can stop back before you leave today to pick it up." She gestures to the dish with a flourish. "Your brand new fingerprint."

I spend the whole day in the library, half-hoping I'll look up and see Alex, but I know it's too soon. There's too much cleaning up to be done after the storm, too much debris and sadness to wade through.

Risha comes to get me at the end of the day, and we walk back to the Finger Factory while everyone else is heading for their bikes to go home.

The print is ready. I reach for it, but Risha pulls back the forceps. "Ah, ah, AH!" She shakes her head. "This isn't like a glove you can put on and take off all day. You're going to be able to wear it once for a few hours. That's it." She pulls out a shallow glass jar filled with fluid. It's shaped like the tiny container where Mom used to keep her contact lenses before she got her eyes fixed. Risha lowers the tissue into it. "Keep it in here until right before you need it."

She tightens the lid and holds it out to me but then pulls back. "Wait a second. I'm going to start another copy. It'll be easier than starting from scratch if you have a problem with this one." She takes out the tissue, presses it against some kind of glass plate, then puts it back in the jar and hands it over. "All set."

The whole bike ride home, the little jar in my pocket pokes into my hip, reminding me of the crazy thing I am about to try. I tell myself there's time; it may be days, weeks even, before Dad remembers that tour of StormSafe he promised me. There's plenty of time to think about this. Plenty of time to plan.

When I get home, the kitchen door slams closed behind me, and Dad's voice booms out, "Thank goodness!"

He rushes to the entryway, holding a BioWake Cola in one hand and bouncing Remi with the other arm. "Oh." His face falls. "You're not Mirielle."

He paces back toward the kitchen with Remi clinging to his shoulder. "She's out shopping, but she knows I need to be up at headquarters this afternoon." He taps his watch. "I'll have to take the baby with me, I suppose."

I put my backpack on the counter and take a deep breath. This is the opportunity I thought would take weeks to come. It may be my only chance. "I could come with you and help," I blurt out before I have time to think about it any more. "And maybe do that tour you promised?" My heart thuds while I wait for him to answer. The tiny jar in my pocket suddenly feels huge. How could he not see it?

"Well, that's a great idea. Thank you!" Before he even finishes the sentence, he's steering me toward the door. I grab my backpack with my DataSlate and head out to the HV.

Once Remi is strapped in her car seat, Dad pulls out of the garage and starts down the street so fast the tires actually squeal. I wonder what the big hurry is, but his brows are knit together so tightly, the line of his mouth so thin right now, that my question settles back inside me.

We're at the Placid Meadows gate when Dad's DataSlate chimes.

He presses the speaker button, and Mirielle's voice pours out in a recorded message.

"Honey, I am so, so sorry I am running late. We are about to have a storm at the mall, of all things, and I must wait until it passes." Her voice is thinner than usual, like she's scared. But I don't know if that's about the storm or about being late for Dad. "I will see you at home later."

Dad lets out a sharp sigh and veers to the side of the road.

"What are we doing?"

His face is lit by the blue glow of the DataSlate, and he either doesn't hear me or isn't answering. His eyes are trained on the screen, full of columns and numbers and symbols. Dad highlights two of the cells, types in new numbers, and pokes at the CALCU-LATE button.

A new page of numbers appears. He takes another deep breath, and I watch his eyes twitching as they move down the columns. He seems satisfied, and pokes at the APPLY button at the bottom of the screen. I catch a split-second look at the box that appears on the screen next, before Dad notices me reading over his arm and angles the screen away from me.

It was only a second, but it was long enough to read two words: "Satellites responding . . ."

Dad looks down at the DataSlate for another few seconds, then powers it down and puts the car back in drive.

"Did you . . . ?" The words are seared into my mind. *Satellites. Satellites responding.* Responding how? Responding to what? Or to whom? "Did you just . . . do something?"

"I checked on the storm path." He reaches over to turn on the music player. "Don't worry. Mirielle's fine; it took a turn to the east."

It took a turn to the east? All on its own? *Satellites responding.* Responding to commands he entered. He knows how to dissipate storms. Is that what he did? The pieces of this puzzle are popping faster and faster in my brain, like raindrops plunking into a puddle. First one, then two and three at a time, and then so many you forget the surface was ever calm at all.

I stare out the window at the retreating clouds as Dad turns into the long driveway that leads to StormSafe.

"I keep forgetting you haven't been here." He's in a better mood now. "I'll show you around a little before my meeting."

"Great," I say. But it's during his meeting that I expect to see the most. The container in my pocket presses into my hip as I shift in my seat. *Please let this work. Please let it work.*

When we round the final curve in the long driveway, I get my first glimpse of StormSafe headquarters up close.

When I look up from Placid Meadows, the buildings of this place seem to glow, and now I see why. Every wall is made of windows.

Windows like they used to have in houses when Mom and Dad were growing up. Glass ones that squeak if you lick your finger and run it down the pane, windows that smudge and streak and sparkle in the sun. Is it all safety glass?

Dad pulls into a parking space, and we get out of the HV. I balance Remi on my hip and follow Dad up a walkway lined with bright orange poppies. I don't need to check to see if they're symmetrical;

I'm sure every plant is DNA-ture. I wait while Dad presses a finger to the data panel. The door swings open, and there's a receptionist at a long chrome desk. "Hello, Nadia." Dad gives her a wave and heads for the elevator.

Nadia gives a fluttery-fingered wave and tucks a lock of black hair behind her ear. Was she the woman on Dad's DataSlate that night in his office? She doesn't say anything, so I can't compare the voices.

"Want a real quick tour?" He starts down a carpeted hallway. "We've got our conference room down here." He opens a door to a lush room with a long conference table and big leather chairs. "It's the brain center, where we have all our planning and problem-solving sessions."

I step up to the big window and see that this main office isn't all of StormSafe; there are smaller buildings around the parking lot and gardens. "What's in the other buildings?"

"More offices. Some research labs and data centers."

One of the buildings, set apart, looks less modern than the others—just a squat concrete structure, almost like an old storm shelter. There's only a steel door and one window. "What about that one?"

"Nothing exciting, just storage. Come on upstairs," he says, heading back down the hallway. "I'll show you my office."

"What about the Sim Dome?" I ask.

"That's in the basement, but it's in use right now, and I don't want to interrupt."

Dad pushes the elevator button for the eighth floor, and when the bio-scanner beeps, he presses his index finger to the panel. The elevator starts to rise.

Remi reaches for the buttons with chubby hands, too little to understand why her fingers won't get us where we need to go. It needs to be Dad's fingerprint. Or a perfect imitation.

The elevator leads directly to Dad's top-floor office and lab. It's a huge, open space, every wall made of windows with a view over the land. The mahogany desk in the center of the room is an exact copy of the one I hid under in Dad's office at home, and from his chair, he has a view of any weather system approaching.

"Not bad, huh?" Dad takes Remi from my arms and gestures toward the bank of computers. "Go ahead and have a look."

I walk over to the heart of the office—no, more like the brain. Plasma monitors taller than I am grow up out of the floor alongside each workstation. One spews out a constantly scrolling screen of computer-generated weather models. Another three are Doppler radar composites, and two more seem to be live cameras trained on the surrounding landscape. One of those shows the storm Mirielle called about, way off in the distance.

"Amazing, isn't it?" Dad says, bouncing Remi. "This place never sleeps."

"People work here all night?"

"Somebody's here around the clock, and the rest of us check in from home often. This is all tied into the wireless network so it can be controlled remotely." He motions for me to take Remi. "I have to get to that meeting."

I put Remi down on the soft rug by the couch with a couple of toys, and Dad heads for the elevator.

"Will you be long?" I call after him as the door opens. "I mean . . . I wondered if she'll need to take her nap here."

Dad shakes his head. "No, I should only be about twenty minutes." He steps into the shiny silver box, and the door closes.

"Twenty minutes," I whisper to Remi, who's chewing on her toy dolphin's tail. How could that be enough time when I don't even know what I need to do?

I arrange couch cushions around Remi to make a sort of play area, and then I head for one of the lab counters. I pull the jar from my pocket and unscrew the top slowly, as if something might jump out the minute it's open. When I lift the lid, the sharp, sour smell of preservative fluid invades my nose, but even with watering eyes, I can see it suspended in the chemical broth.

My new fingerprint.

I didn't think to bring forceps or tweezers, so I reach into the container, grasp the new tissue between the fingernails of my thumb and forefinger, and pull it out. It hangs like a wet scrap of cloud.

I take a quick glance at Remi—still playing with the dolphin, but her eyelids look heavy—and then as delicately as I possibly can, I spread the new skin over the tip of the index finger on my left hand. It's so thin and elastic that it wraps right around, and when I press the edges together, they stick.

I try bending my finger, pointing, wiggling it. The new print doesn't fall off, doesn't loosen at all. It feels like part of me. *Thank you, Risha.*

I cross the room, sink into the plush leather chair at Dad's desk, click the login button, and wait.

"Access restricted to Dr. Stephen Meggs," the screen reads. "Provide bio-verification."

I press my finger to the bio-reader and hold my breath.

The computer beeps, and Dad's desktop menu appears. I scan the icons—satellite feeds, data streams, radar from at least eight different sites in the county. Where is the latest data for his storm research?

The antique clock on the wall ticks loudly. Eight minutes have passed. Remi has fallen asleep and is drooling all over her dolphin. I need to find whatever's here and get off this thing.

The radar, satellite, and model applications seem to be the same ones running on the other computers. But in a corner of the screen, there's a folder I didn't see on any of the screens across the room.

STORMBANK

I click to open it and a box filled with dozens of sub-folders spills out on the screen. Each one is labeled with a set of numbers.

5-7-1840

6-12-1899

6-9-1953

No, not just numbers. Dates.

I scan the list.

5-27-1896

4-5-1936

3-18-1925

5-4-2007

6-17-2010

It goes on and on. Dated folder after dated folder inside the STORMBANK file. Does each folder have meteorological data for that particular date?

The clock ticks again. Ten minutes left.

There must be something here about the dissipation project. There has to be.

My eyes dart from file to file. Half the titles are simply project numbers. I can't begin to guess what Re-creation #129 means, so I keep looking, hoping that the right thing will catch my attention. I feel so certain the answer is here.

Remi murmurs in her sleep.

As I'm standing to check on her, the elevator rumbles to this floor and the door begins to slide open. I fly across the room and practically dive for the couch.

I sit next to Remi, my knees tucked up against me, heart pulsing in my throat.

My view of the elevator is blocked by the row of workstations, but I can still hear whoever it is stepping out into the reception area of the office.

"Stephen?" It's a woman's voice. Maybe the one from Dad's DataSlate that night, but I can't be sure.

I hold my breath. Should I answer? I haven't logged off the computer; the storm notes are there on the screen for anyone who approaches.

"Stephen!" The voice is sharper now, colder.

Is it the receptionist from downstairs? I can't just sit here and let her find me shaking. She'll wonder why I didn't answer.

"My dad's in a meeting right now," I call. I take a deep, shaky breath and get ready to face whoever it is when they come around the corner, but there's only quiet.

I wait, listening to my heart in my ears. Where did the woman go?

The clock on the wall ticks again, and I jerk my head to look. It's been sixteen minutes.

I need to log off that computer before Dad gets back.

I walk slowly around the bank of workstations, expecting the visitor woman to be waiting with more questions. But when I get to the elevator, there is no one. The door is closed and rumbling with a distant hum.

Whoever she was, she left without answering. Apparently, she was only interested in Dad.

The clock ticks. Dad could be back any second, but I can't walk away from this. Not now.

I go back to his desk and skim the pages on the screen. Most of it is over-my-head science, but in one file, the words I do understand jump out. They jump out and grab me by the throat, and shake.

Possibilities for Replication: In simulation exercises, researchers successfully recreated the atmospheric conditions that led to the June 17, 2010, EF4 tornado near Deer Creek, Minnesota, through the heating and cooling of particular features of supercell thunderstorms. In the Simulation Dome assessment, this resulted in the genesis of a tornado that would easily be classified NF4 or above.

In the first non-laboratory trial, certain atmospheric variables interfered, resulting in a smaller vortex forming and veering slightly off the intended track so that intervention was necessary to reroute. Still, damage was impressive, and with further development, more precision in both the scope of the storm and the track may be expected.

Damage was impressive?

I look at the date listed next to the words "first non-laboratory trial," and a throbbing pain shoots through my temple. 5-30-2050. That was our first day at camp. The day Risha and I had the picnic with Alex and Tomas. The day we watched from the jungle gym while the kids at the park "sang" the tornado away from the Placid Meadows fence.

When really, the magical storm songs were coming from this office.

My stomach churns with the poison of what I've learned. This makes it look like Dad isn't doing research to get rid of storms anymore. This research is focused on—no, that's impossible. Is it? I look back at the last paragraph, but my head hurts. Letters are swimming out of place, rearranging themselves, and I feel sick.

Bile rises in my throat, but I swallow it down and pull my DataSlate from my bag.

I don't wait for the clock to tick away my last minutes. I need this—all of it. I don't know yet what I can possibly do with it—I don't know yet what it all means or who I can possibly show—but I know I need it.

I jam my DataSlate connector into the port on Dad's computer.

"Transfer file command restricted to Stephen Meggs. Please provide bio-verification."

Come *on*, come *on*, I think, pressing my finger to the reader. After three failed reads, probably because I'm shaking too much to hold still, the computer beeps, my storage drive appears, and I'm able to drag the STORMBANK folder in to copy.

Remi stirs again.

The file transfer bar progresses slowly, and I curse under my breath because I can't make it zip to the end.

Remi's awake fussing, so I start across the room to pick her up, just as the elevator begins to hum.

No!

I fly back to the computer. Remi's crying, wiggling in my arms as I lean over the screen. The files are still copying.

Go. Go, GO.

Just a few more seconds.

But the elevator dings, and there are no more seconds. I pull the DataSlate from the port and ignore the error message that appears. Right now, it doesn't matter if any of the data actually transferred—I need to get off this thing before Dad comes. But it won't shut down.

I try the escape key.

The elevator dings again.

I yank the power cord from the back of the computer, and the screen puffs to black as the door slides open.

Dad steps out. "How are my girls doing?"

I stand up from the leather chair and bounce a little with Remi. I force my voice to sound calm. "We're fine. She's been fussy, so I thought she'd like spinning in your chair, but she wanted to grab everything." I glance at the black screen, praying it will reboot—and not return to the last screen I was on—when the power returns. "She unplugged your computer. Sorry."

"No problem." In four long steps, he's at the desk, putting the cord back where it goes.

The machine hums to life, and I hold my breath.

Dad turns back to me. "Ready to head home?"

I nod. Remi's quieting down in my arms, her head drooping onto my shoulder, and her rhythmic breathing helps my heart settle down, too. "Let me get my stuff."

I reach for my DataSlate and backpack to follow Dad to the elevator. Just before the door slides shut, I see Dad's computer monitor flash back to life on his desk. There is only a log-in screen.

No sign of the data I was never supposed to see.

No evidence at all that I logged in tonight as Stephen Meggs.

Chapter 20

"Jaden, do you have plans after camp tomorrow?" Mirielle passes me the fruit salad at dinner. "I'd love for us to have a girls' afternoon—maybe some shopping?" She winks at me, and for a second, I don't know why. Then I remember "shopping" is code, and she must have found a dance performance for us to go see. I wonder if Aunt Linda is coming, too, but I can't ask now.

"Sure." I should be excited, but mostly, I'm dying to finish dinner so I can be alone and think about everything I saw on Dad's computer. I spoon out a little heap of globe-perfect blueberries and seedless strawberries. Their plastic-smooth surface feels cold on my tongue. I swallow and try not to think of berries warmed by the sun. "Shopping sounds great."

"Terrific idea." Dad's in one of his good moods. He reaches over to Remi's high chair and gives her a grape that looks like it came out of a mold in a factory. "I have a late meeting tomorrow, but I'd love to see all my girls for an early dinner. Why don't you drop by the office after your shopping, and we'll get something in the cafeteria?"

"Wonderful." Mirielle takes the grape from Remi and cuts it into quarters so she can eat it without choking.

"Perfect," I say, but my brain has left the dinner table and gone upstairs, where my DataSlate is waiting.

On the way to my room, I pass Grandma Athena's picture, and somehow her eyes seem sharper than usual. I stop and pick up the frame.

What Alex and I have been trying to do—what we're so close to figuring out—has absolutely consumed me these past weeks. If Mirielle didn't call me to the table for meals, I don't know if I'd even feel hungry. What I've been starving for is information, and the more I get, the more ravenous I am for more.

Tonight, looking into those charcoal eyes that almost pierce the glass, I understand Grandma Athena's passion for science more than ever.

I sigh and put the digital frame back on the shelf. Grandma Athena probably had a whole team of secret government scientists working with her.

Without Alex, I'm completely on my own.

I'm in pajamas, teeth brushed and lasered, and in bed, but as I'm about to power on my DataSlate, there's a knock at the door.

"Come on in." I'm expecting Mirielle with clean laundry, but when the door swings open, it's Dad.

"Hi there."

KATE MESSNER

"Hi." I slide the DataSlate onto my bedside table and pull up the covers. I don't think he's been in this room since I moved in.

He sits down on the edge of my bed and picks up the poetry book. I've gotten careless about leaving it out. I hold my breath as Dad reads the title. He opens his mouth as if he's going to say something, but then closes it. He turns a few pages, and I can tell he's trying hard not to frown at it. Then he puts it down. "Sorry I've been so busy lately. I haven't even had a chance to ask how you've been doing with the move. You like Placid Meadows?"

"Sure. It's great."

He looks back at the book on my nightstand, but then reaches for my DataSlate next to it. My whole insides turn to ice. "Is your work at Eye on Tomorrow going well?"

"Yeah," I say, frantically trying to think of what I can add. What would make this sound like an ordinary father-daughter summer camp conversation? What can I say so it will never occur to him that I know what I know? "It's fantastic. The library, especially."

"Sure is. That's a top-notch facility, all around." He looks down at the DataSlate. *Don't turn it on. Don't turn it on.* "Dad, I'm really tired, okay?"

"Okay." He turns the DataSlate over in his hands and pauses, and a breath catches in my throat.

But he puts it down, the screen still empty black, and walks to the door. "Night, Jaden."

"Night."

I listen to the click of the door, his footsteps on the hardwood

floor of the hallway outside my room, the groan of the spiral staircase as he heads back down to Mirielle.

And then I reach for my DataSlate. The screen lights up, and I
hold my breath until the menu loads.

The files are there.

They copied before I unplugged Dad's computer.

Every last one.

I breathe out.

It is all here. The real storm dissipation simulation report. The
fake one. All the data that goes with those, and the full StormBank.

I open one of the files to make sure it's intact, and out pour the
details of twin tornadoes that hit Gainesville, Texas, in April of 1936.
There's less information for this storm than for more recent tornadoes, but the file still paints a vivid picture.

The debris in the streets was ten feet deep.

The image swirls in my mind—whipping winds and flying
windows—until I shake my head and close the file. I have to try and
get to sleep.

I create a new folder, drag the files inside, and start to type a
label. I can't call it "Family Photos" like Dad. That's a folder he might
open if he picked up my DataSlate in one of his good-father moods.
Instead, I name it "Poetry" and turn off the light.

Tomorrow at camp, I'll try to get permission to run this data
through the Sim Dome. After it works and I have what we need, I'll
go see Alex and tell him, and he won't look at me that awful way he
looked at me before. I can't wave a magic wand and make Newton
okay again, but I can give him this.

I stare at the rectangle of blue-white light the moon casts through my skylight onto the carpeted floor. I try to sleep, but funnel clouds swirl behind my closed eyes.

I turn the lamp back on and reach for the book of poems.

"Geometry" would make my head spin faster tonight, so I flip through the pages for something calmer, quieter, and I find one called "Adolescence." It is about a hot summer night, like this one, about a girl hiding with someone, her cousin, maybe, behind her grandmother's porch. And the older girl whispers secrets to her in the quiet night and firefly light, tells her how soft a boy's lips can be, like the skin of a baby.

I close the book and look up at the ceiling, where there are no fireflies, only straight rows of perfectly round, recessed lights that never flicker.

Amelia kissed a boy once. It was Nico Groves, and it was winter, not summer. She was waiting for her mom to pick her up after a dance at the StormSafe teen center, and she says one minute he was talking to her about his new air-drum kit and the next minute he kissed her right there on the sidewalk. His lips were chapped, rough, she said. She never mentioned baby's skin, but I think she liked it anyway.

I fall asleep thinking about fireflies. And strawberries with raindrop seeds.

First thing in the morning, I hop on my bike, and with the wind blowing my hair from my face, I can think clearly again. I'll go straight to

Van when I get to camp, let him know I need time in the Sim Dome. And then . . . what? I wish Mom were here. My eyes burn thinking about her, how much I miss her, how much I need her.

Maybe today will be the day she answers. With tears spilling down my cheeks, I stop my bike and pull out my DataSlate. I can't help hoping. Maybe, maybe, maybe.

But there are no video-messages. No text messages. Nothing.

I pull up her contact page and press RECORD to try one more time. "Hi, Mom," I say into the screen, and then I am sobbing. All at once, I can't hold it in anymore, and I cry and pictures flash through my head like some awful horror movie. The storm at the barn. Swirling feathers and dust. Newton whimpering in pain. And the look on Alex's face. Two weeks' worth of numbers and funnel clouds and secrets explode inside me, and I drop the DataSlate to my side, my arm hanging limp. And I cry.

I *can't* face all this by myself. But the more I think about it all, the more I realize what's happening, the more I realize I am absolutely alone.

When I'm empty from crying, I breathe in. I pick up the DataSlate—it's still recording—and I take a deep breath. "Mom." My voice breaks. "I *need* you to come home."

I stare at the red record light. I should delete this and do it over. But deep down, I know it won't matter. She'll never get it anyway; it'll be like all the rest, so I just send it. I start pedaling again, and my tears dry in the wind. They leave thin, salty trails down my cheeks.

When I pull into the Eye on Tomorrow campus, I squeeze the

brakes so hard I almost go flying with my backpack over the handle-bars. Alex's mom is pulling away in the truck.

My heart jumps. Alex is here. He must be inside already.

I wave to his mother, and she gives a small, sad wave back before she drives away.

When I get to the auditorium, Alex isn't in his usual spot. He's in the back, way off to one side, a seat that has *don't-sit-by-me* written all over it.

I go to him anyway.

"Can I sit with you?"

His face is impossible to read. Empty like a cloud-gray sky. He shrugs. I take it as a yes and sit down.

I'm terrified to ask, but I force the words out. "How's Newton?"

"Not good."

My throat tightens, and I wait. *Please don't let him be dead.* "Alex?"

He looks straight ahead. "His leg's not healing right, so they have to amputate. He's having surgery this afternoon."

"Oh, Alex, I hope it goes okay." But really, nothing is okay.

I blink away tears as Van jogs down the aisle to the front. He says it's time for another holo-sim lecture, since we're at a turning point where most groups should be switching from theoretical research to practical applications.

When Dad rises out of the floor, my stomach twists.

I turn toward Alex. "I went up to StormSafe with my dad," I whisper. He doesn't respond, and his eyes are focused up front, but I keep talking over Dad's lecture on responsibility and ethics.

"I have . . . stuff from his computer. I have it here, on my DataSlate, and I was going to try and run the sim again. And then I was going to go find you and talk to you."

Alex folds his arms in front of him.

"But you're here." I turn to face front again because I'm too afraid to see his reaction to the last thing I need to say. "Maybe we could work together again?"

Before he can answer, the lights come on. Dad is gone, erased. If only it were that easy.

"All right," Van announces. "Go wherever you need to go today. I know for most of you, that's the lab, but if you have more to do in the library, that's okay, too."

"Library?" I whisper over my shoulder to Alex, hoping he'll say yes.

He doesn't say anything to me on the way out.

But Van does. "Jaden, I need a few minutes with you, okay? I've been trying to check in with all the first years for a quick conference."

Without asking, Alex lifts my backpack from my shoulders. "I'll take this to the library for you. You can meet me there when you're through."

I consider grabbing it back, but I'm so relieved he's talking to me that I just nod and watch him walk out the door.

"So," Van says, motioning me to take a seat again in the empty theater. "Things are going well?"

I nod. "Mostly, I guess."

Van smiles a little. "I know your partner was extremely frustrated when your last Sim Dome experience didn't go as he'd planned, but that's all part of the process. Have you . . . decided to go in another direction now?"

"Kind of, yeah." I consider telling him now about the new data but decide it's too risky. It will make more sense if I share it with him after we try the Sim Dome again, after I have real proof. "Can we get time in the dome soon?"

"I think so." He swipes through a few pages on his DataSlate until he gets to a weekly calendar. "Maybe Thursday? I'll check the master schedule and let you know."

"Thanks."

Van looks at my empty hands. "I was going to do a DataSlate scan. We're required to check in every couple weeks with students who carry them on campus. Don't you usually have yours with you?"

"I do. But Alex took my stuff to the library."

"No problem. I'll catch up with you later." Van stands and heads for the door. "I'm impressed with your work so far, Jaden." He holds it open for me, and the sunshine streams in from outside. It's going to be hot again. Storm weather later on.

"Thanks."

"I'm serious." He gives me a friendly cuff on the shoulder as I turn to head to the library. "If you're not StormSafe scientist material, I don't know who is."

"Hey, Jaden!" Risha races up to me on the quad after Van walks away. "Hold out your hand and close your eyes. I have a present for you."

I do what she says, and two little glass jars drop into my palm. "Same print?"

She nods. "Save them for a rainy day."

Tomas waves from the Finger Factory steps, just as Van walks up to the building. He stands close to Tomas, talking, and Tomas looks down at the steps.

"He's been hanging around Van a lot, huh?"

Risha nods. "Van's kind of taken Tomas under his wing. He says he might know somebody who can pull some strings and get his mom into a treatment center sooner." She gives me a quick hug. "I'll talk to you later, okay?" And she runs off.

Alex is back at our library table as if nothing happened. If it weren't for the healing cuts, the fading bruises on his face and arms, I might be able to pretend it didn't.

He points to a pile of books next to him. My DataSlate is on top. "I unpacked your stuff. I thought we could do a little more work on supercell formation today before we redesign the sim."

I reach for my DataSlate. "Alex, we don't need to do more research," I whisper. "I have whole folders full of—"

He puts a hand over my mouth—gentle but firm—and sweeps his eyes over toward the ceiling. *Shhh.* "Later," he whispers. "Not here."

I'm four or five pages into the supercell reading when the door opens and Van walks in from outside. "Hey, Jaden. Okay if we do that DataSlate scan now?"

"Sure." I hand it to him and get back to my notes.

"Are you kidding?" Alex hisses, staring at me from behind a thick meteorology textbook. "He's going to find those files."

"No, he won't," I whisper. "They're hidden."

"Not very well."

"How do *you* know how well they're hidden?"

"Jaden, that DataSlate's only got one storage chip and there's a search function. You can't hide anything."

"It's *fine*."

He frowns but goes back to his reading. Van is back with the DataSlate in less than half an hour. "All set, Jaden. Looking good."

"Thanks." I take it from him and set it next to the pile of books. "Any chance that Sim Dome spot worked out for us?"

He nods. "You're penciled in for Thursday, first thing at nine."

"Great," Alex says, and looks at his watch. "I know we're not done until noon, but is it okay if I leave now?" He looks up at Van. "My dog's having surgery, and I want to be there. Plus we still have a huge mess to clean up."

Van puts a hand on Alex's shoulder. "You do what you need to do, man. We're glad to see you back. Let me know if there's anything I can do to help."

Alex packs up, and they walk out together as a bank of clouds moves in from the west and swallows up the sun. My mood dims along with it. How can he leave when we didn't even get a chance to talk?

But then I remember the barn, and the house, and his family and the millions of pieces that need to be put back together.

I remember Newton.

And I feel ridiculous for thinking that Alex talking to me—no matter what it's about—would be more important.

I read through another chapter of one of the reference books, but my heart isn't in it this afternoon, so I reach for my DataSlate instead and pull up a notes page.

The Poetry file is still there, lurking in the corner of the screen, looking innocent.

The library clock ticks—twenty minutes left for today. Not enough time to start research from a new source, so instead, I decide I'll read through the entries in the StormBank file more thoroughly. Part of me—probably the same part that wants to believe in fairies and mermaids and unicorns—still hopes there's an explanation, that my father isn't what all this makes him look like.

Another part of me is afraid. Afraid that even though there are no fairies or mermaids or unicorns, there *are* human monsters. Afraid that my father might be one of them.

But maybe, maybe, maybe. Maybe there is something I'm missing, something more. Something to explain it all away.

I click on the Poetry folder.

It is completely empty.

The files are gone.

Chapter 21

The Sim Dome and reception building are blurry through my tears as I head for my bike, but I recognize the burly figure walking toward me.

Van says nothing about me crying, but his mouth twists into a little smile. "Enjoy your weekend, Jaden. Don't work too hard."

I want to scream. I want to turn around and run after him and push him to the ground.

He deleted the files! He stole them from me! I want to tear them back out of his hands, but I know they're not there. They're not anywhere I'll ever find them again.

And I can't say a word. Because I stole the files first.

Van must know that.

Soon, so will Dad, if he doesn't already.

I pedal home as hard as I can, pumping so hard my legs burn, but no matter how hard I push, I can't outpace the voices in my head.

Stupid.

How could you bring it without making a backup?

Failure.

I slam the door, hard, before I realize Mirielle's waiting for me in the kitchen. "My goodness, Jaden! It must be sweltering outside. You are all . . . eesh . . ." She makes a face and shakes her hands. "Have a drink of cold water and put on some clean clothes so we can pick up Aunt Linda and go."

The ballet.

All I want to do is close myself in my room and think about how to undo this mess, this stupid mess I made.

Instead, I am going to the ballet.

Mirielle hands me a glass of water. Excuses race through my brain like data scrolling on a storm map, and my mouth is about to choose one when I remember the other part of tonight's plan.

I'd love to see all my girls for an early dinner.

We're eating with Dad. At StormSafe.

It's crazy to think I might have another chance to get onto that computer, but I think it anyway.

I need to get that file back. Maybe I'll have a chance tonight. Unless Van has already told Dad what I did.

And *then* what? My stomach twists in fear—but fear of *what*? Am I really afraid of my own father? I shake the thought from my head and take a long drink of water.

"I'll be right down." On the way to my room, I pass Grandma Athena. I fight an urge to stop and talk with her, ask her what I should do. She might have been the only one who'd understand.

I race up the stairs, drop my backpack, and pull out the glass jars from Risha. I open my dresser drawer, shove one of the jars inside a sock and push it to the back of the drawer. I change my clothes and tuck the other jar into my pocket. I keep moving, moving, moving as if I can outrace my own thoughts by rushing around my room, but my twisting insides follow me from the closet to the dresser to the door. It's true. I'm afraid of him.

I check my DataSlate. Nothing from Mom.

Nothing at all.

I tuck it back into my bag and race down to the kitchen. "I'm ready."

The ballet is in a public school basement—a concrete cave of a room with horrible acoustics, but no one seems to mind. Mirielle's wearing a long, black dress with a jingly silver necklace that Remi keeps trying to put in her mouth, and Aunt Linda has on a gauzy white blouse and denim skirt. The best I could do was a clean pair of jeans, but people are dressed every which way, and somehow, no one in the folding-chair audience looks out of place.

The dancers aren't as smooth or as talented as the ones on TV. Their costumes aren't as elaborate, but energy pulses through their bodies, and there is something about them—some spirit or will or determination—that makes it impossible for me to look away. Their movements are fierce and gentle, all at once, and when I applaud at the end of the hour-long performance, my cheeks are wet.

"Remi needs a quick diaper change before we meet your father," Mirielle says, standing up.

· · 186 · ·

Aunt Linda and I join the rest of the audience folding up chairs and leaning them against the old wooden stage. Watching the dancers was like a dream—but now that the soothing orchestra sounds have been replaced by clanging metal, I'm awake, and everything is still wrong. Has Van told Dad yet what I did?

"Wasn't that wonderful?" Aunt Linda leans a chair against the stage, starting a new row. "Just the spirit of those dancers . . ."

I toss another one against hers. "Yeah . . ."

"What's on your mind, Jaden?" Aunt Linda reaches for the chair I've just stacked upside down and flips it the right way. "Seems like you're somewhere else."

"Do you know much about Dad's work at StormSafe?" I blurt out.

She leans against the stage and pushes her hands deep into the pockets of her skirt. "Well . . . yes and no. What are you wondering?"

"Well, I . . ." I need to tell someone. And somehow, I trust her. "I was on the computer in Dad's office. . . ."

She raises her eyebrows, but I don't stop talking.

"There are files on there about the tornadoes. About controlling them."

She nods. "You know that's his area of research, right? Always has been. He's been fascinated by the idea of weather manipulation since he was a boy, back when your grandmother was studying it."

"That's what she was doing? I thought it was secret." But now that it's not, I understand a little more. Dad's password, his crazy focus on all this, makes so much more sense. "Dad's a lot like her, isn't he?"

"Very much. So much it scares me." Her mouth tightens into a grimace.

"He scares me, too." There. I said it out loud.

Aunt Linda's eyes fill with concern, and she leans close. "Jaden, did something happen?"

Yes, something did. Something *is* happening, a whole whirlwind of somethings that I can't sort out. But I shake my head. "No. Nothing really. It's just . . ." The chairs are all picked up, and most people are leaving. Mirielle's done changing Remi but is talking with one of the dancers in the hallway. I don't understand enough about what I saw in Dad's office to even start explaining, so I don't try. "It feels like StormSafe has taken over his brain or something. Like he's . . . possessed." The word sounds silly, and I expect Aunt Linda to brush it off, but she doesn't.

Instead, she pulls herself up to sit on the stage and looks out at the empty room. "Your dad had a lot to deal with at a terribly young age."

"I know. Mom told me Grandma died when he was twelve."

She shakes her head. "Your father lost his mother long before that." She looks at me. "I'm going to tell you something because . . ." She bites her lip. "Because you need to know where your dad comes from. But more than that, you need to know that I'm here if you ever need someone. Do you understand that?"

I nod. But somehow, her words make me more afraid, not less. Does she think I'm not *safe* living with Dad?

Aunt Linda looks back out at the empty room as if she's staring through time. "Athena was part of a group of elite scientists working to harness weather for military purposes. To control the winds and the rain. That job was everything she'd dreamed about when she was in school. She'd never planned to have a child so soon."

I nod. "You told me she was gone a lot."

"All the time. The project started when your dad was a few months old; your grandfather was away serving in the military, and Athena would leave your dad with me for months and months at a time. When the war in Afghanistan expanded to Iraq, she was gone more than ever. She'd come home and take him back for a little while to cuddle him and play mother. As he got older and could understand, she'd do little science experiments with him and tell him about the exciting work she was doing. Then she'd take off again. He cried every time she left."

Out in the hallway, Mirielle sways back and forth with Remi as she chats. It's hard to imagine Dad ever being small. Or crying.

"It seemed like it would never end. Even as the troops were being pulled out of Iraq, Athena kept canceling visits home, writing e-mails instead, telling us she was on the verge of a huge breakthrough."

I climb up to sit next to Aunt Linda on the stage. The old varnished wood feels warm and shiny-smooth under my hands. "What was the breakthrough?"

"I don't know. The next news we heard was that your grandfather's helicopter had crashed in the mountains between Afghanistan and Pakistan. It was awful for everyone, but most of all your dad, because Athena barely took a break for the funeral. She poured herself into her work and almost never slept from what I heard. We saw her once more, when it all fell apart."

"Was she home visiting when she had that car accident?"

"It wasn't an accident, Jaden." Aunt Linda blinks fast, and tears streak down her cheeks. "Less than a year after your grandfather died, the government declared Athena's research project a failed effort and canceled it." She shakes her head, and even though it all happened so long ago, I reach out for her hand. "She must have felt like she couldn't go on after she lost her husband and her life's work one after the other. There was a huge storm the day she came home, tornadoes dropping all over the county, but she drove through it from the airport. She had supper with us and told us the project was canceled but not to worry; she'd finish the job on her own terms. She was so calm." Aunt Linda shakes her head slowly. "But her eyes looked far away, like she was already someplace else. She gave your dad a present."

A worn wooden image flashes through my mind. Words in fancy script.

Stormy. Rain. Change.

"A barometer?"

She nods. "He carried it everywhere. He loved it."

"He still does."

Aunt Linda closes her eyes, and I wait. "And then she left. The weather was wild, but I couldn't stop her. She walked out the door and drove away. The next morning, the police found her car at the bottom of a ravine. The storms that night were . . . Pieces of her laptop computer and papers were scattered over half the county. But they never found her body."

I shiver and picture Grandma Athena's ghostly photo in the frame. I don't know how I will sit in the living room again.

"There you are! Sorry I was so long visiting," Mirielle calls from across the room, and starts walking our way.

"I thought you should know," Aunt Linda tells me quietly, as she eases herself down from the stage. "A person never really gets over something like that. And your dad . . ." She pauses. "If you ever need me, I'll be there for you."

"Ready to go?" Mirielle steps up, bouncing Remi on her hip. "Let's get some dinner."

By the time we drop off Aunt Linda at her house and drive up to StormSafe, it's quarter to five. Dad meets us at the door. "I can't stop for dinner. Sorry. Something's come up." His body language makes it clear we're not invited in.

"Don't be silly, Stephen." Mirielle switches Remi to her other hip. "What is this thing that is so important?"

Dad lifts his DataSlate up so quickly I'm afraid it'll hit Remi, but it misses. She reaches for it and laughs, but Dad doesn't even look at her. "Were you even listening when I told you about the problem with funding for Phase Two?" he says in a voice that's getting louder and tighter by the second. "It hasn't gone away."

"But surely you can take a break. You need to eat." Mirielle reaches out for Dad's arm but he yanks it back.

"What I *need* to do is get back to work. Now." He speaks to her as if she's four years old. "I will see you in the morning."

She glares at him, and for a second, I see a fire in Mirielle that I never would have guessed was there. But then she turns and heads for the HV.

I follow her and feel the weight of my DataSlate in my backpack. Heavy with everything I've lost and with what I learned tonight. What Aunt Linda told me about Grandma makes me wonder how damaged Dad might be, and what he's capable of. What I saw and heard in his office . . . I can't begin to sort it all out now. I can't even look back at the data because it's gone.

It's a quiet drive home until we turn into the Placid Meadows gate. Mirielle flashes Lou her resident card, and as the gate starts to swing open, I see movement in the brush near the main road.

"Mirielle, wait!" She's already started pulling into Placid Meadows but stops and looks over at me. "I . . . it's nice out, and I could use some air. I'm going to get out here and walk back, okay?" I pull my backpack over my shoulder.

She raises her eyebrows. "You won't be long?"

"No, and I'm not hungry yet anyway. I may go to the park or something, see if Risha's around. If that's okay."

"Of course." I watch her pull away and wait until Lou is back in his booth playing a game on his DataSlate. Then I duck back out the gate and into the trees.

"Alex?" I whisper as loud as I dare.

"Here." A hand closes on my wrist and tugs me deeper into the brush, behind a big old tree stump that's turned into a nursery for mushrooms and moss. I lean against it, and the dampness seeps through my jeans.

"What are you doing?" I ask, looking at the DataSlate in his hands. "And . . . how's Newton?"

He takes a deep breath. "He made it through the surgery okay. He's gotta stay quiet for a couple days, and then I guess he'll learn to get around on three legs." The rest of his air rushes out. He leans against the tree stump, close enough that our knees brush. "Jaden, I have to tell you something."

"What?"

Alex squeezes his eyes shut for a second, then looks straight at me. "I stole files from your DataSlate."

I grab his arm. "What?! That was *you*?"

He closes his eyes again. "When you stayed back to talk to Van this morning and I took it to the library for you? I . . . copied some files."

I stare at the DataSlate in his hands, almost afraid to hope. "You copied them onto there?"

He nods. "I know it was a crappy thing to do, but—"

"And you have them on there, *now*?"

"I felt like I *had* to, Jaden. I didn't know at first what you'd found, but I figured it was important, and I was right. This information . . . It's *exactly* what we need." His eyes plead with me to understand what he says next. "I didn't know if you'd show me or not. He is your dad, after all. But I had to do it. For *my* dad. And everybody else in my family. This is our lives, Jaden, it's—"

"But why would you erase the files from my device? Why not

leave them in case I was going to try to help, too? I *was*, you know."

His eyes cloud with confusion. "I didn't erase anything. I only copied it."

"You did so—when I turned it on after—" I interrupt my own thought: after Van borrowed it for the check, after Van said good-bye to me, smiling. It *was* him. "Never mind. It was Van."

Alex's eyes puzzle back and forth for a few seconds, and then his face falls open with understanding. "He erased your files."

I nod and shift my weight. A sharp edge of the tree stump is sticking into my hip, so I stand up and walk over to a pair of close-together cedars that didn't get cut down. "I don't know how he could have known, why he chose that day to check . . . and I can't believe I was dumb enough not to back them up. But . . ." I look at the DataSlate in his hands. "You copied everything?"

He hands it to me. "Everything."

I click on the folder, but Alex tugs my sleeve. "Not here."

"Well, I can't take it home. Not after—"

An HV turns into the gate, and I cover the DataSlate's screen with my jacket so we can't be seen.

"We need to go someplace to look at this, where we can talk about it." Alex ducks under a branch and starts heading out of the woods.

I follow him, my shoes squishing into the damp leaf litter beneath the trees. "There's campus if we can wait until tomorrow, but—"

He holds a branch out of my way and grabs my arm as I start to pass. "We *can't* wait, Jaden. *This* can't wait." Even in the shadows, intensity flashes in his eyes. "It's waited too long already."

He's right. "Then let's go now."

"To campus? It's closed for the afternoon. Everything will be locked. The outside gate, even."

I pull the jar from my pocket. "I have the right fingerprint to get in."

Alex's eyes get huge. "Your dad's?"

"Risha made it for me."

He looks at me, hard. "You're willing to do this? To risk it?"

"Yes." I am terrified, but I mean it. "My dad's gone, working on some . . . I don't know . . . but something that made him cancel dinner. He won't be home for hours, maybe not even until tomorrow. We'll have the library and the Sim Dome and whatever else we need. Come on."

This time I lift up the branch, and Alex starts to duck under, but then he stops and stands straight again, his face inches from mine in the woodsy darkness, and whispers, "Thank you."

He leans in, and his lips touch mine, gentle as the breeze, warm as summer grass.

He pulls away and ducks under the branch, a shadow walking in front of me. I put two fingers to my tingling lips and follow him out of the trees.

Chapter 22

I wave to Lou as we walk past the gate, but as soon as he looks away, we run all the way to the house. The straps of my backpack dig into my shoulders, and by the time we creep into the garage, my hair is damp with sweat.

We lift bikes from the rack, coast down the driveway, and pedal down the street. As we pass Risha's house, I squeeze the hand brakes. "Wait. Let's get Risha, okay?" Alex nods and waits for me at the bottom of the driveway.

Risha answers the doorbell two seconds after the first ring, as if she'd been waiting for us instead of eating dinner with her family.

"Jaden!" She pulls me into a hug that smells like curry, and I whisper what's happening. I tell her everything we know and step back and wait for her look of shock, but it never comes. "Whatever you need," she says, already heading to the garage for her bike. "Count me in."

We pedal the last few blocks. The breeze has died down to nothing, and the air sticks to my skin.

When we pull up to the locked front gate of Eye on Tomorrow,

I pull the jar from my pocket, wrap Dad's print around my fingertip, and press it to the biometrics panel. "I guess this counts as a rainy day, huh?" Risha looks pleased when it works on the first try. The light turns green, and the gate swings open.

"Come with me," Alex whispers, and heads straight for the library.

"Not the library, Alex. It's not—"

"Shhh. I know where we can go."

We follow the path to the library, but instead of reaching for the door, Alex veers off around the side of the building. In the back, old-fashioned fire-escape stairs lead up to the roof.

"Oh, good call. I haven't been up here since I came for my orientation tour a couple of years ago," Risha says.

She and Alex take the steps two at a time, and by the time I catch up to them at the top of the fifth flight, I'm panting. When I look up, my breath catches in my throat.

The roof is enormous and . . . amazing. A gravel pathway winds through patches of garden with lush red and pink flowers. And flowers aren't the only things growing out of the patches of green. What looks at first like some kind of sculpture garden is actually a line of old-style anemometers. They remind me of little kids' pinwheel toys, twirling and dancing in the wind, spinning like little girls in fancy dresses. I'm dizzy just watching them.

"What is all this?" I ask.

"Ms. Walpole's outdoor classroom for the community education center." He looks up at the hazy sky. "No cameras in the ceiling here."

"They run weather programs for younger kids up here," Risha says.

Alex takes my backpack and Risha's and tosses them onto a picnic table near the stairs.

"It's incredible." And beautiful, in a way I wouldn't have expected.

With the weight of my bag off my shoulders, I almost forget for a minute why we're here. I walk to the edge of the roof and look out over miles of land that used to be full of people, buzzing with lives. The roads are so quiet now it's spooky. An abandoned water tower rises up out of the dirt like a spider grown too tall to be stable, whose legs might crumble into dust any minute. The old university campus is being renovated into another energy farm. There's a scattering of patched-up homes where people are still trying to pretend this is a fine place to live, to raise a family. Will it ever be again?

"Hey, we have to get to work, but come check this out first." Alex crosses the roof to a circle of tall rectangular stones, all standing on edge and pointing at the open sky. In the center is an angled, steel rod. "It's a gnomon," he says. "Like a pointer. The whole thing is a sundial. The ancients used them—"

"—to tell time with the shadows. I know." I walk around the circle, running my hand over the rough stones. They feel so old, so yesterday, to be part of a camp with a focus on tomorrow. "Why is this here?"

"History of earth science. History of weather." Risha walks the shadow cast by the gnomon as if it's a balance beam. "Van laughs at it, but Ms. Walpole's in charge of the rooftop classroom and always says you can't just know where you're going. You need to know where you came from, too. Alex, remember that one time—"

"*Shhhh!*" He holds up his hand to quiet her, then closes his eyes, listening.

I hear it, too. Footsteps clanging on the metal fire escape stairs. I duck behind one of the stone sundial markers and hold my breath. Risha and Alex huddle behind the next one in the circle.

The thumping, clanging steps get louder—then change to the sounds of crunching gravel. Someone is on the roof.

The footsteps get louder. Closer. And pause.

I peer out from behind the marker and see a long shadow falling across the pathway. The shadow turns, and I can make out a pony-tail. Van.

A DataSlate chimes and I duck back behind the stone. My stomach twists so violently I want to cry out. We left our backpacks on the picnic table. Van had to have heard that. He'll find them, find our DataSlates, and know we're here. And there's no way for us to get past him because the only entrance to the roof is that one set of—

"Yeah, what's up?" Van's voice rings out over the quiet roof. I peer out from behind the marker again, enough this time to see not only his shadow but the real Van, talking into a DataSlate. It was his. Not ours.

"I know. I'm leaving now. I was on my way out and heard noise on the library roof, so I came up to check it out. Musta been crows or something." He shoves his hand in his pocket and turns, and I pull my head back behind the stone. *Don't come over here. Don't come over here.*

His shoes crunch on the gravel again, but I can't tell if they're coming closer or going away. Another pause.

"Well, you'll be happy enough when you hear what I found out from my young friend Tomas today. Mr. Hazen's accepting our offer." Another pause. "I know. I told you he's a good kid . . . yeah . . . and he headed off a real mess letting me know about your little security breach. . . . No, he has no idea what it was really about. I just sent him to listen in on them, told him I was trying to keep his buddy out of trouble and needed his help. It's all good. And I told you I took the DataSlate and deleted it just in case. I don't think she would have understood it anyway."

I look at Alex, and the hurt in his face tells me that he's put the pieces together, too. Tomas. Waiting outside the first aid clinic while Alex and I talked. That's how Van knew I'd stolen Dad's files. And now his family is selling their farm, too.

"So here's where we are on the other thing," Van says. "I promised Tomas you'd hook his mom up with that clinic in New York as soon as they sign the contracts. I told you I'd take care of it." A pause. Then he laughs. "Okay, I'm sure the wind did some convincing, too, but hey. Done is done. And now we can move forward." More gravel crunching. Getting closer this time.

I look over at Risha. Her brown eyes are huge. And scared. Behind her, Alex has his eyes closed as if he's praying. Or maybe he can't stand to look at Van.

"Well, I don't think they'll be an issue for long." The footsteps move away again. "Yeah, I know it's gonna be a busy night. I'm on my way."

The footsteps crunch all the way back to the stairs—then pause near what must be the picnic table. Did he see our backpacks? My neck prickles with fear, but I lean out just far enough to see Van bending over near the gate, picking a stone out of his shoe. Then he starts down the stairs, and his footsteps clang away to quiet.

By the time I turn back to Risha and Alex, my neck is stiff from being twisted around so long, and Van must be long, long gone. Risha unfolds her legs and crawls to the edge of the roof to peer toward the gate.

"His HV's gone," she whispers.

Alex stares off into the clouds. On his cheek, the shiny trail of a tear ends in a smudge of dirt, where he must have wiped it away.

"Alex," I say quietly. "He couldn't have known what he was *really* telling Van about the DataSlate. Tomas must have . . ." I don't know what to say.

"Don't." He blinks fast and hard a few times, then stands up and turns away from me. "I don't want to talk about him."

"Alex, put yourself in his shoes for a minute." Risha follows him across the roof. "His mom is sick, and they need help. She needs treatment. What were they supposed to do?"

I should follow them, should say something to make it better, but I'm the one whose father has done all this. I'm the reason Tomas's family and Alex's are under pressure to give up the life their families have had for years. I'm the reason we're hiding up here on a roof and—

"Jaden, come on." They're back at the picnic table, and Risha is motioning for me. Even though guilt is churning in my stomach, I stand up and go to them.

"Let's just do this." Alex powers up his DataSlate and blinks hard. It's as if he's pulled a shade down over all his feelings about Tomas. "We came here to figure this out. Let's do it."

Holding the DataSlate between us, he clicks the first folder on the list, and numbers pour out like milk spilling from a cup.

"So what we have here is . . ." His dark eyes are focused, his jaw clenched in concentration. I peel my eyes away from his face to watch the stream of numbers rushing down the screen. "This is data for . . ." He frowns and taps the folder, labeled 6-17-2010.

Inside are four documents: CONDITIONS PRECEDING, STORM DATA, SUMMARY/RESULTS, and APPLICATIONS. I tap on SUMMARY/RESULTS, and a document fills the screen.

An EF4 tornado touched down near Deer Creek, Minnesota, on June 17, 2010, destroying several houses along Otter Tail County Road 143. One fatality was reported, and damage to trees, farms, and vehicles was extensive.

I watch Alex read, and slowly, like stars appearing through clouds, I see him begin to understand. "This data is unbelievable," he whispers. "Every detail. Atmospheric pressure, updraft activity. Everything."

He scrolls through the other folders and shakes his head. "This is crazy. It's . . . it looks like he's been *collecting* storms." He hands me the DataSlate. "Tell me what you see then."

What I see . . . makes my head spin. All the dates I had time to look at in Dad's office are here.

5-7-1840

5-27-1896

6-12-1899

3-18-1925

4-5-1936

6-9-1953

5-4-2007

There are more current folders, too. The more recent the storm, the more data fills the folder.

4-1-2019

10-10-2020

3-15-2022

9-1-2031

5-30-2050

It's like turning pages in a history book, past to present, closer and closer to today. When my eyes reach the bottom of the screen, I gasp. The final date in the list is from the day Risha and I hid in the old barn storm cellar. The day Alex's family farm blew away.

I look more closely, and other dates start to stand out, too.

10-10-2020.

That's the date of the worst storm ever to hit Paris. It was a year before city traffic was back to normal, another three before they finished rebuilding the Eiffel Tower.

4-1-2019.

Mom's talked about this one, too—the April Fool's Day storm that hit Vermont when she was in high school.

Alex reaches past me and touches the 6-17-2010 file again. "Jaden, *look.*" His voice shakes with anger as he taps open the documents inside, one after another. CONDITIONS PRECEDING has a narrative of the weather conditions leading up to the storms. STORM DATA has a table of temperatures, pressure gradients, and wind speeds. Where did Dad get all this? And why? *Why?*

The APPLICATIONS folder is full of projections for how the data and other information from a storm might be used "in future research and development."

"Future research and development?" My voice shakes.

Alex pulls the DataSlate from me. He taps through, opening the dated folders. Each one holds the recipe for a perfect storm.

He points to one of the number-filled boxes. "This is *everything*. Everything you'd need to . . ."

It's too awful to be real, but he's waiting, so I whisper the words anyway.

"Everything you'd need to make it happen again." As soon as I say the words aloud, I know it's true. And that thought that's wormed its way into my brain changes everything I thought I knew about my father. "He's collected all these monster storms . . ."

Alex nods, his jaw set. "So he can bring them back."

"This doesn't make sense," Risha says slowly. "It's not like he can *make* the weather. He just sends it . . . away from here."

"And *toward* somebody else." Alex's hand goes to the scar on his forehead, and he brushes his thumb against it. "He's turning existing storms into monsters, intensifying them with this histori-cal storm data, and then redirecting them."

"But why would he want to do that?" Risha says. "There's no point."

I wish with everything I am that I could agree with her. But I know better. So does Alex.

"No point?" Alex stands so quickly he almost knocks the DataSlate from the table. "You don't think they see a point in send-ing storms toward the farms?" He flings his arm toward the stairs Van climbed down a few minutes ago. "There's a point."

She doesn't want to believe it; I can tell from her face. But it's too clear to miss. The more tornadoes hit the farms, the more people have to buy DNA-ture. The more damage, the more danger, and the more reason to give up and clear the way for Phase Two of Placid Meadows.

"It's about the land," I say quietly. "Placid Meadows, Phase Two."

"It can't be," Risha says, shaking her head. "Jaden, there's no way he'd do this. It's not like your father needs the money."

"It's not about money." I think about what Aunt Linda told me about Grandma, how she ignored everything except her research. How she even forgot about being a mother. "He's obsessed. Obsessed

with getting that land, with building Phase Two of Placid Meadows."
I almost whisper the words, but I know in my bones they're true.

Risha stares at me. "Who could care so much about a project they'd forget about *people*?"

I know the answer to her question. My father. And a long time ago, his mother, too. But I don't say so out loud. I just shrug.

"I still can't believe . . ." Risha looks at me. She wants it to be a mistake, almost as much as I do. "Jaden . . . your dad's spent most of his life trying to disperse storms, hasn't he? Wasn't he figuring out how to *stop* a tornado's rotation?"

"He *was*." I can't stop staring at the screen, can't stop my stomach from churning with truth. "It looks like he's moved on." Finally, I tear my eyes from the columns of numbers and look up at Alex. The words feel like I could choke on them. "The recent storms have all been hitting the farms, haven't they?"

"Four since last month. Worst few weeks we've ever had." He stares off to the west, where clouds are gathering again on the horizon. "My dad kept saying, 'Somebody up there ain't happy with us.'" He chokes out a cold laugh. "I guess he was right."

I push the heels of my hands into my closed eyes so hard that lights dance. Explosions of yellow and blue. I hear more tapping on the DataSlate. Risha's sigh. Finally, I open my eyes and take a shaky breath. "We need to tell somebody."

Alex's voice is bitter. "*Who*, Jaden? Who do we need to tell? The police your father probably has in his pocket? Or maybe we should report him to *Van*? He's good at taking care of things. And he's been *so* helpful with our work in the Sim Dome."

"That's it!" I grab Alex's DataSlate and pull my own from my backpack so I can start copying the data. "Let me get this transferred so we have a second copy, just in case. We'll go to the Sim Dome and run the command codes from this file to show what it is. It will prove what my father has been doing with the storms. We'll keep a data record of the whole thing. Nobody will have tampered with those results because no one expects us to have this." I hold up the DataSlates as the files copy. "If this is really a code to re-create the storm, then we'll have evidence."

Chapter 23

My hands shake as I plug my DataSlate into the computer port inside the clear safety glass of the Sim Dome observation box. "There. It's loading."

I'm praying this works. And at the same time, I'm trying not to think about what I'm doing to my own father—what the world will find out about him—if it does.

I'm still wearing Dad's fingerprint tissue. It's weird, like part of him is here watching us. Risha stopped me when I started to peel it off, though. She's right; we may need it again depending on what happens.

"It's all set." Alex nudges me, and I look down at the computer screen.

DATA LOADED

Below it, a green button reads: BEGIN SIMULATION.

My finger hovers above the touch pad. Will this work?

We chose the ten-ten-twenty storm; it will be the easiest to recognize. Once we see how closely it follows the real event, the triple tornadoes that converged on Paris on October 10, 2020, we'll have a better idea what we're dealing with here.

"Go on," Alex whispers. He holds up his DataSlate, its red record light flashing. "Let's see what we've got."

I tap the button, the gentlest tap. But like that old saying about a butterfly flapping its wings and triggering a storm on the other side of the world, a quiet tap is all it takes.

Alex, Risha, and I stand behind the safety glass and watch.

Storm clouds gather in the dome above us first, and the sim lights cast the familiar yellow-gray, just-before-a-storm glow.

"Rotation's starting." Alex's eyes are trained on the part of the cloud where the vapor has begun to swirl in slow, ominous circles over our heads.

The cloud grows, the funnel forms, and faux trees bend in the wind. Then a swirling, gray rope touches down.

"There's one," I whisper. It whips through a neighborhood like a moody robber, stealing some houses, leaving others untouched.

"Two." Risha points to the edge of the town, where a second funnel cloud is forming. This one starts as a loose, smoky swirl; then a tighter, more organized vortex grows up from the ground like a plant that's been nurtured and watered and fed all the right things.

I wasn't even born when the real 10-10-20 storm hit, but I've heard so much about it that seeing these twin tornadoes converge is like watching a movie I've already seen a hundred times.

Swirling dust.

Flattened buildings.

Trees flying through the air, roots first.

All of it.

Now the third tornado forms and makes a beeline for its siblings.

Within seconds, the three have merged into a wide, churning block of chaos. It starts a slow, steady course in our direction, sucking up entire houses so only their flat, chalky foundations remain.

The monster storm is almost to the edge of the Sim Dome, where I know it will be sucked back up into the ceiling.

Alex leans down over the DataSlate and starts poking at buttons.

"What are you doing?" I ask. "We have to let this one finish before you view another one."

"I'm not calling up another one." Alex doesn't look up at me; his fingers tap the touch screen furiously. "I'm entering the last command code that was listed in the folder."

"What does it do?" I ask.

"That," says Alex, tapping a few more times, "is what I want to know." He tilts the DataSlate in my direction so I can see the page he's brought up. It says SI CODE.

"S-I?" I stare at the letters, but no words form in my brain.

"*S* for storm?" Risha tips her head. "And *I* . . . I don't know."

Alex taps INTRODUCE VARIABLE and suddenly, the huge tornado turns back from the edge of the dome, almost as if it's a living thing and knows what it needs to stay alive. It grows and swirls back through the Sim Community, fueled by destruction, leveling nearly everything it missed the first time.

Finally, on the other side, the growling black cloud climbs back up into the sky.

We are all quiet, staring at what remains.

A few scattered boards. Some flat foundations. There isn't much.

There wasn't much left of the Champs-Élysées or Eiffel Tower back in 2020, either.

But that tornado had slipped back into the clouds after a single pass through the city. This one swept through twice, stronger the second time around. It had grown, intensified.

And suddenly, the letters have words to go with them.

S.I.

Storm Intensification.

Here is the evidence. My father *has* been re-creating storms.

Bringing old monsters back from the dead.

Feeding them numbers to make them stronger, bigger.

Deadlier.

"Intensity. That command intensified the storm." I shake my head as Alex bends down over the DataSlate again. "Did you hear me? You recorded, right? That simulation proves everything."

"We need more than one," Alex says, scrolling through the list of dates, whispering the storm dates one by one. Finally, he clicks on the first folder we opened—for the 2010 Minnesota storm. "Let's run this one."

He chooses a set of data, but before anything can load, a weather alert sounds its shrill, blaring tones over and over, and the warning appears on screen.

Issued: 7:09 PM, June 29

The National Storm Center has issued a SEVERE TORNADO WARNING for all of Kingfisher, Oklahoma, Lincoln, and Logan counties. A powerful storm has been identified via radar and is making its way east. This system has already spawned several powerful tornadoes. Residents are advised to take shelter in safe rooms immediately. More information will be released as it becomes available.

Alex taps the screen to pull up the latest radar images.

"Whoa . . ." I suck in my breath and stare at the green and red blob. It's one of the most organized storm systems I've ever seen—on a screen or in real life.

I look out at the battered Sim Community and wonder whose real-life town will look like this tonight. Whose car will lift from the pavement, hurtle through the air, and wrap itself around a tree? Whose house will be ripped from its foundation and dashed to pieces? "Put a track on it."

Alex taps a button on the DataSlate to bring up the storm's projected path.

The track makes it pass north of Placid Meadows—everything

does—but then the storm's path swings east, and Alex's body tenses beside me.

"The farm," he whispers. "It's going straight for the farm." He squints at the screen, then looks up at me, his eyes bright with fear.

"It's okay, Alex. Their alert will have gone off, too," Risha says. "They're probably already in the safe room."

Alex wheels around to face her. "There *is* no alert at my house. Mom and Dad's DataSlates are still buried under the wooden beams from the porch. And the safe room . . . the safe room door hasn't even been replaced yet." He stands so fast his chair clatters over. He grabs his DataSlate, trips over the backpacks on the floor, scoops his up, and flings open the door. "I have to go warn them."

I catch his sleeve. "Wait!" My throat is dry, and the colors of the radar are still dancing in front of my eyes.

"*What?*"

I swallow hard. The storm is enormous. What if it's one of Dad's? The thought makes me want to pound my fists and scream. But more than that, it makes me want to help. I unplug my DataSlate from the system and shove it into my backpack.

"I'm coming with you."

Chapter 24

I race for our bikes leaning against the library, but Alex grabs my elbow. "No bikes. We can't take them through the gap in the fence."

"I'll come too." Risha's voice wavers in a way I've never heard before. "Just . . . let me check in with my parents so they don't freak."

"There's no time. But go. Track the storm from your house; it'll help in case we can't get a strong signal out there once it gets bad." I give her a quick, tight hug. "Keep your DataSlate on. We'll call."

I turn and run with Alex out the gate, all the way to the fence.

"When you ran that track on the storm, how fast was it moving? How long do we have?" I ask as he climbs through to the other side.

"Looked like twenty minutes, max."

By the time we reach the tree that bridges the river, my heart sounds like thunder in my ears. We have to slow down to cross.

One foot.

Then the next ahead of it.

The river is swollen and fast.

Thunder booms to the north, and in front of me, Alex teeters.

"Careful!" I grab the strap of his backpack to steady him. He reaches back to take my hand and doesn't let go, even after we've reached solid ground on the other side. We run, and he squeezes my hand as if holding on will keep the storm away.

But it doesn't.

When we reach the farm, loose bits of roofing from the last storm are flying up from the ground like ghosts out of a grave. The chickens are out of the temporary pen Alex and his dad built, clucking around in a panic. A stack of wood that used to be barn walls and hayloft floor groans in the wind and topples, and the chickens scatter in an explosion of feathers.

"Mom! Dad! Julia!" Alex calls into the trailer his uncle brought over so they'd have somewhere to sleep while they rebuilt. There's no answer. "Newton!"

"They had to have gotten the warning somehow! They must've left already!" I shout over a gust of wind that pushes me toward the remains of the house.

Alex runs to the trailer door and flings it open, still shouting. He tugs it shut, but the wind blasts it back open and rips the flimsy aluminum door from its frame. It clatters across the dust and comes to rest against an uprooted tree from the last storm.

"Alex, they're gone! I'm sure they're safe somewhere!"

But he's not listening. His eyes are focused beyond me, off to the north, and his mouth is gaping open.

I turn around in time to see the sky shape itself into a nightmare.

A wall of death-black cloud sits on the horizon. Slow-swirling charcoal fingers reach down from it. They point to the ground, hungry for dust and trees and buildings. The fingers close into thick fists, swirling, churning toward the farms.

I watch, transfixed, as the drifting clouds organize themselves into a thick funnel, spinning faster and faster, stretching closer and closer to earth until it touches, and there's an explosion of dirt and tree limbs, a second swirling circle around the tornado.

The monster barrels on toward two houses, a silo, a barn.

"No. No," I whisper, as if it might hear me and change its mind. As if anything with a soul could tear the roof off a house, hurl the walls off into fields, and keep marching on.

The tornado plows through a field, sucks up barn pieces. Nourished by splintered wood and twisted tractor metal, it grows. And I feel like I'm shrinking, about to be swallowed up. Was this the kind of storm Grandma Athena drove out into the night she died?

A flash of blue-bright-white pops at the edge of the funnel. An electrical explosion? A natural gas line?

A shower of sparks rains out one side of the surging mass of dark cloud. Pieces of roof and support beams and window frames swirl around the heart of the storm, tossed aside every so often when it's sick of playing with them.

Whose house was that?

Did they make it to a safe room?

Is the safe room still there?

"Come on!" Alex starts to run."We have to get to shelter!"

I shout over the wind,"I thought your safe room door was—"

"Watch it!" Alex grabs my arm and yanks so hard I fall backward into the swirling dirt, just in time to miss being blindsided by a piece of barn siding that whips past in the wind. I land on my backpack, and a corner of my DataSlate jabs into my shoulder blade. I cry out, half in pain, half in fear that it's broken. But there's no time to check. Alex pulls me up, and we start running again.

"Our safe room's no good." He ducks into the trees past the clearing where the gazebo used to be. "We need to get to Tomas's place. We'll bang on the door and hope they hear."

Over our heads, trees bend and groan, grinding against one another in the wind. When they can't bend any more, a loud, deep crack splits the air, then smaller cracks as a tree falls, snapping branches in its path.

We burst out of the clearing in time to see the door ripped from the barn at Tomas's farm. It flies and bounces, top over bottom, cartwheeling across the field.

"Over here!" Alex pulls me toward the farmhouse door and bangs with both fists. "Tomas! Mr. Hazen! TOMAS!!"

Alex jiggles the lock one last time, then backs up to the driveway. "Stand back." He runs, throws his shoulder at the door. There's a sick thud of flesh and bone on a solid surface but no crack of wood splintering.

"Hold on!" I run to the barn, though the opening where the door used to be, and look wildly around. Flying branches have already smashed two windows, and wind screams through the broken glass, churning loose hay into a frenzy.

There! Still hanging on the wall is an ax, and I lunge for it, trying not to think of what the storm at Alex's barn did to the tools on the wall, how it collected them like a cache of weapons and drove them into the wood, blades first.

"Here!" I run back out and practically throw it into Alex's hands. He raises it over his head and swings.

THWACK!

The wood splinters on the first hit.

He aims lower, closer to the lock.

THWACK!

THWACK!

Beads of sweat fly from his forehead in the wind, and his breathing is fast and heavy, but he swings again—

THWACK!

—and the door makes a loud *CRACK!*

He kicks once, twice, and the third time it falls. "Go!" He pushes me ahead of him. "To the right and down!"

The safe room door is obvious—the only one plated in double-reinforced steel.

It's locked.

Alex shoves me aside and bangs until the heels of his hands start bleeding.

"They can't hear!" I scream, because the wind here is louder. "We need to go someplace else!"

"There is nowhere else!" Alex shouts.

I see the wooden board a fraction of a second before it hits the window. "Alex!"

I pull him down on top of me as it crashes through the glass.

The board flies over us and pierces the video screen in the living room.

"We have to go!" I pull him toward the door.

"The truck!" Next to the barn is a green pickup, miraculously, still unharmed, and we push back out into the wind. The whirling dust stings my eyes, and tears dry on my face as I run.

"Get in!" Alex screams, and runs to the driver's side.

I reach for the handle and fight the wind to pull open the door, but this is no shelter. Even a smaller tornado could pick it up and fling it a quarter of a mile.

I force the door closed, panting, and stare through the windshield.

My heart drops right into my stomach.

The tornado is closer, wider, swirling faster than before.

Right behind it is a second one.

Not far off to the left is a third.

All of them, NF5's, at least.

All of them heading straight for us.

Chapter 25

The truck's engine rumbles to life. "You have *keys*?" I stare. It's an old-time ignition—no fingerprint panel.

"These keys are always in the truck! Hold on!" Alex flings his backpack onto the seat between us, yanks the truck into reverse, and jerks us away from the barn. The tires spin, and we fly down the driveway onto the main road, away from the storm.

The DataSlate in my backpack pokes into my hurt shoulder, but I leave it on. Somehow, I can't let go of it right now, even to put it next to me on the seat. I reach for my seat belt, and Alex almost laughs—as if seat belts will protect us from the storm—but he puts his on, too.

"Where are we going?" I ask.

"I don't know." His jaw looked so set, his eyes burned with so much confidence driving out of there that I was sure he'd have an answer, but he's as terrified as I am, and for a moment, all that matters is easing that fear for him. I try to make my voice as light as it can possibly be with three tornadoes gunning for us in the rear-view mirror.

"Since when do fourteen-year-olds drive?"

He brakes to go around a sharp turn. "I've been driving this thing since I was eleven. Tomas and I'd sneak out and run it up and down the dirt roads while his dad was working in the barn." He almost smiles.

"Well, I guess that comes in handy when—"

He slams on the brakes so we don't hit a twisted piece of swing set that must have blown out of someone's yard. The seat belt catches me, and my shoulder stings.

"You okay?" Alex asks.

I don't answer. I'm staring at the piece of swing set, three twisted metal support bars coming off a crosspiece that still has a swing attached. The painted wooden seat is splintered, but not so much that you can't see the painted handprints that decorate it.

A big green hand. A smaller blue hand. And two tiny prints, pink and purple.

Whose handprints are these? Are they safe?

How many more swing sets and barns and houses will be swallowed up before this night is through?

Alex drives around it, and I twist in my seat to look back.

The three tornadoes are lined up, still coming our way, but something is different. It looks like they've slowed down, maybe even stopped. Will they die out before they get to Alex's farm? *Oh, please, please.* I stare out the rear window at the funnels growing more distant.

But instead of relief, I feel a chill of terror. They may have stopped, but they are growing. Churning with more intense energy. And they are coming together.

Oh, God, make them stop, make them stop. I try to pray them away, will them to be sucked back up into the sky before they do any more harm. But even as I pray, I recognize what is happening . . . three tornadoes that merge. The monster that hit Paris in 2020. A sick feeling swirls in my gut.

This is no act of God.

"Alex, look."

He puts a shaking hand over my seat and twists to stare behind him. "Ten-ten-twenty," he breathes.

Stalled for a moment, the three tornadoes dance, whirling, crunching, spinning closer together and apart, together and apart, until two of them touch, like tops spinning on a table that collide. But these tornadoes don't stop spinning; they swallow each other up, fatter, stronger, and hungrier. Even though they're not here yet, the wind is picking up.

"We have to get out of here!" Alex throws the truck into gear. "Maybe we can get back to the campus, or maybe—"

"Alex! You *know* this storm!" The truck shakes in a gust of wind, and I fling my arm back, pointing at the swelling monster behind us. "You know what it did in '20. It's going to start moving again any minute. It's going do the same thing unless somebody stops it!"

"We have to find shelter!" he screams. "We can't stop that thing! I'm taking us back to campus, or Risha's place, or—"

He turns to the left, back toward the entrance to Placid Meadows, but I reach over, grab the steering wheel, and jerk it to the right instead, toward the curve in the road that leads to StormSafe.

"What are you doing?!"

"Just go!" A thick branch flies out of the woods toward the driver's side window. Alex stomps on the accelerator, and instead of bursting through the glass, the branch clangs into the metal truck bed.

"Go!" I urge him on, and he keeps driving until we reach the first sign for StormSafe. Then he slams on the brakes. "Jaden, what are you *doing*? We need shelter, and this locked compound isn't it. We'll be trapped outside, and even if we get in, what are we supposed to do?" He pounds his hand on the steering wheel and winces. "We need to get to a safe room now! We can't stop this thing!"

"Maybe we can't!" Tears stream down my face. Tears for Tomas and his family, whose house will probably be gone within seconds once the storm starts its march forward again. Tears for Alex's parents and Julia and Newton, wherever they are. Tears for the little girls whose swing set blew into the road. Tears for this whole world, where no one can even go outside without the risk that they might be swallowed up into the sky.

And tears for myself.

Burning, shameful tears because I know the truth, that my father has waved his magic wand at this sad, hot, churning world and made it even worse.

"Maybe we *can't*! But look at it, Alex! It's going to come! We're not going to make it anywhere safe. There's no time. And when the third tornado merges—"

"Stop it! We don't *know* that's what—"

"Yes, we *do!*" I swipe at the tears in my eyes and scream over the roar of the storm. "You *know* what's going to happen! We have to find my father!"

"Your *father?*" His eyes are furious. "You think your father is going to help?"

"Listen, please. We have to . . . we can *talk* to him. Once he knows it's out . . . that people know, he'll have to—"

"Have to *what*, Jaden? *Kill* us?" he spits out.

"Stop!" I scream. "Just stop!" I choke back sobs and press my hands into my eyes to make it all vanish.

It doesn't. And all I can do, all I can hope to do, is try.

"I know you think he's a horrible human being." My voice shakes. "And right now, I do, too. But he's my *father*, Alex. My father, who used to throw me up in the air and sing me to sleep and"—I swallow hard—"and love me, the same way your dad loves you. We have to find him. He can fix this . . . he . . . he *has* to! He *will!*"

I let my head sink back into my hands, but I can still hear Alex's angry, ragged breaths. And then his voice.

"I don't believe it. Not for a second."

"But we have to at least—"

"What we have to do is get out of here!" He yanks the truck's gearshift into reverse.

"Stop!" I scream.

And he does. But he looks at me with eyes that are colder than any weather I've ever seen. "I'm leaving. *Now.*"

I squeeze my eyes shut tight for a second, then open them, throw off my seat belt, and reach for the door handle. The wind flings it open, and I hear Alex shout "No!" but the wind swallows his voice, and I jump down before I can think about it. Before I can think how stupid and dangerous it is. Before I can think about flying tree limbs or barn pieces or the three tornadoes that are about to merge into a single, churning monster and come for me.

I don't think about any of it, and I don't look back. I just run.

The wet strap from my backpack flies loose and slaps at my face over and over. I tighten it and keep running. The wind batters me back and forth across the road, like a cat playing with a half-dead mouse. If there were traffic, if there were anyone else crazy enough to be out, I'd have been run over a dozen times by now.

But I keep running. My backpack thumps against me, soaked, heavier with every step.

Horizontal rain stings my face, and my wet clothes cling. I've sucked in so much water with every desperate breath, it's a wonder I'm not drowning.

Another tree branch flies into the road a few feet in front of me, and I leap aside to keep from tripping.

My backpack strap flies loose again. I can't run with it slapping at me, and I can't keep stopping to tighten it, so I pull out my Data-Slate. As quickly as I can, I stuff it into the waistband in the back of my jeans and pull my shirt down over it. I fling the backpack off into the wind and step back onto the road, but an HV is barreling around a curve, so I leap back into the brush just in time to avoid being flattened by the only other person crazy enough to be out.

When its taillights are lost in the blur of rain, I step back out and run as fast as I can. My lungs are full of needles. My legs are burning. And my heart is breaking, wondering where Alex has gone. Whether he'll make it.

But all I can do is run.

Finally, I round the last curve, and the big steel-and-glass building looms up out of the gray.

The storm is raging, growling, roaring behind me, but I force myself to slow down as I near the entrance.

It's after hours.

The gate is closed and unmanned. But there are HVs in the lot.

I unfold my hand, cramped from being clenched in a fist so long. The bio-print is wrinkled and wet, half falling off, but I stretch it, smooth it as much as I can, and raise my finger to the bio-scan.

The gate slides open with a grinding sound, and a snapped-off pine bough goes flying through ahead of me, as if it had been waiting.

Inside, I stand dripping and panting in front of the gleaming building, unscathed by the winds howling just down the road.

Dad's office on the top floor is dark, but the lights on the ground level glow through the pounding rain. A silhouette passes across a window, and I duck behind one of the shrubs along the sidewalk. The shape passes down the long hallway toward the wood-paneled conference room at the end.

At first I can't believe there's still power in the midst of this storm, but then I remember it's StormSafe. No matter how big this storm grows when the three winding ropes merge, it will never get past the gate. Dad will make sure of that much.

Dad.

I have to find Dad.

I look back. The third tornado swirls closer to the first two. Closer—then away—as if they are dancing. But I know how this dance will end if it goes on.

I have to find Dad.

I crawl out from the bushes and hold my breath, watching the windows of the reception area. There's no activity—just quiet yellow rectangles—so I creep forward and peer inside.

Even the reception desk is empty. Are they all still in that meeting Dad was busy with earlier, when we were supposed to have dinner? And how could that have been just an hour and a half ago, when it feels like the whole world has changed?

I drop to the ground and crawl along the wall. Mud soaks through my pants, and my knees are caked with it by the time I reach what would be the end of the long hallway—the conference room.

I hold my breath and rise up enough so my eyes clear the edge of the window.

The fat leather chairs are all full except for one at the end. On one side of the table are two women I don't recognize. I don't let myself stop to stare, to wonder if one of them is the DataSlate woman whose voice I heard that night in the office. I have to find Dad. Four men face the other way, so I'm looking at the backs of their heads. The first three don't look familiar, but the last one has Van's thick ponytail.

There are papers at the empty seat. And a half-empty bottle of BioWake Cola.

Where's Dad?

I stand up, and my eyes dart from the main headquarters to the outbuildings, trying to remember what was what from our tour.

The buildings are all dark, except for the little one way down at the edge of the property where a rectangle of light glows in the lone window. Dad said it was only a storage room. Why would he be there now?

I run through rain-soaked shrubs, grass that's surrendered to the mud, until I'm crouched by the door. Even though it is made of reinforced steel, low notes of Mozart ooze out around the edges, and I know I've found him.

I reach for the door but feel a rush of fear. I pull my hand back before it touches the cool metal handle.

Who is this man behind the door?

I squeeze my eyes shut and let rain and tears wash my face clean of Alex's harsh words.

He is still my father.

I take a deep breath and hope the air filling my lungs can fill me with something stronger. Faith enough to believe.

He is still my father.

He has the same passion for science.

He still makes funny faces at babies and likes ice cream with sprinkles.

He still loves Mozart.

And I am trying to believe that he still loves me.

I raise my trembling hand to the door and turn the handle.

It's unlocked.

There is no bio-scan on this door.

No excuse not to keep going, to talk to him.

Halfway open, the door hinges let out a low groan, and I freeze, but the only sounds are Mozart and the faint clicking of quick fingers on a computer keyboard in a far corner.

I step inside and stand still as death. My heart explodes in my chest, thumping so loud in my throat and my ears, I'm surprised I can still hear the music.

The steel door swings silently shut behind me.

This room looks a lot like Dad's office, with its giant flat-screen monitors. They swirl with bright green-and-red radar images, but I can't tell if the storm is still stalled.

I try to quiet my breathing.

On the other side of the monitors, the keyboard sound grows louder, as if someone is banging on the keys. Frustrated. Or excited.

What is he doing?

Maybe—

I feel hope rising inside me. Hope that he's calling off the storms on his own. Maybe he never meant to create this nightmare. Maybe—

The tapping stops. There is a sharp huff of breath. A slamming sound, like a book being thrown onto a counter. And my heart goes wild all over again.

What was I thinking coming here?

There is still time for me to go back through the reinforced door, to go back to the reception area and wait out the storm. Time for me to play dumb and pretend I was out wandering and had to rush for shelter when I saw the tornado. Time for me to run.

But I don't. I can do this.

Dad, I'll say, *I came tonight because I know. I know everything. About your files and the storms and the farms. We need to make this right. Everything can be okay again. I need your help.*

I take a long breath and step toward the monitors.

The typing on the other side stops, and my heart stops for a second, too, but I make my feet keep moving.

The Mozart rises to a crescendo. I step around the wall of weather data.

And I freeze.

The person at the computer is not my father.

But she has the same charcoal eyes.

She speaks in a voice I've heard twice before. Once on Dad's DataSlate. And once in real life . . . in his office here at StormSafe the night I came to help with Remi.

"I thought you might show up." She stands to look at me, tucking in a sky-blue blouse that feels out of place with her dark eyes and sharp chin. Her skin is tight and pale. "Stephen said you'd never put it all together, but as usual, he was wrong." She chuckles but there's no warmth in her laugh. "Never underestimate a Meggs woman." She shakes her head, tucks a curl of gray hair behind one ear, and narrows her eyes. "You don't know who I am, do you?"

Somehow, I make my head move up and down, because I do know.

I walk by her photograph every day on my way to bed.

I know. Even though it's impossible.

"You're Grandma Athena."

Chapter 26

Smart as a whip, just like they said." She cackles, sits, and spins her chair back toward the computer, and pecks at the keyboard so hard her fingers must hurt.

"Grandma Athena." I whisper the words and wonder how they could be true. But there is no mistaking the woman in front of me, no mistaking the intensity of her eyes.

"Shhh! Be quiet." Her voice is like ice. Cold. Sharp. "There's something not quite . . ." She trails off, reaches for a DataSlate, and frowns down at it. Her fingers fly, writing a message to someone, and I hear the chime that means it's sent. She calls up a radar screen, and I try to peer over her shoulder, but all I catch is a flash of green before she slams it down on the counter. "Gah! Weakening like nobody's business. Sloppy." She wheels around to face me again. "I know why you're here."

I shake my head weakly. How could this woman, this stranger, know anything about me? How could she even be alive?

She smiles, a thin, chapped line across her face, as if she's read my mind. "You look like you've seen a ghost." She whirls around in the chair again, dashes off a sequence of something on the keyboard. "Why isn't he answering?" She picks up the DataSlate, tosses it back on the desk, and stands to face me. "You thought I was dead."

"Well, yeah. They said . . . I mean, the car accident . . ."

"Brilliant, wasn't it? They knew I'd never give up. They knew I'd never rest until—"

My head is spinning. "*Who* knew you'd never rest?"

"Our *fine* and *dedicated* government leaders." She spits the words; they drip with sarcasm. "They canceled my project, the fools, but they couldn't take back what I'd already learned. I was this close." She holds up her thumb and forefingers, a hair's width apart. "This close to a breakthrough, when they cut the funding and threatened to throw me in prison if I didn't step back from my research. They didn't care that your grandfather had given his life for his country or that I was about to create a weapon so powerful that no American would have to die in battle ever again." Her eyes drift off somewhere behind me, somewhere a long time ago. "They never understood the possibilities. The power we can have."

Her eyes focus on me again. "That's why I had to die."

"You faked the car crash?"

"Oh, there was nothing fake about the crash. That car exploded at the bottom of the gorge like nothing you've ever seen."

"But you weren't in it."

"The car was rigged. Empty. I was on a plane headed for Russia. Viktor, a colleague I'd met at one of the international symposiums, assured me that his government would be happy to fund my work.

It went beautifully, and a few years ago, I sent for your father. He was overjoyed to find me alive. And he was eager to help."

She grabs the DataSlate from the desk again and looks as if she's about to throw it through the lone window. "Though he's proving to be rather worthless tonight."

"I just . . ." I shake my head, trying to loosen the nest of cobwebs sticking my thoughts together. "I can't believe you're here."

"Oh, Jaden. Never trust a death certificate unless you've seen the body for yourself." She grins, a smile so cold it makes me shiver. I take a step backward, toward the door. "But you should know that. You're a smart girl, aren't you?"

It felt like a rhetorical question, but she stares at me, waiting for an answer.

"Well, yeah, I guess."

"How smart?" Her eyes burn into me, and my throat is dry enough to catch fire.

She stands, clutching the DataSlate so tightly the tendons in her hands stick out. She takes a step toward me.

"What do you mean?" I step back. My knees wobble.

"Knock off the big eyes, Jaden. I know why you're here. You stole your father's data, ran a simulation or two with it, and figured out we're in the business of storm creation and enhancement, and not storm dissipation. Now you've come here to save the world. Am I correct?" She steps toward me again. Her eyes keep switching from brown to gray to black, like a river all churned up.

"I . . ." My DataSlate presses against my back. Can she see it under my wet shirt? My head spins with the impossibility of it all. Of her knowing what I did. Of her even being here. Alive.

Another step forward. "I knew you'd be trouble from the minute I walked in on you in your father's office. So stupid of him to leave you alone. I told him so, but he said you were too young, too green and book-smart to be any threat to the program." Another step. "He was wrong, wasn't he?"

A gust of wind rattles the window. I want to fling it open, leap out, and run. This woman, my grandmother, feels like the most dangerous person I have ever met. And yet I stand here rooted to the floor. Is it because I need answers more than safety? "How do you know all this?"

"How do you think?" She turns to the closest monitor, taps the screen once, twice, and an image of the Eye on Tomorrow quad appears. She taps again. It changes to the inside of the library, looking down on the table where Alex and I always sat. Our table, where Ms. Walpole put her finger to her lips to let us know we weren't alone. But there must have been more cameras, more microphones than she knew about.

Another tap, and the inside of the Sim Dome appears. Grandma Athena double-taps, and there is sound. The quiet hum of the fans; otherwise, the empty room is quiet. But I know what she must have heard earlier, and even thinking about it makes me feel like something's pressing on my chest, squeezing out all the air.

"You've been spying on us?" I glare at her.

"Spying?" She laughs again, a cackle that chills my blood. "It's not spying, my dear, when you install cameras in facilities that you own. Why on earth do you think we've poured so much money into Eye on Tomorrow if not to know where our brightest young minds are leading one another?"

Eye on Tomorrow. The multimillion dollar campus. The high-tech equipment. It's never been about encouraging problem solving and exceptional thinking. It's about controlling it.

I stare at the screen. The safety-glass cube where I sat, so close to Alex, working together, figuring all this out with our carefully designed scientific experiments.

Grandma Athena was the variable we never could have imagined.

"It's almost charming, really." She stands and walks to the big screen. "How you put your brainy little heads together and thought you'd found the magic formula." She taps it twice, and there's video of the Placid Meadows gate. She zooms in then, to a shadowy but perfectly clear image of Alex and me in the woods near the entrance.

Grandma Athena smiles a bitter smile as Alex steps closer to me. "Just like Romeo and Juliet, star-crossed lovers caught in a storm." She crosses her arms over her DataSlate as Alex leans into me on the video and kisses me, and at that moment, anger fills me like wind.

"No!" I scream and fly at the monitor with my hands outstretched. It barely moves half an inch.

Grandma Athena's laugh is like dry sandpaper, and I can't control myself. I lunge toward her, but her wiry body is livelier than it looks. She leaps to the side, and I stumble into the desk.

The DataSlate lets out a high warning tone in her hands. Hers is set so loud she doesn't hear mine, muffled under my clothes.

Grandma Athena stares at the screen, completely unconcerned about where I am or what I might do.

I hate her.

I hate that this stranger with my father's eyes knows me well enough to know I will not come at her again.

Instead, I peer over her shoulder at the radar alert that fills the screen, and what I see makes me want to explode.

The three tornadoes have merged into one. One churning, raging, chewing-up, spitting-out monster.

"Finally." Grandma Athena taps the DataSlate screen, hard and fast, then harder and faster when it doesn't seem to do what she wants the first time. "Why isn't it tracking? And where the devil is Stephen?"

She punches out a message, then stares at it with eyes so intense I'm surprised it doesn't burst into flames. Her fingers grow white, tightening around the DataSlate as if that will make it respond, and a whole minute ticks by.

Finally, she grunts, a sharp, irritated sound, and pulls open a desk drawer. From inside, she takes a slender metal rod, no longer than my forearm. She presses a button on the side, and the tip glows ice blue. "Do you know what this is?"

My blank stare answers, and she goes on. "A company in Russia makes them. It's a Shock Wand, capable of delivering a high-powered, deeply debilitating electrical charge. A fatal one, if it's turned up a bit. I'm going to find your father." She levels it straight at me. "You will stay here." She nods toward a painted green chair in the corner of the room. "Sit down."

I hesitate a second too long. She jerks the wand, and a sharp current of pain runs through my shoulder where the tip grazes me.

"Now!" she says. I move away from the door and sit.

She lowers the wand long enough to reach under the desk and pull out a length of thick rope—the kind you use to tie a boat to a mooring—and flits around the chair like some tiny evil bird, pulling the rope tighter and tighter, lashing me to it, pinning my arms to my sides. She leans in, tugs the rope into a tighter knot. It scratches against my rib cage, right through my shirt.

I glare at her, and for the first time, she smiles. "You know, your father showed me video files of you when he came to Russia."

She's tied me to a chair, and now she wants to reminisce? "What videos?"

"Just some footage of the two of you, reading stories, playing on the porch. But I could tell you were a spirited child. I'd wondered about you, and then I felt like I was finally able to know you a bit."

You don't know me at all, I think. But what I say is, "I wish I had known you were alive."

For a second, her face softens, and it feels like my only chance.

"Grandma, please let me go," I say. "You can't do this. You can't just—"

She slaps me across the cheek, hard and sharp. "Don't even think of telling me what I can and can't do," she whispers, her coffee-scented breath hot on my face. "I lost my husband in battle because America's weapons weren't strong enough to end the war. I have worked my whole life to change that, to build what we've created here. Nothing else matters now. Nothing."

She fumbles with a set of old-fashioned metal keys and heads for the door. I need to keep her here, keep her talking. "How come there's no bio-scan here?" I blurt out.

"Because you need fingerprints to make them work." She holds up one hand. Her fingertips are all scar tissue. "I burned them off when I moved away—too hard to disappear otherwise." She fiddles with the keys again, laughing under her breath.

She is insane. Absolutely insane.

Still . . . she's my grandmother. How could I not matter? Not at all?

My cheek still burns, but I squeeze my eyes shut. "You don't want to do this."

"Oh, I do," she says quietly.

"Grandma, *please!*"

The words seem to press a button inside her—the wrong one— and her face hardens, though her voice stays quiet. "Stay where you are, or you'll be sorry." She raises the Shock Wand to remind me how sorry. "I'll be back." She grabs her DataSlate and takes one last look at the screen on the desktop computer, still swirling with green- and-red radar images. "Here." She turns it so it's facing my chair. "You can watch the radar while you wait for me to come back."

Chapter 27

She leaves and pulls the door closed with a heavy *thunk*. I hear the *snick* of her key in the lock, and I am trapped in what must be the only room Dad's fingerprint can't open.

My legs aren't tied, so I straddle the chair and try to wiggle free. If I can get even a little slack, I might be able to get out.

But Grandma is as good at knots as she is at meteorology. The only way I can even stand is if the chair comes with me. I throw my weight forward so the back legs come up off the floor. I do it again. And again, rocking back and forth until the chair tips forward, and I'm standing with it lashed to my back.

I turn and twist, but the sharp fibers of the rope cut into my wrists, and the knots only get tighter as sweat drips into my eyes.

I let the chair clunk back to the floor and sit again, facing away from the table. If I curl my fingers in and stretch, I can feel the knot that binds my hands. I finger the rough edges of rope—is there anything here that might unravel? I tug my hands apart, but again, the ropes dig into my skin, and I feel the stickiness of blood between my wrists.

There has to be something in this awful room that can set me free. A pair of scissors. A box cutter. Anything.

I rock forward to stand again and make a slow turn with the chair on my back. There's not much here. The desk. The chair. The monitors. And a single frame on the wall, a photograph of a storm at night. Lightning blazes out in crazy jags from the bottom of a dark cloud, and the sky below it glows yellow-blue. At the bottom of the photograph in silver letters against the black silhouette of the mountains is a quote.

I believe in one thing only, the power of human will.

—*Joseph Stalin*

The photograph, the lightning, the words, are so full of my grandmother's terrifying spirit, I have to look away.

I have to *get* away. *How?*

I turn full circle, back to the desk. There's only one drawer across the top. I wiggle around until my fingers, stretched out as far as they can behind my back, close around the knob.

I pull it open and turn to look. Empty, except for a few pens and a slip of paper the size of a credit card that reads "Bio-scan override code: 4687291." This must be how Grandma gets into areas like Dad's office without a fingerprint scan. It's nothing that can help me now, not in this room with Grandma's olden-days lock, but I wiggle the paper scrap into my back pocket before I let the chair thump to the floor again.

Out of breath, I sit, helpless, and stare at the computer screen's radar swirls. My eyes burn with tears, and the colors blur together, but then I see something that nearly makes my heart stop. I blink—hard, over and over—until the tears spill out so I can see.

The storm is moving again.

No. No. No.

Let me be reading it wrong. Please. Please let me be wrong.

I throw all my weight forward, too fast this time. The chair's legs fly out from under me, and I fall. My temple cracks against the corner of the desk before I hit the floor on my side.

Lying there, my head throbbing, my arm radiating pain underneath me, all I can see is the hook of that storm. It is still growing.

I ignore the pain in my shoulder, throw all my weight forward, and roll onto my knees with the chair on my back. My forehead presses against the cold concrete floor, and I summon every bit of strength I have to push up with my legs. Up, up, until I'm standing before the desk again, facing the screen.

The storm is moving again, headed straight toward Alex's farm.

I want to scream, but instead I spin around and smash the chair into the edge of the desk. Some way, some how, I have to get loose. Without any idea what I'll do or where I'll go or how I could possibly fix this, I throw my weight at the desk again.

The chair smashes into it, over and over and over, until my wrists feel broken and I have to stop. The splintering noises I pray for never come; there's only the hard, cold thunk of solid wood on wood, over and over and over.

My DataSlate has worked its way out of my jeans. It clunks off the edge of the desk to the floor. The jolt turns it on, and the screen blinks up at me.

Dad's files.

Dad's files are here.

If this little rectangle of titanium and wires holds the power to turn this storm toward the farms, it must also hold the power to turn it back.

If I can get to the computer in Dad's office, I can try to reverse what they've done.

The lightning in Grandma's picture blurs and dances through my tears, and it makes me want to smash the photo, smash everything Grandma's ever done, onto this polished concrete floor.

Suddenly, the power of *my* will feels strong enough to shatter glass.

Glass.

I stare at the reflection of the radar in the glass that covers Grandma's storm.

This. This is what I need.

The picture hangs at eye level, so the lower edge of the frame is even with my chest. I sidestep over to it, knees bent so my shoulder is pressed against the wall. I spring upward as hard and fast as I can.

My shoulder knocks the picture up, off its hanger. It bounces off me onto the floor and shatters.

Jagged shards of glass cover the floor. They crunch under my feet as I make my way to the biggest, sharpest piece. I kick it into a far corner where there aren't so many shards, lower myself to my knees, then roll onto my side. Writhing and twisting and wiggling, I back my way into the corner until my fingers touch sharp, cool edges.

I'm facing the desk, but I try not to let my eyes fall on the radar screen as I maneuver the glass between my wrists and little by little by little, pick at the rough fibers of the rope. I can't see how much progress I'm making, and it feels like it's already been too long when there's a thump at the door, and I freeze.

My heart wants to burst out of my chest and run, but I hold my breath and wait.

There's another thud and a scraping sound—a tree branch or piece of roofing the wind has thrown against the building—and only then do I let myself look at the computer screen again.

The whole county is swallowed up in green and red, and the hook of that monster is inching closer to Alex's farm.

I can't afford to be careful anymore. Every time the glass slips, I feel the warmth of blood spilling from the cuts in my hands. But the rope is weakening; it's starting to give. I keep slicing back and forth until there's a muffled pop, and my hands—finally—are free.

Cutting the rope that binds my chest is faster with two hands, and soon the chair clatters to the floor. I grab the DataSlate with blood-smeared hands, fly to the door, and grab the handle.

Locked from the outside with Grandma's keys.

This time, I scream.

I scream long and loud, and even though I know the window must be StormSafe indestructible, I slam the DataSlate onto the desk, grab the chair that held me captive, and fling it at the glass.

It shatters. Shatters into a million pieces.

The wind swoops in with a howling whistle, and for a second, I can only stare. I guess you don't need safety glass if you believe the storms will always stay away.

I grab my DataSlate, climb out the window, and run for the main building.

Chapter 28

The lights are still on, but the conference room is empty, and when I peer in the main doors, the reception desk is quiet, too. Dad's print wore off my finger long ago, so I tuck the DataSlate under my arm, pull Grandma's override card from my pocket, and look up to the sky.

Please work. Please.

I punch in the numbers and hold my breath until there's a beep and a click, and I push open the door. I run for the elevator, tap in the numbers there, and again, the beep of clearance—of course she would have access to everything.

My skin prickles as I press the button for the top floor and wait, willing it to rise faster, willing this office to be empty when I get to the top.

The DataSlate chimes in my hands and scares me so much I almost drop it. The message is short, from Risha:

Alex is here. Where are you?!?

Six words. But they are from Risha. And the tears I've been fighting for hours come back in a flood. Maybe because the cold, awful fear that something happened to Alex has melted now. Maybe because for the first time since he drove away, I feel like I am not alone.

I write back:

StormSafe HQ.

Even as I'm entering the text, I can't believe what I'm about to do. Break into my father's office. Hack into his computer. And—*please, let it work*—reverse his awful commands.

The elevator dings, and I finish:

In Dad's office—trying to retrack storm.

I tuck the DataSlate back into my pants as the door opens.

The only light comes from the wall of radar screens. They cast a green glow over the beige carpet, and shadows swirl on the walls.

I head straight for Dad's desk. The computer is logged off, but sure enough, right next to the bio-scanner is a data panel, and when I punch in the code from Grandma's card, the welcome screen appears.

ATHENA MEGGS, FULL CLEARANCE

It believes that I'm her.

A message pops up on the screen: DISABLE REMOTE ACCESS? CANCEL OR OK. I click on OK. Now everything will be up to me, and the thought makes me want to run, but I stay.

My hand trembles as I tap the screen, scrolling through folders and files, looking for the program to remotely operate the satellites.

I call up a search and type in everything I can think of: satellite, dissipation, redirection, downdraft, warming.

Nothing.

I pull up a database of the entire server and start scanning, but there must be thousands of files here. Programs with names I don't recognize. Documents full of numerical models, charts, and statistics. I'm not even halfway through the list, when my DataSlate chimes again.

It's Risha. Three words this time.

We are coming.

Another sob rises in my throat. I'm relieved and thankful and terrified, and before I can type back, I whirl around to look at the radar.

The main storm is moving slowly, giving people plenty of time to watch and be afraid and understand what nightmare is coming.

And it's spawned a slew of baby tornadoes, all over the county.

No matter how desperate I am for help, no matter how hungry I am for someone to be here with me, I can't let them do it. There is no way Risha and Alex can get here safely. None.

No! Storm is too big. Stay there.

I send the message and get an immediate auto-reply.

RECIPIENT NOT AVAILABLE

"No!" I shout, and my voice echoes in the empty office. The only answer is the hum of the computers that are my only hope.

I turn back to the screen on Dad's desk.

Be here. Be here. I scroll through the last half of the files. There must be a thousand documents and databases, and nothing that gives any clue it might be the program that whispers to satellites, tells them where to send their energy, how to turn away a storm.

What am I doing here? I bang my fist on the desk. Looking for answers in this jumble of files is like searching for a single blade of grass swirling in a storm. But I keep looking. What else can I do?

Finally, near the end of the list of folders, my eyes land on one labeled REDIRECTION and I click it open. There are fifty files, maybe more. I tap the one called SAT INPUT—it takes forever to open—and scan the screen that appears.

At the top are three satellite icons, each labeled with latitude and longitude.

With a trembling finger, I point to one of the satellites—which one? I can only guess—and tap.

The screen fills with scrolling numbers that make me want to put my head down and cry. It's some manic feed of temperatures, humidity, atmospheric pressure, cyclonic measurements, and who knows what else. What am I supposed to do with all this?

I swallow hard, reach for my DataSlate, and pull up the page with Dad's redirection codes. There must be a hundred different sequences.

I choose one.

I choose, because the only alternative is doing nothing.

Please let it work.

Please let it work.

I chant the words over and over, like some magical mantra, as I type in the code, number by letter by number. One wrong stroke, and I could make it bigger instead of turning it away.

When the last string of numbers is lined up at the bottom of the page, I hold my finger over the on-screen button.

EXECUTE SATELLITE COMMAND

I can barely breathe. *What if I've done it wrong? Who am I to even think I can do this?*

Before the voices in my head can get louder, I hold my breath and tap.

The screen flashes white, then blurs with a wild scroll of numbers, commands set into motion.

I look up at the ceiling and imagine the satellite miles overhead, stopping in its course, turning, rotating, blasting heat energy down, down, down into the cloud that gave birth to this monster.

When the numbers stop streaming, the screen reads.

COMMAND EXECUTED

Nothing more.

Did it work? I stand and run to the window, but there's no way to tell if anything's better. The wind is still blowing the rain at the building in horizontal sheets.

Stop. Stop. Stop.

A gust of wind rattles the window. It reminds me of another window, the one I threw the chair through, and I can't help wondering if Grandma Athena has come back to find it yet. If she's wondering where I escaped.

Or if she already knows.

I look up at the ceiling. No cameras, at least not that I can see. But no matter what, I'm running out of time.

I turn back to the radar image of the storm. It's actually slowed and—Is it possible? Do I dare hope?—looks like it's turning around. I tap the screen twice to put a track on the storm. The dotted line moves back across the screen.

"No!!"

Straight for Placid Meadows.

Placid Meadows, where concrete houses and storms that never cross the fence make everyone feel safe enough to ignore the warnings.

Placid Meadows, where toddlers giggle and shout nursery rhymes at the sky, even as the dark clouds swirl.

Placid Meadows, where Mirielle is probably nursing Remi on the couch right now.

Where Risha and her family and Alex are about to be—

"No!" I yell at the screen. "No! No! No!!!"

But the storm on the screen swells into something broader, stronger than it was even half an hour ago.

I leap back into the chair at Dad's computer and pull up the folder again, but all of these numbers mean nothing. Do I dare even try?

Above the humming of the computer and the beating of my heart and the rain pounding the window, I hear another sound that makes my heart freeze in my chest.

The elevator door sliding open.

I dive under the desk, shaking, and wait.

Chapter 29

Jaden! Are you here? Jaden!"

Alex's voice washes over me, and I scramble out from under the desk. "Over here!"

They are soaking wet, both of them. Risha's hair is plastered to her forehead, and Alex's face shines with rainwater or sweat, or both, as he takes in the huge room.

"How did you get in here?"

Risha holds up her finger. Her hand is shaking. "I made another print this week. Just in case."

"You guys, I tried to tell you not to come. The storm is—"

"We couldn't even see it until we were out of Placid Meadows." Risha's whole body is trembling. "Jaden, it was . . . It had to have been an NF-7 at least, it was just—"

"We're fine," Alex interrupts. "But for a minute there . . ." He shakes his head. "We thought we were okay, but then it turned, and I had to gun the truck, but we made it. I could tell it was still growing, so—" He stops when he sees the radar on the big screen. I watch him process the mix of images, the moving blobs of green and red, and

I hold my breath, waiting for him to see the path this storm is on now. He curses, and Risha rushes over to face a radar image of something too terrible for words.

She lets out a scream that shatters my heart like the glass in Grandma's picture. The scream of someone whose whole world is about to be destroyed. The scream of someone who knows she may never see her parents again.

She drops to the floor, sobbing.

I run to her, put my arms around her. Her body is hot with fear, cold with rain and air-conditioning, and she shakes harder.

"Risha, call on your DataSlate. Warn them!"

She tries twice but can't get a message through.

I jump to my feet and grab Alex's hand. "We have to stop it."

He steps up to the computer. "Where's the program to redirect? We'll have to find a track that—"

"No!"

He wheels around, bewildered. "Jaden, if we don't change this course, then—"

"Changing it won't help. We have to stop it. We have to kill this storm." I say the words out loud, even though I know they're impossible.

Alex shakes his head. "We can't. We never got to run the simulation successfully. We have no idea what the outcome would be, and we—"

"We have to try, Alex! Look!" I fling my arm toward the radar wall, where Risha is still crumpled on the floor. "We have to try. Otherwise, we're sending it *at* somebody, and even if that's not us,

· · 252 · ·

it's still somebody, and then we're just like—" The words get stuck in my throat. "Just like my father."

Alex closes his eyes, squeezes them tight, and I can almost see thoughts swirling behind his dark lashes. Finally, he shakes his head and opens them. "We can't take that chance. What if we end up making it worse?"

"But what if—"

"Jaden, no. There's no precedent for this. There's no research to support it. There's no—just, no!" He bends down and starts scrolling through the folders still up on Dad's screen. The dozens of data files with different codes. "Did you use one of these before?"

"Yes. And look what happened, Alex! We can't do this again. We have to—"

"Just wait!" He holds up one hand and keeps scrolling with the other. Risha has managed to pull herself together enough to stand behind us, her face red and puffy. Alex pulls her forward so she can see the screen, too. "There has to be a path here that doesn't hit any developed areas. Everybody, look. There has to be."

"Which one?" I throw my hands up. "Alex, there must be two hundred separate codes there. We can't keep trying them all until— There's no time for this!"

"Wait." Risha reaches a thin arm between us and scrolls back up through the list. Her bracelets clink together, and her eyes focus on the data scrolling past on the screen. The numbers, the patterns seem to calm her. "Which one did you run before, Jaden?"

"I don't even know. About halfway down, maybe?"

She scrolls halfway and leans in, squinting at the numbers. Then she picks up her DataSlate, calls up a map, taps at it a few times. "Yes," she whispers, and leans in to point at the computer screen again. "These numbers . . ." She runs her finger down the center part of the list. ". . . are all sequential in terms of geographic coordinates." She taps at one of them. "This must be the code you ran. It corresponds with the latitude and longitude of Placid Meadows."

"So that means . . ." I pull up a map of Logan County on the DataSlate and choose the satellite view, the one that shows all the roads and buildings. "If we can find a path without people . . ." In my mind, I draw imaginary lines from where the storm is now, trying every direction. But eventually, no matter which way it goes, the storm is going to hit someone. "It won't work. No path goes on forever."

"It doesn't have to. Hold on." Alex pulls up Dad's historical storms database. "The path just needs to be long enough for the storm's energy to run out. No tornado can last forever, and we already know what this one's got in it. It's already happened once." He calls up the 10-10-20 storm and runs his finger down the screen, stopping at a line close to the bottom. "Thirty-eight miles. We need a path that's empty for thirty-eight miles."

I look down at the map in my hands. It feels impossibly full of buildings. The path might as well be a million miles. "I can't—" The wind gusts, and the sound of rain on the roof turns harder, louder, like someone throwing stones. Hail.

"We have to hurry!" Alex brings the redirection folder back up. "I'll get this ready so when you find the coordinates, we can just do it."

· · 254 · ·

Risha leans in to look at the DataSlate, so close her hair brushes against mine. "What about here?" She drags the line I've drawn a bit farther southeast, and we zoom in to see the track. It would take the storm mostly through woods near one of the energy farms, then past what looks like a few orchards from the satellite view, and close—too close—to one old farmhouse.

"That won't work." I point to the energy farm.

"They all have huge safe rooms," Alex says. "They'll get a warning."

"What about that house?" I point.

"It's not perfect, but we have to do something. That's the only building in the path," Risha argues. "It's thirty miles out. The storm will be starting to weaken, and they'll have plenty of warning time."

She starts to pull the DataSlate from me, but I hold on. "But it's still somebody's—"

"Jaden, will you look!" She lets go and points to the radar wall, where the storm on its current path is churning toward Placid Meadows. Ten minutes, maybe less, from swallowing up Risha's family. From Mirielle and Remi, who are sure they're safe inside the gates. None of them will ever see it coming.

I hand her the DataSlate, and she slides it onto the desk in front of Alex.

"Okay . . ." The computer screen reflects in his dark eyes. "What am I looking for here?"

Risha reads him the coordinates, and he scrolls down the list of command codes until he hits the one that matches. "Here?"

She double-checks it. "That's it."

He clicks it open, copies the code, and taps back to the command entry field. "Jaden, you just typed it in here before?"

"Yeah. Then run it." I look away from the screen, toward the radar, and hear his fingers tap against it.

Then quiet. Except for all of our breathing. All of our hoping.

Then the hum of the computer processing.

Risha and Alex turn to watch the radar. We hold our breath, and it feels like all of the air in the room has gone still while we wait.

The storm on the screen inches closer to Placid Meadows.

"Why isn't it turning?" Risha's voice trembles.

"It will." I take her hand, and she squeezes so hard she crushes my fingers, but I don't let go. "It should. Any second."

But it doesn't.

"It's not going to stop." She doesn't scream or cry or yell at the screen. Her voice is flat, as if she's already died with them. "It's going to hit them."

Turn, turn, turn, I think, staring at the ceiling, imagining the satellites miles above us. Why aren't they doing their job? "Wait, look!" Alex's voice brings me back to the screen, and just as the storm is about to hit the fence, it slows, like it did that day in the park, the day Risha and I listened as the moms and kids shouted their rhyme to the sky. It listened.

And it's listening now.

"Oh, thank God, thank God!" Risha's tears flow again, this time tears of thankfulness. She takes a deep breath and walks to the window. Her fingers trace raindrops down the glass.

Alex sinks back into the chair as if the storm sucked away all his energy when it turned.

I stay at the radar screen, watching the storm pick up its pace, starting a race in its new direction, ready to devour the new meal set before it.

I pick up my DataSlate and zoom in to follow its path as it moves.

The trees planted alongside Placid Meadows. When the sun comes up tomorrow, they'll be in splinters scattered over miles.

Better trees than farms, though.

I follow the path past the energy farm. Criminals or not, I hope they all get to their safe room in time.

I swipe the screen through ten, twenty, thirty miles of woods until the trees thin and arrange themselves into lines, and I know this is the orchard that the storm will level soon—in twenty minutes, maybe twenty-five.

Past the orchard and just a hair off to the east is the one house still in the path.

I zoom into the satellite view, hoping in a corner of my heart that I'll see a FOR SALE sign or already-broken windows and an empty garage to tell me no one lives there.

In another corner lives the cold, raw fear of what else I might see. Cars in the driveway. Dogs on a leash, waiting for someone to come play. Swing sets and tricycles.

I take a deep breath and zoom in as far as the satellite view allows.

And there is something I hadn't imagined even in the darkest corner of my heart.

A house with peeling white paint.

A stable and a brown mare.

A split-rail fence that I reached over with a handful of sugar cubes.

A rickety farm stand with a sign that I can't read in the satellite image, a sign I don't need to see to know that it offers sweet raspberries, fresh peaches, and compliments.

This is Aunt Linda's house.

And we have just sent a storm to swallow it up.

Chapter 30

This can't be happening. Not now. Not when it was all supposed to be over. I let out a moan.

"What?" Alex jumps from the chair, but even his shoulder brushing mine can't warm the chill that's settled on me.

"This house." I tap the screen, and it zooms in closer. The wreath Mom sent last Christmas is still on the door. A bird has built a nest in its gentle curve. "It's my great-aunt Linda's."

Aunt Linda, who fed me pie in that kitchen. Who gave me the poetry book, the one thing that's made Oklahoma feel a little like home. Who told me the truth.

Alex's face darkens. He stares at the screen, processing the information, then hands the DataSlate to me. "Call her. She may not even be home."

I nod and bring up her contact page. The call goes through, straight to Aunt Linda's video-mail, and I've never been more relieved. "Leave a message!" she says, but I don't. If she were home, she'd have answered.

"Feel better?" Alex asks, and I nod.

But then my DataSlate dings with a new message. "That's weird," I say. "I've had it on all day."

"We've probably been getting interference," Risha says, turning away from the window. "I couldn't get through before." Her eyes have relaxed some; they aren't as puffy, and her breathing is finally back to normal. "My DataSlate never connects right on storm nights."

"It's my father." Where is he? Is he on his way up here? I need to know, but I can't bring myself to open the message. Can't make myself let him into this room, even if it's only a recording. I can't help imagining him, looking right through the dark, shiny screen, seeing us here, seeing everything we've done.

But Alex is insistent. "Play it."

So I do.

Dad's face fills the screen. He's not 3-D like he is on the holo-sim at Eye on Tomorrow, but otherwise, it's just as realistic.

Only where did he record this? The shelf behind him is full of old dishes. He's definitely not here at StormSafe. And it's not our house in Placid Meadows, either.

"Jaden," Dad says from the screen in my hands. "I know where you are." He puts a hand up toward the camera in a gesture meant to keep me from freaking out, meant to keep me from throwing the DataSlate across the room and running like I want to. "I need you to stay there for now. You're not in trouble, and I—" He takes a deep breath, and instead of the usual fire in his eyes, the focused intensity, there is something else. Are they shining with *tears*? "I don't want you in danger. I can explain things to you later. It's not what it looks like." His voice breaks, and he looks down.

Alex laughs a quick, bitter laugh and walks away, but Risha stays by me and listens as Dad goes on. "But no matter what, I'm sure you're going to want to go home with Mom. She's on her way here now. So as I said, please stay where you are. Mom will be here in"— he looks at his watch—"ten to fifteen minutes, and after she and I talk, she'll be right there to pick you up."

The screen goes black.

Mom?

Mom is in town? Does that mean she was getting all my messages but couldn't respond? Did she get the last one? Does she already know what Dad has done?

And Grandma! Does Mom know Grandma Athena is alive?

Where *is* Grandma Athena now? I picture her bony fingers, curled around the Shock Wand, and I shiver.

"We can't stay here." I run to the window, where the rain should be letting up, but it's swirling harder, faster in the wind. "My grandmother might come back."

"Your grandmother?" Risha looks bewildered, and I realize I never told them. There was no time. There is no time now.

"We just—we have to go."

"Now that the storm's gone, let's go back to your house. Wouldn't that make more sense than you waiting here for them to come pick you up?"

"They're not *at* the house." It wasn't Dad and Mirielle's house in the video; there are no painted plates in Mirielle's shiny steel kitchen.

But where are they? I rewind the video-message and zoom in to see the background more clearly.

A wooden shelf.

Faded red apples on the wallpaper.

I suck in my breath. Not there. No.

Then I see the coffee mug with Emily Dickinson's face and know it's real.

Dad is at Aunt Linda's house.

And Mom is on her way. Or *was* . . . I check the time-stamp on the video. 7:22 PM. It's 7:45 now. Plenty of time for Mom to have arrived, sat down at Linda's big, wooden kitchen table with a cup of tea. Time for her to be devoured by a giant storm.

I lunge toward the radar screen. The storm is racing forward, showing no signs of weakening.

Alex points to the DataSlate in my hands. "Try calling again." His voice is so steady and calm I could scream.

I pull up Aunt Linda's contact page again.

No response.

I call up Mom's.

Nothing.

And Dad's.

Nothing.

I slam the DataSlate down on the desk and start typing blindly at the computer keyboard.

"Jaden, what are you doing?! You can't just—"

"Yes, I can!" I swipe at the tears filling my eyes, blurring my vision, and pull up the last sequence of numbers we entered, the code to turn the storm. I feed it back to the machine in reverse order. If we sent this storm to Aunt Linda's, then we can take it away, erase its path as if it never planned to flatten the white farmhouse at all. As if it never found this course toward the building with everyone I love inside.

That is the story I tell myself, and I am willing it to be true.

I finish the code, press the command button before Alex can protest again, and turn to watch the radar screen.

Like before, the storm inches forward a few more seconds before it slows and then stops, and then changes direction. And only then do I realize I was holding my breath. Aunt Linda is safe. My mother is safe. My father is . . . safe.

"Are you *insane*?!" Alex pushes me from the computer and starts entering code. "You have it coming right back at us!"

I stare at the radar image.

The storm had been so real when it was chasing us down the road, but between then and now, it's started to feel like something artificial. Something that lives in the colors of a map instead of in the real world.

My eyes trace its new path, back through the woods, along the road, around a curve, and up the driveway to the compound where we sit watching. It is headed straight for StormSafe. Straight for us.

It feels real again.

"What have you *done*?" Alex is tapping the computer screen but can't get back to the page that will let him redirect the storm.

"I had to do something!" My throat closes tight. I slump against the window and watch the clouds swirling above us. Then I whirl back to Alex. "Wait! Stop the redirection codes—what we need to do here—it's what we've needed to do all along! We have to run the dissipation code instead."

Risha shakes her head. "But that's not—"

"Not tested, I know! But it's all we have. Otherwise we can keep turning this storm around and redirecting it every two minutes, and we're going to end up with more people in danger. We have to—" I'm so certain of what I'm about to say that it surprises even me. "We have to take it out."

Chapter 31

Alex doesn't say a word. He walks to the window, presses his forehead to the glass, and closes his eyes.

Risha stares at the computer screen with big eyes, as if she expects it to make the decision all by itself.

"We have to do this." I say it again and look at my watch. For another six minutes, the storm will be swallowing up nothing but forest and fields before it gets back to the populated area. We have six minutes. "There is no. Other. Choice."

Finally, Alex turns away from the window. "It goes against everything we know. Running untested code to drive a real satellite? Testing an unproven theory on an event that's already in progress? Jaden, it's just—"

"It's our only chance! Look!" I fling a hand at the radar screen. The storm hasn't weakened; if anything, it's feeding off the chaos of being directed and redirected in a way nature never intended. "We can't keep recoding it over and over again. There's always going to be somebody in the way, and I can't—" I choke on the words, but I force them out. "I can't be responsible for this anymore."

Risha steps to my side, so we're both facing Alex. "She's right. How close were you to figuring this out?"

"More than close." Alex taps his fingers against the glass. "We . . . I'm sure we have it. But we haven't run a simulation, and—"

"We have it right, Alex. You know we do."

"I know. I'm just afraid that—" He whirls around to face me. "There's another Sim Dome here, right? We could run the code there first and then as long as—"

A gust of wind shakes the building and interrupts him before I have a chance to do it myself. There is no time.

"Where's the code?" Risha asks.

The windows shudder and rattle.

Windows. *The windows jerk free to hover near the ceiling . . .*

I call up the file and stare hard at the numbers, and somehow, they whisper back to me.

Yes. This. Yes.

Almost like a poem.

The ceiling floats away with a sigh.

This is what we need to do. It will work. It *has* to work.

I hand Risha my DataSlate and watch her dark eyes flicking up and down the rows of numbers. She gives one quick, sharp nod when they add up. "This looks perfect. I say we do it."

But Alex doesn't move from the window. I walk over to him and slowly, tentatively, put a hand on his arm.

Still gazing out at the storm, he nods. "You're right." He turns and heads for the computer, but just as I'm about to follow him, a flash of sky blue catches my eye through the rain and I stare out the window.

The rain pours down in sheets, and the wind has picked up enough to send branches whipping down from the treetops and roofing shingles flying like playing cards. The sky is even darker off to the north. The storm is coming. We need to move, to act now if we're even going to try to disperse it, but I can't take my eyes off the figure in blue, making her way through the torrents, toward the main door of the building.

"Hurry. She's coming," I whisper, even though Risha and Alex don't know who she is, and there's no time to explain. I shake my head to clear my thoughts, push off from the window, and rush to join them at the computer. Alex has already keyed in half of the long string of numbers. He hands me the DataSlate.

"Read me the next line, starting at oh-four-six-dash-two-seven-one," he says.

"Oh-four-six . . ." My eyes focus on the numbers, but in my mind, I'm picturing Grandma Athena pushing her way through the wind to the front door. Does she know the bio-scan override code by memory? She's probably in by now, probably through the door with her Shock Wand.

"Jaden!" Alex's sharp voice brings me back to the numbers. He's almost shouting now to be heard over the wind's steady, whooshing roar.

"Sorry. It was oh-four-six-dash-two-seven-one . . ."

A *thunk* against the window makes me jump. I almost drop the DataSlate but manage to fumble it in my hands and get hold of it again. "What *was* that?"

"Piece of the roof came off, it looked like." Risha takes the

DataSlate from my shaking hands and reads Alex another line of numbers. She's about to start the next line when the lights flicker and go out.

The computer's hum dies, and all we can hear is the growing roar from outside.

The windows shake.

There are more clunks and scrapes from the roof, as if pieces of it are breaking free to escape from the cruel winds.

Risha's free hand finds mine, and I hold on.

"The generator will kick in any second." Alex waits. "There has to be a generator. There must be, right?"

My heart sinks. There doesn't have to be a generator because there wasn't supposed to be a need for one. The storms were never supposed to come here.

Dad didn't count on this.

There is no generator. Only the faint glow of the DataSlate.

I let go of Risha's sweaty hand and go to the window. There, eight stories down and off into the trees, is the only other light in the compound. It is the building where I found Grandma Athena.

It must have a generator. And it has a computer.

"There's a light on down there; it's the only building with power!"

"We can't go out there!" Alex shouts.

"It's moving faster!" Risha holds up her DataSlate with a radar image. The storm is coming.

"We *have* to leave! Otherwise, we're trapped on the eighth floor of a glass building!" I scream. "Come on!"

We run, dodging desks and radar screens, past the elevators—there's no hope of them working now—and to the fire exit door that leads to the stairs.

"This way!" I tug it open. "Here!"

Behind us, there's a tremendous crash of glass on glass, and even though I can't see it, I know that one of the windows we'd been looking through is gone, shattered.

When the stairway door closes behind us, everything goes dark.

I've been clinging to Alex's hand but I let go so I can turn on my DataSlate and give us at least a little light.

Risha stumbles behind me. I feel her hands on my back, catching herself, and I grab the railing and hold on. I stumble down a few steps, but Alex reaches back to steady me, and we go down, down, down, until finally, there are no more stairs to descend.

"Ready?" I turn off the DataSlate, tuck it into the back of my jeans, and reach for the door handle.

"Wait!" Alex shouts into the darkness. "That's going to lead straight outside. Do you know where we're going?"

"The building's to the left—maybe thirty yards. We'll have to run!"

"And hold on to each other!" Risha screams.

"I've got my shoulder against the door!" Alex shouts. "On the count of three, you turn the handle, and I'll push it open, and then we need to grab on to one another and go!"

"I'm ready!" I try to ignore the noise from beyond the door, the wind that sounds ever more like that legendary freight train, ever more like a monster from mythology, ready to swallow us up. "All set?"

"Do it!" Alex shouts.

I turn the handle and we push, but nothing happens. Even when I hear Alex grunt from the effort of pushing, pushing his whole body against the door, it doesn't move except to pop open for a split second to mock us and then slam shut.

"Again! Together!" Alex cries. "One!"

The door is cold against my shoulder.

"Two!"

I think about three. Think that *if* we are successful, *if* this goes the right way, we'll fly out of here into a monster storm, and then what?

"Three!"

The door pops open like before, but this time, we are pushing, all of us, and we keep it from slamming shut. Then a swirl of wind comes, and the door that we could barely push open all together flies off its hinges as if it's nothing more than the lid of a shoe box.

And we are out.

Thrown into the wildest storm I have ever seen.

Forget freight trains. Forget Greek monsters.

It feels like the atmosphere itself has come to life, furious, ready to whip us all off the face of the earth in revenge.

Alex is shouting something at me, but I can't hear.

"What?" I scream, but it's no use. Our voices are sucked into the sky. Alex grabs my upper arm tight and pulls me away from the door. His fingers dig into my flesh so hard it hurts, and thank God for that. It feels like I'll be carried off if he ever lets go.

"This way!" I scream, but he can't hear, so I point frantically toward the outbuilding, its light flickering through the rain. I push into the wind and pull Alex along.

The closer we get, the more my stomach clenches. Is she in there?

From the second Alex and I made it out the door, I have been waiting, watching for that glimpse of sky blue. Where is she?

Alex suddenly yanks his hand away from me and pushes Risha to the side. A branch flies close to her head. But it misses her, and we press forward through the blinding rain.

I tug Alex's sleeve and point to the cold yellow light flickering through the rain. I pull Alex and Risha in that direction.

The wind blows rain into my face. I raise an arm to wipe my eyes and finally see the squat little building with its shiny steel door.

Is Grandma waiting on the other side?

There's no time to wonder, no time to worry. The solar energy panels on the next building crackle and send up a shower of sparks.

Alex reaches for the door handle, yanks it open, and pulls Risha and me inside so fast we tumble on top of him. The wind screams through the room, celebrating its newly conquered territory.

The steel door swings open and bangs shut wildly in the wind, and every time it flies open, there are great green flashes of lightning outside. Faster and faster, closer together.

The storm is coming for us.

As if it knows our plans.

And desperately wants us to fail.

But at least our voices are back. "It's over here, hurry!" I lead Alex and Risha around the radar screen to the computer desk where I first saw her. The chair I threw is still toppled on its side in a heap of broken glass. The wind's whipping through the broken window in weird whistling-glass noises. And perhaps the most eerie thing of all is the computer.

Still humming quietly against the wall.

Waiting for Grandma to come back. Where is she now?

Alex kneels down in front of it and starts pressing keys. "Here's the program. Got numbers for me?"

I pull out the DataSlate and start reading numbers, leaning over him. "Oh-four-six-dash-two-seven-one."

"Got it."

"Then five-four-zero—"

The wind shifts, and sheets of rain pour in the broken window. It stings our faces, soaks the floor and the desk.

"It's going to short out the equipment!" Risha screams. She tries to use her skinny body to shield the computer. "Hurry up!"

"FIVE-FOUR-ZERO-TWO-SEVEN!" I scream. There's a terrible scraping, crunching sound above us that can only be pieces of roof, giving up to the wind. But Alex keeps punching in numbers. I can see the strain in his eyes, the urgent effort to focus on getting this right.

The wind is blowing in the open window so hard we can barely stand.

"Then ZERO-ZERO-ONE-ZERO-FIVE— Watch out!!" I drop the DataSlate and throw my body against Risha to shove her out of the way of the radar wall, toppling in a great shattering of glass to the concrete floor.

"Jaden, what's next?!" Alex shouts.

I grab the DataSlate. Thank God it didn't break. "NINE-FOUR-THREE-ZERO-TWO!" I force myself to keep my head down, keep reading numbers, no matter what falls around me, no matter how many branches fly past my head. No matter how sure I am that we will fail. I keep going.

"SIX-FOUR—" The wall behind us explodes in a deep rumble and tears away from the rest of the structure. The wind howls in victory. The roar of the storm is louder, the lightning more frequent; it feels like we'll be hit any second. When I look up, I see why.

I stop shouting numbers because it's too late.

It's here.

"Get down!" Alex screams and tries to pull me under the heavy wooden desk, but I can only stare at the great raging whirlwind bearing down on the main building we just left.

The storm pushes forward. A violent cloud of debris swirls around its base, branches and shrubs, shingles and twisted HV parts, bits of people's lives that will never come together again.

When it reaches the main StormSafe building, it pauses.

Just for a split second.

As if whole walls of glass are a delicacy it wants to savor.

Then it plunges into the first wall. The glass crunches like falling icicles, and the shining pieces are sucked into the vortex and become part of the tornado, sharp and fast.

In twenty seconds, the building is gone.

"Get down, it's coming!" Alex pulls my arm so hard I fall to the ground beside him.

Risha drops and flattens herself next to us. "Ow!" she cries, rubbing her side. She must have landed on something. Broken glass? "You guys, look!" She bends over and pulls with all her weight on a latch screwed into one of the floorboards. "Storm shelter!" The door swings open, and we pile down a steep set of steps behind her.

It is nothing like the storm cellar at Alex's barn. No daybed. No food. But it has metal bars poured into the concrete, for holding on. And on a heavy desk in the corner, it has the one thing we need most right now.

A computer.

I race to it, wait for a home screen to load, and squeeze my eyes shut as tight as I can, as if refusing to watch will keep the tornado from jumping the last stretch of lawn, keep it from coming here where I've brought Alex and Risha.

The wind screams overhead, and I scream back. "No!!"

Because I know now what is about to happen if we cannot destroy this storm.

It is going to kill us.

Storm cellar or not. It's too big. Too strong.

It will devour us. Me, and the two people who are here with me. *Because* of me.

I squeeze my eyes shut tighter.

Please, please, please, don't let them die because of me.

When I open my eyes, the computer has booted up, and I find the file Alex was working on upstairs. "It auto-saved!" For once, it feels like someone might be on our side. "Get the last line of numbers, quick!"

Alex pages through DataSlate screens, one after another.

"Hurry up!"

The wind and rain, already impossibly loud, scream louder, and there's clunking, clanking coming from over our heads. Something—lots of somethings—being flung around like play toys, until finally, in an almighty howl of wind, the whole of the little building—everything above us, is ripped from the foundation and sucked into the sky.

I fall to the floor, grab on to one of the metal bars, and hold on. But impossibly, the wind lets up, and when I dare to peek into the screaming, high-whistling swirl above me, all I can do is stare.

The storm has lifted up; the tornado is no longer touching down, though it's close, and it is absolutely, directly on top of us.

The air feels heavy, like every last molecule of oxygen has been sucked into the sky, and this gray cloud has us encircled like a tomb.

Blue lightning flashes from the sides of the tornado. We are surrounded by a circular wall of clouds and electricity.

"We're inside," I whisper, and only then do I become aware of Alex and Risha on the ground next to me, staring into the sky, too.

"It's . . . it's beautiful," Risha says. But she is also the first to get her wits back. "But it's still moving. It could touch back down any second, and we'll have the other side to deal with. *Finish!* While we still have the computer!"

It's a miracle it still works; if the winds had raged on the ground a half-second more, it would be up there, swirling over our heads.

But it's here, and I crawl to it. There are two lines left to copy from the DataSlate. Alex reads, and I enter them with shaking, blood-stained hands.

"SEVEN-THREE-ONE," he finishes.

I stare at the columns of numbers and let my finger hover over the words EXECUTE COMMAND.

What if?

What if we are wrong?

This storm over our heads will go . . . where? And will we strengthen it along the way?

Alex's hand presses down gently on my shoulder. "It will work."

I tap the button.

Drop to my knees.

And wait.

The wind starts to blow again as the second wall of the storm moves over us.

Let it work. Please let it work.

I keep my head down and listen. I send all my hopes up into the sky.

Wind howls. Rain pelts down. The computer flies off the desk— "Look out!"—and Risha yanks Alex out of the way the instant before it explodes in a shower of sparks on the concrete floor.

We huddle close and hold on, waiting for the wind to rip us apart.

But it doesn't happen. The monster never quite comes back.

There are more distant pops from electrical explosions in blown circuits and transmitters. Branches and bits of ceiling and roofing and God knows what else bang and scrape against the one wall that remains.

But the sounds start to fade.

And we are still here.

We lift our heads and watch the storm sweep away from us, back toward Placid Meadows.

"No, no!" Risha says, and starts to lunge for the computer, in pieces on the floor now.

"No, wait." Alex's eyes are trained on the top of the storm cloud. "It's going to be okay. Watch."

And yes. The churning gray monster is tired. It slugs away from us another quarter of a mile, stirring up dust and last year's leaves.

And finally, it lifts its tail up from the ground and snakes back up into its cloud.

And is gone.

Chapter 32

There are no words to describe this sound.

The quiet after a storm has gone.

The absence of everything—birds chirping, HV motors idling, air conditioners humming.

Here in this broken shelter full of leaves and branches, shattered glass, and bits of buildings the tornado threw at us as it passed, there is almost total quiet.

Only the sound of our breathing—Alex and Risha and me, huddling together.

It feels like time should have stopped when the storm rose back into the sky, like this problem should be solved forever now that it's gone.

But I know it's not.

I know the storms will come again, on the next day when the clouds start swirling and the conditions are just right. They will come.

But right now, it's too soon to talk of next times. I am too thankful to do anything except stay here with my head on Alex's shoulder, breathing this same air with him, holding on to Risha's hand, and feeling her bracelets, cool against my wrist.

Alex is the first to speak. "Thank God we had the numbers right."

A few minutes later, Risha is the second.

"Look." She points up, out of the shelter. We uncurl ourselves like fern fronds in spring and stretch our necks up, up to the line her finger traces toward the clouds in the east.

A smudge of broken rainbow leans against the storm-bruised sky, faint color in the day's last light. I stare hard at it, willing the colors to brighten.

They don't.

I am thankful anyway. Because hope has to start somewhere. And a glimmer is better than nothing at all.

It is the sound of tires crunching over broken boards and branches that finally brings us up out of the shelter to meet Aunt Linda's blue farm truck. Mom jumps out and looks as if she can't decide whether to hug us or kill us.

"Jaden!" She flies at me and pulls me into a hug that comes dangerously close to accomplishing the latter, but I manage to push away so I don't suffocate.

"You got my messages!"

Her eyes fill with tears. "I'm sorry I didn't come home sooner. I thought you were probably getting used to everything. A new house and Mirielle and—"

"Mirielle! Remi! Are they okay? Were they with you and Dad? Or are they home at Placid Meadows? And where's Dad?"

My stomach tightens. Is he okay? Is he back in his office at Placid Meadows sending down another storm?

Mom presses her hands against her eyes and shakes her head a little. "Mirielle and Remi are fine. They're safe. So is Dad, but . . . there's . . . we have a lot to talk about, Jaden." She moves her hands and smiles a weak, exhausted smile. "And I need to say hello to your friends, too."

"This is Risha. And Alex." I wait while she shakes their hands. "Mom, where is everybody? What's going on?"

"What's going on," she says, "is that we need to get the three of you someplace safe, where we can clean up those cuts, and you can eat something." She looks at my matted hair. "And take a shower. Pile in." She opens the truck door. "We'll talk on the way back to Linda's house."

Chapter 33

Dear Dad,

I hope things are going okay for you. I wish ...

I stop and stare out the window, where fat raindrops are starting to fall, pelting the red leaves on our sugar maple in the yard. A
long time ago, I used to love the way September storms would make
Vermont's autumn leaves shine.

Thunder rumbles, and I set the pencil down.

It feels weird writing to him like this instead of talking at my
DataSlate for a video-message, but it makes sense that one of Dad's
restrictions at the energy farm includes the use of any electronic
communication devices.

At first when Dad turned himself in and came clean about the
technology he developed with Grandma Athena, it didn't look like
he'd be doing time.

After all, it was the government that opened the floodgates on
weather manipulation research when it changed the laws and even
paid StormSafe to redirect hurricanes in the Gulf when they were

headed for populated areas. They wanted Dad's technology, so they pretty much gave him free reign, extended his patent for the Sim Dome, and didn't ask questions about how he made Placid Meadows so safe. It was the National Storm Center that funded Dad's tornado dissipation project when he came back from Russia. Weather manipulation won't be a crime until the new legislation takes effect next year.

But lying under oath has always been against the law, and Dad had testified before Congress about the failure of his dissipation research. He lied about the project he scrapped so he could go on to something bigger, technology that would let him rule the storms instead of simply sending them home to the clouds. The project Grandma Athena had always dreamed of. What she'd given up her life to do. And Dad finally got the attention he never had from her when he was a kid.

It's crazy that after all he did, all the lives he destroyed with his pet storms, that it was the lying that landed him on one of those energy farm bikes, sentenced to pedal for power in the sun for the next five years, paying back in sweat what he stole from society with his crimes.

Only he can never really pay it back. I think of Alex and Tomas whose family farms were ravaged and almost stolen away, of the countless people who lost their homes in Dad's redirected storms. Of Newton.

Thank God for Ms. Walpole, who helped Tomas's family get their farm deed back, along with a settlement so StormSafe will pay for his mother's treatment in New York, and then some. He and Alex have had a chance to talk, too. I was right; Tomas trusted Van and had no idea what he and my father were doing.

Lightning flashes, and my stomach twists, even though the only storms around tonight are small ones. I run my hand over the cover of the poetry book I brought home with me from Dad's, and I breathe in slowly. It will be a long time before my heart remembers that storms aren't all evil. That they can be ordinary rain, with thunder and lightning and a bit of wind.

I pick up the pencil again.

Set it down.

What do you write to someone who is so much like you and yet nothing like you at all? What do you say to a parent who is no one that you want to grow up to be?

And what can I say about this summer that was supposed to be our time to reconnect?

I've only been home—real home with Mom—two months, but Eye on Tomorrow already seems like forever ago. Placid Meadows, the campus, the playground . . . they all feel like memories of some high-definition dream.

That afternoon when the storm was raging, when we crouched clinging to metal bars in the storm cellar, I wanted to wake up like Dorothy from *The Wizard of Oz* and find a cold compress on my forehead because it was never real.

Just a dream.

Did Dad ever really want to know me again? Or was I there like all the others—another Eye on Tomorrow kid to watch and shape and ultimately hire to help keep secrets?

Mom unloaded the truth on the way back to Aunt Linda's house that night. When she left for Costa Rica, she hadn't known how Dad's research was evolving, how his interests had taken such a dark turn. When she finally got my message—the video-message of me crying by the side of the road—she called Mirielle, who broke into Dad's office—I still don't know how but it doesn't surprise me that she figured it out—and pieced together what was happening. That's when she learned, all at once, that her dead mother-in-law was alive and that her husband was not doing the work he said he was.

She told Mom everything. And Mom borrowed an HV, drove straight to the airport, and caught the next flight home.

Aunt Linda had picked her up at the airport, and when Dad met them at her house, Mom gave him a raging earful about the promises he'd made to her, to me, about my summer and keeping me safe.

And that's when Grandma Athena's message got through. Her face appeared on Dad's DataSlate, right there in Aunt Linda's kitchen, talking about how the storm wasn't performing as they'd planned, how she locked me in the outbuilding. I was more of a problem than he'd imagined, she said, and so the two of them would need to talk. Dad swore up and down to Mom that she never really would have hurt me. I don't think I believe it.

Dear Dad,
    I hope things are going okay for you. I wish this summer could have been different. I really wish...

I roll the pencil between my fingers, then snap it in half.

Thunder rumbles again, and rain pours down my window in thick rivers. Everything outside looks warped and blurry and wet.

What do I wish? I wish Eye on Tomorrow had been real, a legitimate opportunity for kids like me and Risha, Tomas and Alex, to collaborate and solve this world's problems.

I wish Dad was the father he used to be, or pretended to be anyway, the dad with the strong shoulders and rainbow sprinkles.

I wish that his corporation never existed. That he'd never gone to Russia and found Grandma Athena.

I wish I had a grandmother like Risha's, who stirred curry stews and kissed my head, instead of one who tied me to chairs.

And yet . . . I wish I'd had a chance to talk with her, really talk with her, about her life and her ideas and her choices, before she died.

I pick up a jagged pencil piece and turn it over in my hands.

It's been two months, but we haven't had a funeral yet. Mom and I will have to go make arrangements because with Dad locked up, we're the only ones who can take care of her burial.

Mom's waiting to book plane tickets. The storm was so huge it's taken them weeks to clear the debris. If Grandma had entered the main StormSafe building, or if she were right outside, she'd have been buried under a mountain of glass and steel when the tornado hit.

"Jaden?" Mom knocks at my bedroom door, then walks in with a pile of clean clothes and balances it on my dresser. "Done with the letter?"

I push the paper away. "I don't think I have anything to say."

I run my finger over the end of the pencil piece, then pick up the other one and try to fit them back together, but splintery edges stick out. Breaks are never truly clean.

"Did he really used to love me?" I try to say it as if I don't care, but my shuddery voice gives everything away.

"Yes." Her eyes are sad. "He really did and he still does, Jaden."

I almost laugh.

"Truly." Mom puts a hand on each of my cheeks so I have no choice but to look right at her. "It wasn't until that night you were in danger—you, his little girl—that he could finally see what he had done. Remember what he looked like when he called you on the videophone?"

I nod. I remember. I could never forget the first time I ever saw my father cry.

"He loves you. Nothing excuses what he's done, but he's damaged, Jaden. His thinking. Athena is—was—I can't get used to the idea of having her alive and now gone again—she was larger than life somehow. It's like . . . I don't know . . . like she had some spell cast over him."

"Yeah," I whisper. And I almost understand. I know that feeling of wanting a parent back so badly. Wanting to be celebrated and loved. It's a feeling he never really knew. Mom pushes my hair behind my ear, and all at once, I'm filled up with tears at how lucky I am that I do know.

The house videophone buzzes in the hallway, and as Mom leaves to answer it, my DataSlate dings with a video-message from Alex.

· · 286 · ·

"Hey, Jaden! I gotta show you what came in the mail today."

Video-Alex holds up a fat off-white envelope, and I cheer, even though I know he can't hear me. "All *right!*" Risha and I both got similar envelopes two days ago, invitations to spend three weeks interning at the National Storm Center's new weather modification research facility this winter, and permission documents for Mom to sign. According to the paperwork, Ms. Walpole recommended all three of us, based on our "outstanding commitment to research." Everything in the NSC envelope makes me hope this is the program that Eye on Tomorrow was supposed to be.

"So I guess I'll be seeing you in a couple months!" Video-Alex winks, and the screen goes black.

I stare out the window and smile at the rain, just thin trickles down the glass now, and the clouds are thinning. It really was a small storm this time. Nothing more.

I pick up the longer of the two pencil pieces and go back to Dad's letter.

I ask him about Mirielle and Remi. They've been to visit him, Mom says, even though Mirielle isn't sure if she'll stay or take Remi back to France. I write a few lines about school, about the new schedule I'm on this fall with home connection three days a week and morning classes in person the other two. I ask how things are at the energy farm, then erase that because they're probably not great.

I'm about to sign it when Mom comes back through the door. The lines in her face are tight.

"Who was on the videophone?" I ask.

"Logan County Sheriff's office. They finished clearing all the debris from StormSafe, and Grandma . . ." Mom pauses.

They must have found the body.

Mom bites her lip. "I'm . . . not sure how to tell you this."

I stare at her for a second. Does she think I'm going to be that upset over losing a grandmother I never knew, until the night she almost killed me? "Mom, it's okay. I was there when the building went down. I know she never could have survived. Is the funeral going to be soon?"

"We'll go down for a service on Monday," Mom says. "Closed casket."

I nod, remembering the flying debris, the minefield of broken glass and twisted metal that night. "Her body was in pretty bad shape, huh?"

Mom shakes her head. "They didn't find her body."

A million thoughts swim through my head. The storm was huge; it could have picked her up and dropped her anywhere. But one thought rises to the surface—not so much a thought in words as a mental movie of Grandma Athena, standing in the outbuilding, her mouth a straight line, her hands on her hips.

Her laugh.

Never trust a death certificate.

Could she possibly have survived that monster?

My stomach twists.

Could she still be out there somewhere?

Mom goes on. "We can still have the service. But closed casket. It's not a problem."

Not a problem. I let Mom go on thinking that. She's probably right.

"When will we leave?"

"Sunday. You should call your friends. You'll have some time to see them, too." Mom leaves and closes the door behind her.

An image of Grandma's face floats through my mind, but I imagine the wind blowing it away like Risha's dandelion fluff. Like the magical numbers on her bracelet, zeros and ones, swirling through the air until the ceiling lifts away, and they arrange themselves into something that makes sense, into a world mended and whole again.

But it took decades to make this mess. It will take time for us to go back.

No. To move forward.

It'll take time and research and work. And hope. Failing and trying again and probably wanting to scream because it can't happen fast enough. It won't be impossible, but it will feel that way sometimes; I already know that. And I know I want to be part of it. I need to be.

I reach for my DataSlate to call Alex and Risha. Outside, the sun streams through a gap in the clouds. Puddles glimmer on the sidewalk, and half a rainbow arcs over the woods. This one is brighter than before.

And today feels like a good day to start.

Acknowledgments

Many thanks to all whose work, research, and support helped me to write this book, especially Dr. Howard Bluestein from the University of Oklahoma's School of Meteorology, who took time out of a stormy week in September 2010 to meet with me and answer my long list of questions, most of which began with the words, "So what if . . ." Dr. Bluestein also reviewed sections of this manuscript for scientific accuracy relating to the formation of tornadoes (even though the actual weather manipulation that happens in the book isn't possible at this time). His meteorological expertise is most appreciated, and any errors that remain are my responsibility alone.

I'm grateful to senior meteorology student Tim Marquis for the weather school and National Severe Storms Laboratory tour that provided much of the inspiration for the Eye on Tomorrow campus. The following books were also helpful: *Tornado Alley: Monster Storms of the Great Plains* by Howard B. Bluestein (Oxford University Press, 2006), *The Tornado: Nature's Ultimate Windstorm* by Thomas P. Grazulis (University of Oklahoma Press, 2003), and *Storm Warning: The Story of a Killer Tornado* by Nancy Mathis (Touchstone, 2008).

Acknowledgments

As someone who loves both science and art, I am fascinated by the idea of intersections between the two. Richard Holmes's *The Age of Wonder: How the Romantic Generation Discovered the Beauty and Terror of Science* (Pantheon, 2009) got me thinking about it in new ways.

I am grateful to poet Rita Dove for the gift of her work and for permission to include the excerpt from "Geometry" that Jaden reads in her faded paper book.

Thanks to student beta-reader Theo Gardner-Puschak for sharing his thoughts on the manuscript and to critique partners and writer friends Loree Griffin Burns, Eric Luper, Liza Martz, Ammi-Joan Paquette, Marjorie Light, Stephanie Gorin, and Linda Urban. You all make me a more thoughtful writer, and I'm grateful for your friendship.

Thanks to my agent, Jennifer Laughran, for supporting my writing, helping me weather storms, and generally being amazing; to my brilliant editor, Mary Kate Castellani, for asking just the right questions; and to Emily Easton, Beth Eller, Katie Fee, Kate Lied, Amanda Hong, Nicole Gastonguay, and the rest of the team at Walker/Bloomsbury, and to cover illustrator Vincent Chong.

A special thanks to Elizabeth Bluemle and Josie Leavitt of Flying Pig Bookstore, Marc and Sarah Galvin of The Bookstore Plus, and all the other independent booksellers who work hard for authors, books, kids, and communities every day. You rock.

Finally, thanks to Tom, Jake, and Ella. I saved you for last because the very best part of this book journey is sharing it with you.

KATE MESSNER is a former middle-school English teacher and the author of the E. B. White Read Aloud Award winner *The Brilliant Fall of Gianna Z., Sugar and Ice, Eye of the Storm,* and *Wake Up Missing.* She lives on Lake Champlain with her husband and two kids. When she's not reading or writing, she loves hiking, kayaking, biking, and watching thunderstorms over the lake.

www.katemessner.com

@KateMessner

Don't miss Kate Messner's latest adventure

"Combines a fascinating concept with page-turning suspense. . . . A wild roller-coaster ride." —MARGARET PETERSON HADDIX, author of The Missing series

Wake Up Missing

KATE MESSNER

Don't miss the sweeter side of
Kate Messner!

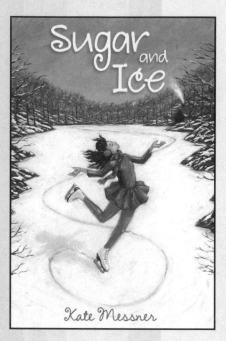

"Laced with humor and heart. . . .
An insightful and affecting read."
—*Booklist*

"A title that remains in your mind
long after you've put it down."
—Fuse 8